ROUGH ICE

Diamonds in the Rough

Ken Jungersen

ROUGH ICE

ISBN: 9781728886268

DEDICATION

This book is for Nancy.

ROUGH ICE is the first book that I wrote. It has a storied history in that my agent of the past turned down a book deal with a movie contract because the publisher wanted the ending changed. Without consulting me, he turned the deal down. I know that he meant well.

Subsequently I rewrote the ending. But the exigencies of life precluded me securing another agent. And so, ROUGH ICE, along with other manuscripts, lay on a shelf in a box.

Unlike my first wife, Nancy took an interest in my love of writing. When she read the manuscript for ROUGH ICE her reaction was, "This is better than most of the things I buy. Why aren't you doing anything with it?"

Well – now I'm doing something with it.

Thanks for the encouragement, Nancy!

ROUGH ICE

ACKNOWLEDGMENTS

Rough Ice is a work of fiction. Names, characters, locations and incidents described are used fictitiously and any resemblance to actual persons, living or dead, or events is coincidental.

Technical details in various parts of the book may at first seem incredible, yet they are plausible. The modifications made to the 747 are theoretically possible. The virtually unknown technique used to mark the diamonds was developed by my father and it does work. The remote diamond mining camp in the Guyana highlands of South America existed on a lessor scale and was my home for well over a year.

The book is set in the pre-September 11th days when security screenings and indeed overall airport security was more lax.

I owe my thanks to many people, too many to name, but they know who they are. One deserves special note though. This dedicated United Airlines flight engineer came out to his 747 an hour early to do some studying of his own. Instead, he found himself teaching a novice about cockpit procedures and letting that novice help start the engines and prepare the big plane for flight. It should be noted that he bears no resemblance to the flight engineer in the story.

Ken Jungersen

ROUGH ICE

Prologue

9 July

Steaming cup of coffee in hand, the lithe woman gazed through the thin curtains at the cobbled street beyond. Two children had just emerged from the old building opposite. A man in dark clothes appeared from nowhere and strode purposefully along the sidewalk. Reaching the kids, he hustled them back inside the building.

Suddenly alert, the woman's eyes scanned up and down the sloping street. No one else was in sight. Nor was there any traffic. Turning in as relaxed a fashion as possible, she withdrew from near the window, setting down the coffee as she passed a table.

She walked calmly down a narrow hall, pausing at an open doorway. There were three men sitting in the little room engrossed in conversation that halted when she appeared. An assortment of automatic weapons lay on a table by the far wall.

The bearded man seated nearest the door smiled at her. "Thought you'd never get that coffee of yours refilled," he said in

Spanish.

She returned his smile. "I've a new pot brewing. Why don't you finish checking out the weapons? I'll just slip out and check the mail."

"Now?"

"Si." She stated flatly and continued down the corridor. But at the end of the hall, instead of opening the apartment's door, she slipped down the steps into the basement. Urgency gripped her as she moved quickly through the semi-darkness of the dank space. Along the wall furthest from the street there was a little alcove piled high with cartons. She pulled some aside far enough to slip into the space behind them. There her hands felt along the old bricks of the wall until finding a rusty metal door that was about two-foot square. Locating the catch, she pulled it open on well-oiled hinges.

Finding the pencil flash that she had left there for just such an eventuality, she switched it on. A plastic bag lay in the narrow passage. She opened it and pulled out a silenced Mauser and two spare clips. She tucked the latter into the back pocket of her form hugging jeans and climbed into the cramped confines of the dusty passage. Twisting awkwardly in the musty darkness, she reached to pull the metal door closed behind her. Just as her fingers found the rusty metal, she heard a dull crash above. There were some startled shouts, the staccato buzz of a machine pistol, then relative silence.

By then she had the door latched and was shuffling along the passage on hands and knees, the Mauser held awkwardly in one hand and the pencil flash in her teeth. After about ten feet the passage widened by about a foot to either side. The top and bottom also expanded until it was about six feet from floor to ceiling. She thanked God that the old landlady who owned the apartment block had confided about how her husband had used the passageway to hide Jews from the Nazis during World War II.

Continuing along the passage, she brushed aside cobwebs, listening intently. At any moment the little doorway behind her might swing open, bringing near certain death or capture. And yet, she remained remarkably calm and poised as she hurried through the eerie confines of the passage where others had sought refuge so long ago.

She didn't know exactly how far she had gone when the passage suddenly narrowed back down to the same two-foot square dimensions, but she knew that she had passed beneath the entire courtyard of the apartment block and was below the building opposite the one she had just left. Reaching the metal plate at the end of the passage, she switched off the pencil flash and gently pressed an ear to the cold steel. There was only silence. Mauser at the ready, she found the catch and eased the door open. Darkness greeted her.

Slowly opening the door on its creaking hinges she found it blocked after only a few inches. Something had been piled up in front of it. She cursed softly, as she pressed harder. The door refused to open further. For an instant, panic seized her thoughts, but she quickly recovered, mind racing.

Twisting about in the cramped space, she put her feet against the metal and thrust hard against the doorplate. It gave a little. At that instant the doorway at the distant end of the passage was flung open and a powerful beam of light stabbed into the murky darkness behind her. Bracing herself, she slammed her feet into the doorplate with all her might. A box crashed to the floor and the door flew open. Behind her there were shouted warnings in French and adamant commands to stop.

The woman ignored them and scrambled out into the dark room beyond the long passageway. She slammed the door home. The first bullet ricocheted off the closing door and sang off into the darkness. The rest slammed harmlessly into the old metal with a loud hammering that ceased as suddenly as it had begun. Thinking quickly, she heaved a mass of boxes in front of the passage's exit, then she rushed to the stairs and bounded up to the top. There she hesitated only a second before opening the door and looking into an apartment that apparently had exactly the same layout as the one she had just left. There were voices in the living room, but no one had heard her. Nor did anyone react as she slipped a man's jacket off a hook and left the apartment. In the hallway, she brushed off some cobwebs and dust and slipped into the jacket, which was too big. She found a wad of crumpled Francs in the pocket. The Mauser vanished into the waistband at the small of her back. The cold steel of the weapon and its stubby silencer seemed to thrill her as she strode purposefully through the door and into the street.

The BaBuuu BaBuuu wail of police units could be heard as she strutted cockily down the cobbled street and entered a little bistro. A police van roared past the windows as she settled down and ordered some wine and cheese.

Louisa Lopez Sanchez smiled seductively at the young waiter as he brought her order. He blushed as she unabashedly ran the tip of her tongue along her lips, then retreated to the kitchen.

Louisa chuckled as she reached for the wineglass. Men were such fools, easily manipulated by a good-looking woman, and by no stretch of the imagination could she be called anything less. Though she barely topped 5 feet in her stocking feet, they were five feet of sculpted curves and toned body capped with raven hair that hung loosely around the shoulders. Dark, captivating eyes highlighted a face that could only be described as beautiful. She wore gunmetal, wire-rimmed glasses and several silver rings. In short, to look at her one would scarcely believe that she personally had slain at least a dozen people and was directly responsible for the deaths of several more.

Louisa munched on some cheese as she thought about the impact of the raid she had just narrowly escaped. Obviously one of the three men in the apartment had sold out. Not knowing whom precluded any warning of the impending strike. It mattered not who was the traitor now, because the loyal ones were suddenly useless to her; being either dead or captured. The one consolation was that none of them could further damage the ETA, the Basque separatist movement that she had devoutly served for half of her thirty-five years.

This raid was but one of many that had taken place in France and Spain during the past several months. Authorities in both countries were trying hard to crush the ETA. She thought about her options in light of the current government pressure. Some restructuring would be needed and it would be safest if done in a country other than France or Spain. She would miss Paris, but sacrifices had to be made. Money would be needed too. Lots of it.

Two police officers walked by outside, peering through the window as they went. She smiled seductively at them and toasted them. They nodded and moved on, gripping their machine pistols lightly. Louisa laughed quietly as she thought how childishly easy her escape had been! And this from the elite French thugs!

Somewhat more pensively, she pondered how she would help rebuild the ETA.

ROUGH ICE

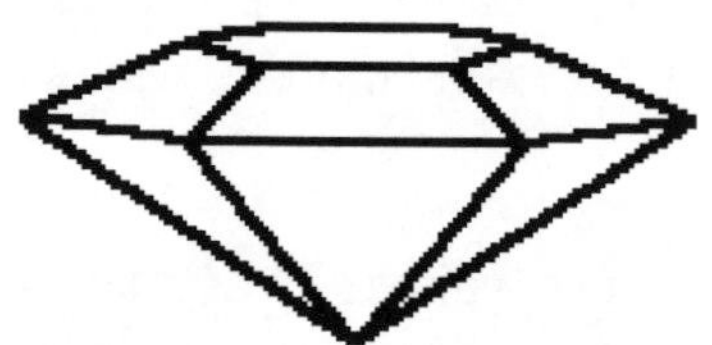

BOOK ONE

GROUNDWORK

CHAPTER ONE

22 August

Rainbows of color burst forth from each exquisite facet as the practiced hand slowly twirled the gemstone. Fire and brilliance dueled throughout the diamond as light danced across its surfaces and penetrated to its very heart.

"Not bad," commented the nattily dressed gentleman as he gazed at the gem through the diamond loupe held in his left hand. The words seemed hopelessly inadequate. So too was the lackluster way in which they were spoken. But then, the speaker was an infinitely cautious person. He disdained actions or sign of emotion that might betray his true character or intents. It followed that Collins, the name he used with his host, was false.

"Not bad," his host mimicked with an irritated snort. "That diamond, or piece of 'ice' as you would perhaps put it in your crude fashion, is flawless. It ranks among the finest blue-white gems I've had the pleasure of seeing." The obese speaker spoke gruffly in heavily accented Oxford English. A stubby fingered hand reached out to retrieve the bauble as he haughtily added, "And I have seen more than most, my dear mister Collins."

The man who called himself Collins shrugged impassively. The steady gaze from his blue-gray eyes was cold, imperious; his voice equally so. "By now I'd have thought it blatantly obvious that we've painfully little in common, van Troje. Least of all your obsessive attachment to ***ICE***," he emphasized the offensive word, "be it cut or rough." He dropped the diamond loupe onto the leather desktop. Why, he wondered, did the Dutchman always insist on opening their meetings by handing him some magnificent gemstone to ogle? Perhaps he strove to impress his wealth with such displays.

A somewhat rankled van Troje strove to maintain his calm as he almost reverently returned the diamond to the black velvet recess of its little case. The lid snapped shut with a muted 'click.' He was unaccustomed to blithely accepting such insolence. People just did not treat Nicco van Troje like that. Quite the contrary, they generally groveled to gain his favor. Being perhaps Amsterdam's most influential diamond merchant and one of the city's more influential citizens made him a powerful individual. Those who worked in the city's diamond trade had long since learned that his numerous faults and oft offensive ways had to be endured. But van Troje's influence extended beyond the diminishing diamond trade. His immense wealth had provided the means to secure footholds in numerous other business ventures. From restaurants to warehouses to import/export firms, he was a force with which to reckon. He even controlled several businesses in another nearby Diamond center, Antwerp.

Just where all his money came from remained a mystery. Undoubtedly he managed to wring out a more than adequate living from his flourishing international diamond trading and assorted other ventures, but even his business acumen never could have produced the vast wealth he controlled. Rumors that he was acting on behalf of wealthy oil sheiks circulated, but were never substantiated. Nor were tales of astronomical bank deposits in Zurich and Geneva. Thus rumors abounded while facts remained scarce. It all made for good copy in local papers, yet it never seemed to tarnish the name of Nicco van Troje. He remained an elite citizen, a throwback to the past. He was a man whose lifestyle hinted at the aristocratic lineage from which he hailed.

Van Troje's brash visitor knew all this and much more. Diligent research had unveiled a great deal about his host. Of particular interest to him was the fact that the Dutchman showed no aversion to ignoring laws and harbored no scruples where profit was concerned.

Collins had not, however, expected the lengthy preamble to any substantive discussion that opened each meeting. This time he would terminate it early on. He got rigidly to his feet. "I had thought we might do some business. Apparently I was mistaken. A wasted trip and wasted time. I should have stayed in New York. Good day, van Troje." He spun on his heel and made for the door.

This sudden move to leave caught his host off guard. People just did not up and walk out on Nicco van Troje. Under normal circumstances the Dutchman would have let him go, but this was no normal circumstance. Literally millions of tax free dollars hung in the balance. He hurriedly got out of his leather office chair. The speed with which he moved his vast bulk surprised his departing visitor, who half turned when the rotund man stammered, "Wait!"

Already half way round the desk, his heavily jowled face a shade redder, van Troje stopped the moment he realized the American had halted. "Be reasonable, my friend. You should reconsider your position. Hasty decisions are oft regretted later on, my dear mister Collins."

The bait had been taken! The urge to smile was suppressed by the man who called himself Collins. His real name was Larson, Erik Larson, but that was something the Dutchman would never know.

Larson released the door handle, turning to face the avaricious van Troje. "Why on Earth should I?" The supreme arrogance was unmasked. Don't acquiesce too quickly, he told himself. Let him sweat a little.

Van Troje regained his composure. He had not gotten where he was by allowing himself to be caught off guard by the likes of this noisome American. When he responded, his voice was every bit as arrogant. "Because you need me, my friend."

To the Dutchman's surprise, Larson waved away this haughty declaration. "Nonsense. Others can provide the services I seek. No, van Troje, it is you who need me. Without me, a once in a lifetime opportunity will pass you by. Your damned beating about the bush each time we meet bores me. It's a waste of time and I hate to waste time." He started to reach for the polished brass door handle.

"No, my friend, you do indeed need me. I regret that what normally would be viewed as common courtesy, seems to upset you. But you must remember that here, in Amsterdam, life is not yet quite as hectic as in America." Van Troje sought refuge behind his large desk. "Perhaps it would be fairer to say that we need each other, mister Collins. Let's be quite honest. There are very few people who can turn such a fortune in stolen gems into legitimate assets."

"Fewer still can produce them in the first place."

"Point well taken. Let's not quibble over such petty things. There is money to be made here. Much money to be made. I, for my part, will strive to dispense with my usual 'beating about the bush' as you perceive it. You must simply realize that you are in

Europe now. Understand that business is conducted differently here."

Van Troje drew the heavy Burgundy drapes behind his desk before retaking his seat. The room plunged into sudden gloom. A small, gold-fringed desk lamp provided the only illumination.

The drawn curtains struck Larson as incongruous. He was not an Amsterdammer, but he was observant. One of the Dutch quirks noted during his numerous visits was that curtains were rarely drawn. Even in the evening, homes were left open to the scrutiny of neighbor and passerby alike. It was as though people pointedly were declaring they had nothing to hide. The warm glow of lights gave the houses life and created an atmosphere of openness and intimacy he had not experienced elsewhere. But then, van Troje had much to hide.

Larson slowly returned to his chair. "If our talks are to continue, then I insist that you level with me now. Do you or do you not have a suitable conduit in South America?"

The Dutchman allowed himself a little grin as he snipped off the tip of a cigar. With languorous movements he lit it with a gold lighter. He felt back in control. This rude American's abrupt behavior would be tolerated. Or more correctly, it would be tolerated until van Troje gained possession of the diamonds. Then his arrogance would be rewarded properly.

"Naturally, my friend," he said after exhaling a cloud of obnoxious smoke. "And like you and I, the man in charge is not adverse to quick profits, whatever their source."

"He's of no use if he's already suspect in criminal dealings," Larson reminded.

"Do give me some credit. I didn't get where I am by being careless or underestimating the efficiency of law enforcement agencies." He produced a map from his drawer and pushed it across the desktop. "Isolated, quite far north, has a private airstrip, and regularly ships diamonds in the rough. That seems to meet your specifications to a 'T', mister Collins."

A perfect summer day was fading into an equally splendid summer evening. The sun had just slipped below the horizon. Street lamps blazed in its stead. Bridges, their arches illuminated with strings of lights, added to the charm. The cool air was filled with discordant sounds and laced with a variety of scents as Larson walked briskly through the streets of Amsterdam.

Ten minutes earlier he had concluded the afternoon-long meeting with the repulsive van Troje. He had come away with exactly what he wanted. The diamond broker was prepared to use his less reputable sources to obtain some of the more esoteric items needed by Larson. More importantly, he had found a suitable conduit in South America. The former was useful, the latter essential. Larson did not doubt the validity of the choice of recruits for the South American portion of the operation. The greedy Dutchman had entirely too much at stake to steer Larson to the wrong individual. If nothing else, van Troje was inscrutably dishonest. Although thoroughly convinced of that prior to the first of their meetings, Larson had since reinforced that conclusion time and time again. The one thing that really amazed him about his new partner was the way the repulsive Dutchman managed to keep his own name clean, his reputation unscathed. The fat man would be a formidable adversary. Despite their joint venture, Larson planned to regard him as such throughout their dealings.

The just concluded meeting with the wily Dutchman had been

the second in as many weeks. As had been the case at the end of their previous session, Larson suspected that he was being followed. The last time round it had not mattered because he had gone directly to Schipol airport and left the country. This time, things were different. By convenient coincidence Larson had other business to attend to while in Amsterdam. This time the tail would have to go.

The tall American maintained his habitually brisk pace. One of the city's colorful old barrel organs gave the opportunity to verify his suspicions. He strode up to the gaily painted, ornately crafted organ. A neatly lettered sign proudly proclaimed in Dutch and English that it was a hand cranked barrel organ, a hold-out as compared to most of the others scattered about the city that had converted to gas driven motors. The little three-wheeled truck upon which the organ rested was the only concession to progress

Larson quietly listened to a few minutes of the lilting music. Casually glancing round, as though lost in thought, he saw exactly what he expected. It was not the scattered tourists meandering about which caught his eye. They belonged. The nondescript man in equally ignominious clothing a short distance up the street who turned quickly away, suddenly taking an interest in a nearby shop window, did not.

Larson listened contentedly to the music for a few more minutes. Only occasionally did his gaze stray up the darkening street. The man had moved closer only to find a new shop window on which to focus his attention.

Any vestige of doubt extinguished, Larson pulled some coins from his pocket. They clanked into the little cup placed beside the barrel organ on the bed of the little truck for just such a purpose. The wrinkle faced old man who tirelessly cranked the old musical instrument smiled a broken-toothed smile and nodded thanks.

A half hour's brisk walk brought Larson, and a short distance behind him his shadow, to the somewhat less respectable

Walletjes (little walls), Amsterdam's red-light district. Tucked neatly between the high-banked Oudezijds Voorburgwal and Oudezijds Achterburgwal canals, from which the name is derived, the Walletjes offered one of the world's oldest commodities in a genuine setting of old world charm. Relatively neat old houses with pitched gables lined the peopled streets.

Larson slowed his pace. There were girls of every conceivable size, shape, and color. Tall or short, skinny or plump, old or young, stunning or drab, black, white or Oriental, they were all there; something to suit every taste. Dressed in revealing clothes, leather outfits, thigh-high boots, or even barefoot, they were there. A few leaned seductively against convenient walls or cliché-like lamp posts. Others stood in doorways or on street corners. Still others lounged in the district's bars. But those that caught Larson's apparent interest were the numerous scantily clad women seated behind picture windows, most bathed in pale red light, sensuously beckoning prospective customers to enter. These he assiduously eyed as he made his way along the street, politely refusing the services of several eager to please prostitutes as he went. His shadow seemed to be doing better and Larson failed to spot him when he casually looked about. Perhaps he had lost him already.

Numerous windows were curtained off, their owners busily servicing clients. A dozen available prospects passed before Larson halted. He cast a brief look back at the last window he had passed where a peroxide blonde pursed seductive lips. Then his attention fell on the buxom brunette in the window before him. The blonde made an 'oh well' shrug as he entered the dimly lit doorway of her competitor.

The sultry brunette whom Larson had selected, dropped the paperback novel she was reading onto a small wooden table. She got casually to her feet. In a well-practiced procedure she drew the crimson curtains, slipped easily out of her negligee, and locked the door before turning to fully face the well-dressed gentleman. Brown eyes swept up and down his body. The splendid cut of the immaculately tailored, navy blue, three-piece suit, the high gloss of black, hand-sewn, Italian dress boots, the tastefully coordinated silk tie, the flash of the 18 karat gold wristwatch; all were noted appreciably. So too were the physical attributes of the man who wore these items so well; the proud, erect stature, the powerful, broad shoulders, the thick, neatly groomed black hair, the tiny crows feet beside intelligent blue-gray eyes, the handsome features of a face that hinted at Scandinavian ancestry, the two long parallel scars at the edge of his right cheek that were almost hidden by the sideburn.

"An American," she stated with a perceptive nod. "A hundred guilders, Luv. Unless you've a mind for something unusual. That would cost extra. Payment in advance, if you'll please." She spoke pleasantly as she speculatively watched her patron.

"Sounds reasonable enough," Larson replied. The smell of cheap perfume was overpowering. He didn't bother to ask how she knew he was American. His attire, he assumed. From a well-stocked wallet he produced the correct amount, which the girl quickly folded and tucked away in a compartment in a Swiss music box.

When she moved to help him out of his jacket, he gently took her shoulders in his hands to stop her. "No need, dear. Most regrettable, but I won't have time to avail myself of your services tonight. All I want is a small favor."

The brunette stepped slowly back, sudden suspicion and a hint of fear clearly evident in her eyes. She asked, "What kind of favor?"

"A very profitable one considering how easy it is." Larson picked up the sheer negligee from the chair where it lay discarded. He smiled congenially as he handed it to her. "You may as well put this back on."

Still wary, she slipped into the negligee. The garment did little to conceal her ample figure. The black lace bra and panties, and black silk stockings remained in tantalizingly clear view. The tops of her barely covered breasts rose and fell with each breath. Modesty was certainly not among this young woman's hang-ups, Larson mused.

"I presume that you're fairly well acquainted with the peroxide blonde working next door?", he inquired mildly.

The prostitute laughed. "So that's it! You want two girls at once! That can be quite a lot of fun for everyone involved. Of course, it can be arranged. For a price. And here I was beginning to wonder if despite all the finery you were some kind of weirdo or something."

Larson smiled again. "No, I'm not a pervert. Nor am I out to make it with two women at once. Maybe I'm dull, but one has always proved sufficient." The prostitute's spirits waned slightly at the latter confession. "What I would like is childishly simple. Just give your peroxide neighbor a ring on the phone. Ask her to gaze casually out her window. A dull, easily forgotten man with black hair, a gray jacket, brown slacks, and a pale-green shirt should be somewhere about. All I need to know is whether or not he is still around."

"She may have a customer."

"She didn't a minute or two ago," he replied coolly, hoping the blonde whore was still unoccupied and still alertly watching those on the street fronting her domain as she had done when he passed.

The prostitute pursed her lips. At length she nodded. Her dark eyes narrowed. "She'll want something."

"A hundred guilders for her and another two hundred for your added troubles." Larson produced the alligator billfold and extracted the currency.

She took it quickly, as though afraid that he might reconsider. It soon lay tucked away in the beautifully crafted music box. Suspicion vacated the dark eyes. Concern took its place. "You're in some kind of trouble." It was not meant as a question. "Police?"

Ignoring the question, he gestured towards the flame-red telephone. "Please make the call now. I need to know if the gentleman in question is still outside. If he is, then I expect that he may soon leave to report to his superiors. This too I will need to know about." He thought it more likely that his pursuer would be checking for a back entrance. If the tail had any misgivings about Larson having noticed his clumsy efforts, then it would be a natural assumption that he might expect Larson to engage the prostitute and slip out the back door.

The woman studied him as she dialed. This tall American was not so different after all, she concluded. Beneath the fancy clothes and eloquent speech he was just another man haunted by a world filled with a myriad of problems.

The faint sound of a phone ringing could be heard. It was answered on the second ring. Yes, there had been a man walking aimlessly about a few minutes earlier. He might have been dressed as described, but she could not be certain. After passing for the fourth time he lit a smoke and walked away quickly.

The prostitute thanked her friend and told her that the inquiring gentleman had left fifty guilders in appreciation for her help. Larson merely grinned as she said the amount. Surprised to see that her patron understood Dutch from his reaction to her lowering of the fee, the whore winked a heavily mascaraed eye as she thanked her friend and replaced the receiver.

"Excellent," Larson said. "Now, if I could just make one local call myself, everything should be in order. Fifty guilders should defray your phone expenses."

"Amply," the prostitute replied as she again took the offered currency. "Where did you learn to speak Dutch?"

Larson ignored the question. He dialed and waited patiently. When someone answered, he said, "I seem to have picked up a shadow. You know what to do. I won't be long." He replaced the receiver, thanked the prostitute for her cooperation, and unbolted the door. She stopped him with a gentle tug.

"When this, whatever it is, is over, come back and see me. I'll show you a good time. And as a thanks for your generosity tonight, it'll be on the house." She smiled her best seductive smile.

"I might just take you up on that," Larson lied, knowing that he never would return. He opened the door and slipped into the cool night air.

There was no sign of the nondescript man in the drab brown slacks among those on the street. Larson nodded to the prostitute as she opened her curtains to display her wares once more. Keeping to the shadows where possible, he hurried off. He had things to attend to while in Amsterdam. A detailed report about his movements was the last thing he wanted van Troje to receive.

From his vantage point in a dark doorway several houses up the street, the man in the drab brown slacks watched his quarry make a stealthy departure from the prostitute's home. A flicker of a smile crossed his dull features. He was pleased with himself. Another long draw on the carefully concealed cigarette and the butt went spinning into the gutter. He waited a few more seconds to give Larson a fair lead, then he set out in pursuit.

Night had brought a chill to the air. He zipped up his jacket and turned up its collar. He sighed wearily as he threaded his way past some drunks. His was a less than exciting way to make a living, but it did pay the bills, he reflected. At least he was still within sight of his target. Van Troje would be pleased if things continued as well for the remainder of the night.

To his surprise, the American didn't head back into a nicer part of the city. Instead, he worked his way into a more or less deserted warehouse district. The kind of place that seemed dead at night. Perhaps van Troje was not wrong to suspect this finely dressed foreigner after all.

Street lighting was noticeably poorer as Larson moved steadily along the warehouse lined canal. Many buildings were totally dark. The remainder were little better off. The dull glow cast by hopelessly inadequate light bulbs did nothing but serve to heighten the gloom. A perfect setting for mayhem, Larson reflected, as he walked briskly along the dreary street. Given the old warehouses and their high pitched gables towering above him like hulking demons, even he could not help but feel slightly uncomfortable as he walked alone.

Since leaving the prostitute he had occasionally glanced round quickly. The other man was still there. An unfortunate turn of events. Unfortunate, that is, for the hapless person assigned to follow him.

He turned a corner into an even darker side street. It was totally deserted. Overhead, the twin rows of ancient buildings seemed to lean together and almost touch. The illusion was no doubt enhanced by the hoisting beams that jutted far out over the narrow street.

Larson could have virtually disappeared in the foreboding darkness along either side of the nearly black canyon. Rather than choose this obvious method of concealment, he strode purposefully down the center of the street. He had covered some thirty odd yards when his tail rounded the corner. Unlike his quarry, he made full use of the darkness.

He was not alone. Another figure also clung to shadows. When he moved quietly past an unseen doorway on his rubber soled shoes, there was a slight 'swish' as something swung rapidly through the air. Some sixth sense made him half turn, but it was far too late to react. The blackjack caught him neatly below the right ear. A muffled grunt left his lips as he collapsed to the cracked pavement.

His assailant knelt to make certain that he was out cold. He quickly rifled the unconscious man's pockets. The hapless man's billfold and wristwatch were transferred to his own jacket pocket before he rushed up the street to join Larson. When the unfortunate man came to, he would undoubtedly assume he had been mugged. Given the neighborhood, it was an easily reached conclusion.

At the next corner the two Americans stepped into a waiting BMW whose motor turned over at once. The driver slipped the car into gear without looking at either of his passengers. At length he asked, "Everything went smoothly?"

"Like clockwork," Larson replied. "Keith handled our friend's eyes and ears very neatly."

The driver nodded. He swung down a side street that paralleled a canal. The watch and wallet, now minus its cash, went spinning out across the dark water. With the familiarity of a man who knows the streets well, the driver soon negotiated a route to the outskirts of the city.

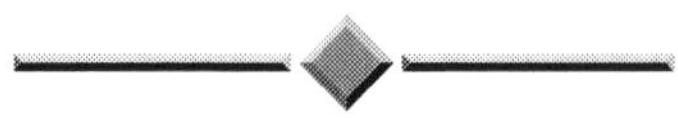

Keeping surreptitiously out of sight, an unseen individual noted the efficient trouncing the diamond trader's lackey received with mild amusement. Whoever the tall American stranger was, he worked smoothly. He would be a dangerous adversary, he thought.

He too had picked up Larson's trail when the American exited the diamond merchant's office. Unlike van Troje's surprisingly clumsy underling, he had moved warily, but not so warily as to draw attention to himself, especially not that of his quarry. He was a professional and as such could not afford careless mistakes. Careless mistakes brought failure, injury, or death in his business.

When the men had piled into the waiting car, he rushed along the street, reaching the end of the block in time to spot the BMW passing a street lamp. He closed his eyes and repeated the license number quietly to himself. It was committed to memory. When he opened his eyes again, the car had vanished.

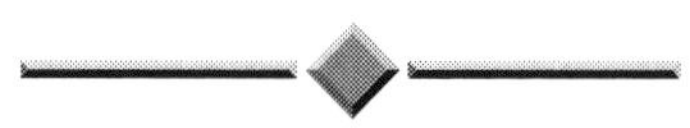

Two hours later a weary and footsore man rode the elevator to the fifth floor apartment that was his home in Amsterdam. His backtracking had been fruitless. The whore, as expected, had not been unable to shed much new light on the identity of this American. The only tidbit gleaned from her was the fact that he understood Dutch. Besides that, she merely expressed surprise that twice in one night prospective customers would engage her services and then fail to avail themselves of her feminine charms.

Entering his apartment, Kurt Schmitt picked up a big manila envelope that lay on the floor of the vestibule, and shuffled into the living room. He lobbed his black leather jacket onto a convenient chair, kicked off his shoes, and tossed the envelope onto a low table beside the couch. He fetched a half empty bottle of Johnnie Walker Black Label, poured himself a generous measure, and flopped onto the comfortable couch. Two camera cases and accessories were pushed aside to make space for his feet that were soon propped across the table. Examination of the manila envelope's contents began after a long, savory sip of the whiskey. The first several pages were transcripts of every long distance telephone call van Troje had made with parties in South America and Africa within the past month. Schmitt skimmed rapidly through them. Nothing startling came to light. Van Troje was not stupid enough to incriminate himself on a phone line that could be tapped. Of minor interest was a series of calls to Guyana, a small country in northern South America. They began the day after Schmitt first observed the American with the diamond merchant.

The transcripts were flung onto the cluttered tabletop. The next few pages were brief dossiers, complete with attached photos of the people van Troje had phoned. Schmitt found the sheet covering the person in Guyana and read it through. The man ran a diamond and gold mining operation near the Brazilian border. He had dealt with van Troje for more than a decade.

The dossiers joined the transcripts. Schmitt scanned the remaining two pages. One listed the last known whereabouts of several suspected smugglers thought to have ties with van Troje. The other said simply that no identity could be linked to the attached photo of the American which Schmitt had submitted for analysis. "Good. Very good," he said quietly to himself as he studied the face. "But that only makes my job all the more interesting, my friend."

Schmitt replenished his drink. Plunking the bottle down, he scooped up the phone and punched in the number.. He drank as he waited.

A disgruntled voice answered the sixth ring. "Yes?"

"I'm afraid it's me again, Peter." Schmitt spoke softly.

"Who else at this ungodly hour?", the man replied sourly. "Surely it could have waited 'til morning."

Schmitt downed the last of the whiskey. "I need a favor."

"Hardly a newsworthy event."

"You still owe me a few, you know."

"Ja . . . Jaaaa. What this time?" The man relented, anxious to crawl back under the covers.

So Schmitt told him. Then he too retired for the night. He slipped quietly into bed. His sleeping lady friend stirred, then resumed her rhythmic breathing.

CHAPTER TWO

23 August

"Kurt! Kurt, wake up!" A feminine voice beckoned. Schmitt blinked awake. Bedraggled hair dripped water as his lady friend proffered the phone in one hand and clutched a towel around herself with the other.

"Thanks," he muttered as he took the phone. She made to return to her shower, but he grabbed her hand and gently held it.

"Schmitt," he grumbled into the phone. He sounded tired as he pressed the phone to his ear.

"Oh . . . did I wake you." The voice on the phone dripped of mock sincerity. "I'm so terribly sorry. Maybe if you'd try sleeping during the night like the rest of us, you'd be conscious by eight," his friend chided with feigned severity.

Schmitt glanced at the digital clock beside the bed. "Seven fifty-three," he corrected. "For what it's worth, I'm sorry about earlier this morning. Any luck?"

"We do function, you know." The sound of shuffling papers could be heard. "Blue BMW. A rental picked up three days ago at Schipol. Went to a Mr. and Mrs. Collins. Americans from New York City. Arrived on KLM for a one week stay. They're registered at the Schiller. What're they to you?"

"Nothing yet."

"And cows will fly. So I'm not to know about it, eh?"

Schmitt smiled. "You're beginning to know me far too well, Peter."

"Too well is a gross understatement. I don't know what you are into this time, but do try and stay clean. This Collins seems to be rather well healed. If you press him too hard, you just might find yourself in hot water. So hot that even I might not be able to pull enough strings to get you out, provided I was so inclined."

"Thanks for the warning, Peter. And thanks for the info."

Schmitt dropped the phone onto its cradle. He drew the soft hand he held to his lips and kissed it gently. "Good morning, Lisbeth." His eyes lovingly surveyed her towel-clad body. "You're starting to form a puddle."

"Thanks to your ignoring the phone."

Schmitt's free hand wrenched the towel from her grasp. He dropped it onto the wet spot on the floor. Admiring eyes snaked up her long legs, past her curvy hips, lingered momentarily at the soft swell of her breasts, and only stopped when their gaze was fixed upon sky-blue eyes framed by auburn hair. "We'd best get you off that nasty cold floor," he said as he pulled her onto the bed, hands beginning to explore every sensuous inch of her curvaceous body. She responded in kind as the sheets were thrust aside.

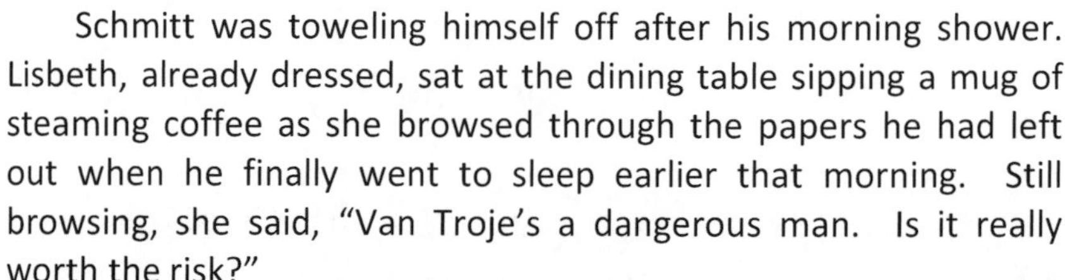

Schmitt was toweling himself off after his morning shower. Lisbeth, already dressed, sat at the dining table sipping a mug of steaming coffee as she browsed through the papers he had left out when he finally went to sleep earlier that morning. Still browsing, she said, "Van Troje's a dangerous man. Is it really worth the risk?"

Casting aside the towel, Schmitt began to dress. "All depends on just how big a deal we can nail him on. De Beers estimates that he accounts for in excess of $5 million in illegal gemstones annually. Interpol figures closer to $4 million. But you must remember that these are, at best, guesses formulated upon the sketchiest information. The actual sum could be higher."

"Or lower," Lisbeth interjected. She had turned to watch him dress through the doorway. She liked the way his muscles rippled when he moved; liked the hard flat stomach, the solid thighs, the powerful arms, the manly face with its rugged, yet handsome, features.

Schmitt ignored the comment and her gaze. "Nobody's been able to touch him. Legal constraints being what they are, I hardly find that surprising. Diamonds aside, it is generally assumed that he is somehow involved with at least another twenty to thirty million worth of narcotics traffic." He dragged a comb through his sandy-brown hair.

"Which makes him all the more dangerous," Lisbeth persisted, concern etched onto her delicate features. "The initial report said that two investigators had 'disappeared' while probing his doings."

"Police inspectors working within the excessively restricted confines of their overworked and underpaid profession."

"And you are naturally so different. At least in your own mind you seem to be. Or had you forgotten that you used to be a police inspector yourself?"

Schmitt walked over to where she sat and kissed her forehead. "Which is precisely why I'll succeed. I know all of the ins and outs. More importantly though, as an independent, I can bend the rules when necessary."

"Ignore them, you mean."

"You've been comparing notes with Peter too often, I fear."

Lisbeth pulled the picture of the man called Collins out of the pile. "Where does he fit in?"

Schmitt shrugged as he moved into the kitchen and poured some coffee. Its aroma always seemed to invigorate him in the mornings. "Not sure yet. About the only damned thing I really know about him is that he sure as hell is not a saintly American tourist here to see the sights. He and van Troje are working some sort of deal. The funny thing is, that based upon last night, they are definitely not the best of bedfellows. Neither trusts the other completely. This American is either obsessively cautious or he's doing more than he wants van Troje to know about. Either way, everything points to a big event in the offing."

"Diamonds or narcotics?"

"I haven't a clue. At least, not yet. I do hope that it is diamonds though, because if I can recover a sizable cache, then I'll collect my usual fee plus a fat bonus from De Beers."

"Always the money." Lisbeth sounded worried. "Don't you

realize that the only reason they pay you the ridiculous fees and bonuses is because people like van Troje are callous killers?"

"It's a living." He spoke between bites of cheese. "Besides, it's what I do best."

"Second best," Lisbeth said coyly.

"I hardly think I could make a living with the other," Schmitt responded with a sheepish grin.

Suddenly serious again, Lisbeth slipped the papers into the manila envelope. "Please let this be the last one. When it's finished don't accept another."

"We'll see." He rinsed his cup and joined her. "I'll need your help today. It seems our mysterious Mr. Collins has a Mrs. I want you to stake out the lobby of the Schiller and if possible get a picture of her without her knowing it. It does not have to be a superb photo, just use your finesse with the lens to the best advantage stealth allows. And for God's sake don't let her know you're there."

"I'm no fool," Lisbeth stated matter-of-factly. "And where will you be?"

"Oh . . . skulking about, mingling with the baser sorts."

Those who knew him said that Kurt Schmitt was part chameleon. He could walk into any room, be it brimming with diplomatic bigwigs or scruffy ruffians, and be right at home, or more aptly put, seem to be. The Zeedijk bar into which he sauntered on the heels of the American, required only that he shelve his manners and interject liberal amounts of profanity into his speech in order to blend in. His leather airman's jacket and navy slacks raised no eyebrows from the rough-hewn clientele. Most were sailors or dockworkers.

The tall American, clad in surprisingly proletariat-like garb, sidled up to the bar. Some bills changed hands and the bartender pointed towards a table along one wall. A longhaired young man sat playfully fondling a buxom brunette. The American, trailed by another man whom Schmitt reasoned to be Collins' heavy handed assistant from the night before, approached the table and struck up a conversation with the young Dutchman.

Schmitt discreetly watched the encounter as he forcefully elbowed his way through the crowd and ordered a shot of whiskey from the barkeep. Still vigilant, he struck up an inane conversation with a burly sailor who leaned forlornly against the end of the bar.

The scraggly youth's sudden interest in the newcomers incensed the brunette, who rose indignantly and stalked haughtily off. The youth was the object of several booming guffaws. The woman plunked herself onto a convenient customer's lap and proceeded to paw him instead.

Minutes later, when the American and his escort exited, Schmitt did not follow. He waited patiently. An hour passed. Then half of the next. The Dutchman downed several drinks in the interim before he popped to his feet and left the clamorous bar. Schmitt threaded his way through the throng in pursuit. A heavy mist hung in the cool night air as he stepped into the street. Collar turned up, he set off.

It turned out to be a short walk. The building the young Dutchman entered was an old assemblage of tiny apartments. Schmitt waited in the shadows as his quarry entered the dimly lit hall and mounted the creaking stairs. He was near the top of the first flight when Schmitt followed silently, keeping his weight near the sides of the steps to lessen the creaks and groans of the old wood. The youth fumbled with a key and opened a door on the second floor. A slight noise made him turn in time to see Schmitt bound up the last steps. Startled and somewhat inebriated, he did not react quickly enough. He found himself thrown roughly through the door.

Stepping quickly into the little apartment, Schmitt shut the door and groped along the wall for a light switch. Just as he found it, the youth rammed into his chest. They crashed against the doorframe. Schmitt recovered quickly, reflexively. He grabbed an exposed wrist, wrenched it down and back, spun the man round, and tripped him with a vicious kick in the shins. A small, rickety table crashed to the floor as the youth went down. Before he could get up again, Schmitt was on top of him, the stubby barrel of a Mauser pressed hard against his temple.

"Lie very still and don't make a sound!" Schmitt commanded in fluent Dutch. The man obeyed. "Much better." The barrel remained firmly in place. "Now . . . I want some answers. Who met you in the bar?"

"You're hurting me!" The foul odored man whined.

"Who?" Schmitt maintained the pressure on the man's temple. His knees ground into his victim's shoulder blades.

"I . . . I . . . don't know. Never saw them before!" The barrel twisted against his temple. "No! I swear it! I never laid eyes on 'em before!"

Surmising that this was in all probability the truth, Schmitt asked, "What did they want from you?"

"Nothing."

The man grunted in pain as Schmitt smashed his face into the floorboards with his free hand. “The truth,” he said patiently.

“Who are you? Police?” He paused as he threw aside that ridiculous possibility. “No, you couldn’t be. Who then?” Blood trickled from his nose.

“I ask the questions. What did they want?”

“Drugs. They wanted a few hits of cocaine.”

“Cocaine?”

“Ja. For a party. They wanted to party.”

The man gasped in pain as Schmitt grabbed his one arm and twisted it round his back. “I don’t like liars. Do you understand?”

“Ja,” he gasped. “They wanted information.”

“What information?”

The young man hesitated. Another jerk on his arm prompted him to speak. “You’re hurting me! They want contact with a courier.”

A further twist on the arm accompanied Schmitt’s next word. “And?”

“You’re breaking my arm!”

“Answer my questions and I’ll stop.”

“O.K.. O.K.! For God’s sake, just don’t hurt me anymore!” He drew a deep breath and went on. “A friend of mine is a courier. Sometimes, anyway.”

“Not good enough.” With practiced proficiency Schmitt jerked the arm just far enough to make it very painful without serious damage to muscle or tissue.

The man cried out. Sobbing, he muttered, “That’s all they

wanted to know!"

"They paid you a considerable sum. There's got to be more to it. I'm growing impatient."

The thought of another wrenching twist with its accompanying spasm of pain, was sufficient to quell any thought of further recalcitrance. "Alright, alright! But for Christ's sake let go my arm!" The pressure eased ever so slightly. The young man sighed heavily. "They knew about my friend, only his name, mind you, but they knew he was a courier. He carries money and things across borders for people. They claimed to be sympathizers who wanted to help. They . . . "

"Sympathizers of what?" Schmitt interrupted.

"The ETA."

"The ETA? What the hell is that?"

"Freedom fighters. Something to do with the Basque country in Spain."

Schmitt was genuinely puzzled. How did some Spanish terrorist faction factor in with van Troje? He was many things; most of them vile, disgusting, and quite beyond the realm of legality, but sponsoring terrorists was a bit out of even his league. Or was it?

"Tell me more," Schmitt demanded after a moment's reflection.

"Jan, my friend, sometimes takes money to places and smuggles weapons or explosives back. He believes in them, sort of anyway."

"Sort of?"

"Ja. The ETA has close ties with the IRA and Jan's grandfather was Irish. He fought and died for that cause. But Jan is smarter than that. He is not one of them, just a paid courier. With all the trouble they've had of late . . . "

"What trouble?" Schmitt demanded.

"The governments in France and Spain have come down hard on ETA since they tried to kill King Juan Carlos in 95. Jan has a reputation for being good. They know they can trust him to deliver. Besides, if he gets caught they disown him. But Jan never gets caught. He's good. In fact, he's doing a run any day now. Libyan cash for a small arms deal in Brussels. That's what they were on about. I swear I can't tell you anything else!"

Schmitt demanded and got the full name and address of the courier. "Presumably, you were going to forewarn this Jan Ruiter fellow?"

The man nodded.

"Don't. If you do, I'll know. Then I'll hunt you down like the vermin you are and exterminate you. Do I make myself perfectly clear?" His tone left little doubt that he could and would make good on any threats.

"Ja," the man croaked feebly.

"Excellent." Keeping his quarry pinned beneath him with his gun-hand, Schmitt deftly relieved the youth of the money the American had paid him. Just a little pressure from his gun barrel was all it took to squelch the man's protest. "Saves you the trouble of having to explain it on your taxes."

Pocketing the cash, Schmitt added, "Don't try to get up until I'm gone and don't forget my warning." Schmitt rose stiffly and let himself out, the Mauser disappearing into his jacket as quickly as it had materialized.

CHAPTER THREE

24 August

The Centraal Station was crowded. Diverse people headed to varied destinations. Tourists festooned with cameras dangling about their necks on colorful straps hurried about. Many, obviously unsure of how to get where they were going, wore slightly exasperated expressions on weary faces. Vendors vied for customers. Beautiful cut flowers created bright splotches of brilliant color.

All in all, Amsterdam's central railroad station was the busy sort of place where one easily escaped notice. There were all sorts present, from executives in designer suits on down to longhaired youths in faded jeans decorated with patches. Almost anyone, if practiced enough, could blend in.

Erik Larson wore ivory slacks, pale blue cotton knit shirt, and mirrored sunglasses. A lightweight nylon carryall was slung over his shoulder, a folded local paper in his hand. To the casual observer he was just another slightly lost traveler being jostled about by the constantly moving throng. He walked slowly, apparently uncertain of his destination. Which, in fact, he was.

The bearded young man he discreetly followed wore faded denim jeans and a soiled white T-shirt bearing the Heineken Beer logo. His quarry also toted a well-worn brown leather satchel, which from the look of it should long since have been relegated to the junk heap. The satchel carrying Dutchman was of average height, but his unusually lean build gave the illusion of greater stature. His was a macabre mug; a bony face with sunken cheeks and an unhealthy pallor. He was either undernourished or a dope addict. Probably both, the American concluded as he continued to follow at a respectable distance.

The young Dutchman stopped by a flower vendor. The battered satchel dropped loudly to the floor beside a white plastic bucket that overflowed with scarlet tulips. He took a step or two to one side to select a bunch of dazzling yellow tulips from yet another bucket. While he paid the vendor, another man, this one dressed in a rumpled gray suit, stopped and placed his satchel beside the young man's. The satchels were identical twins. Every bit of abuse inflicted upon one, had been wrought with equal zeal upon the other.

Tulips in hand, the T-shirted Dutchman retrieved a satchel. Predictably, it was not his own. Larson allowed himself a grin. It was an old trick, but he had to admit that it had been executed smoothly.

He again set off in cautious pursuit of the T-shirted Dutchman, taking special care not to let the gray suited person, who was already headed in the opposite direction, notice his presence.

Outside the station the young Dutchman paused at a snack stand. The satchel dropped lightly to the ground and was securely pinned between his legs. With his free hand he produced some coins and bought a salted herring. Holding the little fish by its tail, he craned his head back. With obvious relish he lowered it into his mouth in what had become the common way for an Amsterdammer to enjoy the tasty tidbit in the centuries since a Dutchman first discovered herring could be preserved by salting in 1384.

After a casual glance upwards at the Centraal Station's ornate facade with its twin towers, one capped in a black point, the other culminating in a white point, he crossed to a nearby signpost where his bicycle was chained. He strapped the satchel on the rusted carrier. Flowers in hand, he mounted and rode slowly out onto Prins Hendrik Kade.

The American noted his departure and walked swiftly toward a parked car. He climbed in beside the driver of the waiting BMW. Neither the driver nor the grim faced individual in the back seat said anything. Their eyes fixated on the retreating form of the cyclist. The driver started the engine, eased it into gear and pulled into the stream of traffic. They knew where the cyclist was headed, but one never took chances when it was not necessary. They would follow in the car.

The dilapidated houseboat lay peacefully in the sun-dappled canal. Schmitt waited until the young man who emerged on deck had mounted an old bicycle and rode off along the canal. Only then did he walk purposefully onboard. The locked door provided only a minor inconvenience. He was soon inside. The interior was a shambles, even more so than the run-down exterior which was hard to believe. Crumpled clothes, yellowed papers, and odds and ends lay heaped everywhere. Cobwebs stretched across corners. The windows were all but obscured by thriving vine-like plants with sinuous tentacles extending about. Densely layered filth gave the few visible panes of glass a frosted appearance.

An overpowering mildewed odor hung in the musty, fetid air. A faint trace of cannabis was discernible. The latter was not so surprising because Schmitt had noted several healthy plants growing in old wooden boxes on deck.

He moved slowly through the cabin. Bizarre posters adorned walls. Some lacy material, probably once white, formed a partition of sorts at the far end. The disarray of pillows and blankets strewn atop two old mattresses beyond, obviously served as a bed. Nearby another door led on deck.

Schmitt thoroughly checked every cabinet and cupboard. He rifled through any papers he found, skimming through those that seemed to offer potential. He did not know precisely what he hoped to discover, but if and when he stumbled upon it, he knew he would recognize it.

The sudden sound of someone on deck startled him. He hurriedly stuffed a handful of papers back into a drawer. After a moment's hesitation he ducked into a closet near the main entrance. From there he reasoned that he could beat a hasty retreat when opportunity allowed. Safely concealed under a pile of dirty laundry in the recesses of the closet, he heard the main door open.

Jan Ruiter felt good as he threaded his way through the

familiar streets on his rusty bicycle. It had been acquired for a mere pittance at the regularly held, police sponsored auction of recovered stray bicycles. It was not much, but it suited his simplistic needs. He rounded another bend and coasted slowly across the pavement to the canal-side where the old houseboat he shared with his equally politically fanatic lover, lay moored.

He rolled the bike down a wide wooden plank that served as boarding ramp and locked it to the stern railing that, like the rest of the boat's exterior, was painted a dull yellow and in desperate need of repair, not to mention a fresh coat of paint. Oblivious of the blue BMW that slowed and parked under some trees a short distance along the canal-side, he took the leather satchel and tulips and entered the houseboat. He barely had time to switch on a lamp beside the entrance before he heard footsteps descending the boarding plank. He tossed the satchel on a table.

Smiling, he opened the door and said in Dutch, "Helena, you're home early!"

The smile waned when he saw the two strangers. He felt foolish with the bouquet of flowers proffered in his outstretched hand. He lowered them while studied the strangers. One was tall and broad shouldered, the other slightly shorter, but every bit as powerful, if not more so. Had Ruiter been observant, he might have noted that both men wore skintight, black nylon gloves. "Wat wenst U? Wie is U?" he demanded.

"Visitors," replied the taller man in English, a congenial smile on his tanned faced.

"There must be the mistake," Ruiter responded in intentionally heavily accented English. "I don't know you."

"You do now," the tall man replied. His right arm shifted ever so slightly so that the sides of the unzipped top of his carryall parted. His hand, which Ruiter suddenly realized had been concealed within the recesses of the bag, gripped a pistol. Its muzzle aimed directly at the Dutchman.

"Who are you?" Ruiter demanded. The sternness in his voice was forced. Fear showed plainly in his dark eyes.

"Inside. Now!", the shorter man said harshly, though his face remained pleasant enough. If anyone took note of Ruiter's visitors all would seem to be in order.

No appreciable alternative available, Ruiter stepped reluctantly backwards. The interior of the houseboat was dismally dark in contrast to the brilliant sunshine outside. Once their eyes adjusted to the gloom, Ruiter's unwelcome visitors beheld the frightful mess with as much disgust as Schmitt had earlier.

Nose wrinkled in disgust, Erik Larson cursed his acute olfactory sense. He shuddered involuntarily as he absorbed the spectacle. The thought that any human being would willingly endure such an existence thoroughly repulsed him. He could not help but feel a sense of pity for the distasteful wretch who stood before him. He thrust the feeling from his mind. This was not the place for emotions, he told himself.

Almost casually, Larson pulled the Luger from the carryall. The perforated cylinder of the silencer screwed to its barrel made it look even more sinister. A similar weapon appeared in his companion's hand. It had been concealed inside the colorful Windbreaker he carried.

His Luger still leveled at Ruiter's chest, Larson grabbed a battered old chair with chipped fluorescent-green paint and spun it around so that it faced him. "Gaat U zitten!", he commanded in fluent Dutch.

"Who are you?" Ruiter persisted as he obediently settled heavily onto the chair. The flowers dropped to the floor. His constantly shifting eyes kept returning to the satchel that lay atop a cluttered table.

"Cover him," Larson said quietly in English. "Let's see what our newfound friend has in his little bag." He placed his Luger atop some papers and unzipped the satchel. About a half dozen small brown parcels lay inside. Thin twine bound each parcel. Taking one, he sliced through the twine with a switchblade. The brown paper peeled away to reveal a stack of well-used, one hundred dollar bills. He rifled through the pack. "There must be roughly five thousand in each. About thirty-five thousand dollars total. Tidy sum to entrust to a bum like this. I must say that I find it to be exceedingly poor judgment on the part of his masters. He strikes me as wholly incompetent."

The remarks had the desired effect. Ruiter's temper rose swiftly. Anger replaced fear. "Who the hell are you people?" This time he spoke in English.

"Quiet!" Larson said sternly. "One more shout like that and it may be your last."

Ruiter fought to contain his rage, something he had never been particularly adept at. "I have done nothing wrong." His English diction markedly improved as he spoke. "You come in here; push guns in my face! I have a right to know what office sent you. Why are you here?"

Larson remained insentient to Ruiter's comments. "In spite of the ongoing crack-down by French and Spanish authorities there are obviously many who believe strongly in the survival of the ETA and all that it stands for. Shrewd planning and persistence will prepare the ETA to strike back harder than ever. I find myself almost admiring them." His cold eyes met Ruiter's. "Thoroughness and planning for contingencies are traits of sage people. Yet, as for myself, the ETA and Spain as a whole could happily annihilate each other and I would lose no sleep. Politics and power struggles never fascinated me.

"You, on the other hand, give a damn about all sorts of wild causes. We know that you sympathize with the Irish Republican Army, the ETA, and various other so called freedom fighters throughout Europe. At times you make trips across borders for several of these organizations, among them the ETA and IRA. This," he gestured to the pile of money now stacked neatly in a cleared space on the table, "is being funneled to an arms dealer in Brussels from points south, specifically Libya."

The shocked expression on Ruiter's gaunt face indicated the veracity of Larson's statements. "Your current assignment is to deliver these funds to a black market arms dealer. The weapons he will provide are then to be moved to Marseilles for delivery to other ETA sympathizers who will smuggle them into the Basque region. Regrettably for your terrorist cause, you will be unable to carry out your end of the bargain. Though I suppose that in the long run, the loss of one weapons shipment will be only a minor setback to your Basque friends. Besides, during the current government onslaught, they would be better advised to lay low and bide their time."

The houseboat rocked gently as a tourist laden tour boat cruised past, its engine purring gently. Moments later a deeper, rumbling boat's engine passed and stopped.

Larson shook his head slowly. "You know, when one is involved in such illegal activities as you are, one should exercise a much greater level of caution than you seem to."

"You son of a bitch!" Ruiter shouted angrily. "Like all police, you're nothing but swine! You'll . . . "

The words died abruptly with a sickening crunch as Larson's companion thrust the silenced barrel of his Luger into the Dutchman's mouth. Teeth shattered, lips turned red. Blood trickled down his chin from the corners of his mouth. It dripped onto his T-shirt.

"We told you not to call out," the man said softly as he withdrew the pistol. He grabbed a soiled shirt from the table and tossed it to the terrified courier. "Clean yourself up, boy."

Ruiter mopped his bruised and bleeding lips and gums. Bloodied pieces of shattered front teeth were spat onto the floor. "Bastards!" He mumbled venomously under his breath.

Larson shook his head sadly. "Some always insist on learning the hard way. Listen carefully, Ruiter. You would be much better off if we were police. Unfortunately for you, we are not. Which leaves you with two options. Cooperate and we leave you without inflicting any further injury. On the other hand, should you insist on making things difficult, I can assure you that my associate here will have no compunctions against extracting the information forcibly. Either way, you'll talk." He turned and began to transfer the bundles of hundred dollar bills to his carryall. "As I was saying, we've learned a great deal about you. Of particular interest to us are the two trips that you made to the United States last year. You visited the contacts for some very prominent sympathizers in Boston. We want to . . ."

There was a loud thump outside on deck. Someone had just jumped aboard. The sound of a few footsteps followed. Then the door at the far end of the large main cabin opened inwards.

"Jan?" a woman's voice called out.

In that split second of unexpected confusion, Ruiter saw what might be his only chance. He lunged at the gunman nearest him, the shorter one. The force of his attack was sufficient to send the man tumbling backwards, tripping over an old packing crate. He landed with a crash that brought a pile of filthy clothing cascading down over him.

The woman reacted with remarkable alacrity. She dove for a dilapidated nightstand beyond the lace partition. The lace ripped off the thumbtacks that held it in place as she rolled across the mattresses and flung open a drawer, spilling its contents. Among the assorted odds and ends lay a Walther P38. Her hands snatched it up, flicked off the safety, and aimed in one swift, fluid motion.

She was incredibly fast, but Larson was that little bit faster because he had the advantage that his weapon had been in hand by the time the door opened. Had it not been, the outcome probably would have been different. Twice his weapon spit fire.

He was vaguely aware that both shots hit the dark eyed woman near the heart. The impacts pitched her onto the pillows where she landed face up, staring eyes fixed at some unseen point on the ceiling. Larson had never killed anyone before, never been directly exposed to brutal murder. The hours and hours of target practice under the close supervision of his proficient associate had honed the skill, but had not prepared him for the gory details as bullets shattered living flesh, splattered blood about, and left a lifeless corpse in their wake. For an instant he stood mesmerized by the horrible sight. He swallowed hard to quell the urge to be violently sick. Bile was choked down. He came back to life, reflexively dodging a flying chair.

Ruiter heard the muted shots. He spun round, grabbed the chair where his interrogation had been unfolding, and hurled it viciously at the tall American. At that instant Ruiter realized that a third intruder had just burst through the doorway at the far end of the cabin. Time for further thought had expired. He ran. Behind him, the wooden door frame splintered as the newcomer fired at him with a silenced weapon.

On deck Ruiter glanced frantically from side to side like a hunted animal. His neighbor on the next houseboat was just tying up his speedboat. The aging Super Sidewinder was his pride and joy. Carefully polished and waxed, the craft gleamed in the sunshine. Its powerful Evinrude Starflite engine had been what they all heard pass only a minute or so ago. His neighbor looked up from the cockpit and waved. "Hallo, Jan," he called cheerfully. "Hoe maakt U het?"

Ruiter did not acknowledge. He vaulted the after-rail of the houseboat and landed in the speedboat's cockpit beside the startled owner.

"Hey! What's the matter? Are you crazy?" The man shouted angrily in Dutch. The sudden appearance of two armed men on Ruiter's houseboat diverted his attention. Ruiter pulled the confused man round to use him as a shield. Simultaneously he activated the electric-start ignition. The boat's powerful eighty-five horsepower outboard engine roared to life.

One arm still locked around his struggling neighbor, he threw the throttle forward. The boat leapt ahead. Ruiter never heard the muffled plops of the weapons leveled at him, but he knew they had been fired. Two holes suddenly perforated the curved windscreen in front of him. A jagged cracked pattern spread outwards from each. It was only then that he realized his neighbor no longer struggled. He let the corpse drop, dully aware of the crimson stains smeared on his T-shirt and jeans. Both hands grasped the wheel as he narrowly avoided collision with a slow moving barge whose grizzled owner shouted a string of obscenities. An angry fist waved at the young lunatic in the power boat.

Ruiter's departure played havoc with the otherwise peaceful canal setting. Aside from the heavily laden barge, he also narrowly missed another motorboat headed in the opposite direction. The smartly dressed young man steering the other boat shook his head in dismay and made some blistering comment about the madman who nearly had collided with them, to his fiancée seated by his side. He twisted his neck round to stare after the disappearing maniac.

Larson brought up his weapon and fired three quick shots at Ruiter as the speedboat lurched into mid-canal. At that instant he noticed the young couple in the other motorboat veering towards the houseboat in order to avoid Ruiter. He pointed at them as their boat came nearer. “Can you make it?” he asked his companion.

The question went unanswered. The man was already taking the two powerful strides that brought him to the rail and propelled him into the air. Arms outstretched, he flew across the water. With a loud bang he landed roughly on the motorboat’s foredeck. He scrambled quickly over the windscreen and into the cockpit where he menacingly brandished his pistol.

The protesting couple soon found themselves over the side in the cool waters of the canal. This accomplished, the gunman spun the wheel, brought the boat around one hundred eighty degrees, and rammed the throttle as far forward as it would go. The inboard engine growled throatily. Spray flew high as the boat zoomed past the barge whose aging skipper launched another verbal tirade.

Cramped in the stench of the bottom of the musty closet, Schmitt listened intently to the flurry of violent activity that ceased as abruptly as it erupted. He contemplated leaving his concealment, but abandoned the thought when he heard the clatter of approaching footsteps. As before, the voices carried clearly through the thin door.

"Is she dead?" The voice was that of the person who had directed the thwarted interrogation.

"Very much so. Nice work, Erik." The second voice was a new one.

"Mmmm. Bit messy though. Especially since that punk from the bar will have to be silenced. Permanently!"

Schmitt could hear drawers being opened and shut, papers being shuffled.

"Why bother? He knows nothing. To him we were just curious strangers."

"Not quite. He knows what sort of conduit we're trying to tap into. That makes him a threat, albeit a minor one."

"Fair enough. I'll start looking as soon as we're through here."

"I'll take care of things here. There's little enough time before the police will arrive. You get going. Do it cleanly."

"What about the other bastard? What if he escapes? He may go to the police."

"He won't." There was an air of finality to the statement. "Now get moving!"

After one set of footsteps withdrew, Schmitt heard only an occasional footfall or indistinguishable sound. The Mauser had been in hand since the beginning. If the closet door opened, he resolved to shoot the American then and there. The door remained closed.

All sound seemed to cease. Seconds passed. A dull crackling sound grew in intensity. A new odor slowly filtered into the closet, that of burnt wood and fabric. Schmitt leapt to his feet and smashed open the door. Smoke swirled throughout the length of the cabin. Red-orange tongues of flame arched upwards from several rapidly spreading fires. The door and walls near the closet were already a sheet of flames. Schmitt jammed his weapon back into its shoulder holster and jumped into the middle of the room. The putrid stench of burnt flesh permeated the acrid smoke. Eyes watering, he stumbled through the stifling heat towards the other exit. Halfway there he saw that flames engulfed it completely. He knew only seconds remained before the entire cabin ignited in the phenomenon known as flashover. There was no time for hesitation. He darted through the flames in front of the nearest window, launched himself into the air, and crashed through the glass, arms shielding his head. Shards of flying glass and woodwork followed him into the murky waters of the canal.

Bobbing to the surface, he quickly swam to the far bank and climbed ashore. An old man offered a helping hand. Schmitt thanked him perfunctorily and hurried away. He had no desire to be caught up in the growing commotion. Police and fire klaxons blared as he slipped up a side street.

The high-speed boat chase soon left the Brouwersgracht behind as it wound through the quaint canals to the distinct displeasure of other, saner, individuals who plied the waters. Only a few startled pedestrians on canal side streets or bridges, who turned upon hearing the repeated blasts of boat whistles and the approaching roar of strained engines, could find anything but contempt for the two powerboaters and the mad race they seemed to be engaged in. With quiet fascination they watched the madmen fly past. Then they went about their own business as though it had never happened. A few envious youngsters ran from one side of a bridge to the other to glimpse a few more precious seconds of the contest.

The streamlined, fire-engine red, Super Sidewinder that Ruiter had appropriated, swung wildly from side to side as it rushed past slow moving barges and tour-boats. More than one boater found himself showered in a spray of cool water as the red blur thundered by.

Arcing onto the broad Singel Canal, Ruiter fought desperately with the tiny wheel only to feel his entire body jarred and bumped about as the powerboat side slipped violently. It rammed broadside into a stark white, glass-topped tour-boat. Metal screeched and tore. Terrified tourists who were getting vastly more excitement for their money than they had bargained for, screamed in panic. And then the lunatic was off again, the powerboat slowly regaining lost speed.

Seconds later the tourists witnessed another fright. The tour-boat's already dented side, marred by a long, red-lipped gouge, took a further beating. The trim white motorboat added to the damage and confusion with its lesser impact. Then it too shot off along the canal, twin fountains of water soaring out to either side.

The collision cost Ruiter valuable seconds. When he shot a

hasty look backwards, the little white speedboat had narrowed the gap. Although he knew the throttle was already fully open, his hand instinctively pressed against the unyielding lever. The futile gesture only served to maximize his anxiety.

Ahead, behind some trees lining the left bank, the unmistakable spire of the Mint Tower loomed with its black-faced clocks. To the right of the old landmark a large billboard advertisement towered above the buildings Ruiter was oblivious of both as he guided his craft under another low lying bridge. There was a momentary deafening reverberation as the boat roared through the tightly confined space beneath the bridge. He wrestled with the wheel to avoid another crash. He swerved right. Ahead stretched the much wider Amstel River. He opted to follow the river after swinging dangerously close to another tour-boat that had just pulled away from its dock laden with a fresh load of wide-eyed tourists.

Two side canals slipped past. All the while the gap between Ruiter and his pursuer diminished. A third, wider, canal neared. Ruiter suddenly realized that two heavily burdened barges, linked in tandem, soon would block the entrance to the canal. He waited as long as he dared, spun the wheel wildly, and prayed. The red speedboat side slipped in a series of bone jarring bounces. Then it rushed in front of the barges. The Oudeschans Canal seemed to welcome him victoriously.

The newfound exhilaration faded quickly when the skipping hull of the white powerboat managed to defy the odds. It bounded through the impossibly narrow opening just as the barges closed it. Whoever his pursuer was, he must be a suicidally inclined individual. He doggedly clung to Ruiter's tail.

The Dutchman grew more concerned when he realized the white boat had drawn close to his port flank. He tried desperately to clear his thoughts. The determined expression in his pursuer's dark eyes did little to comfort him whenever he glanced nervously back. Another few moments and the white boat would overtake him.

In desperation, he jerked the throttle back suddenly. The battered red hull lowered itself into the canal. Speed dropped rapidly. Caught entirely unprepared, the other craft rushed past to port.

Ruiter cut the wheel and brought the boat around a hundred eighty degrees before ramming the throttle all the way forward again. A skilled boatman he was not. The battered red hull lifted obediently. To his chagrin the white speedboat, maneuvered by more competent hands, made a swifter, larger radius turn. It was almost on top of him before he was up to speed again.

Moments later the scratched white hull swung abruptly toward him. Metal groaned in agony. Wheels bucked in firmly locked hands. The boats parted, steadied, and slammed together again with even more force. Screaming metal sent sparks flying. The hulls clung together momentarily, then slipped apart. Again the white boat angled in. This time it climbed partially over the rail of Ruiter's craft. The whining roar of the engines was deafening.

Still off balance from the impact, Ruiter was not prepared to repel a boarder. He raised an arm defensively in front of his lunging assailant. It did little good. Ruiter crashed to the cramped deck, the full weight of his attacker atop him. There was a thud as his head banged against a metal toolbox. The last image he could recall before blacking out was that of his assailant scrambling to grasp the swinging wheel and bring the boat under control. The last sound he heard was the booming explosion as the abandoned white speedboat, totally out of control, impacted with the side of the next bridge. A terrifying reality became a nightmarish dream world for Ruiter as he lay unconscious atop his neighbor's corpse.

CHAPTER FOUR

25 August

Peter Determeijer was a month shy of fifty and already well on his way to baldness. Heavy lines creased a visage where a crooked nose separated tired gray eyes. He smoked incessantly, the result of too many years spent working on the more distasteful cases he consoled himself. The ever-bountiful drug trade, with its occasional power struggles between rival factions for control of the lucrative business, provided a steady source of homicides that required investigation. In the early seventies, Chinese tongs had risen to prominence in Amsterdam's flourishing narcotics' trade. Their tight-lipped control made a difficult task even more so. But Determeijer was not one to yield easily. He stoically dogged cases. His work took him into the clouded rooms of opium dens and the bizarre nether world of the city's freakier citizens. It was slow, methodical work that craved vast reserves of patience, a trait very much akin to Determeijer. Skill, thoroughness, and an unswerving sense of devotion made him one of the city's most respected homicide investigators.

The bloody daylight killings and the high speed boat chase that had disrupted the quaint waterways the previous day dominated the morning newspapers. The sheer audacity and brutality of the killers made it a case to be solved quickly, the chief inspector had been adamant about that. The killings bore ominous overtones. The charred corpse on the houseboat moored in Brouwersgracht and the neighbor whose corpse had turned up in the battered red speedboat had both died of gunshot wounds. The young man who turned up floating in an inner city canal had suffered a worse fate. From his police record he had been identified as Jan Ruiter, a person no police officer would mourn. His corpse gave them cause for worry though. It bore evidence of forced interrogation that had terminated when someone had wrenched his neck beyond the limits of human anatomy thereby snuffing out his miserable life. Besides this physical abuse, Ruiter had been assaulted chemically. His bloodstream was full of the old fashioned, but in the right hands still effective drug, scopolamine. Both kneecaps had also been shot out at close range after he already had died. A bullet through the kneecap was statutory punishment for a traitor of the Irish Republican Army, a fact that further bewildered authorities. The IRA was supposed to be quietly watching the peace process at work, not blowing people away in other countries.

The investigation's first full day was drawing to a close when the surprising phone call had come. The unidentified caller claimed to have solid information about the triple homicide, but refused to meet Determeijer in his office. Instead, he named a rendezvous point. He would wait thirty minutes. If Determeijer failed to show within the allotted time, then it would be too bad.

Dressed in his habitual dark slacks and ill fitting, charcoal-gray jacket, Determeijer walked briskly along the dark street. A cigarette hung loosely from the side of his square-jawed mouth.

The place selected by the anonymous caller lay near the heart of the medieval city in the Zeedijk district. It was one of the city's numerous bruine cafes (brown cafes). Like similar establishments, its decor was strictly simplistic, its clientele boisterous. Dark wainscoting, scratched and nicked from years of abuse, hemmed in the happily swaying crowd, many of whom talked animatedly with compatriots as generous quantities of beer and alcohol were consumed. Above the darkly stained wainscoting the walls were adorned with cheap prints that depicted everything from sensuous nudes to serene canal-side scenes. Lighting was minimal. Tables and chairs were scarce.

No multilingual signs to attract tourists hung outside. No emblems to proclaim which credit cards were honored adorned the door. This establishment catered to a different clientele and from the looks of them, they were not the nicest assemblage of Amsterdammers that could be gathered. Determeijer recognized several people from their police dossiers.

He slowly forced his way through the smoke-filled room. In a rear corner a young man with disheveled, long, brown hair sat alone at a tiny rectangular table that sported a piece of cheap, soiled carpet in lieu of a tablecloth. How utterly typical, Determeijer thought as he settled into the vacant chair opposite the pitiful youth. He couldn't see the eyes behind the dark sunglasses, but he knew they were scared, darting to and fro like those of a hunted animal. Better than twenty-five years on the force had nurtured in Determeijer a sort of sixth sense. With an amazing penchant for accuracy, he could interpret a person's state of mind and the likely reliability of what the person was about to say, after only a mere moment of contact. The man before him was easy to read. He was agitated, highly nervous. Determeijer caught that on the phone. Seeing the man merely reinforced it. The dark glasses advertised that the wearer had something to hide or wished to hide himself. The set of the stubble covered chin, the slight shake of the hand as it grasped the mug of beer, the hurried way in which the beer was quaffed, all told the story.

Determeijer took a long, thoughtful draw on his cigarette. His eyes bore steadily at where the other man's hid behind the dark glasses, but he knew his gaze would not be met. It was meant to intimidate, to break down barriers. A barman appeared behind the detective.

"Een Hollandse jenever," the detective said.

"Twee," the young added hastily, holding up two fingers. The hand was quickly withdrawn when its owner realized it visibly shook.

The barman grunted something and cut a path back to the bar.

"Determeijer." The voice was strained, barely audible above the deafening din of innumerable conversations, "I can help. They're out to kill me too."

The detective took his time absorbing the statement. At length he pulled the cigarette from his mouth. A practiced tap with his index finger sent the long tip of ash swirling towards the scuffed floor. The cigarette returned to the corner of his mouth before he spoke. "Now why would someone want to do that, son?"

"Don't you see? I told you on the phone. I know! I know!" The cloying smell of fear, of abject terror, pervaded. Determeijer knew it well, all too well.

"Just what is it that you know?" He asked mildly as the drinks came.

"The killers! I know who!"

"You mentioned that on the phone," Determeijer reminded patiently. "I mean, what do you specifically know about the murders? Who did the killing? Why did they do it? And, for that matter, where do you fit in?" Determeijer lifted his small tulip-shaped glass. "Op Uw gezondheid!" He said with a curt nod.

His companion scooped up his glass, spilling some of the chilled contents and swallowed the remainder in one gulp. "Ruiter . . . Jan . . . was a sort of friend. It was my fault. I helped them." He pounded the table angrily with a fist.

Determeijer signaled the barman for two more drinks. "Easy, son. Let's get the story straight. Start from the beginning. The whole thing, if you'll please."

The distraught young man nodded quickly. "Alright. O.K.." He swallowed hard. "The bastards were fishing for information. Passing around bills and drinks freely. I . . ."

"What information?" Determeijer cut in.

"The ETA! The God damned ETA!"

"You mean IRA, don't you?"

"No I damned well don't! Jan hasn't worked for the Irish bastards since the peace crap started a couple of years back."

This information intrigued Determeijer. If true, it indicated the hallmark IRA-style shooting of the victim's kneecaps was a red herring. "Who or what the hell is the ETA?"

"Basque liberation movement, the ones that've been catching hell of late. The people who killed Jan knew a conduit for ETA moneys was here. In Amsterdam, that is. Tapping into it was what it was all about. Said it was important, they did. Said they had important information that needed to be passed on. Information that could save many in the organization."

The fresh drinks came and were consumed rapidly. Determeijer hoped the alcohol would relax his jittery informant, making it easier to extract information from him. "I've read about the crack-down on the ETA. They've mostly gone to ground or fled the region," he said as he contemplated the implications of what the young man might be involved with.

"Sure, but their sort don't play without having a hole card. They've got to watch their asses every step of the way. The Spaniards would love to eliminate them and be done with the whole mess. Anyways, the ETA is very much alive and well."

"Then Ruiter was indeed mixed up with the Basque cause?"

The young man nodded as he wiped away some stray drops of jenever from his chin with a dirty sleeve. "A courier." He waved for the barkeep to fetch another round. Free drinks were not to be missed under any circumstances. "Jan got into it through his old lady. He carried things across borders. Listen, what Jan did does not make a tinker's damn. He's dead. The bastards that iced him and his old lady are bad news. They're evil! One of them was by my flat late last night. Which means I'm next on the extermination list. I mean . . . I was their link with Ruiter. I know who they are. I'm a loose end."

Determeijer stroked his chin thoughtfully. "What happened at your flat last night?"

The informant shook his head and gesticulated with his hands, "No! No! No! Nothing happened there last night! Don't you understand? I saw the bastard! Do I look crazy? I ran! He never saw me and he never will." He paused as a new thought occurred to him. "Oh yeah, you should know about the other one too. Same night as the others. Only he didn't pay for info. He just knocked me about a bit and threatened worse if I didn't tell him what I'd told the others."

"And?" Determeijer felt certain he knew the identity of the man who had conducted the rough interrogation.

"I damned well told him!"

"I can arrange protection, son, but I'll need to know who

we're dealing with. You said you knew the murderers."

"I don't want any bloody protection!" He hissed vehemently. "I want you to get the SOBs! That's all. Just get them!" The loud outburst ended as suddenly as it began. The bartender added two more tiny glasses to the growing number on the tiny table and slipped quietly away. He had no desire to become involved in whatever was transpiring.

Determeijer remained unperturbed by the emotional outburst. "Get who?" He asked quietly.

"I don't know their blasted names!" The voice dripped exasperation. "Their kind don't exactly go round introducing themselves and handin' out business cards to one and all, now do they?" He belted down another drink in a single gulp. "But I do know a little. They were Americans. Rich Americans."

"Because they were buying drinks and passing money?"

"No. Because of the tall one's ticker."

"His ticker?" Determeijer sipped his drink, savoring the flavor of the yellowish liquid.

"His ticker. His watch, man! It was gold."

Still eyeing the remainder of the delightful jenever swishing round in the little glass, Determeijer dropped his cigarette butt to the floor and crushed it beneath his heel. "How do you know it was gold, son?"

"Pssssh! How do I know? Look at me Determeijer. I'm no damned go to church every Sunday saint, am I? I've stolen more bloody watches than there are hours in a week. I know prime stuff when I see it. That ticker cost him ten thousand, if not more."

"Guilders?"

"Dollars! A Piaget it was. Fine piece too. I'd have taken it from him out on the streets after I saw it, but I'm not crazy, am I? I saw the look in his eyes. He and especially the shorter one, they're trouble those two. I should never have told them about Jan."

The detective scribbled some notes on his pad. "How about their appearances? Describe them."

"Good clothes. Tailored maybe. Not the stuff I'm used to. The taller one, the Piaget, spoke Dutch fairly well, but with an accent. In his late-forties maybe. The other one, a bit younger, never said much. Darker complexioned though, but he never said much."

"How about their faces?"

The man shook his head jerkily. "I don't know. Nothing unusual comes to mind. They had ordinary faces." He paused. "Look, I've told you what I can. Can't be many dark-haired Americans in the city with gold watches like that one. Check the hotels. Just find him!"

It was Determeijer's turn to shake his head. "You ask the impossible. I'll need something more to go on. Why not come back to my office? We can sit down in peace and try to revive your memory. Besides, even assuming that my men turned up an American with a gold Piaget watch, without you to identify him for us, I would have nothing to arrest him for. We need each other to get Ruiter's killers. I offer protection."

"Me? Police protection?" He made a futile attempt at a laugh. "You've got to be insane. No, I take care of myself. I just wanted to talk with you so that you can get the bastards. Until you do, I have to keep running. You worry about getting them. That's your job. Me? I'm getting out of Amsterdam. I've got friends in Rotterdam." He got suddenly to his feet. "I've been here too long already. Stay put 'til I'm gone."

Determeijer nodded philosophically. “As you wish, son. But keep my offer in mind. You know where to reach me. These are dangerous people, son. Very dangerous.”

The young man spun round and made his way through the crowd towards the door. The detective signaled the barman for another drink and continued to make notes on his pad. Among other things, he wanted to run a thorough check in the police records to learn the identity of his informant. He was certain that he would find the face among the thousands on file. Whether or not the young man wanted it, he would have police protection. Not so much because Determeijer cared about the well-being of a self-confessed hood, but because whoever the killers were, they might try for him again.

He was still writing when he heard the first horrified scream. Determeijer scooped up his notepad and leapt to his feet. He plowed through the crowded cafe, elbowing and shoving people. Several glasses crashed to the floor. Angry people, their drinks spilled all over them, shouted venomously at the maniacal detective.

Outside, he thrust through a mass of gathering spectators. In the tiny clearing around which they were assembling, lay the object of the commotion.

The stubble covered chin hung open, the dark glasses lay shattered on the pavement, dark eyes, forever blinded, stared blankly up at the heavens. Three tightly grouped holes penetrated the soiled shirt, an expanding dark stain surrounding them. The young man had died instantaneously.

Gun drawn, Determeijer lunged away from the center of the commotion. But he knew it was a futile gesture. Trained eyes sought a face that might trigger a mental alarm. There was no such face. Only bewildered, scared expressions greeted him. The murder had been executed cleanly, efficiently. He slipped his weapon back into its holster and wove his way back through the onlookers to the body.

He knelt beside the corpse and hurriedly rifled through the deceased's pockets. There was no identification. Only some crumpled twenty-five-guilder notes, a few coins, a set of keys, and an abundance of lint were to be found. The detective cursed aloud. Somebody was killing on a wholesale basis and the only tangible clue as to the reason was a vague connection with a supposedly resurgent ETA. But what was the root cause? Factional infighting within the ranks of the Basque fanatics? A French or Spanish anti-terrorist unit operating illegally to eradicate the ETA on Dutch soil? Neither thought struck him as plausible, but what then, he wondered.

The Schiller Hotel dated from 1892 and was one of the few structures on the Rembrandtsplein to survive the devastating effects of World War II. It possessed a certain grace born of age, not to be found in some of the newer buildings nearby. Its pleasant surroundings offered old-fashioned Bohemian comforts to a clientele that counted many writers and artists amongst its ranks. A large sidewalk terrace fronted the hotel, providing a perfect spot from which to sit and watch the world of *Rembrandtsplein*, the heart of Amsterdam's throbbing nightlife and theater district.

Among the hotel's owners through the years was a prolific painter whose oils and watercolors remained, a lasting legacy. The rooms were comfortable, blessed with a coziness not found in most hotels. Pastoral paintings of the Dutch countryside adorned their walls. Such aesthetic touches made the Schiller a natural choice for Erik Larson. The accommodations were more than adequate, the service amiable; the atmosphere perfection itself.

The afternoon had been spent lazily marveling at the treasures housed within the vast galleries of the Victorian-styled building of the *Rijksmuseum*. The magnificent works of the seventeenth century masters provided the high point of the visit.

The leisurely afternoon proved a welcome change of pace after the distasteful events of the previous day. The typically Dutch fare served stylishly in the elegant second-floor restaurant at the Schiller also provided a needed diversion from nagging thoughts of death and killing that plagued Larson. He mustered a smile as he raised his glass to toast his lovely spouse, Kristine.

Their glasses clinked gently together. Their eyes met. At length Kristine said, "I'm glad to see you smile again. Did you know that was the first time all day?"

"I really haven't been keeping count." His voice was sullen, uncharacteristically soft.

She reached across the tablecloth and gently took his hand. "It's done. We can't change that now, darling. You, yourself said how imperative it was for everyone to be prepared to deal with worst case scenarios."

"I am well aware of that fact. I suppose I'm just being silly. Don't let me spoil dinner."

She smiled warmly. "Then cheer up. Things could be much worse. Besides, you took reasonable precautions. Harry was watching the street entrance to the houseboat. You couldn't have known the girl was next door and would jump across before he could slow her up and warn you. You did what you had to do, Erik. Nothing more. It was her or you. There was no alternative."

"I know. I guess I just had some nonsensical delusion that such things could be avoided. There is a certain sterility attached when one watches a murder on film. A sense of detached safety, I suppose. You see it portrayed so often that it finally loses meaning, one becomes blasé. I honestly think that I half-expected it to be the same in reality; a neat sterile event. Something from which one could remain wholly detached. But it wasn't like that at all. It was a grisly mess. I don't envy our two, shall we say, assistants."

"At least Keith extracted the information we needed prior to dispatching that filthy wretch," she said.

Larson mustered a feeble smile. "Always pays to hire the best. I just hope he fairs as well with tonight's little foray."

"He will. By now the deed should be done." She released his hand and took another forkful of the delicious *lamstongen met rozinnensaus*. The lamb's tongue was superb, but what made it so especially palatable was the sauce. The flavorful combination of garlic, cumin, raisins, white wine, and other ingredients left taste buds in ecstasy.

Each enjoyed a few tasty bites in silence. From the outset, Erik Larson knew that sooner or later killing was bound to become a necessary recourse. Actually, he thought to himself as he munched on some succulent vegetables, eliminating Ruiter and his distasteful cohorts was the best way to ensure absolute silence. With that rationalization, Larson cast aside the last vestiges of moral scruples that had inhibited his sanctioning of cold-blooded murder by his associates. Henceforth, it would be deemed an acceptable tool to be used if and when expediency dictated.

Between mouthfuls he looked admiringly at his wife. The dark, chocolate-brown color of her hair and the new coiffure she had selected were nice, but he favored her natural color and usual styling better. His own doctored appearance was probably just as strange in her eyes. Another part of the innumerable precautions he would be glad to see ended when the operation itself was finally put behind them.

Erik finally broke the awkward silence. "Truly superb meal, don't you think?"

"Unquestionably. It's a shame we've got to move on tomorrow."

"All part of the game plan. Besides, before long, we'll be back."

She noticed his glance at the gold face of his watch for the fifth time since the main course had arrived. "I'm sure everything's gone well. Keith will handle it cleanly, professionally."

He smiled. The troublesome memory of the grisly dead woman aboard the horrid houseboat was thrust aside for the umpteenth time. He raised his glass. "To success!" The wine's excellent bouquet was not missed by his attuned sense as he spoke.

"To success!" Kristine repeated with feeling.

The pervasive smell of cigarette smoke alerted Schmitt as the door to the apartment swung open. The Mauser was instantly in hand. Senses on high, he cautiously entered.

The intruder sat comfortably ensconced in the sofa. He looked bemusedly at the stubby weapon pointed at him.

"I could have you arrested for carrying that thing," he said.

Schmitt holstered the weapon. "I thought policemen frowned on breaking and entering."

"Among other things," the man conceded. He forced a tired smile. "I'll forget I saw the gun, you forget how I got here."

Schmitt fetched a glass and picked up the Black Label bottle from the table where his guest had left it. "May I?"

"It ***is*** your whiskey."

Schmitt helped himself to a generous measure. He strode over to the window and looked out at the sleeping city beyond.

"Where's Lisbeth?" The man asked from the recesses of the sofa.

"Rotterdam. She got an assignment from the magazine, packed her cameras, and caught a morning train." Schmitt already missed her. He turned to face his visitor. "But that's not what brought you here."

"Hardly." Determeijer methodically lit another cigarette and inhaled deeply before elaborating. From the number of butts in the stone ashtray, Schmitt deduced the detective had been in the apartment at least two hours. "I want to know just what the hell you're up to." His tone embodied frustration laced with a hint of anger.

"Conducting an investigation," Schmitt replied coolly.

Determeijer exploded. "A triple homicide one afternoon! A professional murder the next! And ***you're*** conducting an investigation! Into what!?!"

"Take it easy, Peter."

"Take it easy! Four brutal murders in two days! One practically in front of my face!"

Schmitt's brows arched ever so slightly. The fourth corpse could only belong to the youth the American had marked for death. "I didn't kill them, Peter."

"No, of course not! But you damn well know who did! Perhaps you've forgotten you requested a complete rundown on Ruiter yesterday morning, only hours before he was slaughtered. And tonight's hit. You talked, and I use the word liberally, with the victim night before last. Now he's dead."

Schmitt sipped his whiskey impassively. The detective was no fool. "How do you figure I talked to him?" He asked.

Determeijer snickered derisively. "I know your methods, Kurt. You've a penchant for encouraging cooperation. Now I want some answers."

"Or?"

"Or I'll haul you in as an accessory. Several witnesses saw a man answering your description leap out of the burning houseboat. In itself, that's enough. The bloodied glass splinters in your bathroom garbage pail tend to reinforce matters."

"Thorough as usual. That's what I've always liked about you, Peter. You don't leave a stone unturned."

Determeijer ignored the praise. He leaned forward. The harshness in his voice abated. "I'm not unreasonable, Kurt, but I cannot sit back and ignore your connection. I've a sworn duty. I can overlook your illegal weapons and occasional strayings from what would be considered *normal* investigative procedures. Many's the time you've been a big help to myself and to the city. However, even that does not change multiple murder. Like it or not, I've got to know what is going on here. For instance, where does Nicco van Troje fit in? Or the damned ETA, for that matter? Van Troje has never been mixed up with that lot or their ilk."

It hardly surprised Schmitt to learn that Determeijer had

sifted through his reports and dossiers. He remained silent as he pondered just how much it was prudent to tell his friend.

"Be reasonable, Kurt," Determeijer prodded gently. "Those documents in the dresser mean you're working with Interpol's blessing. Any idiot can see van Troje is the focal point. You're probably trying to expose his smuggling operations. A most dangerous game. He is incredibly adept at crushing those who threaten him." He snubbed out his cigarette. A wisp of blue smoke curled upwards and dispersed. "Ruiter was some kind of courier for those Basque fanatics. And yet, the bullets through his kneecaps were meant to identify him as a traitor to the IRA. I don't make any connections, but obviously you do."

Schmitt smiled wryly. "I wish that were true. I do know that the ETA is involved. Aside from that minor data, so far, all I've got is a collection of disjointed bits and pieces."

The detective's glass was empty. He reached for the bottle, then thought better of it. "The American, this Collins fellow, is one of those pieces." It was not a question. "Before being slaughtered tonight, my informant said that a rich American with an expensive gold watch had bought information from him. His rich American and yours are obviously one and the same."

Schmitt shook his head slowly. "You'd have a hell of a time proving his complicity, let alone guilt. Besides, van Troje is the one you should really be after. He's the man behind the whole thing. Take the American now, and he slips through the net once again."

"This Collins bastard killed four times!"

"You know as well as I, that given the tenuous case that you can build against him, he'll be free faster than your men can round him up."

Determeijer looked exasperated. "So am I to just throw my

hands up and forget any of this ever happened? Is that your brilliant solution?"

"No. Just don't botch things by barging in on him quite yet. I need more time to put all of the incongruous pieces together. Take this bullshit with the IRA. The kneecap thing with its sinister overtones of the IRA is just a ruse to throw any police investigation off. If Collins genuinely were connected with those people, then he sure as hell would have known who Ruiter was. There would have been no need to fish for his actual identity. Yet Collins and his henchmen have gone to great pains to find out just who was the courier for the **ETA**, not the IRA. Once killed, his body could have easily vanished, yet they just dumped it in a canal, using it to advertise the fact that Ruiter was supposedly executed by his old good-natured IRA buddies. The whole damned thing stinks. I make it as a smoke screen. They want you looking for Irish fanatics when the real game is with the Spanish variety."

"But why some obscure group that no one's heard of? Why this ETA?"

Schmitt shrugged. "Who knows? I did some quick research and I do know that ETA stands for *Euskadi ta Askatasuna.* The group has its roots in the days when Franco ruled Spain. Seems the Basque region was semi-autonomous before then, but Franco greatly limited that freedom. I guess it was almost inevitable that any proud people would resent that intrusion and seek to change it."

"Hence the birth of ETA."

"Right on target, Peter. Limited home rule was granted in '82 and ETA more or less vanished for a while. When it resurfaced in 1994 there were indications of some kind of alignment with the IRA's leadership. Whether the meetings were just to learn about tactics or forge some kind of alliance is not known. It is known that Libya, Lebanon, and Nicaragua have all provided training to

ETA members at one time or another. Funding has generally been self-provided by various methods ranging from extortion to bank robbery and kidnappings. There are indications, corroborated by events here in the last few days, that outside sympathizers supply monies too.

"The ETA has been hit hard of late as both French and Spanish units have tried to eradicate the group. The biggest trouble is that no one knows just how big ETA is or who all those involved are. Even within the organization, it appears that the group is splintered into separate parts that have contact with, but do not know all about each other."

"Smart." The detective commented.

"Yeah, I suppose so. The bottom line is that the ETA is little known outside of the Basque country and is hardly likely to have ties with a twisted diamond merchant in Amsterdam. Yet Collins went to great pains to trace an ETA conduit that he knew to be here."

"But why?"

"I don't know. Not yet, anyway. I'm fairly certain that this Collins guy is relatively small fry. Time will tell where he fits in with Van Troje. Van Troje is the driving force and I need time to get him."

"Hmmmph." Determeijer snorted.

"There's something else you should consider, Peter. I found Collins. Without my work, you'd have nothing to go on. All I want is a chance to capitalize on that work. You owe me that much."

"You honestly think you'll get van Troje?" Determeijer asked.

"Won't be easy," Schmitt admitted, "but I think so." A broad smile spread across his features as he added, "I only collect the big payoffs when I deliver."

Not amused, Determeijer fell silent. He scooped up his glass and the Black Label. The last of the whiskey slopped into the glass and vanished in one gulp. A certain sense of renewed determination became evident in his mannerisms. He placed glass and bottle gently on the table, then rose stiffly. Tired gray eyes met Schmitt's expectant gaze. "Alright, you'll have some time. How much, I won't say. I cannot and will not impede the progress of my colleagues. Should they stumble onto Collins, or you for that matter, then justice must run its course. My only pledge to you is that I'll not hasten its course with regards to your link with Collins, unless, that is, something should happen to you." He paused, then in an unusually emotional voice, added, "May God help you."

Schmitt realized the tremendous trust the balding detective was exhibiting. Feeling somewhat ashamed that he had not told his friend everything he knew or suspected, he quietly muttered, "Thanks, Peter." But the words fell on deaf ears. Determeijer had already shouldered into his overcoat and headed out the door.

No sooner had Determeijer left than Schmitt pulled a plastic bag from his jacket pocket. A small cordials' glass lay in the bag. Schmitt removed the glass without touching its outer surfaces. It was placed with reverent care on the dining table. The waiter had demanded 100 guilders to spirit it away from the American's table. The maitre 'D had demanded another 200. It was a damned expensive little glass he reflected as he lobbed his jacket onto a chair.

Schmitt fetched his briefcase, laid out an array of

implements, and went to work. Shortly, three bands of wide Scotch tape were neatly attached to three index cards. Only one of the fingerprints was reasonably clear and even that was slightly smudged near the top. But it would have to do.

He labeled the cards, scribbled an explanatory note on another card, then tossed the lot into an envelope together with several other cards containing other prints. A Paris address and appropriate special delivery postage were applied.

Though already fatigued, Schmitt ventured back out into the night and posted the letter at the main post office.

CHAPTER FIVE

31 August

Schmitt lazed over the remnants of his light breakfast. He watched in wistful fascination as Lisbeth tinkered with a recalcitrant camera. Like every successful artist, she knew the tools of her trade inside out. She also possessed an enviable flair for composition with the lens.

He popped another chunk of cheese into his mouth just as the doorbell rang. Lisbeth was up in a flash. Schmitt merely twisted round to see who was there when she opened the door. It was a messenger. Lisbeth thanked him and brought the big manila envelope over to the dining table.

A switchblade magically appeared in Schmitt's hand. It neatly slit the envelope open and disappeared. He withdrew the packet of papers and flipped quickly through them, tossing most carelessly on the tabletop as he advanced through the mass.

Lisbeth looked slightly puzzled. "Why're you being so

uncustomarily sloppy?"

"Only with the chaff. Ah, here we are." He kept one report in hand, discarding the rest. "The others were just red herrings. Fingerprints of people who mean absolutely nothing."

"To screen the identity of the person that has really piqued your interest. You're a devious one, Kurt."

"So I'm told." He agreed.

"Doesn't it ever bother you that some poor devil has been working hard to prepare all the others?"

"Probably kept several people going at odd hours," Schmitt added as his thoughts concentrated on the document.

"You're incorrigible!"

Schmitt looked up briefly. He endeavored to look stern, but with Lisbeth that was difficult. "Are you going to babble all day? Or do you want to know the condensed, yet compelling, life history of our mysterious Mr. Collins?"

"Frankly, I wish I'd never heard of him or van Troje, but at this point, the more we know, the better. At least I hope so. Thank God, he's left the country."

"Temporarily."

Lisbeth hated it when he mocked her concern. "Oh, shut up and read!"

"Very well. For openers, it seems our Mr. Collins is better known as Erik Larson, ex-aircraft engineer. Hails from a wealthy, society-type family. An only child, he graduated near the top of his class from MIT. Went to work for Boeing in Seattle, Washington. He worked on the 747 and 767 projects during his tenure there. In the late eighties he came under suspicion of peddling technical data to competitors. Cleared of all charges, but within a year he was unemployed.

"Applied for positions with Lockheed and McDonnell Douglas. Rejected flatly by both. Airbus Industries did likewise, and here it gets interesting. There's an excerpt from their file. They declined because of . . . quote . . . the applicant's questionable loyalties. Past experience cautions that financially motivated disclosures of sensitive technical specifications could occur. Acumen and talent, however desirable, cannot subordinate trustworthiness . . . end quote."

"The implicit message being that they were among the buyers while he was at Boeing. Theft being condoned so long as it proves beneficial." She frowned. "It makes no real sense though. Surely, even then, a good engineer must have been well paid. Besides which, you mentioned a wealthy family."

"True, but apparently Larson, a.k.a. Collins, enjoys the finer things in life, perhaps too fine for his means. For instance, Peter mentioned that Larson wears a very expensive gold watch. It also says here that he owns two Mercedes Benzs and a Jaguar. Top that off with a twin-engined turboprop and you have some expensive toys. He likes to travel; our own observation has shown that here too his tastes exceed the mundane by a wide margin. It says that he's a private pilot qualified for everything up to and including small business jets. In short, he lives exceptionally well and relishes it."

"You forget to mention, that he's not bad looking either." Lisbeth feigned swooning. "Catch me, Kurt, I think I'm in love."

"With a killer?"

Her eyes spit fire. "You never quit, do you?"

"Besides, he's taken. Or had you forgotten that rather gorgeous . . ." He ducked as she swung. "Just joking. Getting back to our report here, we see that friend Larson has held several consulting positions with various engineering firms since his termination by Boeing. None lasted more than a year. Current status is either unemployed or self-employed. Yet, he maintains his somewhat enviable lifestyle. One wonders how?"

"Family money." Lisbeth ventured.

Schmitt backtracked to an earlier page. "Parents killed in an auto accident. The entire estate went to the father's beloved Alma Mater. Our boy got a paltry $100,000."

"Poor baby." Lisbeth said with a pout.

"Yeah, the way he spends money, that wouldn't go far. The question now is, where does all this leave us?"

"With a spoiled rich kid who flaunts expensive hobbies and lacks the money to pay for them."

"I meant, how does he fit in with van Troje? Surely it can't be a simple case of smuggling. And then there's the ETA wildcard. Larson has gone to great pains to make a connection with someone in a money and weapons conduit for the Basque gents who are supposedly cowering in fear these days. Why? What possible gain? Somehow we're failing to make a logical connection because there has to be more, a whole lot more."

Lisbeth got up and walked round behind him, her arms snaking down about his neck and chest. "Cynicism is your most detestable trait, Kurt. Always, with you, there have to be double entendres; never is the obvious acceptable. Although you hate to admit it, it does not always have to be so complex. The ETA thing could just be a red herring. This could just be a matter of smuggling diamonds." She kissed his ear, letting her tongue trace its outer surface. "How about some undercover work, sleuth?"

CHAPTER SIX

11 September

Like most bars, the Boston establishment into which Larson and Malin strode, sported subdued lighting and a causal atmosphere. Being mid-afternoon on a weekday it came as no surprise that only a scattering of customers were present. Three of these men stood silently round a red-felted pool table studiously watching as the fourth player lined up a tricky bank shot. The remaining two customers, beers in hand, stood near the alcove intently studying the contest.

None of these people took much interest in the strangers who sidled up to the bar. The bartender, a strapping man with a nose that had been broken more than once in his life, finished putting the last few clean glasses into an overhead rack before asking, "What'll be your pleasure, lads?" His voice bore an unmistakable Irish accent.

"Two Bushmills." Larson said as he settled onto a barstool. Malin, his swarthy associate, contented himself with leaning lightly against the polished bar.

"Bushmills is it? And you gents with no hint of an Irish accent. However, your taste in whiskey is commendable." The bartender busied himself with pouring three generous measures. "I hope you've no objection to my joining you?"

"None so long as the round is on the house and may God bless all here." Larson spoke the words gleaned from Ruiter slowly, eyes locked on those of the bartender.

"So be it." Glasses clinked. "God bless all here." Whiskey slaked thirsts.

The bartender cast a glance at his pool playing patrons. They remained engrossed in their game. His voice was a mere whisper when he spoke again. "Who sent you? No word has come."

"I need to contact Murphy."

"Murphy? Now who would that be?"

"I don't relish games."

"I don't like folks who come in for Bushmills on the house when no one told me to expect them."

"Fair enough. Murphy is the gentleman who pays for the Bushmills here and, shall we say, sends his regards and donations to the needy people overseas regularly."

The bartender's hard eyes studied the two strangers intently. Suspicion was more than evident in his gaze. "Who sent you?"

Larson ignored the question. "His office is somewhere nearby and I want to speak with him now!"

"Is that a fact? And let's suppose I tell you and your pal here to go to hell! Get out before I throw you out!"

Malin turned so that the folded newspaper he idly carried pointed towards the bartender. The black perforated cylinder of the silencer poked out just enough to have the intended effect on the big man. He stood very still, eyes glaring.

"Tell the others over there to finish their drinks and leave. And no cute things. I assure you, that my friend here will kill you without hesitation. Nod if you understand."

Brute physical strength was no match for a bullet at close range. Clenched fists whitened at the knuckles. The big man grudgingly nodded.

"Good. Tell them."

"Sean! Michael! The rest of you! I've got to close up for a wee bit. Finish your beers and be off with you."

This bit of news was not well received. "What the hell do you mean breaking up a game in progress? Rules of tavern keeping must say that you can't do such a thing! We'll keep an eye on things while you do what it is you must."

"The hell you will!" The bartender bellowed. "Out I say and OUT I MEAN!"

"I've got fifty bucks wagered!" Protested one of the spectators.

"My heart's a bleedin'. Now get OUT!" The bartender's menacing scowl and vehemence left no further room for debate. With angry grumbles the men swilled the last of their beers, threw the cues on the table, and marched off.

When they had gone, Larson went over and bolted the door.

As he did so, Malin guided the bartender from behind the bar. Keeping a respectable distance, he motioned for the big man to sit down at one of the small, round tables. The weapon kept the bartender's hatred at bay as the shorter man stood watch over him.

Larson joined them and said, "I need to speak with Murphy. There have been leaks. Friends have been compromised. Good men are dead. Others are under police surveillance and that makes them useless too. I have information that I must relay to Murphy personally and promptly."

"Tell me what you want him to know. If my path should cross that of a man name of Murphy, then I'll pass along your regards."

Larson shook his head. "No offense, but I can't trust the likes of you. Now I know Murphy's office is nearby. The three of us are going to go there now with you leading the way. Bear in mind that my associate here will be just a couple of steps behind you as we go. If you try anything, the first shot will sever your spine. The second and third shots will obliterate your kneecaps. Do you understand?"

The big man leaned angrily forward. He knew well the symbolism embodied by shooting out a man's kneecaps. "I'm no cursed traitor!"

"Then prove it. Take us to Murphy."

The squat, old office building sat only a few blocks from the bar. Its aging brick exterior had more character than newer glass and steel towers nearby that dwarfed it in size. Inside, polished marble and woodwork, vastly superior to anything its loftier neighbors might sport, greeted visitors.

The suite of offices to which the burly bartender led them lay on the third floor overlooking the street. The gleaming brass nameplate on the wall outside read, 'Donnelley, Dobson, and Murphy - Attorneys at Law'. Beyond the door lay a small reception area resplendent with verdant butterfly palms. With a surprising lack of fanfare, the pert receptionist admitted them to see Mr. Murphy.

When they entered the office, which as it turned out was on the corner of the building and overlooked both streets outside, they found Murphy poring over some briefs. His reading glasses landed lightly atop the papers as he rose to greet his unexpected visitors. His short stature and slight, almost malnourished build hardly made him an impressive man. Until, that is, one locked horns with his eyes. They were of the bluest blue, highly intelligent and extremely powerful. So too was his handshake as he grasped Larson's hand and pumped it vigorously.

"What might I be able to do for you gentlemen on this glorious afternoon?" The voice was surprisingly deep.

The bartender briefly stated how Larson had known the password for a courier and then demanded to see Murphy. The attorney nodded thoughtfully as he listened. His attention fixed on Larson. Suspicion was evident.

"I repeat myself, what might I do for you gentlemen this glorious afternoon?"

"Much, I hope," Larson replied. "First off though, I would think it prudent if your tavern-keeper here, and my bodyguard were to leave us while we talk."

"As you wish." He waved the others out. Closing the door behind them, he locked it. From a small drawer in a magazine covered table he produced a small electronic device. Approaching the slightly bewildered Larson, he passed the device up and down and all around. Satisfied with his findings, he returned the device to the drawer.

"I could have told you that I'm not wired."

"Ah, but you see, if you were, then I'd expect you to say precisely that and nothin' less. This way my spirits can relax as we talk. Can I offer you a drink?"

He crossed to an antique mahogany cabinet replete with intricate carving. Bushmills splashed into two crystal glasses. One was passed to Larson before as he motioned his guest to a black leather chair.

"To a better day!"

"Amen to that!"

"Now, for the third and final time, I'll ask what in bloody blazes I can do for you on this glorious day?"

"Mr. Murphy, my name is Collins, Thomas Collins."

The other man laughed. "You're joking?"

"It seems my parents had a penchant for humor. Needless to say, I go by the formal Thomas at all times."

"The cruelties of life are many. Sad to think that one's own flesh and blood would perpetrate such a joke, and on their very own offspring, no less!"

Despite everything, Larson found himself warming to the short man with the intensely blue eyes and graying hair. "I've seen worse. A family in the town where I grew up was named Gunn, G . . . U . . . N . . . N. Their son was Tommy and their daughter, Brenda, or Bren Gunn for short."

More laughter filled the room. "A rich life they lead, no doubt!"

"No doubt." Larson drank some more of the Irish whiskey. He made a mental note to get some Bushmills for his private stock.

"Well, Thomas, old son. Levity aside, I suppose we've some serious talking to do."

"That we have."

"Me mum always said, the easiest way to do things was to start at the beginning." All levity drained from the man's demeanor. "Suppose you do that and tell me how it is that you know what was presumed to be a very hush, hush password sequence."

"Without wanting to seem coy, I honestly can't answer. I assume that the people who employ my services wrangled the information out of someone within your organization's ranks." Larson had become a fluent, convincing liar. "You see, Mr. Murphy, in all candor, I don't give a damn about any of the terrorist organizations that your network of sympathizers sponsor. Not the Kurdistan Worker's Party, the ETA, or the IRA, or for that matter any other such group of politically motivated lunatics."

Murphy's brows arched slightly upon hearing this. "Is that a fact, now? Then I'm sure I'll find your explanation of what brings you to my office fascinating in the extreme."

"My employers are wealthy men, Mr. Murphy. They share a kindred spirit with you and one of the causes to which you funnel assistance."

"And what cause might that be? The mission fund at me church, perhaps?"

"The mission fund for the Basque liberation movement would be more on target."

Murphy studied him briefly. "Do I take it that your employers are a wee bit shy and wish to make an anonymous donation to charity?"

"Of a sort. They wish to meet or rather, have me meet, with the powers that be within the organization itself in Paris or wherever convenient."

"They don't want much do they, Thomas?"

"Frankly, I don't know how dicey a thing it would be to set up. Nor do I relish sitting down with a known terrorist or freedom fighter or whatever you choose to call your friends overseas. All part of the joys of being a hired hand, I guess. To answer your next question, I am authorized to tell you that my employers feel strongly that the current pressure to eradicate the ETA is doomed to failure. Spain will not back off, but neither will they destroy the organization. Hence, my employers envision the need for renewed resources within the ETA. The coffers will need replenishment for when the crackdown eases. They want to make a lucrative proposition to the powers that be within the ETA. The monies involved reach into seven figures. More than that I can only disclose to a person known as *The Black Widow*, whoever the hell that is."

Leaning forward, elbows on his desk, fingers steepled, Murphy pondered what Larson had said. The prospects were intriguing. "You are unusually well informed."

"My employers are extremely cautious men."

"Undoubtedly. Tell me, Thomas, why should I trust you?" He peered over his steepled fingertips as he spoke.

"If I were not legitimately what I claim to be, why the hell would I be here? How would I know the things I know? Police? FBI? Putting a gun to your bartender's head to force him to bring us here and then baiting you would hardly stand up in a court of law. Spanish or French Secret Service? Perhaps? Although the same legal niceties apply, unless you think it's some dastardly plot to execute *The Black Widow*. Given the fact that I'm willing to meet her on her turf, unarmed, and alone, I should think that nonsensical scenario can be laid to rest. As I see it, either I'm an off-the-wall nutcase or I'm legit. The real question is, are you willing to pass up massive financial support for the cause?"

A smile spread slowly over Murphy's face. "Did you ever study law, Thomas?"

"No."

"I think you may just have missed your calling. With a bit of polish you could make a fine defense attorney."

Almost exactly one week to the very minute since he left the offices of Donnelley, Dobson, and Murphy - Attorneys at Law, Larson was back; this time sans Malin and the bartender. His host poured healthy measures of Bushmills and toasted Larson's health as the two bantered amicably for a few minutes.

The devil-may-care glint in his eye, Murphy turned from the window where he stood watching a striking blond walk past on the opposite side of the street. "Will you look at that, now. Seems they get fairer all the time and me, I just get older and more crotchety with each passin' day. A pity for sure.

"Have you ever been to the Denmark, Thomas?"

"No. Not yet."

A far off look glazed Murphy's eyes. "I've been several times on business. Like everywhere, it changes each time one returns. They say change and growth are good. They may have a point, but I hope that the marvelous scenery doesn't change too much, leastwise not in my lifetime. Ah, it's a grand place, rich in history. I'm sure you'll like it when you see it first-hand sometime."

He sighed, turning to face Larson and switched abruptly to business. "I expect that you and your mysterious employers will be pleased to know your request for a meeting has been granted."

"Excellent."

"Mmmmm. You travel alone." He passed across a folded piece of paper. "Be in Copenhagen on the twenty-first. At half past two PM, you call that number. You'll be told what hotel to check in with."

"And?"

"And you wait, Thomas. *The Black Widow* is a busy person. She may see you that evening, the next day, or later. Or if she smells a trap, never. That's the long and the short of it."

Larson nodded as he pocketed the slip of paper. "So be it. Tell her I'll be in Copenhagen on the twenty-first. She'll hear from me at two-thirty PM."

"The address below, the one here in Boston, that'll be how you reach me from now on. One of our people collects the mail there daily. Future contacts between us must run that route. Understood?"

Larson nodded again. He rose and took Murphy's proffered hand. "Thanks for your help."

"Don't mention it. The devil himself would be welcome if he'd further any cause that we support."

Larson started to leave when Murphy added, “I pray you are what you claim to be, old son.” A chilling iciness crept into his usually urbane voice. “Because if you’re not, your soul will be screamin’ for mercy long before the last breath leaves your body.” The coldness vanished as abruptly as it had appeared. “God bless you, Tom Collins.”

CHAPTER SEVEN

23 September

The little hotel in which Larson found himself hardly could be considered to his liking. It lay off the side of a side street, far from the usual haunts of tourists or executives. The room was small, positively cramped by Larson's standards. Old wallpaper, peeled in places, adorned walls whose only decorations were three cheap prints of the Danish countryside.

Larson sat sullenly reading a dog-eared paperback edition of *The Odessa File*, an old favorite. Occasionally he glanced out of his second story window at the quiet street beyond. Like the hotel, the buildings along the narrow street were old. He wondered who among the passersby might be ETA members keeping tabs on him.

Since his arrival nearly forty-eight hours earlier nothing had happened. Only at mealtimes did he venture from his room. On those occasions, he dined nearby and always checked with the old man at reception to see if anyone had called during his absence. The old gentleman spoke poor English, but after the first confused exchange, he understood what Larson was after. No one had called.

Innumerable games of solitaire had helped pass the time when he had wanted a break from reading. He was on his third novel and had begun to wonder if the ETA people had opted to forego the intriguing offer relayed them via Murphy in Boston.

Afternoon was fast fading to evening. When he reached the end of the next chapter, he decided, it would be as good a time as any to break the monotony with dinner.

Just then the phone rang harshly in the otherwise silent room. He answered on the second ring. "Hello?"

"Hello, yourself." A man's voice mocked. "Be at the *Holmens* Bridge near the inner harbor in thirty minutes. And be alone." The connection clicked off before Larson could even acknowledge the message.

Slipping a bookmark into his book, he tossed it on the nightstand. Almost unconsciously, he consulted his watch before picking up his map of Copenhagen. A minute or so later he had located his destination. It lay in the heart of the city, right near the stock exchange. He hoped a cab could be quickly had. Fetching his overcoat and briefcase from the closet, he switched off the light and made to open the door.

As he unbolted it, the door heaved inward and sent him crashing to the floor. Before he could react, two powerful individuals pinioned his arms to the floor. None-too-gently they began a thorough search of his person. They were no novices. He doubted anything would have been missed. The body search revealed nothing untoward.

"Clean." The one announced to yet a third man who had entered the room behind them. This third man had drawn the faded curtains and switched on the glaring overhead light.

"Is he, now?"

"Who the hell are you?" Larson grunted indignantly.

The blond-haired man, who looked to be about thirty, ignored him. He picked up the briefcase from where it had landed. Noting that it was locked, his cold stare fell on the prostrate Larson. "A pity to ruin such a handsome leather case, don't you think? The combination, Mister Thomas Collins." His accent was impossible to place, but it was not Danish, though he looked the part.

Seeing little point in refusing, Larson gave the man the combination.

The blond-haired man opened the case and shuffled through its contents. Using a small device fished out of a pocket, he electronically scanned the case for bugs. At length he seemed satisfied. "A wise man, you are. No tricks up your sleeves." To the others he added, "Bring him."

Strong hands hefted Larson to his feet. The blond-haired man paused by the door. Staring straight at Larson, he said, "We're taking you for a short ride. Make any move or gesture that I don't like and you die on the spot. Do you understand, my friend?"

"All too well." Larson found it uncomfortable to be on the receiving end of such harsh treatment.

"Good. Then be a good boy and follow me." He spun on his heel and led the way along the gloomy corridor.

It was completely dark by the time Larson was hustled out of the car and into a foreboding brick building. The circuitous route the driver had taken through the labyrinth of darkening streets made it impossible to judge even approximately where he was in the strange Scandinavian city.

His guides shuffled him along an ill-lit corridor and down a flight of stairs into a musty basement. At least two doors were secured behind him by the time Larson was led into a small, whitewashed room as scantily furnished as the Amsterdam whore had been dressed. Only the blond-haired man entered the room with Larson. He nodded curtly to a surprisingly attractive woman seated on a metal chair behind a beat-up, gray, metal desk. She wore a light sweater with a Nordic design and tight jeans that followed every curve.

The woman returned his gesture. She stood up and offered her hand in a gesture that was almost sensual the way she executed it. Her handshake was remarkably firm; the intensity of her dark eyes riveting.

“A pleasure to finally meet you.” She spoke with only a hint of a Spanish accent. She gestured him to a chair and settled back into her own. “We’re most anxious to learn the details of your intriguing proposal.”

Larson caught himself staring. “You'll forgive me, but . . .”

A warm smile crept across her features as she interrupted. “But you expected some old hag or at the very least a homely spinster out to wreak havoc on the world because of her own physical shortcomings.” She laughed mirthlessly as the smile vanished. “More than one police officer has died or missed opportunities because of the same stupid assumption.”

"Sorry. I meant no . . ."

"Of course not. No man ever does, does he? Yet, the thoughts are always there, be they spoken or just pondered. Let me set your mind at ease. Brains and beauty can go hand in hand. And a woman can be every bit as ruthless as a man. Maybe even more so."

Larson felt extremely uncomfortable. This woman exuded sexuality, yet she was every bit the hardened killer that he had read about with a sense of disbelief. He tried to seize control of the encounter. "Naturally, Miss Sanchez. My own wife is . . ."

"***Mrs***. Sanchez, Collins, although my husband was slaughtered several years ago by the oppressors that we fight. That ugly reality, coupled with my penchant for deadly efficiency, is why I am called *The Black Widow* by friends and foe."

"I'm sorry. Anyway, I trust you've received our token gesture of friendship?" Larson said evenly, still striving to gain some semblance of control. Some of the money stolen from Ruiter in Amsterdam had magnanimously been sent to ETA coffers via Murphy in Boston. Though he hated to part with so much cash, the money would, he hoped, assuage any misgivings that Murphy and the other ETA people might yet harbor.

"The $15,000 is already being put to charitable use." Louisa eased back into her chair. "I must apologize for your necessarily unfriendly reception at your hotel. Given the aggressive nature of the French and Spanish authorities of late, one has to be extremely cautious in our trade."

Larson shrugged as he settled reluctantly into an aging armchair whose thinly worn fabric warned that the chair was long past its prime. He wasn't surprised to find himself seated on a cushion of hard springs that creaked noisily with every movement. The irritating smell of mildew surrounded him.

"Perfectly in order." Larson placed his black leather attaché case on his lap, dialed the correct combination, and flicked open the shiny brass latches. "My employers will be so glad to know that their moneys are being put to charitable use, perhaps even for the benefit of widows and orphans."

A wry smile flickered across the woman's features. "It may indeed *create* some widows and orphans in the Basque country or elsewhere.

"Now, Tom Collins, just what's your game? It seems your performance in Boston left our mutual friend, Murphy, with the sense that you are your own employer. In fact, that you. . ."

"Pardon my interrupting, but Murphy is mistaken. I'm just a minor cog in the machine. An easily replaced part of the much larger whole."

Again the flicker of a wry smile. "Oh, surely you sell yourself short, Collins. You're extremely cautious, there's a bit of the charmed one in you, and that's a fact. For example, try as we might, no one in our organization has been able to verify your identity." She passed across an eight-by-ten photo of Larson obviously taken in Murphy's office. "Money has a strange way of opening doors, Collins. Blackmail works where money doesn't. We've a good many sources within various police and security organizations, yet none could tell us anything about you. Even with such a fine portrait as this. A minor cog, you say. I say balderdash! If you be a cog, then I'm a haggard old spinster."

Even behind the glasses, her dark eyes seemed to turn icy cold as they studied the unflinching Larson. For so petite a person, she could be incredibly intimidating. She continued, "And yet, you weave an interesting tale. And then there is the matter of your welcome donation to our cause and your impeccable logic with Mr. Murphy." She hefted a cassette tape, then let it slip from her delicate looking fingers to clatter onto the desk. "Murphy sends very thorough reports. He does indeed. So tell me, Collins, why risk death to talk with me? You're not Basque. What is your real game? Why do ***you*** want to help the ETA?"

Larson cleared his throat. The chilled atmosphere seemed to have warmed considerably, almost to the point of discomfort. He fought hard to suppress the cloying sense of fear that the woman's eyes and demeanor had aroused. "I don't give a damn about you or your cause. Such political polarization can be a liability; a luxury I can ill afford. It hardly surprises me that even with well-placed informers, you've been unable to learn anything about me. If I was on file everywhere, then I'd be of little use to my employers, now would I? Quite frankly, I wish I was elsewhere right now, because chatting with a woman, however attractive, who can only be deemed a political fanatic and terrorist of the first order, hardly appeals."

"You're a bold one, I'll grant that. My thanks for at least ranking me in the first order though. And for the complement about my appearance. No woman minds that."

"Given the almost legendary exploits credited to you, I think it well deserved. Now Mrs. Sanchez, if you've no wish to hear me out, I'll bid you adieu and ask that your men return me to my hotel so that I can get the hell out of Denmark."

"Feisty too! I admire that." Her eyes seem to warm a little. "Don't be rushing off just yet, Tom Collins. Speak your piece, then we'll both see what happens. But first, tell me this, why since your 'employers' could not see fit to speak in person, did they not just forward their scheme through our Boston conduit?"

"Too risky."

Her left brow arched slightly. Larson noted the quizzical movement and hastily added, "The operation is a sensitive one. The fewer people involved, the better for all concerned."

"Which brings us to the meat and potatoes, eh Collins?"

Larson had rehearsed his presentation in his mind many times over. Details had been hashed out with Kristine. Yet he found himself strangely nervous as he began his pitch. Butterflies roamed freely in his stomach. "Only a fool would believe that the Spanish government will yield without being forced to," he stated flatly. "Events of the last year prove the government's resolve to eradicate your organization and the movement for which it stands. Without money the ETA will not survive the current campaign against it. And when I say money, I don't mean paltry sums like the $15,000 we sent you. I'm talking about real money! That, along with intensive training in Libya, and the new weaponry that the money will buy, can spell success in the foreseeable future."

Louisa nodded. "It takes no genius to know that without money, we cannot exist. At least not on an effective level. Tell me something new."

"And, without wishing to belittle your efforts, relatively petty extortion and bank robberies are hardly methods to raise the kind of money that the ETA needs."

"Without being ungrateful, benefactors such as your 'employer,' hardly supply enough funding to carry on our work."

Larson met her intense gaze. "Maybe that's because outside of your homeland and the surrounding region, damn near no one has ever heard of you."

"Am I to assume that your employers wish to change this?"

"Very much so! To begin with, even if the rest of the world knew you existed, then hearing about petty bank robberies and blackmailing rich families would do little to generate sympathy. No, what is needed is a platform to put ETA on the world stage in a forum that will guarantee media coverage and publicity that will generate sympathy for the movement. We need to put ETA on the lips of people everywhere. We need to generate political pressure against Spain from around the globe, but specifically from the United States."

Louisa smiled. "And so you promise me the sun, the moon, and the stars?"

Larson returned the smile. Strange how this woman could change so abruptly! "Not quite. But my employers do envision a strategy that should accomplish these things while propelling ETA into the big time, giving ETA a whole new stature on the world stage."

Larson brushed an unruly lock of hair back into place. From the attaché case he took and unfolded a large detailed diagram that he placed on the desk. His chair creaked loudly, protesting his every movement.

Louisa leaned forward and studied the document briefly. Peering over the rim of the glasses, she coyly said, "A nice drawing. Are we planning a trip, you and I?"

"The project my employers envision is a sporting one. If successful, it will provide your coffers with a great deal of cash money while generating enormous public exposure and with it, sympathy for your plight. As noted, your message will be front page news the world over and will dominate the TV news casts as well"

"Money and publicity, both in grand measure, you say. But how? Details Collins!"

"To begin with, you'll have to convince your associates that the time has come to up the stakes. The ETA must be prepared to wage war on a new level. The first step will be a traditional bombing campaign directed against Barcelona. It should be planned to begin sometime early next February. The pyrotechnics will get Spanish attention. What will follow will get that of the world.

"Several weeks after the campaign begins, the exact date will be relayed through the Boston conduit a week beforehand, a handpicked team of your best people will hijack a British Airways 747 bound for the United States."

Louisa held up a hand. "Why British?"

"A British carrier will guarantee an audience in Britain, a nation that could bring considerable pressure to bear against Spain. Let's not forget British and Spanish differences about Gibraltar. A British flight also is more likely to have a high percentage of US citizens aboard and we want lots of American hostages too." He pointed at the drawing. "The diagram here illustrates a standard seating configuration for one of their planes and includes other salient facts and features of the airliner. Your team will force the plane to land at the Dallas-Fort Worth International Airport. There they will demand a half million dollars ransom from the U.S. government."

"Just a minute, Collins. The American government harbors the nasty position that dealing with what it deems terrorists is a bad thing. The administration has been good to some freedom fighters up to a point. The Irish Sinn Fein has even been granted certain privileges in the US of late, but bringing our fight to American soil . . . well . . . that'd be another matter entirely."

"As a rule of thumb, that's true. But this will be different. They'll have a big planeload of hostages, many of them foreign nationals, to consider. The ramifications of failure resulting in their deaths or injury would be great. Far too great! The assembled sympathizers, my employers that is, are convinced that with appropriate media hype, they can force concessions. A further ransom, the amount determined by you and your associates, will be demanded of the Spanish government. The official line will be that the ransom moneys will go toward furthering the cause of peace in the Basque region. The propaganda possibilities are endless and, for once, the ETA is guaranteed a worldwide audience.

"The only other crucial demand is for a business jet of the

type specified in the mission implementation signal we send via Boston the week before the mission goes off. This jet will fly the team and ransom to safety."

"But the risks?" Louisa shook her head wearily as she pondered the possibilities. She had orchestrated numerous ETA operations, including several assassinations and a car bombing in April 1995 that injured eight. Bold terror was her business. A hijacking onto distant foreign soil seemed reckless. Stealthy bombings and assassinations were more her style.

Larson held up a hand to squelch the lithe woman's objections. "Without risk, there is no gain. Besides, any risks taken will be well worth the effort. To begin with, my employers will match every dollar of the American share of the ransom with three of their own. That ups the American portion of the revenue to an even two million dollars. Plus whatever you feel the Spaniards will be willing to cough up to avoid a bloody catastrophe on American soil." Louisa drew a breath to comment, but maintaining the initiative, Larson waved her to silence. "Surely you know that you already have influential friends in the US administration. They may not be able to vocally cheer your people on, but they can do much. And then there is the little matter of my employers. Influential men and women, one and all. They will bring significant pressure against the US government to secure a hasty payoff. To further insure success of the mission, the getaway jet provided by authorities in Texas will have a crew sympathetic to your cause."

"But how?"

"Trust me." Larson lied with a passion and eloquence that seemed to assuage all fears. "My employers are powerful people. They fervently believe in your cause and are intent on doing their part to further it. Arrangements will be made. The getaway jet's crew will provide a swift and safe exit from the continent.

"Beyond that, there is the media circus that such events

inevitably draw. It will be manipulated to your best advantage. The aim is to stir widespread sympathy for the cause."

Louisa stared at the diagram. "And have your employers got any inkling of the kind of security at airports these days?"

"No one said that it would be an easy operation, Mrs. Sanchez. But therein lies the sport of it, the challenge! Knowing the reputation of the infamous Black Widow, I'm certain you and your people will devise some vastly clever method. Semtex explosive perhaps? Whatever suits the occasion. You've some proficient experts in such matters on your staff. However, you should be advised that my employers feel very strongly that actual use of extreme violence would only serve to weaken the media extravaganza of this grandstand play."

"I take it, they don't consider blowing innocents apart on Barcelona's streets extreme violence then?"

Larson smiled ever so weakly. "Perhaps I should restate that. During the actual hijacking, violence and casualties should be avoided if at all possible. The bombing campaign that opens the show is another matter entirely. Yet, here too, some semblance of sensibility needs to reign. Trigger the car bombs or whatever at times when only a handful on innocents will be dismembered or killed."

This drew a wicked chuckle from the dark-haired woman behind the desk. "Why on a particular day? What difference can it possibly make?" Her mind methodically sought potential solutions to securing the plane as she asked the questions. Potential members of her organization suitable to the task were already being considered in the back of her devious mind. And yet, she knew that the final call was not hers alone. She would have others to sell the bold scheme to. Given Spanish recalcitrance and the ongoing crackdown, she thought it an easy sale, at least to some elements within the organization.

Larson's eyes widened. He was fast becoming a consummate actor. "All the difference in the world! My employers must know precisely which day the thing goes off if they are to orchestrate the escape route, etc. Without perfect timing, the whole operation could crumble. Disaster easily could supplant victory!"

Louisa pursed her soft lips in thought. "A reasonable answer. I find only one glaring flaw in the entire scheme. Assuming total success, what's to stop your people from seizing the ransom moneys from our team?"

The tall American grinned. The quarry was toying with the lucrative bait. "Several things. To begin with, my employers are wealthy men. They would have little use for your hard won moneys. Beyond that, there is the cold hard fact that they intend to profit from your success in the long haul. An independent Basque state opens many interesting paths for investments of most lucrative potential. Yes, they believe in you, but they also believe in making lots and lots of money.

"Perhaps the best reason is that the ransom will not be paid to the team aboard the aircraft. It will be delivered to the place of your choice on a timetable ***you*** establish once the operation is underway. When it has been paid, the team simply vacates the jet with a few first class passengers along to insure continued cooperation. Then they are whisked to safety. The matching moneys will be forwarded through the Boston conduit."

"You have a remarkable penchant for making the nearly impossible sound highly probable, Collins."

"Trust me when I tell you that a great deal of effort has gone into evaluating the operation. If everything goes according to plan, the operation nets needed publicity and lots of revenue." He pulled some papers from the attaché case. The chair persisted with its vexing creaking. "Now, Mrs. Sanchez, if we could gloss over the more mundane details of the proposed operation I can be on my merry way."

Louisa leaned pensively back in her chair. "You presume a great deal. We may not wish to mount your affair."

"You'll mount it. Given the hammering your organization has had of late, you cannot afford not to." A chill crept into his voice. "Let's face it, you need support from people like my employers to carry on this jolly little war of yours. Let's not play childish games. Organizations like yours only exist so long as suckers like the poor bastards for whom I work are willing to play along and foot the bills. Who the heck knows why they do it? Cheap thrills? To get richer? Or maybe they genuinely are sympathetic? But whatever the reason, you know and I know that without filthy rich people like them coughing up cash and lots of it, the big top comes down on your little circus in a big hurry."

The dark eyes met Larson's steady glare for a moment, then shifted to the blond-haired man by the door. He had remained silent throughout the exchange. "Feisty, eh Gregorio?" She spoke in Spanish

"Never truer words spoken." The man replied flatly in the same tongue.

"Mmmm. And your assessment?"

The blond man was Louisa's right-hand man, one of the few whom she wholly trusted. Born and raised in the confusion that was akin to the Basque region since Franco had radically restricted the area's semi-autonomous rule, he was inured to violence, quick death, and risk.

"God knows positive publicity in America could not harm us. Nor could infusions of cash. As for risks? We take 'em daily for vastly lesser rewards. Boldness and surprise might make it work. On the whole, it may just have merit. God knows sitting back and worrying about when or where the next raid is coming won't get us anywhere."

"Mmmmm." Attention returned to Larson and she spoke in English again. "And when would your employers expect an answer?"

"Preferably now. But realistically within two weeks via the Boston conduit."

"Seems fair enough, Collins. We'll take it under advisement. Murphy will have our answer in ten days' time. Now, I believe you were about to expand on the background information?"

The next thirty minutes passed with Larson reiterating the important points and outlining useful security details. When the session finally ended he was extremely glad to be out of the clutches of the ETA people and back in his shabby hotel room. He checked out immediately, moving to vastly more luxurious accommodations at the elegant Hotel D'Angletere. Comfortably ensconced there, he booked a flight to New York for the next day. Which left him the balance of the evening to dine in the style to which he was accustomed in the magnificent old hotel's restaurant.

As he sipped an excellent Brandy with his scrumptious dessert he reviewed the day's events. The meeting had gone essentially as planned. The competence of the ETA's Black Widow and her associates had impressed Larson. He had expected fanatical crazies, not the calculating professionalism embodied by the strangely haunting woman and the man called Gregorio. They would be deadly adversaries, of that he came away convinced.

CHAPTER EIGHT

3 April

A brisk spring morning greeted Bostonians as they started another average week. The brilliant sunshine promised warmer temperatures as the day progressed. It was a welcome thought.

A dark-brown, suede jacket and a similarly colored pair of corduroys kept the man comfortably warm as he strode down the sloping street. He was glad that the seemingly endless winter had finally relented. The green leaves unfurling on the trees were welcome splashes of color, a stark contrast to the blandness of winter. He began to whistle a lilting tune as he continued on his way, hands plunged into pockets. If the box was empty, as was usually the case, he promised himself a long walk along the Charles River before succumbing to the unavoidable, another day at the office where he worked as a legal assistant for an attorney named Murphy. Long walks seemed to invigorate him. They were one of the things he missed most when winter descended upon the city with its icy gusts of numbing cold and its drab hues of gray.

A gentle breeze ruffled his thick black hair as he crossed Charles Street and proceeded along it to the corner of Pickney Street. Still whistling his merry tune he entered the same building that he entered every morning before making his way to his office. The sign outside proclaimed, 'Beacon Hill Personal Mailboxes.'

The black haired man's appearance at the mail receiving service was duly noted with weary monotony by special agent Drake of the FBI. Ritualistically, he sat well back from the glass panes of the bay window on the second story of the building across the street from the establishment. It was a dreary routine that had lasted nearly two months. Surveillance began when the man had become suspect as a possible conduit for ETA sympathizers to funnel moneys to the newly resurgent Basque group. Only days before the new bombing campaign in Barcelona had begun, his box number had turned up on an intercepted document in Paris. Substantive evidence remained lacking, but the connection was irrefutable. The ETA was back in business with a vengeance and somehow he was a part of it. Primarily as a courtesy to the Spanish, the U.S. government placed the man under surveillance. As luck would have it, Drake drew the dreary assignment.

It was relatively easy work. The target was the quintessential creature of habit. He was dull and boring in the extreme. Only on the days when some piece of correspondence or package awaited his arrival at the Charles Street location did the routine vary. Then nothing could be counted upon and Drake and his partner were hard pressed to keep tabs on their quarry. Thus far, this had happened on only three occasions. On two of these he had eluded them. Yet Drake would swear that he had been oblivious to their presence. The third time had been a wasted effort, the small package had been delivered to the wrong Mr. Smith. They had trailed him to the nearest Post Office where he properly enough rerouted the errant item. Aside from his evasive behavior of the two other occasions, he seemed a model citizen. But model citizens did not take such abnormal precautions against being followed.

On this particular day the man emerged with a small white envelope clutched lightly in his hand. Drake cursed softly. He had a headache and the beginnings of a cold. A quiet day would have been much more agreeable. He took several quick photos of the man with a 35mm Nikon, dropped the camera on the couch by the door, grabbed his jacket, and hurried onto the landing and down the stairs.

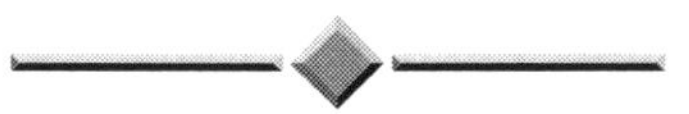

Walking slowly along the redbrick sidewalk, the man tore open the envelope. After removing the single page inside, he discarded the envelope in the nearest garbage can that was cleverly concealed in an old barrel. Anything for the colonial look he mused as he unfolded the sheet. The message was brief. At precisely ten AM that same morning he was to be at the phone booth on the corner of River and Mount Vernon Streets. As he read the note he paused in front of the black iron bars of the ancient looking Charles Street Station Post Office. He glanced at his Bulova. Twenty minutes remained before the appointed time.

He folded the typed message and slipped it into his pocket. Turning round he strode casually back up Charles Street in the direction of the Boston Common. He was unaware Drake slowly followed his progress from half a block away on the opposite side of the street. He was equally oblivious to the fact that Drake's partner, who had nonchalantly fished the discarded envelope out of the trash bin, preceded him by about the same distance.

The three men, separate, yet essentially moving as one, progressed slowly along the street with its charming buildings and gas streetlights. The target's slack pace made it awkward for the two special agents to maintain their positions without being obvious about it, but they were well trained in such arts.

Several blocks up the street stood an old building, once a church from the look of it. Three shops now lined its length. The first sold antiques. Its marvelous window display had offered the opportunity to stop and browse, thereby helping to slow the pace, to the leading agent. Above the second shop hung a black sign lettered in gold. It needlessly proclaimed the establishment to be a flower shop. The numerous buckets brimming with freshly cut flowers that flanked the doorway and the faint scent that wafted through the air told all. The quarry paused ever so briefly to look at the flowers, seemed to change his mind, and moved on. Obviously strong-willed where treats were concerned, he ignored the ice cream shop occupying the corner of the building. Instead, he turned down Mount Vernon Street.

A short distance brought him to the prescribed meeting place. According to his watch he was still three minutes early. He paced aimlessly near the designated phone. He noted with dull interest that the old firehouse behind the phone dated from 1947. He ran an idle hand along the bright- red, arched doorway to the old fire station and continued his pacing.

Across the way a svelte brunette in a stunning scarlet dress, who had apparently paused to admire the unusual yellow house on the corner there, turned and headed towards him. Her bearing was proud, her walk almost regal. This, he thought, was a woman of breeding. Undoubtedly her lineage could be traced to some moneyed and powerful aristocratic family. Even without the expensive designer clothes that seemed elegantly at home on her lithe form, she would exude class. Such was the conclusion the man drew as his eyes admiringly ogled her. Not wanting to appear rude he forced himself to glance away once or twice as she drew nearer.

Only when she spoke his name did he realize that she was his contact. Her greeting was civil, but frigid, the tone hinting at distaste. Without further conversation she handed him a folded manila envelope. A seal covered all of the seams on the envelope's back. "Personal courier for the *Black Widow*. Post haste. She must have it in her hands no later than Thursday. Understood?"

"Yeah. Understood," he replied as he took the envelope. "Say, why the cold treatment? We're on the same side, baby."

"Are we?" Her response was positively frostbitten. "I hardly think that you and I have *anything* in common. And I am quite certain that we have nothing further to discuss. You have your assignment. Execute it." She turned abruptly to leave him standing there fighting to control mounting indignant rage.

"Haughty bitch!" The angry words fell on deaf ears.

Special agent Drake watched the brief encounter from the far side of Charles Street. A practiced hand wielded a miniature camera fashioned to look like a Dunhill lighter. A couple of pictures were quickly snapped, then he used it to light the menthol cigarette already placed between his thin lips. Marvelous little gadget, he thought, pocketing it again. James Bond eat your heart out!

The occasional gadgetry employed in his profession never ceased to amaze him. He often wondered where they dreamed up some of the more nonsensical ideas. He drew the smoke deep into his lungs as he watched the attractive woman end the encounter. She started in his direction.

Drake turned slightly. His large frame was reflected in a shop window. Out of habit he straightened his tie and tugged down on the gray vest to eliminate some folds. His short, hair was disheveled. His bushy brows arched. What the hell, he told himself, you're going to tail her, not try to pick her up.

He started lazily along the street. Passing his partner who had doubled back, headed in the opposite direction, he said, "I've got the girl. Stick with him."

"Like glue." The other federal agent crossed the street to tail the man who was headed toward the Charles River that lay at its opposite end.

The well-dressed woman passed the sedately paced Drake. He was vaguely aware of a faint, alluring scent. He glanced at her just as she looked his way. Eyes made contact. A hint of a smile flashed across her pretty features before she turned and moved on her way. Drake found himself somehow flattered. High-class all the way, he thought as he began a discrete pursuit.

Before long the lady reached the entrance to the large underground parking lot that lay hidden beneath the manicured park known as the Boston Common. Opting not to wait for the elevator, she rapidly descended two flights of stairs, oblivious to the occasional obscene graffiti scrawled on the walls.

Before descending into the underground parking garage, Drake hailed a cab, whipped out his identification, and instructed the driver to wait near the garage's exit. By the time he bounded down the stairs, his quarry was already far away on the multi-pillared second level. It did not help him any that the place was crowded to near capacity. Entering the parking level Drake glanced around. A splash of red tagged the woman's position for a brief instant before she was obscured by a van. He hurried along to catch up. It was imperative that he maintain surveillance. He wanted to know the make and color of the car and, if feasible, its license number. With that information stashed in his memory he would dash for the waiting cab and follow.

That was the theory. Reality would not cooperate. Rounding the customized van, Drake, much to his intense chagrin, found that he had been duped. The woman rushed forward and delivered a vicious kick to his groin. The spasm of intense pain doubled him over reflexively. It was then that the swinging bag in her hands crashed into the base of his skull. Drake slammed into the side of the adjacent car, his right hand instinctively reaching for his shoulder holster. Before he could do more than grasp the butt of the pistol, the woman, previously assessed as a cultured and refined person incapable of violence, delivered a series of devastating karate blows and kicks. The fragrant scent of her perfume enthralled his clouding senses as he crashed onto the cold, unforgiving pavement.

After checking that apparently no one had taken note of the scuffle, the brunette knelt beside the prostrate Drake. His pockets were rifled, yielding his FBI identification and wallet. They disappeared in her purse. The sound of pounding feet seemed suddenly to echo throughout the cavernous underground garage. They grew louder and closer as she used her handkerchief to pull the agent's weapon from its holster and pressed it into his limp hand. She had just straightened when a man in his late thirties came running up.

Between heaving breaths he stammered, "You all right, miss?"

The brunette hesitated for the fleetingest of seconds. "Oh my goodness! Nothing like this has ever happened to me before." She feigned terrified fear. "He . . . he tried to accost me. Thank God for all those self-defense courses my husband insisted I take."

The hirsute man looked down at Drake's crumpled form. "Worth every penny from the looks of things." The gun caught his attention. "Good Lord! He could have shot you!" He stooped and yanked the weapon from the motionless hand. His breathing was gaining some semblance of normalcy, his heart and lungs settling back into more sane circulatory and respiratory routines, the sudden burst of unaccustomed exertion over. An admiring gaze at last soaked in the beauty of the woman before him. She was older than first glances would register, but still quite beautiful. "Remarkable. C'mon, let's go call the cops." He moved to take her arm, a friendly, helpful expression on his face.

She withdrew, taking a step backwards. "No. I can't get involved in this sort of thing. The media never let go. I'd better just slip quietly away." She smiled warmly. Men were always suckers for a congenial smile, she mused as she continued, "Thanks for the concern." Gesturing toward Drake's pathetic looking form, she added, "Be a dear and let the police know about that fiend. Take credit for helping to subdue him, whatever. I'm sure he must have a lengthy criminal record." Again the smile that could assuage the concerns of the most recalcitrant of men. "Be a hero." With that she disappeared. Two other businessmen in conservative suits, attracted by the commotion, approached.

Pistol clutched loosely in hand, the would-be rescuer stood awkwardly over the still unconscious Drake. His cheek twitched nervously as he turned to face the newcomers. "This guy tried to attack a woman. That one over yonder," he said, jerking his head in the direction of the disappearing brunette.

"Lucky for her that you were here. I doubt I'd have had the nerve to tackle an armed man. Nice going, fella."

"Yeah. Well done. We'll have the guy at the booth call the police," added the other businessman.

It was then and there that the man holding Drake's weapon decided to take the stunning woman's advice. It wasn't often one would get the chance to play hero. The kids probably would be thrilled to see dad's picture in the papers and on TV. He could picture it all already. It was a lie he would soon learn to regret.

Kristine Larson drove the rented Buick Regal all the way to Logan International Airport before she pulled curbside to examine the wallet and identification taken from her unconscious pursuer. Since leaving the Common's underground parking garage, her hands trembled ever so slightly. The methodical training had paid off. Long hours spent watching, practicing, and finally perfecting violent skills had not been wasted. As when a child, she had been an avid pupil and had learned well. The slight trembling was simply the result of suppressed tension mixed with a tinge of genuine excitement born of the thrill associated with living out what for the average person would only be experienced in the pages of a novel or on a movie or television screen.

The hands that held the items no longer trembled. She quickly digested the pertinent facts they disclosed. A rush of air expelled from her lips as she realized that it was a federal agent she had laid out cold in the parking garage. Concern dispelled any remnants of excitement as the items vanished once more into the neatly organized recesses of her Gucci purse.

Kristine was absolutely calm and composed as she returned the rented car and entered the main terminal building. She soon found a convenient phone. The number punched in belonged to a New Jersey Ramada Inn. After a brief wait she was connected with the correct room. Hellos were exchanged and then both parties paused. Kristine looked casually around to make certain that no one was within earshot.

At length she said, "We may have a slight problem." She spoke in hushed tones so as not to be overheard by passersby.

"I'm listening." It was great just to hear Erik's steady voice.

"The meet was observed by a federal agent. He followed me to the car. I knocked him cold, but I don't like it."

"Don't panic," Larson said slowly, his own mind racing. Would the final instructions Kristine had hand-delivered reach the terrorists? If not, would the absence of the ETA action adversely affect the underlying plot? The date was near. Great effort had been expended in order to arrange a bona fide terrorist action to bedevil authorities. "They can't touch us. The leak has to be at the other end. It was a calculated risk given the pressure to stamp them out. Unfortunate turn of events, but it's inconsequential. Our tremendous edge is only slightly diminished nothing more. Once you're sure that no one else is following you, continue as planned. I'll see you this evening, darling. Keep up the good work."

"I'll be careful. Good-bye." After a casual glance about, she strode confidently into the airport throng. Via a circuitous route, she made her way to a ladies room. Drake's things, minus the cash he carried, landed in a trashcan.

Out of sight in one of the stalls, the carryall she brought came into play. A hook caught the top of the door. It soon sported a mirror. Medium-heeled alligator skinned shoes were exchanged for high-heeled, black leather ones. The Gucci purse was replaced by a purse of a different color and style. She slipped out of her dress. A pleated skirt, silk blouse, and matching jacket took its place. The emerald studs in her earrings became half-carat diamond studs. The emerald ring with its beautiful stone surrounded by a ring of small diamonds was exchanged for an exquisite one-and-half carat diamond solitaire set in platinum. The silver banded Tiffany watch was traded for a gold Piaget similar to that worn by her spouse, though slimmer, with a narrower band.

Next on the agenda was hair. Liberal amounts of hairspray and deft work with brush and pic soon transformed her flowing tresses into a wholly different look. The hair implements returned to their respective compartments, she set about to alter her face.

As a rule she preferred a modicum of make-up. Circumstances dictated otherwise. Larger quantities made possible the alterations needed to elude any would-be pursuer. She was grateful for the intimate knowledge of stage make-up garnered from a close friend with whom she had roomed and worked on university productions of Camelot and Hamlet. Such practical knowledge, augmented by further in-depth study and uncounted hours of practice, made her a competent artisan.

Kristine leaned forward and spread her eyelids apart on first one, then the other eye. A large scleral contact lens dropped away from each. Brown eyes suddenly became their true emerald-green shade. She blinked several times, glad to be momentarily rid of the uncomfortable lenses. Another pair soon replaced them. Dull gray eyes stared into the mirror as she removed all vestiges of her make-up and began anew. When she had finished, her facial features looked remarkably different. Highlighting stressed varied natural attributes, giving the illusion that the face now reflected in the little mirror bore little resemblance to the other that had been there only minutes before.

Long, red, lacquered fingernails peeled off to expose shorter, natural nails painted a distinctly different shade. A detailed final inspection in the mirror told her that all was in order. The mirror and hook returned to their respective places in the case. Then the red exterior of the case peeled off to reveal a black Samsonite finish. The remarkably rapid transformation was complete. Bag in hand, she calmly exited the ladies' room to resume her itinerary.

From his adjacent hotel room Schmitt listened to the telephone conversation. The minute bug was concealed in Larson's phone.

Three days had passed since he had spotted Larson exiting van Troje's office. The half-year hiatus between Larson's last known visit to Amsterdam puzzled Schmitt. He had begun to think the deal, whatever it was, had soured. And yet, the ETA had returned to the headlines with a new wave of bombings. The connection with Larson was tenuous at best, but could it be ignored?

Larson's return was encouraging. The realization that Larson held the key to the operation and possibly to the renewal of violence in Barcelona, spurred Schmitt to follow when the American boarded a KLM flight bound for New York. In the intervening days he had shadowed Larson's movements. These included a visit to a Hoboken, New Jersey apartment where a handful of apparent hostages were being held. Schmitt had no way of knowing who they were or where they fit into the overall picture, but they could only mean that the actual caper was in the offing.

The telephone conversation he had just heard reinforced that conclusion. The sheer scope of the operation continued to amaze him as bit by bit he located seemingly discordant pieces of an enormous puzzle. It pleased him that the months of uncertainty were nearing an end.

Thoughts pondering the importance of the woman's call, he completed a detailed longhand report of his findings and suspicions. Within the hour it would be posted to Lisbeth. She would keep it together with the remainder of his detailed reports on the case. If he failed to contact her within a given time frame, she would phone a special number and arrange immediate delivery of the documents to Interpol.

Schmitt already had fed them routine progress reports, but they were sketchy to say the least. Any hard facts were withheld. He always played in close to the chest like that to insure that he alone could orchestrate the final moves and thereby reap the rewards of his efforts. Such methods did little to endear him to anyone; the fact that he almost invariably delivered did.

It was early evening when Schmitt followed Larson out of the hotel. A light rain began as Schmitt tailed the American's van for many miles. He was mildly surprised to see the van pull up at a

Post Office. There were unquestionably innumerable places nearer the hotel where one could post a letter. Interest piqued, Schmitt watched Larson bound up the few steps, drop a letter in the box by the door, and return to the van.

Schmitt yearned to know the contents of that letter or at the very least the identity of the addressee. Unattainable goals, he consoled himself as he swung the rented Ford from the curb and trailed his quarry back to the hotel.

Two days later the letter would be opened and read at the Washington, DC headquarters of the Federal Bureau of Investigation, the addressee. The single, neatly typed page was unsigned and devoid of fingerprints. It caused considerable concern. It read:

> "The Communist Chinese delegation on international trade due to arrive in San Francisco 7 April, has been targeted for extinction by certain members of our pro-Nationalist Chinese movement. Further detail would endanger not only the writer, but friends and relatives.
>
> "These overzealous extremists must not succeed. The ultimate goal is laudable; the means deplorable. The writer hopes that forewarned will be fore-armed."

The letter was, of course, wholly fictitious, but once read in Washington, its implications could not lightly be ignored. Chinese / Taiwanese relations were very strained. Trouble seemed almost imminent when the Chinese government opted to do missile tests a scant twenty-one miles off Taiwan in early March, a mere three weeks ago. The scenario was simply too real, the potential consequences too great. On the third day after its posting, the FBI's 50 member anti-terrorist team, HRT, would be dispatched to the West Coast. Which placed the elite specialists precisely where Erik Larson wanted them.

CHAPTER NINE

10 April

6:38 PM

Somewhere over Canada

The event began when the British Airways 747 was about halfway enroute from London to Los Angeles. Six passengers, four men and two women, all from the economy section, rendezvoused by the aft lavatories. They marvelously illustrated the proletariat. Simple, inexpensive clothes draped these exceedingly average looking people. All were obviously working class, from the lower ranks if appearances were to be believed. Ambition would never mar their lives. In fact, they seemed the type slated to eke out a living and remain ignominiously within their little niche in society's fabric.

Each had brought some item or items from his or her seat to the congregation. They huddled together briefly, bodies forming a living screen. Concealed by the human shield, the collection of items was expertly combined to make three distinct parcels. Each consisted of wads of plastic explosive connected to a detonator with a dead-man's switch triggering device. The detonators had been electric razors and a portable radio. The plastic explosive itself - wrapped candy and a sealed box of child's modeling clay. The straps from which each assembly hung were borrowed from cameras and a carryall.

Weapons assembled, the six paired off. One pair remained near the tail of the big jet, while the others boldly advanced along either of the two aisles, the person clutching the dead-man's switch leading. These same people loudly announced the lethal nature of the parcels they now sported as they advanced. Frightened gasps accompanied the terrorists as they walked steadily forward. The terse tone of the dark-haired man leading the starboard procession bore the ring of utter conviction when he announced that neither he nor his friends would hesitate to release the tiny switches clasped firmly within their fists if there was the slightest resistance. He calmly explained that any one of the explosive packs would be sufficient to devastate the aircraft. No one decided to test the terrorists' resolve. Nor did anyone think to question whether or not the masses of purported explosives, into which the detonators were set, were in fact, genuine. There were no heroes.

8:19 PM

The Oval Office, The White House

The President busily reviewed material for a morning meeting with the Saudi Arabian Foreign Minister. The talks would center upon the continued U.S. military presence in the Persian Gulf and continued access to Saudi Arabian facilities that had begun with the Gulf War in 1991. The outcome could prove pivotal to U.S. aspirations in the volatile region.

He felt the prospects for a mutually beneficial agreement were reasonably good. The thorough review would enable him to present his case effectively. Foreign policy had been heralded as a major weakness of the President during his election campaign. It followed that he habitually made every effort to project strength, sagacity, and competence in handling the nation's foreign affairs. Determination to prove would-be detractors wrong, was a potent thing in his skilled hands.

Consequently his spirits were rather good when two close and influential aides interrupted his study of the prepared reports. He looked up from the work atop the ornately carved, antique desk. The American flag and the presidential flags flanked him. Framed by the magnificent desk, the flags, and the golden drapes, he seemed the quintessential symbol of officialdom.

"We're sorry to barge in on you, mister President, but I'm afraid we've got a bit of a problem."

The President leaned back in his chair, flexing weary shoulders, somewhat grateful for any reprieve from the classified documents spread before him. "Fair enough, Herb." He smiled affably. His was the sort of reassuring smile that put people's minds at ease. "Let's hear it."

Herbert Bartlett was a balding man of little stature who had long since lost the battle with his waistline. A worried expression perpetually graced his round face. It was a deceptive characteristic, because under pressure he rarely showed any sign of stress. He rubbed his stubby-fingered hands together as he settled onto a chair opposite the Chief Executive. This tiny gesture with his hands betrayed agitation. Either the situation was pretty bad or Bartlett had yet to develop a viable solution. Or perhaps both. His voice was its usual eternally dull monotone. "A British Airways 747 has been skyjacked by the ETA."

"The who?"

"It's a Basque separatist group."

The other nattily attired aide, John Herrin, added. "They're bound for Dallas/Fort Worth." He too sat facing his boss.

All trace of good spirits vanished. "Have the British and Spanish authorities been informed?" It was a superfluous question.

Herrin nodded. His gaunt features were, as always, deadly serious. "State is handling that aspect of the situation. The Spanish government's line is that the event began on foreign soil on a foreign airline - so they're sorry, but will step-up security at home. They, the British that is, want to know what we intend to do." He hesitated, then added, "The British kind of hinted, broadly hinted that is, that they feel we have not toed a hard enough line against terrorists to date."

A wry smile graced the president' face. "Nothing's ever easy, is it? Senate committees probing and prodding for any indiscretion in my family's past, the media carrying on its own blitz along the same lines . . . God, you'd think they believed they'd elected some spiritual knight in shining white armor, not a flesh and blood man cursed with the foibles of any normal human being. Now this, the media will use it to further chink away at our foreign policy's merits. So will our adversary in the other party come the next election. Ah, the perks of power!" His gaze caught that of his advisors again. "Given that it is a British airliner, presumably laden with principally British nationals, any indication of what the British would like us to do?"

"They've made it quite clear that they favor non-acquiescence backed by strong force."

It was the President's turn to nod thoughtfully. "Understandable. Keeps in line with their policy of refusal to kow-tow to terrorists. Also maintains our stated policy position. Their support simplifies matters greatly since I assume that most of the hostages are British. Just what are we dealing with?"

"The ETA claims to have a substantial amount of explosives aboard the plane. They're demanding one million dollars from us and another million from the Spanish government. The ransom is to be delivered through an elaborate procedure in Sweden. The only thing they want in Texas, where the actual terrorist team will land, is a fully fueled business jet with a pilot. And, of course, full media coverage. They want maximum publicity for this grandstand play of theirs. If these demands aren't met by midnight tomorrow, the plane and hostages will be sacrificed for the cause." Herrin was concise, yet thorough, traits developed during nearly two decades as a legal consultant with a major oil company.

"Quite a theatrical stand."

"Yeah," Bartlett agreed, "but one wrought with political sensitivities. There are those who will condemn any action against the terrorists because of various warped reasoning, be it sympathy for the Basque rebels or whatever. Another factor is that roughly three quarters of the hostages are foreign nationals, mostly British. If any die as a result of actions on our part, we may find ourselves harangued by the foreign media, despite the official support already expressed to State. A disaster could have serious ramifications on many fronts, particularly our remaining forces in Europe. The fact that the perpetrators are a little known Basque group makes it even more ticklish. It's a little like a David and Goliath thing. In a worst case scenario, the media blitz could prove most embarrassing if not downright harmful for the country and for the next election. You know how they can twist something like this around. Make the terrorists sound like heroic freedom fighters, that kind of crap."

"Only too well," the President conceded. Bitter memories of press attacks on his own integrity flashed through his thoughts. "On the other hand, deviation from our own stated policy on terrorism would invite further problems. We must show that such flagrant abuses won't be tolerated. Our resolve must remain firm. What options are available?"

"Essentially, we've got only one, if indeed we do act. Operation Blue Light is the logical choice. They're supposedly the best we've got for this kind of thing." Herrin replied.

"What about the FBI's HRT unit? I've heard good things about them."

"Already engaged to counter a potential threat on the West Coast. Besides, Blue Light is a tailor-made unit. They've trained for exactly this type of mission. From the special equipment requisite to the job, to the esoteric skills needed to employ that equipment, they're the ones we want." Bartlett sounded confident in his assessment. Generally, his judgment was sound.

"I've seen them in action." Herrin added. "It was a privilege to watch those men at work. I've never experienced anything quite like it. For instance, in one exercise they led me into a group of rooms where numerous life-size photos of people were mounted on pasteboard backing and stands. I was told to arm the dummies of my choice with cardboard weapons lying on a table. Then I was to position the dummies wherever I desired. I was led into an isolated corner. The lights went out. All of a sudden,"

Herrin was gesticulating with his hands as the incredible memory played through his mind, "a door burst open. Flickering red-orange tongues of flame lanced the darkness, the air reeked of burnt cordite, and my ears hurt from the reverberating thunder of automatic weapons' fire within close quarters. The whole thing lasted no more than a few seconds. Then the lights came on again. Decked out in night-fighting gear, complete with strange looking goggles for infrared light or some such thing, weapons held in steady hands, a team of their men stood in the rooms. Even more frightening, or impressive depending upon one's viewpoint, were the armed dummies, that is, the fake terrorists. A cluster of bullet holes perforated the pasteboard where their heads should have been.

"In those few seconds, they made a believer out of me."

"And you of me, John," the President stated solemnly. "Give the necessary orders. They'll be acting upon my authority and with my best wishes for success. No word to the media aside from the fact that we're consulting the British and Spanish governments. See that State informs both of our decision immediately. And make damned sure that they're kept fully updated the moment any information becomes available. You might also have State convey the notion that any advice members of Britain's SAS might have to offer would be greatly appreciated by our boys. The SAS has enjoyed noteworthy success with this sort of thing in the past and asking for help might assuage British sensibilities. Oh, and make sure that our field commander understands fully that if any such advice is forthcoming, I expect him to weigh it judiciously and to implement it if at all feasible."

"If I'm not mistaken, a four-man team of SAS advisors has already been dispatched from London. Two of them assisted the Germans with the strike at Mogadishu."

"Great. Glad to hear it." The President leaned forward again, resting both arms on the reports spread before him. The gesture was an informal dismissal. "Keep me posted."

8:41 PM

Fort Bragg, North Carolina

The duty officer sat in a typically utilitarian military building huddled amongst many other similar structures. They and the training grounds surrounding the lot were part of a compound within the immensely larger expanse of Fort Bragg proper. An imposing fourteen-foot high fence isolated them from the rest of the base. There were undoubtedly other, less obvious, safeguards to discourage the curious.

Predictably, the goings on within the compound were of a highly secretive nature. Few outsiders gained access. Those who did were carefully screened. Members of the media were strictly taboo. The individuals who trained within the specialized surroundings were all handpicked for their intelligence, physical condition, and above all the ability to keep the nature of their work absolutely secret. Their number was about 300 and they were drawn from all branches of the service; Army, Navy, Air Force, and Marines.

These specially selected individuals endured a rigorous training regimen to prepare them for highly specialized missions. Their operational code name was Blue Light.

Project Blue Light evolved to provide America with a capable unit of exceptionally skilled fighting men. Their purpose was to deal effectively with particularly difficult operations that required fast, hard-hitting action on a limited scale. In time of war, the destruction of vital installations behind enemy lines would be their forte. In peacetime, suppression of terrorists and daring raids to free hostages became their focus. Theirs was a close knit organization, one consigned mostly to honing skills that rarely, if ever, were called upon. It was an elite group that only the President could call into action.

Since Blue Light's inception in 1977, such calls to action came rarely. The Iranian Hostage Crisis offered their first true test. It proved less than glorious. The devastating disaster that befell 97 members of the unit on the night of 24 to 25 April 1980 would cast a dark cloud over the unit. The tragic mishaps their strike team suffered at an obscure point in the Iranian desert, designated Desert One, would raise serious questions about Blue Light, also known as Delta Team, and military capabilities in general. Since that disappointing day the persons at Fort Bragg's little compound had patiently awaited other calls to duty, hoping for one through which their prowess could be shown to equal their counterparts in Great Britain, Germany, and Israel. When the long awaited Presidential call came, pity the target.

The duty officer sat bolt upright as he heard the appropriate code words delivered. The hint of a smile graced his lean features as he picked up the phone to alert his CO. The time seemed at hand.

10:17 PM

Fort Bragg, North Carolina

Two McDonnell Douglas C-9B Skytrain IIs rolled down the runway and rose into the night sky. Sixty-five members of Blue Light were divided between the two gray and white jets. Also aboard was a plethora of specially developed equipment specifically designed for anti-terrorist strike operations. Spirits were high as the two aircraft set course for the Dallas/Fort Worth International Airport. The chance for redemption seemed at hand.

Dried streaks of reddish mud covered the sides of the old, rusting Ford pick-up truck. Larger chunks of mud caked around the wheels and wheel wells. The pick-up stood parked among some persimmon trees at the side of a dirt track that saw little use. Its owner had hiked up the small rise at the foot of which the convenient persimmon trees grew. Atop the knoll he found concealment for himself within a thicket. A small space had been cleared to make room for a folding campstool within the tangled mass of the thicket. The man's behind had only vacated the canvas seat a few times since he began his stint on watch. Nature had called on those occasions, the pile of crushed Budweiser cans thrown behind him testimony as to why.

Faded jeans, still damp from brushing through tall grass and briar wet from an afternoon shower, clung annoyingly to his legs. The accompanying itch only accentuated the discomfort. Yet he remained on the stool, a brand new pair of expensive Zeiss night binoculars frequently scanning the heavens. With only the stool, binoculars, beer cooler, and a walkie-talkie for company, he had been in the thicket since four PM. A thousand more intriguing ways to spend an afternoon and evening came to mind. When they did, he consoled himself with the thought that the miserable hours in the thicket would earn him a dollar for each of them, one thousand dollars cash money. The fancy binoculars and radio were a bonus. Though he hadn't much use for either, he figured they could be sold for additional profit.

And so it was that Billy Morrow came to be involved with something he knew had to be illegal. Of course, the law had never warranted much respect from the sandy-haired Morrow in his 23 years. He was a simple man of limited means and limited skills. Several brushes with the law spawned a deep hatred of those who enforced it and the establishment that hired them.

Legal or not, there were a thousand tax-free dollars to be made for himself and each of his like minded brothers. Seth, the youngest, was set up like Billy some five miles to the north, while Erwin, the eldest, sat comfortably in his old rattletrap that in better days had been a Chrysler New Yorker. It was Erwin's turn to take up station near Jamison's Country Store. He had undoubtedly doffed his rain soaked clothes after Billy had relieved him at the thicket. When the time came, if indeed it came at all, he would climb the creaking wooden steps in front of the old relic of a business and place the call on the pay phone set on the narrow porch. It was all so simple, Billy Morrow thought as he maintained his vigil. He wondered why the man with the Yankee accent was so damned interested in a particular jet or jets leaving the airfield at Fort Bragg. It didn't seem to make much sense.

The sky had cleared as dusk descended, which made the job

somewhat easier. It also dismissed all fears of a thorough soaking such as that dealt Erwin earlier on. Several aircraft had crossed the star speckled heavens, but none matched the specific outline of the aircraft in question. Binoculars brought up again, bull neck craned, Morrow located another approaching jet. At first he didn't think so, then as seconds passed he became convinced that it was the one he was posted to spot. And then the second one was visible too!

"Hot damn!" He spit out a wad of chewing tobacco and grabbed the walkie-talkie. "Hey, Erwin! You there, brother?"

The weary voice of his brother crackled out of the tiny speaker. "Yo, Billy. See somethin'?"

"You bet yer sweet ass! Two of 'em!"

"Fer sure?"

"Plain as daylight in these fancy spyglasses here. They're the ones that bastard wants ta know 'bout. Now we can all git home."

"Right O, Billy. I'll call 'im now. Bye."

"Bye, yerself," Billy said happily as he got stiffly to his feet and gathered his things. "Easiest thousand bucks I'll ever make," he announced to the insects buzzing around him.

10:30 PM

New York, NY

A phone rang in the rented loft. It did so every hour with boring routine. Each time it was automatically answered by the telephone answering machine that was the only item the new tenant had installed on his one and only visit. Each time the machine was fed a coded signal to trigger a playback of any messages left by callers. Each time there had been none. At least not until the 10:30 PM call. The solitary message given with a distinct southern drawl was brief. The target planes were up at about 10:20 PM. Positive Identification had been made. Then the caller hung up.

11:03 PM

The White House, Washington, DC

The President had only just retired to his private quarters. Another long day in the job yearned for since school days was about over. It had been a tough one and the next promised more of the same, but such was the life of the nation's Chief Executive.

The endurance and abilities of those elected to the post were taxed regularly.

The First Lady had just vanished into the ornate bathroom when the phone buzzed. The President paused in the act of removing a brightly hued silk tie. He shrugged good-naturedly at himself in the mirror and reached for the nearest extension.

"Sorry to disturb you." It was John Herrin.

"That's your job, John."

"Maybe. Anyway, the situation in Texas has altered. For the worse, I fear."

"I'm listening."

"The hijacked plane is on the ground now. It was taxied off to an isolated part of the airport. Everything's quiet out there, for the moment. The complication comes via the British Foreign Ministry. They've just notified State that some distant cousin of the Royal family is aboard that plane. They don't think the ETA knows of the young man's presence, otherwise they would certainly have exploited the fact. But it does put a whole new perspective on things. Britain still favors force, but given the new complexion of things, the Prime Minister respectfully has asked that a British strike team be allowed to make the assault."

The President finished removing his tie and hung it neatly away. With one hand he began to unbutton his shirt. "They want the SAS to do the dirty work, is that it?"

"Essentially. State seems to feel we should oblige. I just conferred with the Secretary himself." Herrin hesitated, then added, "I'm inclined to agree. It puts the monkey on their back, while still pointedly asserting our policy of refusal to deal with terrorists."

"Mmmm. It does that. Actually, the PM is going out on a bit

of a limb with it. If the SAS should fail, the blame for any debacle falls squarely on 10 Downing Street. On the other hand, if we turn down the request and our lads screw up, we really look bad. In effect, we've little choice if we wish to play it safe. Have State approve the British operation. Offer any and all assistance required. And keep Blue Light on scene. They may still be useful. Tell the Secretary to squelch any red tape that might hinder the operation and make damned sure that the press doesn't muddy the waters or threaten operational security."

"Understood. I'll get right on it. Thanks."

"Keep me informed, John. Let's pray those brave men can carry it off without a bloodbath."

"Amen to that. I'll have an update prepared for your breakfast briefing. Good-night, mister President."

ROUGH ICE

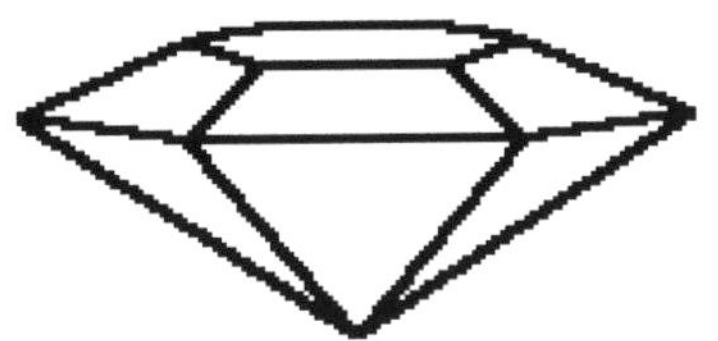

BOOK TWO

EXECUTION

CHAPTER TEN

11 April

6:00 to 8:00 AM

New York

The customized Ford van provided an easy target for Schmitt. Carefully keeping a respectable distance from it, he threaded his way through the thickening traffic on the Shore Parkway.

The sun had only just risen. The air was still cool, particularly so in Schmitt's rented Ford, whose power window refused to go back up after he paid the toll collector at the Verazano Narrows Bridge. At least the blast of chilled air helped to revive him from his sleepy stupor. Larson's earlier than expected departure had almost caught him by surprise. Schmitt thanked God that he had slipped the motion sensor into Larson's entry so that any movement in or out of the hotel room would trigger a beeping signal in his own. Still half-dressed he had hastily thrown his belongings into his single suitcase and rushed to checkout. His bill settled in cash, Larson had bumped into him at the reception desk, so near had the two men been.

The van slowed and stopped in front of John F. Kennedy International Airport's main terminal. Schmitt pulled curbside some hundred feet behind. He watched as Larson and another man stepped out. It struck him as odd that their luggage was passed through the front door of the van instead of just opening the big sliding door on the right-hand side.

Someone rapped sharply on his own windshield. It was a black police officer. "You'll have to move. This is strictly an unloading zone, buddy." He pointed to a nearby sign that confirmed his point.

Schmitt jumped out and rounded the car. "Right you are, officer. And I was just about to do precisely that." He pulled out his bag and dropped it roughly on the curb.

The cop placed his hands on hips. "And what about the car?" He hated being treated in a flippant manner.

Schmitt shot a glance toward the van. It had just pulled away. Larson and the other man, both immaculately attired, were passing through the terminal's glass doors. Lowering his voice to a conspiratorial level, Schmitt said, "Listen, I'm with the FBI. We've got a sting operation going down! Don't blow months of work by making waves. Put a ticket on the car and act like some son-of-a-bitch left it there."

"What the . . .?" Confusion replaced annoyance.

"No time to explain. Just tell the field office that McMurdo is in the terminal." Schmitt called over his shoulder as he hurried away, bag in hand.

Larson had just slipped his boarding pass into his jacket when Schmitt entered the terminal. Larson's associate already was headed for the escalator. Schmitt looked up at the departure schedule. The airline had three flights going out that morning; bound for Germany, Brazil, and Hong Kong. Which one? Schmitt wondered.

He skirted to the fore of the rapidly growing first class ticket line. Several people voiced objections to his brashness. The cheery-faced woman at the counter said, "I'm afraid you'll have to wait your turn, sir."

"Thank God I made it on time." Schmitt sounded profoundly relieved. "I'm on the same flight as my associates over there." He jerked a thumb at Larson's retreating form. I can't afford to miss it."

The attendant forced a smile. She hated it when people seemed to think that they were the only one's with problems and expected everyone else to bend over backwards to help. Still, her job dictated tact. "Flight 923 for Rio doesn't even begin to board for another twenty or thirty minutes. Now if you'll please be so good as to wait your turn."

Schmitt looked dumbly at his watch. "Oh my. I'm terribly sorry, I thought it was already boarding." He turned to the disgruntled people in line. "Truly sorry. Just a mistake." He picked up his suitcase and moved away from the counter. Several first class ticket-holders shook their heads in disgust.

Schmitt made his way to another line and patiently awaited his turn to buy an economy class ticket on the Rio flight.

The lengthy corridor seemed endless. Schmitt threaded his way cautiously through the other travelers as he followed the man who had arrived with Larson. They had left Larson seated in the first class lounge where it seemed safe to assume that he would remain until the flight was called. The other man entered a glass-enclosed newsstand and concession. Schmitt lounged outside, surreptitiously observing the man who moved aimlessly about picking up items, then replacing them. He frequently set down his flight bag and the little parcel he toted. After one such move he failed to pick up the parcel. Schmitt watched as the man gently nudged the package under a display rack with the side of his shoe.

"There you are!" A big hand locked round Schmitt's upper arm. It was the cop. "No one around here knows a damned thing about any McMurdo! Let's see some ID."

Schmitt twisted loose. "I told you, I'm in the midst of a sensitive investigation."

"I've had enough of that crap. Get some ID out."

The man exited the newsstand, gave the black cop with Schmitt a disinterested glance, and headed back towards the Atlas Airways first class lounge. The Rio flight was called as he passed.

"That's my flight." Schmitt said angrily. "You'll screw up everything if you make me miss it!"

"Listen, buddy. You claimed to be FBI. That car out there is a rental. The papers in the ashtray don't confirm nothing of what you said. The security office knows nothing about McMurdo or any sting operation."

"I'm undercover!" Schmitt looked exasperated as he pleaded. "I've got to go!" He turned and started to move toward the entrance to the newsstand.

"Freeze!" The officer commanded.

Schmitt spun round. "The men I'm tailing are international terrorist! Murderers!" This drew a startled look from a curious old woman who turned and fled. "They've already killed several people in Amsterdam. But don't take my word for it, check out the package that bastard just left in there!" He was fast losing his patience.

"I've had enough of your story telling bullshit. Hands against that pillar, feet spread wide!" Schmitt rolled his eyes and reluctantly complied. "Wider!"

"You're making a big mistake."

"Yeah, well we'll just see about that." Skilled hands began a thorough frisk. "Hello there, what's this?" He yanked a specially made switchblade from the inside of Schmitt's sock where a rubber band secured it firmly. Its blade and case were a tough new plastic resin and had not tripped the metal detectors upon entering the terminal. Schmitt cursed himself for not having dumped it in a trash receptacle already.

"I can explain that, officer." He started to turn, but found himself pushed roughly against the pillar. The cold steel of handcuffs slapped round his wrists.

"Sure you can. I'll bet you can explain lots o' things. Let's go, buddy."

Schmitt licked his lips nervously. "At least check out the package he left in there."

"So you can try to run off again? Move it!" The cop prodded Schmitt away from the newsstand. The crowd of spectators who had watched the bizarre incident in fascination began to disperse.

The scene viewed from the sloped, tinted windows of the control tower's 'cab' was a familiar one. Aircraft moved about on the maze of taxiways, while a steady stream of cars and busses poured in and out of the airport along the curved access road. People toting luggage, cameras, and other travel paraphernalia streamed into and out of the various terminal buildings. The early morning rush was well underway. Over the next few hours the load would peak, then gradually let up, giving the tower personnel a chance to relax a bit before their shift ended.

Another routine day. Then, without preamble, Atlas Airways flight 923, which was almost in take-off position, broke radio contact and came to an abrupt halt on the taxiway.

The wavy-haired ground controller made repeated attempts to re-establish communications with the inert 747, all to no avail. One favorable sign was that the pilot had not discretely dropped his flaps to indicate a hijack was in progress.

The subdued whine of the engines was clearly audible above the soft music being piped into the wide cabin of the 747. The aircraft rocked gently as it moved along the taxiway. Larson sat rigidly in his seat. His Moroccan leather flight bag stood between his legs, its top unzipped. He slipped on a pair of skintight gloves. A camera lay on his lap. A tiny red light atop it suddenly began flashing.

Larson tossed the camera aside, bent forward, and slipped into what resembled a medical oxygen mask. He produced a can of aerosol deodorant, or rather a canister made to resemble one, snapped off the spray nozzle, and lobbed the hissing canister back toward the base of the spiral stairway that led to the plane's upper deck.

Across the aisle his companion mimicked his movements. Both leapt to their feet, grabbed their flight bags, and moved aft. The familiar sounds of the aircraft were joined by the loud hiss of escaping compressed gas as the two canisters spewed forth their contents.

Without warning, the aircraft jerked violently to a halt on the taxiway. Both men had to steady themselves against seatbacks before continuing. All around them, passengers lapsed into unconsciousness.

Simultaneously with events below, the flight deck was suddenly filled with the hissing sound of gas being released. In the few split seconds before the startled flight crew realized what was happening, it was too late.

Larson stepped across a fallen flight attendant and moved quickly towards the azure curtains separating first class from the economy sections. In the opposite aisle his accomplice did the same. In perfect unison they reached into their bags, pulled out two more aerosol cans, snapped the tops off, and brushed the curtains aside. The people in the forward end of the section were already under the effect of the quick acting gas. Several had lapsed into unconsciousness.

From the growing commotion towards the rear of the aircraft, Larson could see that they would have to act fast. Lobbing the first of his two canisters down to the rear of the section, he raced down the aisle. People all about dropped unconscious as he threw the second canister deep into the heart of the next cabin section.

Two flight attendants lay sprawled in a heap on the floor as Larson passed the galley between the last two sections. One had spilled a basket of headsets she had been carrying when the gas overcame her. Everyone in the second economy section was succumbing when he and his accomplice entered the third and final section, their last gas canisters at the ready. Buttons off, these angrily hissing items were tossed into the midst of the screaming throng. A few moments later the screams died away. Silence reigned; the airliner was theirs.

The plush upper lounge was deserted. Larson's flight bag sailed across the room into a convenient couch. He turned to the wood-grained door in the forward bulkhead. A brass plate read: "Flight Deck - No Admittance."

The door opened freely. At his feet lay the crumpled form of one of the flight crew. He stepped across the limp form as the man in the pilot's seat turned to greet him with a thumbs up gesture. Like Larson, he wore a tiny gas mask.

What the flight deck lacked in size was more than compensated for in technical complexity. Row after row of dials, knobs, and switches dominated the right hand wall. Below this intimidating array a narrow workspace completed the flight engineer's domain.

Countless switches also covered the ceiling between the pilot and co-pilot's seats. Directly beneath them a console sprouted the four levers governing the huge Pratt and Whitney turbofan engines suspended below the wings. Each of these power plants would deliver 47,000 pounds of thrust on demand, an awesome force harnessed to do the seemingly impossible - make the enormous aircraft fly.

Ahead of the four levers a column of dials related vital data about each. This was the heart and soul of the aircraft.

Four full minutes had ticked by since the last canisters of gas had expelled their highly effective contents. The gas oxidized in about two and a half. Larson cautiously lifted an edge of his mask. An experimental sniff found no telltale scent. He peeled off the uncomfortable mask. The others followed suit.

Larson slid confidently into the co-pilot's seat. To no one in particular, he said, "So far, so good." The offered headset was donned.

A small gadget snapped onto its tiny microphone. The gadget electronically mired a voice so that any voiceprint made from the tower tapes would be useless to the authorities.

Having drawn a remarkably relaxed breath, he depressed the transmit button. He feigned his best Irish accent when he began. "Kennedy Ground Control, this is Atlas 923, do you read?"

The response was immediate. "Atlas 923, Kennedy Ground Control. What the hell happened? We've been trying to raise you for nearly five minutes!"

"Forgive the suspense. I'm sure you'll agree that this is a rather large aircraft with a great many passengers. With that in mind, I'm certain that you'll also concur that subduing the lot and taking them and the aircraft hostage in less than five minutes is not a small accomplishment. We of the *Euskadi ta Askatasun*, better known as the ETA, are most efficient. So far, no one has been hurt. To keep it that way you had best listen very carefully." Larson spoke slowly, distinctly, so that nothing could be misunderstood.

CHAPTER ELEVEN

11 April

8:00 to 8:20 AM

The ground controller's face was aghast as he turned to look at his shift supervisor. She took the headset from him, motioning him out of the seat as she grabbed a pencil from among those strewn about the workspace. In twenty-two years of working air traffic control, the last six of which spent as a shift supervisor, Judy McArthur had coped with innumerable problems including a fiery crash on take-off. None mustered her ire like a hijacking. It was the lowest form of human endeavor. She wondered what sort of fanatics had commandeered Atlas 923. Would their demands be financial like their comrades in Texas?

The 747 stood plainly visible far away on the airfield as she gazed through the canted window. Vibrant gray eyes reflected sudden anxiety by their uncharacteristically frequent blinks. Two months hence she would celebrate her forty-sixth birthday and the irrepressible question that leapt to mind was that of how much longer she could cope with such tension and stress. The day-to-day workload imposed by the busy airport was bad enough, but events such as this made the position of tower supervisor unsavory, to say the least. Responsibility was no problem, but the sense of utter helplessness inevitably attached to such events, made it a heavy burden for a conscientious person.

McArthur generally dressed simply. A charcoal-gray skirt and a cheerful pastel-yellow blouse suited her well. The matching blazer, as usual, hung neatly in her small office two stories below. Silky, chestnut hair just brushed her shoulders. Still its natural color, upon closer examination, the occasional gray strand could be found making an inroad. Her figure and features were average, nonetheless she was the sort of person who stood out in a group. A bubbly, always eager to help, demeanor made her an ever popular personage. As tower supervisor she developed a close rapport with her co-workers and held their admiration and respect.

The deep voice from the stricken jet resumed. McArthur noted the salient facts on a notepad even though all transmissions to and from the tower were routinely recorded for reference when needed.

"If the passengers and crew are to be released safely, then each of our demands must be followed with strict compliance. Our sphere of influence should you fail to do so is not, however, limited to our hostages here on the field. Several explosive devices have been planted around the airport and surrounding communities. Any interference with us will result in their detonation. Many, many people will be killed or maimed if this becomes necessary. Add to that the cost in damaged or destroyed property, a figure we conservatively place in the realm of nearly a billion dollars, and compliance becomes a relatively cheap, painless solution." McArthur found herself staring at the equally shaken controller by her side as the steady, almost cocky voice proceeded. "Our initial demands are as follows. First and foremost, the area around this aircraft is to be completely cleared and kept that way. Anyone or anything approaching our site will be considered evidence of hostile intent. Severe penalties will be immediate. Second, we want the airport administrator in the tower promptly. Upon his arrival the remainder of our requirements will be released.

"In the interim, a small demonstration of our capabilities might serve to avoid future misunderstandings." There was a momentary pause. "Exactly three minutes from now, the central newsstand area in the International Arrivals Building will be history. One minute later the main lobby area of the old Pan American Terminal will be decimated. I suggest immediate evacuation of both areas. We'll talk again after the fireworks. Atlas 923, over and out."

McArthur's face was ashen as she tore off the headset. The enormity of the threats boggled the mind. In a blur of motion she was across the tiny room, tearing the airport security hotline phone from its cradle. Blunt instructions were relayed to the duty officer. The 'cab' coordinator alerted the FBI on the direct phone link to the local office while the ground controller began to clear the area near the besieged aircraft.

Her next move was to contact the airport administrator's office. She stood nervously, the seconds passing with alarming rapidity. An eternity expired before the line came to life. "Kennedy International Airport, Administrator's Office. Can I help you?"

"Emergency! This is McArthur at ATC. Get Fredericks, and for God's sake hurry!"

The secretary caught the urgency, for Fredericks was on the line almost instantaneously.

"Bill, Judy McArthur. Atlas 923 to Rio has been seized on the runway by ETA terrorists, the same bastards who're putting on the show in Texas. They claim that the central newsstand in the IAB and the main concourse of building 53 will be obliterated within the next couple of minutes. Evacuations are underway."

"Good God!" Fredericks sounded as though someone had punched him hard in the gut. "Have the authorities been alerted?"

"Naturally. Bill, I think they're for real. I'd stake my reputation on it. The guy is too damned sure of himself for a hoax. His voice sounds somewhat funny, but it smacks of invincibility." As she spoke, McArthur looked out across the expansive airfield at the 747.

"Try and talk them out of destroying anything. Bullshit 'em. Tell 'em we'll co-operate in any way humanly possible."

"They want you here in the 'cab' for some reason, Bill. Specifically demanded that you get over here pronto. Don't ask me why."

"Hold it," Fredericks said. He buzzed his secretary. "Have a car and driver out front immediately! Then get on the horn to the main office. Tell them we've got a code 25 and related code 28 in progress. I'll be in the 'cab' when they want me." He punched the blinking light on the phone unit and reconnected with the tower. "Stall for time. I'm on my way!"

Fredericks bolted from his overly soft chair as he flung the phone back onto its cradle.

The tiny office was functionally furnished, no more. Schmitt sat on an uncomfortable wooden chair that looked to date from the early 1940s. The big cop stood smugly beside him. A harried looking man studied them both across the cluttered desktop.

"And you claim that you're pursuing an international terrorist? Is that it?" The man spoke with the 'I've heard it all before' monotone of a longtime law enforcement officer inured to cockamamie stories.

"Listen to me." Schmitt leaned forward, his hands still manacled. "I've been conducting this investigation for several months. The man I'm tailing has already butchered four people in Amsterdam. I believe he is somehow connected with the ETA. skyjacking underway in Texas. A second, similar strike may be in the offing here. You can verify my identity and the rudimentary facts of my story by phoning police inspector Peter Determeijer in Amsterdam."

"Oh, we'll verify your identity, mister Schmitt, if indeed that *is* your *real* name."

Schmitt cast a quick glance at the wall clock. The flight should have departed already. It was too late to cling to Larson's trail. And then something jarred his memory. "The parcel! Someone's got to check it out!"

"What parcel?" The FBI agent sounded tired.

"Suspect claims that one of some terrorists left a parcel in the central newsstand here in the IAB," the cop volunteered.

"And?"

"I saw nothing. Figured it to be another corny ruse."

"Did you check it out at all?"

The sureness melted from the voice. "Not closely."

"Then get the hell out there!" The phone rang at that precise instant. The agent answered it on the first ring. "Yeah? A code 25 ***AND*** a code 28? Sweet Jesus! I'm on my way." He slammed the receiver down. "Hold it!" He shouted at the retreating form of the cop. "Uncuff him!" Then to Schmitt, "Follow me, buddy." He grabbed his jacket and bolted from the office.

"Hurry up with the detonator." Larson commanded superfluously. His assistant from below labored as fast as he could. Larson turned to the flight engineer, a man recruited for the crucial task of securing the flight deck. "Let's get this bird turned onto the runway. I want her parked right on the intersection with 4 - Left. That'll leave plenty of room for our take-off run while placing us a bit further from any easy covert access point."

The engines increased their shrill note as they were throttled up a little. Brakes were released and the big jet lumbered forward onto runway 31 - Left, aligned itself, and rolled about two thousand feet down the seemingly endless strip of pavement. It halted precisely at the indicated point, a position that placed it well over a half mile from the nearest terminal building and also maintained a respectable distance from most of the small service and equipment sheds scattered about the vast airport grounds. Only one such structure lay within a thousand feet of their chosen location. To approach it unseen would require supernatural powers.

Once the aircraft had eased to a halt, Larson added, "Cut the air conditioning on the lower deck. Then shut down main engines. Keep the APU (auxiliary Power Unit - a small engine located in a 747's tail) running. We don't want to waste fuel. There's a long flight ahead and we'll need every drop."

"Coming up on three minutes," Larson's accomplice from the lower deck reminded. Harry Higgins was his name. The lean built Higgins possessed certain esoteric qualifications that had led to his recruitment for the operation. He was a better than average pilot, but more importantly, he had certain questionable connections through which less than common items such as the gas used to subdue passengers and crew, could be had if the price was right. Higgins' flying experience included many unlogged hours flying old transports, such as the venerable Douglas Dakota, laden with illegal drugs into the southern United States.

"To the second, if you please."

Higgins watched the digital readout on his watch's liquid crystal display flow from number to number. The detonator he clutched was fashioned within the shell of a compact cassette recorder. Underneath the back cover where the battery compartment should have been, five toggle switches lined the space. At the appointed moment Higgins threw the switch labeled 'A'. Sixty seconds later the switch labeled 'B' was thrown.

All hell broke loose in the main terminal building. What had been the central newsstand now plastered surrounding walls or lay strewn about the floor. Windows in nearby shops shattered. So too did the windows overlooking the exits from the customs area below. Shattered glass and debris showered the area. Burning magazines and newspapers lay among scattered candy bars, souvenirs, and bits of terminal ceiling. Smoke filled the air along with the choking stench of burning plastics. The crackling of burning debris was effectively drowned out by the screams of scores of terrified people jamming terminal exits. Mass panic was on the verge of erupting, the orderly evacuation having ended abruptly with the intense thunderclap and rippling concussion of the explosion.

Airport personnel and security officers quickly extinguished the scattered fires in the central concourse and surrounding shops, but the damage was heavy.

They were still hard at work exactly sixty seconds later when Thor's hammer struck again. A second thunderclap erupted within the main concourse area of the terminal building that once served the now defunct aviation pioneer, Pan American. The devastation was near complete. Burning debris lay everywhere. Nearly all of the large plate glass windows that hemmed in the forward portion of the building were cracked or completely shattered by the concussion of the shock wave from the blast.

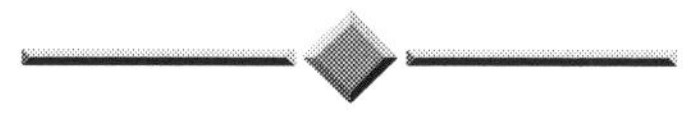

The control tower's elevator stopped three floors short of the 'cab', a fact that irked Fredericks whenever he had occasion to visit the FAA dominated facility. The twin bomb threats had been executed while he was enroute. Preliminary word of the destruction had reached him via the squad car's radio. The media would undoubtedly already have picked up on the unfolding events. Before long throngs of reporters and camera operators would besiege the administration building demanding information. They always seemed to complicate matters for him, he thought as the elevator doors slid open. Perhaps the terrorists had realized the advantages of removing him from the administration building for negotiations.

Nearly five minutes had elapsed since the detonations. He tried to quicken his pace as he scrambled up the three flights of stairs to the 'cab,' but his bulk protested the effort. Years had passed since physical exertion of any consequence had been undertaken by the aging administrator and it showed. Nearing the top step he stumbled out of breath, pushed himself upright, and forced tired legs to carry him into the 'cab.'

McArthur turned as Fredericks stumbled in. The two had worked together for a good many years. In all that time she had never seen the obese man look so intensely worried. Fear and worry rarely surfaced on the balding administrator. Perhaps, thought McArthur, these emotions were kept at bay by the man's stubborn, often arrogant, behavior. She and Fredericks were different as night and day. No love was lost between them, yet each respected the other for his or her abilities and accomplishments. Those abilities were now being tested to the full.

Fredericks puffed heavily as he leaned for support against a console. McArthur said, "Just before the first blast they moved the plane onto 31 - Left and parked at the intersection with 4 - Left. We tried to reach them and stop the fireworks. No response." She handed the administrator a headset and moved so that he could take a vacant seat. "You'd better sit down, Bill. They want you to contact them now that you're here."

Breathing slightly less laboriously, Fredericks dropped onto the seat that creaked under the sudden burden. "Anything from security about the severity of the damage?"

"Not much detail yet. But one look outside at the fleeing crowds and you can imagine it isn't pretty in there." McArthur gestured towards the hundreds of people fleeing the building below. It was not a pretty sight. They pushed and shoved one another as they fled in panic. In the vast parking lots, cars were pulling out everywhere, heading in every conceivable direction, creating one massive logjam of traffic.

Fredericks gazed at the scene in growing contempt. "What kind of senseless bastards are we dealing with. Just look at what they've already done. And for what?" His voice trailed away with a question that went unanswered. The ground controller tapped his shoulder and told him that Atlas 923 was on the line.

Headsets throughout the little room listened to Larson's electronically altered voice. "Kennedy Ground Control, this is Atlas 923, do you read?"

"Kennedy Ground Control, we read! Too damned well by far, 923! Name's Fredericks, airport administrator. Just what the devil are you trying to do to my facility?" He visibly strained to contain his famous temper.

"Just making sure that we understand each other, Fredericks. The pyrotechnics should be sobering proof that we can strike at will at any time that you fail to obey our instructions. Any deviation will be regarded as a provocation. If provoked we are prepared to destroy and kill to defend ourselves. Several additional charges lie peppered throughout the area. Each is placed to imperil a great many people and do lots of costly damage if triggered. And, incidentally, if we deem their use prudent, no warning will be given. Do we understand each other, Fredericks?"

"You bastards are mad! Only someone crazier than yourself would seriously believe such a load of crap!"

"Mad?" The voice replied calmly. "Cautious would be a more accurate term. Extremely cautious, and yes, you had better take me very seriously. If you need further proof of my sincerity, then I can easily arrange another demonstration. Just keep in mind, Fredericks, any casualties will be killed or injured purely because of your ignorance. It will be as though you, yourself, threw the switch. In short, people will die if you don't take me seriously."

There was a brief silence as the terrorist let the inherent menace of his words hit home. At length he continued. "In addition to the local charges, we have another little surprise that should keep both you and the US Federal authorities from antagonizing us. A series of remote charges lines our intended flight path. Most are set on timers that will automatically detonate them within the next eighteen hours if we are not on schedule. These charges can be anywhere. Office buildings, restaurants, shopping centers, theaters, schools, or any other of countless potential targets. Any interference with our operation that delays our departure means that they all go off. With them ride the fates of hundreds, perhaps thousands of innocent people.

"Additional remote charges can be controlled manually. They enable prompt retaliatory action. We realize that on the surface these threats may seem wild and wholly implausible. Here again, in the interest of avoiding bloodshed, we are willing to demonstrate our capabilities. We will detonate one of our remotes to convince you and the authorities that our threats are not idle ones. To prove that our long range defenses are not limited to a one shot deal, we'll even let you select the target region, Fredericks. Northern Virginia or Florida? Choose now!"

"What the devil are you getting at?" The administrator stammered.

"Pick one. Now!" The voice commanded.

Fredericks shook his fleshy face, heavily jowled cheeks quivering like Jell-O. "Virginia.," he said dryly, praying that no one would come to harm as a result.

"So be it. At precisely 8:30 AM a charge will detonate in the long-term parking area of Dulles airport. We provide the delay in triggering the device purely for humanitarian reasons. I suggest that you notify the people at Dulles to have the area cordoned off.

"By now I should think it painfully obvious that compliance is the only way to avoid a catastrophe. The detonation at 8:30 should further reinforce that conclusion." The deep voice was perfectly relaxed. Not once had it faltered. Fredericks stared at McArthur in disbelief as the full impact of what they were hearing began to filter through his rage-clouded mind. It was like a nightmare resplendent with bizarre, insurmountable obstacles. If only he would awaken soon. The steady voice droned on, it was worse than a nightmare because it was stark reality.

"Our demands are as follows. Demand number one. You will arrange to have between ten and eleven million dollars worth of uncut, blue-white diamonds brought to the airport. The diamonds are to be no smaller than five carats, no larger than fifteen carats. They must be flawless, first class gemstone quality. Nice and clear, no milky colored stones will be accepted. A knowledgeable diamond expert is among our team, so don't expect to pass off any paste or industrial grade stones.

"Demand number two. The gems are to be delivered to us in no more than three hours. It is now 8:17 A.M.. You have until 11:20 A.M. to have the diamonds delivered to us. This deadline must not be missed. Unlike our brethren aboard the other flight in Texas, we have a tight schedule to follow in the name of our glorious cause. The first remote timed device will trigger before we can deactivate it, if we are not underway by the appointed time. Any failure to meet that deadline will be solely your responsibility. Any blood spilled, will be on your hands.

"Demand number three. There is a yellow and brown, customized Ford van parked by the Port Authority Police and Aeronautical building. License number YJR-874, New Jersey plates. On my signal it will begin to drive towards the nearest gate leading out to the runways. You will clear it for immediate passage. I am in constant communication with our teammates in the van. Any hint of trouble for them will result in severe retributions. Have you any relevant questions thus far, Fredericks?"

McArthur could see that the administrator smoldered as he scribbled down the license number and description of the van.

"You're damned right I've got some relevant questions, you Irish bastards! How in hell am I supposed to get the diamonds, let alone getting them delivered out here in only three hours? Your shenanigans have already snarled vehicular traffic throughout the access roads. If we're to have any hope of getting the diamonds you want, we'll need more time." Fredericks' face was bright red, beads of perspiration rolled down the puffy cheeks. He yanked a handkerchief from his pocket and mopped his brow.

"Getting the diamonds is your problem. However, once you've relayed the gravity of the situation confronting you here, I'm certain that the proper authorities will accede to our demands and cough up the diamonds post haste. Not because they want to, but because they have no choice. Have a police helicopter pick up the gemstones in Manhattan. Have it land at this end of building 53 where we can see it upon arrival. Final delivery instructions will be relayed at that time.

"One more thing, Fredericks, tell the federal boys that marking the diamonds with radioactivity will be a waste of time. If they arrive hot, they may as well not arrive at all."

"Whether or not you get any diamonds is entirely out of my hands. Whether or not you get that van and God knows whatever equipage it carries *IS* within my control. If indeed, you were so omnipotent, the van would not be a factor. Since you need it and whatever vile persons are in it, then to allow its passage would strengthen your hand. The bastards in that van aren't holding women and children hostages to shield themselves, not yet at any rate. And by God I'll not allow them to bring you whatever weapons you've got squirreled away with them. Do ***I*** make myself perfectly clear?" Every effort to sound tough and unyielding went into Fredericks' words. As he spoke he scribbled a note to McArthur, 'Get a description of the van to the Port Authority Police commander and have him surround it.' She nodded and moved to a phone.

The hint of apprehension Fredericks hoped would infect the terrorist's voice was conspicuously absent. "So be it, Fredericks. We can play hard ball. Just remember that you are initiating the conflict."

"You're bluffing." The room seemed oppressively balmy.

"The I.A.B. and building 53 fireworks were not bluff."

"Fancy demonstrations. Nothing more. Without the van and its contents, you are nothing. You're weak, impotent, exposed, and highly vulnerable."

"I'm about to order my van to move. Don't be a fool."

The 'cab' took on a deathly silence. Attention riveted on Fredericks. He sensed the spotlight effect and hated the arrogant terrorist all the more for it. The ball was in his court and the wrong play could spell disaster. He felt as though the weight of the world rested squarely on his shoulders. He thought of the other hijackings he had endured during the eternity since his tenure in airport administration had begun. Never before had he himself felt so threatened, so violated, so integrally involved.

"The van will be stopped," he spoke as forcefully as his highly emotional state would allow.

The terrorist's voice remained unperturbed. "As a courtesy to those who might otherwise die because of your misjudgment, I give you sixty seconds to clear the TWA hanger. It will be decimated. During or after that sixty seconds, if the van is touched, the devil himself would have a hard time distinguishing what's left of your airport from Hell."

Fredericks spun round in the chair. "Evacuate building 12!"

The order was superfluous. The quick-witted McArthur was already on the line to the huge hanger building. Sixty seconds was about as good as no warning at all, she thought bitterly as she spread the alarm to the airport's fire units.

CHAPTER TWELVE

11 April

8:21 to 8:30 AM

The blast in the T.W.A. hanger detonated within a Tristar's starboard engine. The engine exploded sending shrapnel in every direction. Three fleeing workers clad in grimy coveralls bearing the airline's red-lettered logo, were caught in the spray of metal. The blast itself was many times greater than the two previous ones. Not only was the engine obliterated, but the wing itself was nearly sheared completely off. Fuel in the wing tanks and lines burst into flame.

Within seconds the entire area around the crippled aircraft was ablaze with burning jet fuel. The injured workmen were helped to safety as the inferno rapidly engulfed the entire airliner. There was a second loud explosion when the port wing tanks let go, followed shortly by a third when another pocket of fuel ignited. Both blasts sent showers of flaming fuel in all directions.

The floor of the hanger soon became a sea of raging fire. The leaping flames spread rapidly towards another plane within the enormous structure. The heat was so intense that it seemed unlikely the flames could be stanched before claiming another victim. Workmen wrestled with fire hoses. The second L-1011 was coaxed to life. It rolled quickly out of the smoke filled building to safety.

The people in the Kennedy control tower 'cab' watched as the hanger belched acrid black smoke. The expanding column was a stark contrast to the building's light colored walls. Infuriated, Fredericks crushed a pencil in his large hand and flung the fragments against the console. His puffy face turned beet red. His intention had been to call the terrorists' bluff, but there had been none to call.

Deep-set eyes glared venomously at the distant 747. What sort of demonic individuals were out there? The hijack was less than thirty minutes in progress, and the damage already surpassed every previous siege in his experience by immeasurable bounds. The voice he had learned to hate interrupted his thoughts.

"Kennedy control, this is Atlas 923. The van will now begin its move. I trust no further destruction will be warranted. 923 out."

The console's speaker fell silent.

"You murderous bastard!" Fredericks growled gutturally as his fist pounded the workspace, scattering pencils and pens. Coffee slopped onto the gray metal surface.

"Bill, what about the van? The commander will need immediate instructions." Judy McArthur reminded softly, acutely aware of the 'administrator's anguish.

The reply was slow, pained. "I don't have any real option. I can't risk any more violence on this scale." He gestured vaguely at the smoking hulk of the hanger in the distance. "What if the son of a bitch can make good on all his threats? He's so damnably cocksure. Christ, who knows? Next time lots of people might die. Notify security at the gate that the van is to be passed unmolested."

The abhorrent, yet inescapable decision made, Fredericks crossed to the water cooler. A chilled cupful seemed to help his suddenly parched throat. McArthur was by his side, fully aware of just how untenable a position the administrator found himself in.

"What's our status?" Fredericks asked.

"All incoming is stacked. Outgoing flights have been diverted to 31 - Right."

"Mrs. McArthur?" The young ground controller who had been handling Atlas 923 at the outset, nervously broke in. "Security reports all small fires in both terminals are out. Damage is pretty heavy, but there were no serious injuries."

"Thanks, Dan."

The obese administrator shook his head gravely, cheeks aquiver. The need to explain himself surfaced momentarily. "I just couldn't gamble with other people's lives." His eyes beseechingly sought hers. "What else could I have done?"

"Nothing." She agreed somberly, her gaze straying beyond him to the growing column of smoke belching from the T.W.A. hanger.

"Anyway, my ass is the one in the sling. I made the call. But we can debate that later on. The Feds will want a complete rundown on the demands. I'll use your office, Judy.

"In the interim, have all incoming flights diverted elsewhere. Get the last fully loaded aircraft the hell out of here. Leave any partially loaded or newly landed aircraft where they are. The passengers should be safe aboard the planes. As soon as the last plane is off, close the field to all operations pending further notice."

CHAPTER THIRTEEN

11 April

8:10 to 8:55 AM

"Comfy?" Keith Malin asked as he flipped lazily through a dog-eared copy of PLAYBOY magazine.

Someone stirred in the rear of the van. "I just luv sittin' with me arse on a pile o' lumpy gear. Care ta switch, mate?"

"I'll pass on that," Malin said. Movement outside drew his eyes from the curvaceous body of Miss April. He watched as a person got into a nearby car and drove off. Admiring eyes returned to the magazine.

"Might 'ave figured as much. Just like that time in Kinshasa, you always get the best." Mark Price shifted uneasily in the darkness. Discomfort was part and parcel of his profession.

A smile lit Malin's rugged face. "Oh, I dunno. Yours had a fine ebony bod and a set of tits that'd do any woman proud."

"And a face like a pig," Price grunted.

"I keep tellin' ya, ya don't hafta look at the mantelpiece while you're stokin' the fire."

Price chuckled. "Tis a good thing we met, Keith. I don't know what I'd do without that lightnin' wit o' yours. Glad we're workin' together again."

Malin gave Miss April a last loving look before tossing the magazine aside. He flexed his shoulders. "Thank old Dave Luftin for that. The crop-dusting pilot with an extra." The 'extra' was Luftin's sideline business of recruiting mercenaries.

"Bit different this time though, eh?"

"Yeah, we're both getting too old to be playing soldier."

"Bullshit! Besides, you know what I meant. The operation."

"This is no Angola," Malin stated flatly.

"Kind o' like the Seychelles job. Remember ol' Mad Mike Hoare? Twas a grand plan. Bad luck that weapon being turned up at the airport. And us all posin' as rugby players." Price poked his head through the curtains. "It could 'ave worked, you know."

"Perhaps, perhaps not. Least we were lucky to grab that Air India plane and blow the country before we got ourselves massacred."

Price stroked his graying beard thoughtfully. His voice was suddenly melancholy. "Every time I hear that word, massacre I mean, I think o' the lads in Angola." Fourteen of Price's fellow Britons had been mercilessly butchered by their commander because they were reluctant to obey orders. Price, Malin, and other mercenaries had deserted in the confused aftermath.

"Brings ancient memories of Dak Pek for me," Malin stated flatly. God, it seemed a lifetime ago, yet the images remained stark, so incredibly vivid.

In the rear of the van Price nodded knowingly in the dark. "Aye. From what you've told me, that was a ruddy awful place too."

"Under different circumstances it might have been a nice enough place, although the weather left a mite to be desired." Malin smiled wryly as memories flooded back. "Christ, I've never seen anything like the rainy season. The whole damned compound became a sea of mud. Bunkers collapsed. Those that didn't, flooded with muck and mire. Everything constantly wet; the stench of mildew and mold. Great fun!" He turned to look his companion right in the eye. "But I was a Green Beret and man, that made it all worthwhile. I was one of *the* best!."

"Every bloke whatever wore a uniform says his outfit was best," Price, an ex-paratrooper, observed philosophically.

"Yeah, they all say it. Routine bullshit! Special Forces were different. We *were* the best. Hell, Dak Pek was the most isolated, northernmost outpost our boys set up. Twelve of us, just twelve, ran the whole place."

"With a little help from the Vietnamese Army and the local militiamen," Price commented as he ducked back into the rear of the van, plunked himself down on a duffel bag, fumbled briefly in the near darkness for a pack of Camels, and lit his smoke.

"A dozen slant-eyed regulars and a few hundred ill-trained Montagnard militiamen of the potent sounding Civilian Irregular Defense Group. That was our help. Despite the fancy title, the strikers were little better than a bunch of civilians carrying weapons. *We*, the Green Berets, were what made it work. *We* knocked back the more daring VC probes. *We* coordinated defenses for the sixteen mountain villages scattered within a mile's radius of the post. *We* sent the support fire with our 81mms when the villages were besieged by the bastards. And *we* had to endure the nightly harassment. Charlie sent in a few mortar rounds or launched some form of assault damned near every stinking night."

Noting his companion's increased agitation, Price tactfully shifted the conversation's direction. "All ancient history now, I'm afraid. Makes one feel very old and wonder if we shouldn't long since have retired to some saner occupation. But then fer us, 'at'd be painfully boring, wouldn't it? Least this one'll be a short, quiet, private little war, eh Keith?"

"Maybe too quiet," Malin said sullenly. He hated to think of himself as old, but the fact remained, he was old enough to be a grandfather.

Price checked his chronometer. Nearly an hour had passed since Malin had placed the second of the two airport explosive devices assigned to him. Since then, the two had killed time with inane banter in the stuffy confines of the parked van. Price knew Malin hated waiting to go into action. He was the type who wanted to charge into battle and resolve the outcome post haste. Price sought to lighten the atmosphere. "Think there'll be any luscious birds where we're headed?"

Malin ignored the question. He stared pensively at the radio and listened to the tower transmissions. Maybe he *was* getting too old for this kind of thing. Hell, his fiftieth birthday was a mere nine months off. No, he told himself, you're not ready for the old age home just yet. The surge of excited anticipation was still there. Physically, his body would be the envy of men half his age. Hell, he could probably outperform even the Green Beret's newest enlistees. So why the twinge of hesitation? Why the hint of reservations? Too damned long a wait, he answered himself.

Unfazed at being ignored, Price went on. "I'll wager there'll be lots o' birds. All kinds, Keith. Pretty ones for you. And big titted ones with faces like pigs for . . ."

"Quiet!" Malin commanded tersely. "It's finally begun!"

The cigarette was snuffed out. Price again poked his head through the curtain so that he too could follow the transmissions.

Malin wished he could witness the results of the charge he had placed in the old Pam Am Terminal. The extinct airline seemed another reminder of his own aging process. He thrust the noisome thought aside and thought of the expanses of glass offered by the architecturally interesting terminal building. They were a challenge. The charge had to create a substantial concussion to blow them out. If successful, it would be a showpiece of his expert demolition skills.

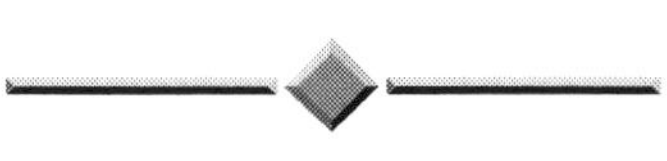

Success or failure of the operation rested squarely on Fredericks' decision as to whether or not to let the van pass. His reticence had forced Larson to play another of his aces, which left only two trumps while still on the ground at Kennedy International. If Fredericks remained adamant in his refusal to pass the van, he would usurp still more of Larson's waning leverage and strength.

Higgins leaned anxiously across Larson's shoulder, his gaze focused on the general area where the van should appear. "There it is! They've let them pass!"

The taut features of Larson's face relaxed into the semblance of a faint smile as he drew a relieved breath. His attention shifted to the flight engineer. "You stay here and watch the field. Listen in on the tower too. Anyone starts this way or you see anything in the least bit suspicious while we've got that door open, let us know at once."

"Don't worry. I want my share just as much as you guys do."

"Let's move it, Harry," Larson said.

After a cursory check of the lower deck, they opened the forward port side door through which they had boarded earlier. The door was on the side of the aircraft turned away from the terminals and other buildings. Beyond the side of the runway, a wide grassy field dropped off into the glistening waters of Jamaica Bay. The other runway, which they blocked, jutted out into the bay on a slender finger of land.

The whining noise of the APU engine in the tail was clearly audible but not overpowering. Warm outside air infiltrated the cool cabin. Larson removed his tailored jacket and cast it aside. Though a comfortable garment, it had outlasted its usefulness.

The gleaming yellow and brown shape of the customized van drew up below. The van was a stretched body affair. Most of the roofline was elevated by a foot and a half with a camper-type addition with metal sides and a curved forward facing window. A low luggage rail ringed the camper top and a shiny chrome ladder on the back provided access to it.

Since its purchase from a used car dealer, the van had undergone additional modifications. One was a three-foot square hatch in the camper roof that Malin was already cranking open. The hatch dropped inside the van and slid back out of sight.

Malin waved a bronzed arm in jubilant greeting. Then he heaved up a coil of nylon rope and some leather work gloves. The next several minutes passed with the four men toiling laboriously to transfer the van's stores to the 747. Most were packed in large, heavy canvas, dark green duffel bags. There were ten of these bags in all, each filled to capacity and bearing a numbered tag. A black wooden case soon joined them in the airliner, as did a couple of Ingram machine pistols and three Savage Model 99-CD rifles, all with spare clips of ammunition in attached pouches.

Once the transfer of gear was completed, the van's hatch cranked shut and the 747's massive door was secured. Larson and Higgins labored quickly to transfer most of the gear up the spiral stairway to the lounge above. Only the wooden case remained below.

In the lounge, four sacks were heaved against the forward bulkhead. The remainder were lined up along a couch in numerical order. For utmost speed and efficiency in locating equipment when the time came, everything was stowed in the order in which it would be required.

Working at a furious pace the two men soon had cut away the Perspex panes in the rearmost window on either side of the lounge. A rope snaked out through one opening. When it was hauled in, a dark blue Plexiglas dome with sponge rubber padding around its base had been secured to it by Price.

Five minutes later it and its identical twin on the opposite side of the cabin had been securely bolted in place over the window openings. The inner sides of the openings were completely covered by thick metal plates, also padded with tightly compressed sponge rubber where they fitted neatly to the curve of the wall. Coaxial cable connections protruded from the center of each steel plate.

More and more equipment rolled out of protective layers of burlap and foam rubber. The men worked with the practiced familiarity akin to people to whom a task has become second nature. Rehearsal had followed rehearsal until the complex installation of the esoteric modifications to the 747 became childishly simple and remarkably swift.

One of the lounge's tables had a set of twin radar screens clamped to it. Cables snaked from them to the two metal plates now securely mounted over the window openings. Beyond the plates, aft-pointing radar antennas were mounted within the protective plastic domes. Also clamped to the wood-grained tabletop was a small Sony television set. A cable stretched from it to the stairway where it disappeared over the coaming. On the lower deck the cable ran along the ceiling to the forward bulkhead where it entered a small rectangular box mounted just below the ceiling. The box had a mirrored panel facing aft through which its hidden camera could monitor activity on the spiral stairway and most of the first class section of the aircraft.

Several cables crisscrossed the carpeted floor of the upper lounge. Duct tape soon held all firmly in place to prevent any mishaps. Tools no longer needed were stuffed into empty sacks together with discarded packing materials.

Radar and video installations complete, the two men returned to the lower level. The only two male flight attendants were located and dragged forward to the door. Duct tape soon had both securely bound hand and foot. They should still be sleeping, blissfully unaware of what had transpired since the release of the gas, when the 747 left Kennedy, a fact that made the bonds seem superfluous, but Larson was a firm believer in leaving absolutely nothing to chance.

The bulky door swung open again. In short order the two hostages had been transferred to the van where Price pulled them inside. The hostages would provide the van with added security in the event that the authorities made the foolish mistake of trying to make an advance towards the 747.

Before closing the hatch in the shiny roof, Price and Malin gave the thumbs up gesture. Larson acknowledged in kind before heaving the jet's door shut. By the time it was fully secure again, the van had pulled out of sight. Larson knew that Malin had moved the vehicle back along the fuselage to a point where the monstrous main landing gear would not obstruct his view. The van would be parked beneath the port wing, between the two enormous engines. There it would remain partially in the shade of the giant wing while Malin and Price guarded the flanks.

Standard anti-terrorist procedure is to approach the stricken aircraft from the rear, where its occupants have a tremendous blind spot. That tactic succeeded in routing the terrorists at Mogadiscio. There, German commandos scaled the wings and swarmed into the aircraft before the hijackers ever had a chance to offer effective resistance. Larson was determined not to repeat the mistakes of others. With two first rate sharpshooters like Malin and Price down on the field itself in the modified van and with a continual radio link, it would be highly unlikely, if not impossible, for anyone to be able to get anywhere near Atlas 923 undetected.

"Just how long have you been onto these bastards?" The FBI agent asked icily.

"A few months," Schmitt replied.

"And in all that time it never once occurred to you that maybe you should forewarn some law enforcement authority?"

Schmitt straightened. His expression hardened. "Listen, Randall. I work alone. I'm independent. I get paid to put the pieces together.

Then, and only then, when I know precisely **what** is going down, **when** it's going down, and **who** is involved, do I turn it loose. It wasn't until word came back there in your office that I fully realized the scope of what I was onto.

"Like it or not, aside from a parking offense and carrying a blade concealed, I've violated no laws or rules other than your own ethical standards. Were our roles reversed, you would have done exactly what I have." Then as an afterthought Schmitt added, "Face it, Randall, if people like you had all the answers, there'd be no need to contract people like me."

David Randall, the FBI representative, swallowed hard. The urge to pick up the gauntlet flung almost contemptuously at him, was suppressed. Randall's features were boringly plain and nondescript. Even his steel-gray eyes were pale and lackluster. His was an easily forgotten face. His voice was habitually cold, impersonal. "If your deductions are correct, then this Larson guy masterminded the mess here and the hijacking in Texas which you say is just a diversion."

"So I would presume," Schmitt agreed. "This is too complex and iffy for the target of my original investigation to be the driving force. Larson ties all the discordant bits and pieces together; the murdered courier in Amsterdam, the ETA hijack in Texas, Amsterdam's diamond trader, the whole works." He intentionally neglected to mention van Troje's name.

The phone buzzed. Randall snatched it off the desktop, listened briefly, muttered thanks, and dropped it back with a dull thud. "The hostages in the apartment you discovered are safe. An airport mechanic's daughter and a security guard's wife. We're tracking down the mechanic and guard."

Schmitt fished a little leatherette notebook from his pocket. Some pages covered with scribbled notes were torn out and passed to Randall. "Best have your people seal off and thoroughly search each of those sites for possible bombs."

Plucking the pages from the outstretched hand, Randall scanned them briefly. His eyes widened when he saw the reference to a Chevy Cavalier left in the long-term parking at Dulles airport. "Where'd you get this info?" He demanded.

"I thought it painfully evident by now that I have been trailing our dear Larson for quite some time now. During the past week he and one of his cronies drove south in their fancied up van. They rented two small cars during their trip. Both were left in long-term parking, the one at Dulles, the other in Miami. The tag numbers, etc. are there. So too are the handful of places, mostly local, where they pointedly stopped and entered with items that were conspicuously absent upon their departure."

"The remote bombs!"

"Bravo, inspector! I should indeed think so," Schmitt agreed. "I've also got a list of the motels they used. He seems to favor Holiday Inn, not that I think that matters much."

Randall was no longer listening. The phone was already in hand, the number punched in.

The next phase of the immediate preparations aboard the jet involved the black wooden box left below earlier. Larson and Higgins opened its hinged lid and carefully withdrew the first two of the slender gray cylinders it contained. There were eight in all. Each sported a pressure gauge that read 2,000 PSI (Pounds per Square Inch) and had a remotely operated release valve near the tip.

In the rear cabin section Larson knelt beside a passenger. He gently pushed the slender legs aside and went to work on the underside of her seat. When he finished, the tank was firmly in place under the seat and still completely invisible unless someone else crawled down into the same position he had, and that seemed highly improbable

The other cylinder they had brought found a similar home in the opposite aisle. The rest of the black box's contents shortly found equally effective concealment in the remaining cabin sections. That task finished, the empty crate was hauled upstairs.

The next phase of their preparations involved the flight deck itself. The windows were all covered with a plastic film that permitted them to see out, but the gold-colored, mirrored outer side of the material made it impossible for anyone to see in. The same material had already been stuck on all other upper deck windows. Protected from view, the work continued. The modular auto-pilot unit was removed. A similar, but not quite identical unit, replaced it. The only visible difference was the electronic jack set in its face. The old unit was placed in the small stowage area aft of the pilot's seat.

Minutes later the VHF radio module joined it there. Its spot in the central console had been taken with a similarly altered unit. Both of the flight deck's auxiliary seats were folded down, a laptop computer strapped to each. Cables soon connected the computers with the newly installed systems. The work was complete.

The transfer of the equipment and the entire installation procedure consumed twenty-eight minutes, two minutes less than expected. Being ahead of schedule was always preferable. Larson was duly pleased with their handiwork. Many long days and nights spent studying a 747's electrical, radio, and auto-navigational systems enabled him to design the requisite modifications. Still, the units were unproven. They had never undergone actual flight tests. Maybe they wouldn't function properly, but then they simply had to, the entire project demanded that they did.

CHAPTER FOURTEEN

11 April

8:55 to 10:30 AM

John Herrin had been conspicuously absent during the President's breakfast meeting, though his concise progress report on the affair in Texas had been there as promised. The President worked in the Oval Office when Herrin knocked and hurried in. A long, sleepless night had taken its inevitable toll, he looked tired. His tie was crooked, something highly irregular for the painfully neat aide.

"Morning, John," the President said somberly. "I understand we've got another little problem brewing in New York."

Herrin dropped wearily onto a chair opposite the ornate chief executive's desk. "A bit of an understatement, sir." He ran hastily through the details of the unfolding situation at Kennedy. In summation he added, "The car bomb blew right on schedule at Dulles. If the rest of their threats are as real, we may have a serious problem on our hands. Worst thing is, thanks to events in Texas and the West Coast, there's not a snowball's chance in hell of our getting a potent strike force on scene until the expiration of the deadline."

"To yield would be a potentially disastrous policy reversal," the President commented dryly.

"Mmmm. However, we have another option albeit one fraught with inherent complications. The British SAS contingent en route to Dallas aboard a Concorde is that option. Given the fact that the terrorists at Kennedy claim to be connected with the ETA strike in Texas, the British might agree to divert the SAS strike team to New York and tackle the events in progress there. They'll have damnably little time to act, but they could be on scene to beat the deadline.

The President smiled wryly. "Which places the Texas event squarely in our bailiwick once more."

"The alternative is to let a local SWAT team try and handle New York. No offense to the cops, but given the sophistication of those involved, I wouldn't want to give odds on a SWAT team's success. Unless we opt to pay these guys off, I feel the British strike team offers our only realistic hope. The ETA tie-in should serve to spur their guys on. Besides, the SAS troops are among the finest in the world.

"Fair enough. Get to it. Just make certain the diamonds are available as a contingency. And keep me posted, John."

"Naturally." Herrin rushed out. He hadn't bothered to mention that he had already contacted the British through State Department channels and had begun to lay the prerequisite groundwork for the co-operative venture.

"The mechanic set the bomb in the TWA hanger. The guard planted one at the base of a fuel storage tank in the tank farm. The local bomb squad is pulling it now." Randall sounded slightly more at ease as he flopped into the chair behind McArthur's steel desk. Because of its convenient location, the Tower Supervisor's office had become his temporary command post. It was a simple office, Spartan in its furnishings. A series of photographs depicting the airport's gradual expansion and change over time adorned the walls. Some thriving African violets brightened the drab, metal desk.

Schmitt looked up from the notes he was compiling. "Just like pulling teeth on a crocodile. Soon as we hear from the teams checking the locales I gave you, the last vestiges of any external leverage fielded by Larson will have vanished."

"The thing that gets me is the planning involved here. According to our office in Miami, the car was packed with a couple of pounds of Semtex. It was rigged so that a call to a cellular phone lying in the trunk would detonate it. Undoubtedly the same set-up used at Dulles. But think of the expense, the intricate attention to detail! This Larson fellow has invested thousands and thousands of dollars in this scheme. And just look at how he's covered damn near every angle!"

"I never disputed his almost fanatical attention to detail."

"One hell of a dangerous person," Randall stated flatly.

Schmitt added another point to the list of notes he had been compiling. "There you are. The essential abbreviated basics of Erik Larson, terrorist extraordinaire." He shoved the page across. "A genius at planning, but blissfully unaware that the potency of his threats is fast waning."

As he scanned the list, Randall commented, "Assuming that the trip you monitored was the only one made to set remote devices, you might just be right about his power being greatly diminished. My main concern at this point is additional stuff on the ground right here. Both of the exemplary blasts that he used to open the whole show were placed just this morning. The one obviously by the men in the van. Suppose those same guys placed additional surprises for us? That's the real danger as I see it." As an afterthought he added, "And let's not forget the hostages."

"Looking for more local charges would be like trying to find a *possible* needle in an unimaginably huge haystack." Schmitt noted as he flicked a piece of lint from his charcoal slacks.

The FBI agent spun round in the padded swivel chair. The stationary jumbo jet still straddled the intersection of the two runways. The surrounding area was clear save for a narrow pile of colorful cargo containers along the edge of the apron about half way between the aircraft and the nearest terminal building. Those containers probably would be unapproachable without detection. The hijackers had selected their ground well. It was no accident that they had placed themselves in so defensible a position, of that Randall was positive. These men were extremely dangerous. Worse still, instinct nurtured during years of field experience told him that the man in charge of the terrorists would not back down. Or would he? It was always the same, he pondered glumly, a high stakes poker game where one had to outwit his opponent. The stakes in this case were higher than usual, there were many, many innocent lives involved. That irked him because he hated the feelings of guilt that always went hand in hand with any injuries or casualties incurred by civilians. At length, he said, "Your list doesn't mention any sympathy for the ETA."

"I doubt he has any."

Randall spun back around to face the man who seemed blessed with all the answers, a trait that did little to enamor him to the FBI agent. "According to you, he's responsible for the ETA action in Texas. He basically sponsored the whole damned thing. He may even be to blame for the damnable bombing campaign in Barcelona!"

"True. But only as a diversion. He drew your best anti-terrorist units away with diversionary moves. A threat to a trade delegation got your HRT unit; the ETA hijack drew Blue Light. Larson went to great expense and trouble to orchestrate events that would pull all viable strike forces away from himself."

"Leaving us the local police SWAT team."

"Are they any good?"

"Of course they are! They're exceptional, but this one may still be a notch or two out of their league."

"Specialists are inherently best suited to deal with special problems."

"This ETA crap still bugs me." Randall knit his brow. "There must be more to Larson's link with them than mere convenience. Think of all the time and trouble he went to. And he called them his 'brethren' and spoke of the 'cause' earlier."

Schmitt waved away the connection. "Attempts to screw you up. Supposed to put the heat on the ETA." He indicated the paper in Randall's hand. "About halfway down, you'll note I wrote that Larson is politically indifferent. No . . . politically inspired fanaticism is not his style. He's in this for the money. Pure capitalism, of sorts."

"Which means he'll be even less predictable."

"And infinitely more dangerous," Schmitt added thoughtfully.

CHAPTER FIFTEEN

11 April

10:30 to 11:15 AM

Colonel Richard Cooke was a stern-faced professional. He was also a much decorated and well-seasoned soldier. Despite his fifty-four years, or maybe because of them, he was every bit as fit and imposing as most of the much younger men in his command. Like every one of them he had volunteered for duty in the elite Special Air Services Regiment and like all the others, he too had passed the rigorous qualification exercises that had a staggering washout rate of ninety percent. Only a special breed of individuals survived the induction period. Those that did relished the fact that they had with a great sense of pride and accomplishment. To fail was not bad, it just meant you were not up to the phenomenally demanding requirements of the regiment. Colonel Cooke could recall one young lieutenant who had washed out after volunteering. Cooke's report on the candidate stated, 'he is a fine officer and an outstanding gentleman. Undoubtedly he will continue to serve Her Majesty's armed Forced with distinction, but he is not for us.'

The Colonel had joined the SAS as a brash young man fresh from Cornwall. He saw action almost immediately in the jungles of Borneo from late 1963 through 1964. His next assignment had taken him into the urban warfare of Aden from 1964 through 1967. Then it was off to the arid landscape of Oman from 1971 through 1974. The streets and countryside of Northern Ireland became his bailiwick during the mid to late seventies. Then in 1978 he joined the special anti-terrorist Counter Revolutionary Warfare Team of the SAS. He helped orchestrate the team's highly successful and much publicized rescue of hostages from the Iranian Embassy in London. Like other members of the SAS he politely shunned the attention garnered by the mission's unprecedented success. Anonymity and secrecy were paramount in his profession.

Cooke's credentials and vast experience made him a natural choice to head up the strike team. Thus, he and the thirty-six-man team had embarked aboard a Concorde bound for the United States. To their surprise they had been diverted to Newark International Airport in New Jersey where a group of US Army Blackhawk helicopters was waiting to take them on the short hop to Kennedy. They came in low from the north and settled on a vacant stretch of the apron fully concealed from those in the hijacked 747.

Colonel Cooke was a solidly built man. He walked with the precise measured gait of authority. Decked out in full battle dress, square chin set, his eyes hard, he cut an imposing figure. He glanced up and down as he reconciled what he could see from the control tower with what was shown on the map of the airport spread across the console before him.

Randall pointed to various spots on the airport map. "The local SWAT team has sharpshooters positioned at the blast fences, here . . . here . . . and here."

"Range?" Cooke demanded tersely.

"Just shy of a half mile for the fence just aft of the jet. A bit further for the others."

Cooke's aquiline nose bobbed up and down almost imperceptibly as he nodded. "What's this?" He indicated a tiny square on the map.

"The localizer transmitter," Judy McArthur, the tower supervisor, volunteered. "It's just a squat, little shed-like building."

"Distance from the airliner?"

"A few hundred feet," she replied.

Cooke glanced at Randall. "No sharpshooters there?"

"Unapproachable." Randall mimicked the Colonel's clipped manner. "Open ground all around."

"The domes. What possible purpose?"

"Observation," Randall ventured.

Schmitt pushed past a burly SAS sergeant who had accompanied Cooke to the over crowded tower. The sergeant was speaking softly in a field radio. "Hardly," Schmitt said matter-of-factly. "They've staked out one or more men in that van. There'd be no need to go to all the trouble of installing the little domes and cutting out two windows. Larson is many things, but he does not seem the type to waste time and effort. Those domes fit perfectly to the skin of the airliner. That means they're custom-made, expensive. They've got definite purpose, but observation here on the field sure as hell doesn't figure into it."

"Then for what?" Colonel Cooke demanded.

"You're the flashy terrorist expert," Schmitt replied coolly, "you tell me." He didn't like being treated like a subordinate and made no secret of it.

Cooke's nostrils flared. Field glasses suddenly hid his dark, brooding eyes as he again studied the target in silence.

The SAS sergeant came closer and snapped to attention. "Sir. Field reconnoiter complete. Two hostiles in the lorry. The two hostages with them are prone on the floor along either side. One hostile up front, the other is in the rear. They aren't saying much. Just occasional banter. Strangely enough one is probably British. Indications are that the lorry is heavily reinforced with emphasis towards the rear compartment."

"Just how in hell . . ." Fredericks began in amazement.

A benign expression graced his face as the sergeant quickly explained. "Special sensing equipment, sir. Tools of the trade, in a manner o' speakin'." Then to Cooke, he continued, "The hostages aboard the aircraft remain immobile. In fact, there is no movement on the entire lower deck. They appear dead, but since they still register significant heat signatures it seems more probable that they're just out cold. Either way it makes any operation a tad easier. An additional two or three prone forms are in the lounge near the aft wall. There are three hostiles in the plane, all on the upper deck. One regularly moves aft into the lounge section for brief intervals, perhaps to check on the hostages there. Again limited conversation. Nothing of particular consequence, although the name 'Harry' came up twice so far. They also referred to one of their members as 'flyboy.' The domes contain something relatively solid and metallic either beneath the surface or behind them. They appear to be tightly secured to the skin of the aircraft with some form of seal round the base. That's all we've got, sir." The SAS sergeant summed up his appraisal of the situation succinctly. "Bit of a sticky mess, sir."

"Indeed. With precious little time to act." The deadline for delivery of the diamonds was frustratingly near. There was little enough time to acquaint his team with the locale and mount a 'routine' operation, let alone formulate a special tactic to accommodate the highly irregular circumstances confronting the Britons. Adaptability was one of the SAS's hallmarks so Cooke tackled the problem with typical aplomb. The trouble was that every basic strategy called for the element of surprise, something that seemed unattainable. Cooke doubted any operation could be executed without significant endangerment of the hostages.

"Quite clever really," the sergeant said suddenly. "The lorry, or minibus as you Americans might call it, eliminates the classical blind spot in a jet." He had distinguished himself in the 1980 hostage rescue at the Iranian Embassy in London.

"Obviously!" Cooke's irritation at having the glaringly evident pointed out, was amply conveyed in the single, harshly uttered word.

Unswayed, the swarthy faced sergeant persisted. "Well, sir, I was just thinkin' 'bout the bloke in charge. He's a clever bastard. But you see, he and the other hostiles in the plane are all concentrated up front lookin' forward and to the sides. True he's staked out two more hostiles in the lorry to watch his ass. Those two are watchin' the rear and flanks. Don't you see the one thing whoever is in charge forgot?" Obviously no one did, so the sergeant went on. "Well, sir, they're focused on, and only dealin' with, two dimensions, an' all the while *we* 'ave three. If you catch my meanin', sir."

"Unless the diamonds have arrived, we've painfully little to discuss." The voice emanating from the speaker had an unearthly quality to it, as though it were being electronically distorted, which in fact, it was.

"I think you'll agree we do, mister Erik Larson." Randall drew out the name to hammer home its immense significance. He expected hesitation born of confusion. There was none.

"I always thought John Doe was the moniker you people assigned to unknowns."

"Let's not play games, Larson. We know your life's history. So why don't you, Harry, and flyboy call it quits now? Oh, and don't waste my time by retorting with some threat of your omnipotence. Each of your fancy remote explosive devices has been disarmed." Randall rushed through the list of locales where charges had been safely removed. "We've also freed the hostages in New Jersey and secured the bomb planted by the tank farm. You're in deep shit, mister, but so far you haven't killed anyone, at least not here yet. Why not hang it up before you cross that line?"

To everyone's surprise the speaker crackled with laughter. When it subsided, the steady voice said, "Bravo! Well done, inspector! By some fluke you've actually managed to locate and disarm our *first* line of defense." The tone harshened. "But only the *first* line. Only a fool would rely solely on a single faceted defense. I'm no fool, nor am I this Erik Larson that you claim to know so much about. You seem pitiably misinformed on many things, Randall. To win this one you would need a minor miracle, and I fear no such miracle is forthcoming."

"Listen, Larson, it's over."

"You bore me, Randall. Our deadline is very near. If you sincerely want to avoid casualties, then I suggest you make a strong effort not to miss it. Atlas 923 out." The speaker went dead.

With a somewhat bemused expression Schmitt leaned against a console in the crowded control tower 'cab'. "A difficult man to rankle."

"Painfully so," Randall said. "Question is, does he have a second line of defense?"

"Improbable," Cooke stated flatly. He was never one to waste words.

"But entirely plausible." Schmitt met the Colonel's gaze. "And, as he so prudently reminded us, the deadline is almost here. Which raises the question Clint Eastwood asked in one of his flics, 'Do you feel lucky?' Well, Colonel, do you?"

Cooke stared contemptuously at Schmitt, but refrained from comment. Randall reflexively consulted his watch. His stomach tingled. The unpleasant possibility of a second line of defense loomed large in his thoughts. The terrorist might just have one. His voice certainly gave no indication of fear or uncertainty.

Randall broke the uncomfortable silence. "What do you think, Colonel? Do we act? It's your call."

Colonel Cooke's SAS strike team had been thoroughly briefed and deployed for their mission. Washington had been consulted and authorization granted the Colonel to take whatever actions deemed appropriate. Given the nature of the situation, the ransom was ready should he opt to hold off. The decision rested squarely with the taciturn officer.

The resolute Cooke stood at ease as he calculated the odds of success. There were so many variables, so many unknowns. No one could blame him if he decided not to act on the grounds that the mission was impossible with a high probability that hostages would be severely endangered. The sergeant's plan was bold, highly risky, and certain to provoke scathing criticism if it failed. It would definitely tax even the remarkable talents of Cooke's command. But like any proud officer, he had eternal faith in his men. He prayed that the regiment's motto, 'Who dares, wins', would prove prophetic.

The control tower 'cab' was abnormally silent. At length Cooke turned to Judy McArthur and queried, "The wind remains the same?"

She checked with the meteorological office. "Essentially unchanged. Four to six knots coming from a heading of nine to ten degrees."

"Thank you." Cooke knit his bushy brow in concentration. He picked up his field radio and contacted his sergeant who was on the field. "Anything new?"

The radio crackled momentarily. "Someone shouted, 'It's blown,' a couple of times. An argument seemed to start, then virtual silence. This Larson chap is a cold bastard to be sure, but I'm inclined to side with his co-hort who shouted, 'It's blown,' along with a few expletives. I think he's down to just the hostages in the plane and the lorry, sir"

"Thanks, sergeant. Stand by for orders."

Cooke was about to set down the radio when the tiny speaker added, "For what it's worth, I think it could be done, sir."

A hint of a smile momentarily graced Cooke's features. Then, decision made, he stated, "So be it. We take 'em!"

Though Cooke did not show it, the nagging sensation that some hostages were going to die or sustain serious injury on this one plagued him. He consoled himself with the true soldier's rationalization that it was a calculated risk well worth the taking.

"It's blown! The whole fuckin' thing is blown!" Higgins shouted angrily.

"Shut up!" Larson commanded just as loudly. "I've got to think!"

"About what, eh? It's ove . . ."

Higgins' gaunt face contorted in pain as Larson viciously backhanded him. Blood trickled from the corner of his mouth.

"Shut up!" Larson placed a finger to his lips, indicating silence. Mind racing, he tried to assess how the authorities possibly could have located the explosive devices or known his identity or known the names Harry and Flyboy. The last piece of the puzzle fitted in place first. When he spoke again it was in a barely audible whisper. "As I see it, there's only one way they could have come up with the names Harry and Flyboy. We have to assume that they've trained a super-sensitive shotgun microphone on us. My fault for not surmising that was probable. Which means anything and everything we say is relayed right to the boys in charge out there. Normal conversation is out. From here out anything of pertinence is written down or whispered damned near inaudibly. Do I make myself clear?"

The flight engineer nodded. Higgins glared menacingly. With the back of his hand he brushed away the trickle of blood. His tongue touched the salty tasting abrasion. "You're crazy!" His voice was a gravelly whisper. "They've pulled the charges! They know who we are!"

"*Most* of the charges. The balance of the stuff Keith placed this morning is still out there."

"Face it, Erik! Someone sold out!"

That thought was a distasteful one. It also failed to make much sense. Besides himself, only Malin knew the location of every charge, and Larson trusted Malin explicitly. Yet the Federal agent neglected to mention the last local device. All of which seemed to confirm that Malin was not the breech. Who was?

Higgins broke his momentary reverie. "Contact them! Negotiate something! We've still got nearly three hundred hostages with us."

"We'll have the gems and depart on schedule," Larson retorted.

"To where?" Higgins' voice level increased with each word. "Surely they know the escape route too. Suppose they don't humor you by coughing up . . ."

The barrel of Larson's pistol jammed hard into Higgins' chest. Speaking in lethally low intonation, he said, "As Keith observed so adroitly on innumerable occasions, this operation is run like a military campaign. Well, mister, I'm the commander-in-chief for the duration. You're a lowly enlisted man. Like it or not, you're in it for the duration too. I've trusted you, counted on you to perform various assignments, and I expect you to obey orders without question. Any further insubordination will force me to take steps neither of us will relish. Do I make myself crystal clear?"

Higgins nodded very slowly. Larson relieved him of his pistol, then stepped carefully past him, keeping his own weapon leveled at his associate. He paused by the door to the lounge. In a normal speaking voice, he said, "Get on the radio and advise our other team members that the authorities are listening in on any audible conversations. Use written henceforth. Do you hear that, Randall? As though we were going to spell things out for you anyway, you pitiable bastard." Then in a whisper, he added, "We're all on edge, but things could be much worse. Just thank God that the deadline is only about ten minutes off. Send the message, then keep an eye on things. I'll be right back."

He pulled the door shut behind him. Alone in the lounge, Larson let out a long sigh. A pistol hung loosely in each hand. He tossed one on the couch while holstering the other. Hands pressed against the port side wall, he stooped downward to peer pensively out the window. Fear knotted his stomach. The sudden turn of events baffled him. None of it made sense. There seemed no logical explanation and his was a mind that thrived on logic's universal applicability.

A gray and white seagull dipped into view as it executed a graceful turn. The bird swerved near the edge of the runway, then veered sharply back out across the still waters of Jamaica Bay.

A small rectangular shadow suddenly crept off the gently swaying grass onto the pavement. Others joined it. Larson stared quizzically for a split second, then pressed his face against the window to look upwards. He could see nothing, but something in his harried mind clicked with a sickening realization. His heart began to pound as he bolted for the flight deck. Only seconds separated him from utter disaster. "The sons of bitches are trying to take us from above!" He shouted as he lunged into the cockpit. "Arm yourselves and take station at the stairs!" He snatched a headset from the console. Pressing the mic button, he shouted, "Paratroopers coming down fast! Take 'em!" He drew a nervous breath and strove to calm himself. "Randall, you son of a whore, you'll pay dearly for this stupidity! Call them off this instant!" He reached round, found the detonator on the flight engineer's workspace, and threw the last switches. "You just kissed another airliner good-bye! More to follow if this plane is boarded!" Larson flung the now useless detonator contemptuously to the floor. The last ace had been played. In a cold sweat he stumbled back to the lounge and took the Ingram machine pistol offered by Higgins.

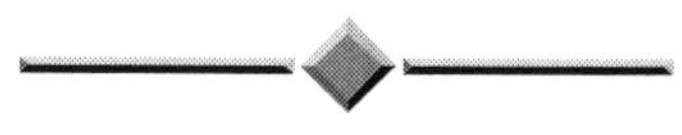

In the van, Malin reacted as though jolted by a sharp electric shock. "Sweet Jesus!" He gunned the ignition and threw the van into drive. Gears meshed with a grinding crunch. Tires squealed and belched acrid blue smoke. "Get that hatch open! For Christ's sake hurry, Price! They're using paratroops!"

A burly SAS sergeant led one of the two, four-man assault teams making the tricky jump. Though encumbered by their weapons and the specialized equipment for blowing an airliner's door off its hinges, they still managed to guide their steerable chutes with remarkable precision, something absolutely imperative if the bold plan formulated in the control tower was to succeed.

Most people would consider the jump suicidally insane, but then most people would not have survived the rigorous training the sergeant and his men had endured. All were expert parachutists. Dangerous jumps such as Hi-Lo in which the jumper left the aircraft at unusually high altitude, but did not deploy his chute until almost splattered on the ground, were stock-in-trade for SAS parachutists. Another specialty was treetop jumping, an insane concept whereby the commando intentionally landed in a forested area, a place every parachutist knows is to be avoided at all costs.

The sergeant's four-man team would have to hit within very close quarters. To compound the difficulty, they had to land on a smooth, slightly angled surface. The 747's wing offered a vast expanse of surface area when viewed by an idle spectator comfortably ensconced within the jet's climate controlled environs. When seen from the perspective of a descending paratrooper whose mission dictated that he and three others hit in rapid succession, it suddenly looked pathetically tiny. Once on the wing the sergeant's team would have only seconds to shed their chutes, blow the door off its hinges, and storm the interior of the aircraft. Any longer time frame than that and the terrorists within would be afforded a chance to react.

The other four-man parachute team drew the chore of immobilizing the terrorists in the van. They would hit first, about fifteen seconds ahead of the sergeant's team. For back up, several crack shots were positioned around the perimeter with laser-sighted sniper rifles. Further support, although it couldn't possibly be brought to bear until the brief firefight should be over, came in the form of two of the American Blackhawks, each carrying eight more eager SAS troops. The sergeant could see the two helos were already airborne. He knew that when he was about two hundred feet from target, which would be the case within seconds, they would swing towards the LZ.

The sergeant skillfully guided his chute towards a point only a few feet from the fuselage. It was then that he saw the fancy van rush out from beneath the wing in a cloud of bluish haze. A gaping hole appeared in its roof as it emerged. He suddenly felt very worried.

The parked Lufthansa 747F was near capacity as workmen guided the last shipping container through its massive cargo orifice. A small crate labeled 'MACHINE PARTS' was in another such container near the big air-freighter's midsection. The explosion was enormous, many times more powerful than any of its predecessors. A fireball rolled heavenwards out of the ruptured fuselage. Flames spread quickly along the aircraft as the tail section sagged gently to the ground. The jet and cargo were total losses.

The van screeched to an abrupt halt as Malin slammed the transmission into park and killed the engine. The windshield shattered in a spray of a million fragments as he ducked into the protected rear of the van. Once there he slid a steel partition that isolated the rear of the van in place. Instantaneously, the partition reverberated with metallic clangs and bangs. Had he run a hand along the previously smooth metal, he would have found it pockmarked with deep dents.

Price, seeing the first chute had already dropped below his line of fire, grabbed an Ingram machine pistol and an M-16 and leapt out through the rear door. Malin tried vainly to stop him, but his shouted order went unheard and unheeded. Without further consideration for Price, he swung his own machine pistol up and emptied the first clip at the last of the already dangerously low first group of paratroopers. He tore the spent clip from the smoking breech, ramming home a fresh one. The stench of burnt cordite hung heavily in the confined space. It was as sweet as any scent he ever smelled. In swift motion he expelled the second clip in a thunderous burst. Malin was in his element.

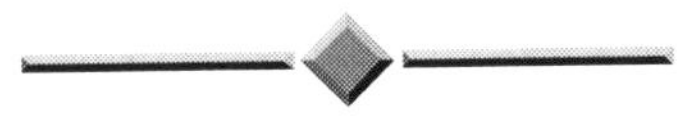

Price hit the pavement lightly on catlike feet, rolled once coming up in a crouch, his M-16 spitting fire at a paratrooper just alighting some fifty feet away. The mercenary's bullets pounded the commando's chest and sent him reeling. Simultaneously, unseen beams of laserlight targeted several rounds from pre-positioned snipers. The bullets hammered into his back and side, slamming him to the ground. His bulletproof vest took the brunt of the sniper fire. After rolling laterally, Price fired at another paratrooper about to alight. The next hail of snipers' bullets tore away the side of Price's face and left him lying limply on the warm pavement, a pool of blood slowly spreading around him.

Malin quickly realized that like himself the paratroopers were decked out in highly effective protective garments. The machine pistol clattered to the floor of the van as he yanked out one of the Smith and Wesson .357 Magnums stuffed in his belt. With a double-handed grip he emptied the chambers on four successive targets just before they were out of his line of sight. Four of the six shots hit their marks. He tossed the empty weapon aside and drew a second from his belt. As he kicked open the swaying rear door he was vaguely aware of the thunderous racket as innumerable rounds tore through the thin outer skin of the van only to be stopped by the extra-heavy armor-like metal plates installed at Larson's behest. He could have kissed Larson for his foresight just then.

The open doors offered Malin an unobstructed line of fire. He knew that the most important thing would be to get the men going for the wing. Without hesitation he ignored those on the ground and picked off first one and then the other remaining SAS paratrooper as they hit the wing and scrambled for the airliner's door. They tumbled off the slanted surface and plunged to the unforgiving pavement. Malin ignored them. Attention was suddenly riveted to those already on the ground. Before he could bring his weapon to bear, he was knocked violently backwards as three rounds pelted a neat line across his chest. He crashed into the steel bulkhead, tripping over one of the hostages.

All breath expelled from aching lungs in a loud gasp. Acting more reflexively than anything else, he twisted up into a sitting position, brought up his double-handed grip, and fired the last two rounds in his weapon. The last visible member of the strike team staggered and dropped to the pavement as Malin reloaded with a Speed-loader.

In the control tower the gaunt-faced Colonel Cooke scooped up the field radio from the console. His voice was typically relaxed, a picture of steely efficiency. "Abort. Scrub the mission. I say again, abort, scrub the mission." Out on the field red flares arched skyward and fell slowly to the tarmac, leaving a thick trail of red smoke to dissipate in their wake. The command to abort came too late to prevent an outburst of small arms fire on the field. He and the others in the tower 'cab' watched the brief firefight unfold.

Only Randall seemed oblivious of the spectacle on the field. Face drenched in perspiration he pleaded with the terrorists not to detonate additional charges. "For God's sake think of the consequences, man," he begged.

"If this aircraft is boarded, the consequences will be solely the fault of your stupidity," the voice from the besieged 747 replied. For the first time it sounded on edge, a small consolation given the circumstances.

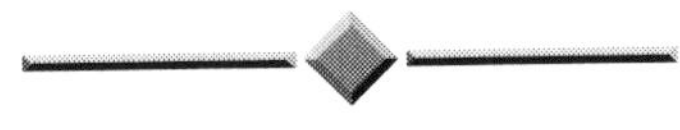

A bullet whined past Malin's ear as he scrambled to the side of the van, sending two rounds into a charging soldier. The mercenary reached around and tugged a loaded M-16 from the van's gun rack. He sighted at the distant spread-eagled form of the only paratrooper to have come into his line of sight. A pained yelp left his lips as a bullet tore a searing quarter inch deep furrow through the side of his left shoulder. The rush of pain made him convulse involuntarily, had he not done so, the next bullet would surely have shattered his forehead. Drawing a deep breath, teeth gritted, Malin emptied his M-16 into his assailant. His rounds found their mark and the hail of shells from that direction ceased as a cloud of swirling gray enveloped the van.

Malin knew other highly skilled assassins still lurked outside, their approach concealed by the twin smoke grenades' noxious cloud. To remain in the van would be suicidal. A stun grenade, followed by a burst of gunfire would sound his death knell. Fast action offered his only hope. Malin rammed in a fresh clip and dropped onto the pavement. Hidden in the swirls of gray he rolled quickly to his right, towards the huge landing gear. Lying spread-eagled on the hard pavement he clutched his weapons and waited, billows of gray fog drifting lazily about.

The sudden absence of sound was deafening. The regular staccato beat of rounds slamming into the van had ceased. So too had all gunfire. The ringing in Malin's ears faded slowly until he was able to hear the faint thump-thump sound of retreating helicopters.

The smoke grenades expelled the last puffs of their contents. Moving air soon thinned the gray cloud. Ghostly shapes soon took shape. Three commandos, hands placed atop their heads, walked slowly away. The one had a pronounced limp. The battle was over.

A baffled Malin climbed gingerly to his feet. Several flares still puffed brilliant red plumes from points on the landward sides. He assumed them to be the recall order. He was equally correct in thinking that had the assault force not been recalled, he would have been a dead man. The M-16 hung loosely in his right hand. The realization of just how narrowly he had escaped death left him slightly sobered. The exhilaration of the early moments of battle deserted him. His arms and legs had a tingly, almost rubbery feel to them.

The carnage spread before him would have made many a person ill. Malin simply looked about in seemingly disaffected detachment. Again Larson's attention to minute detail had paid off. The easily wielded machine pistols were ineffective at the range they had first been used at. The M-16s had the range and accuracy needed, but unless the hits were absolutely perfect, they had limited effectiveness against the bulletproof garments of the assault force. The Smith and Wesson pistols would have met with equally mediocre results had they been loaded with conventional ammunition. Thanks to Larson's foresight they had not been. Highly unconventional ammunition known as KTW bullets made up their loads. The distinctive green Teflon coated slugs could penetrate four bulletproof vests and still have sufficient force to plow through two and a half thick phone books. They were virtually unstoppable. Though ostensibly introduced for the use of law enforcement officers, who saw no practical need for such a bullet, the KTW provided an ideal assassin's bullet. Rather than aid police, the mere existence of such bullets scared them, and not without good reason.

The sun was warm as Malin walked the few paces to where Price lay. He knelt beside the dying mercenary. A few stray locks of brown hair blew across the remnants of his face. It didn't take a doctor to make the prognosis, Price only had a few hours of life remaining, if indeed that. To bring him along would be senseless. To leave him alive meant that information might be gleaned before the inevitable happened. The only recourse was a painful one, but one that every mercenary had to be prepared to render as a kindness and service to fallen comrades. It would not be the first time Malin made such a gesture. He hoped it would be the last.

A grim expression on his sweat streaked face, Malin gathered Price's weaponry and stood up. The barrel of the M-16 lined carefully on Price's still forehead. Malin looked away and grimaced as the shot rang out. The loud report of the weapon reverberated in his ears as he walked slowly away without looking back at Price's corpse.

Five members of the strike team lay scattered about the surrounding pavement. Malin deposited Price's weapons in the van, then cautiously approaching each in turn. The grotesque, inhuman position the one person lay in was enough to tell even the uninitiated that he was dead. Two more men were hit badly, but not severely enough to threaten their lives. A third would require prompt medical attention if he were to live. Malin applied field dressings to the commando's wounds in an effort to retard the man's loss of blood. With a little luck, the soldier would survive to regale comrades with tales of his heroic bravery. The last SAS man, a sergeant, didn't have the luxury of possible life. He was one of the men who had managed to actually land on the wing only to be shot off before he could effect entry to the cabin. The tumble off the wing and subsequent drop to the hard pavement had only hastened the inevitable. He would die within the hour. As with Price, Malin opted to terminate the man's suffering with a single shot.

Another two names would have to be added to the panel at the base of the clock tower at the SAS regimental headquarters in Hereford, England. The name of every member felled since the unit formed during World War II graced the panel.

CHAPTER SIXTEEN

11 April

11:16 to 11:29 AM

"It could have worked." Colonel Cooke's usually stern face was positively stony. He cursed himself for agreeing to abort the mission if any remote explosive devices were triggered once the assault began.

Randall shook his head wearily. "Not without significant endangerment of the hostages and God only knows who else. Face it, your men were under fire before they even hit the deck. A prolonged firefight could only have netted sizable civilian casualties."

"One hell of a fireworks display." Schmitt swung his binoculars away from the blazing hulk of the cargo jet and back to the scene of the aborted siege. "The deadline's almost upon us," he commented to no one in particular. "It would seem that you guys have little choice left but to pay up."

Cooke became surprisingly verbose. "If those bastards get the diamonds and manage to convert them to cash, have you any concept what will 'appen? Today's destruction will be just an infinitesimal sample!"

"They're not affiliated with the ETA or any other terrorist group for that matter, Colonel. They're just a bunch of greedy bastards using a convenient political smoke-screen to help cover their tracks."

"Speculation?" Cooke was back in form.

"Call it an educated guess," Schmitt responded. He grudgingly found himself liking the Colonel.

Randall pulled Judy McArthur aside. "Can they fly the plane with those gizmos stuck on the upper sides?"

"Sure. Why not? The slipstream might rip them off if they're not properly mounted and they will create some drag, but as long as they stay below, say, ten thousand feet, they should be alright."

"Higher and the pressure difference will blow them out?"

She nodded. "Unless they've got them mounted with an airtight seal able to withstand the cabin pressurization at higher altitudes, yes."

"And if they stick within safer altitudes, they sacrifice range?"

"Substantially. Oh, they may exceed the ten thousand feet I just mentioned, but unless they can get that baby over thirty thousand they'll be greatly limited in range. Those machines routinely cruise at thirty-five thousand feet."

"Can you put together an estimate of the reduced range?"

"Given a little time I can give you a crude figure, but it could be way off the mark."

"Just do the best that you can." He spun on Schmitt. "You seem blessed with all the answers. Where will they head from here?"

A wistful smile graced Schmitt's features. "I've one or two ideas. I'd say that makes me an invaluable part of the investigation, wouldn't you?" He paused, inhaling slowly. "Since you'll be paying them off, I want an agreement drawn up whereby I get a set percentage for recovery of the ransom."

"You're a mercenary bastard," Randall commented sourly.

Schmitt shrugged off the insult. He had learned to ignore the inevitable jibes his profession garnered from outsiders who viewed him as nothing more than a scavenging vulture. "It's a living," he said dryly.

A briefcase containing $10.1 million in uncut diamonds was reluctantly passed to the bearded terrorist from the battered van, the exterior of which was perforated like a Swiss cheese. He cautiously transferred the velvet pouches with the gemstones to a leather case of his own before heaving the briefcase provided by the FBI off toward the side of the runway. Any hidden device, signaling or otherwise, had been rendered useless.

The grinning terrorist climbed into his battered van and drove back to the 747.

While Larson busied himself with examining the quality and quantity of the ransom diamonds, Higgins opened the port side door above the wing where two men had managed to land. A careful inspection of the massive wing's surface revealed only slight indentations where the men had hit. There were no bullet holes or other visible damage. Higgins picked up the equipment bag the one man had dropped and flung it aft onto the runway. The inspection complete, he returned to the vastly more hospitable environs of the cabin.

At the same time Malin busily inspected the landing gear, underside of the aircraft, and the massive engines for signs of damage. A stray bullet had nicked the one strut just above the massive tires. Another had hit a few inches further up, near a seal. A minute trickle of hydraulic fluid made its way down the side of the strut. It would not be a problem, he decided and continued his inspection. No other damage to the aircraft could be found from below. He was grateful that no stray gunfire had hit any of the enormous tires. Before reporting his findings to Larson, Malin dragged the bodies of the dead and wounded clear of the runway. The man he had applied the field dressings to was still alive, his eyes looked feebly at the terrorist as he hauled him to safety. Malin knelt beside the SAS soldier and offered a sip of cool water from a Thermos. The man drank gratefully.

"Not much longer now," Malin stated as he rose. "They'll get you fixed up again in no time." He turned and took up station in the van once more. Maybe Price had been right, he was getting too old for this sort of thing.

Less than fifteen minutes had elapsed since the ransom was delivered, when the terrorists radioed the tower. The now familiar voice had lost all signs of the nervous inflection that had surfaced briefly earlier on. "A random sampling of the diamonds indicates that the lot is within specifications. First rate merchandise. I congratulate you on your wise decision not to attempt further futilities. Our mission here is now complete. Shortly we will be underway. Basically, our flight path will take us down the Eastern seaboard, across the Caribbean to South America. A detailed flight plan can be found in the rear compartment of the van. I expect you to use it to clear an air corridor for us. No aircraft, civil or military, are to approach within fifteen miles of us at any time. Our modifications to this aircraft enable us to detect any violations of this stipulation.

"Caracas, Venezuela is our current destination. Upon arrival there we will release half our hostages as a sign of good faith. In return we expect a prompt, uneventful, refueling. Our final destination will be disclosed at that time.

"That's all you need to know right now. No point in idle banter between us. Let's just leave it with a final warning. Make no mistake, we can still inflict damage and casualties at will, so heed our instructions to the letter.

"Flight 923 will now begin its take-off procedures." The speaker fell silent.

CHAPTER SEVENTEEN

11 April

11:30 AM to 12:30 PM

Take-offs and landings rarely attract much attention from airport personnel. That which is commonplace seldom does. Atlas Flight 923 was an exception. Unlike the thousands that had preceded it down runway 31 Left, it drew attention, lots of it. Ground, fire, rescue, security, and tower personnel alike watched in almost reverent silence as the 747 rolled down the long runway, rose skyward, and gradually disappeared in the distance. For them, the worst should be over. They had weathered the storm.

McArthur's little office was crowded, though the congenial McArthur was conspicuously absent. Fredericks had just ambled in. His fleshy face registered relief. His presence was ignored. Unperturbed, he stood clumsily by the door, his vast bulk leaned against the doorframe.

"At least the respective governments are in agreement. A bit of a rarity these days." Randall rubbed his neck.

Schmitt shook his head. "Makes no difference. You're all assuming Larson is going to be true to his word, that Caracas is his real destination. Presumably once he's on the ground, a second rescue attempt could be mounted. With no one in an armored van to guard the flanks he and his cohorts should be infinitely more vulnerable."

"Extremely vulnerable," Cooke offered. "A far less theatrical operation will be possible." The Colonel shuddered to think what kind of press coverage the foiled parachute drop would get. It would undoubtedly be played to the hilt, heralded as a grandstand play concocted by glory hungry soldiers with mock heroics in mind. The thought angered him. His men were all hard-core professionals. One didn't make it into the SAS otherwise. They gave their all for Queen and country and Cooke was damned proud of them.

Schmitt smiled bemusedly. "Providing Larson plays right into your hands."

"He might." Cooke remained stone-faced.

"He also might not oblige you. I think that far more probable."

Fredericks pushed his bulk off the doorframe. Open hands seemed to plead, as did beseeching eyes. "You've all missed the point here," he interjected. "Doesn't anyone see? This bunch is different. Force another direct armed confrontation and there'll probably be lots of dead people. Innocent people! Does life matter so little?"

Cooke's nostrils flared, his features drew tight. He would brook no further abuse. "I beg you to remember *mister* Fredericks, that *you* allowed the weapons to reach them. The only resultant non-terrorist deaths thus far are two of *my* men. No innocent people have been killed!" Cooke checked his mounting volume. "Those bloody bastards on the plane have to be stopped! Eliminated. That's my job, Fredericks. Damnably ugly work. The devil's own at times. Don't ever affront my dignity again by questioning my concern for life."

A bewildered Fredericks remained silent. It was one of the rare moments in his life when words failed him. He suddenly felt guilty, inherently responsible for the death of the Britons on the runway. He wanted to say how sorry he was, to apologize for questioning the underlying motives. Stubborn false pride born of years of arrogance would not allow such a display. His fleshy face beet red, head bent forward, eyes avoiding those around him, he retreated from the suddenly oppressively hot office.

When the door closed, Schmitt clapped. "Bravo, Colonel! That pompous old fool needed someone to take him down a few notches. He's done little to make the past couple of hours easier for anyone."

Cooke looked slightly embarrassed. "I'm afraid I let a spot of temper flare." He forced a weak smile as he slipped on his tan beret and with a practiced hand adjusted it to precisely the correct rakish angle. The badge bearing his Regiment's winged dagger and motto, 'Who Dares, Wins,' hung proudly on the beret.

"I think all of us need to vent some frustration occasionally," Randall muttered. "Trouble is, most of the time restraint prevents what needs to be said from being said." Innumerable tempting situations sprang to mind. Anyone trying to enforce the law constantly was stymied by legal nuances and vexing hurdles. Better than most, Randall could sympathize with the British officer who had revealed that his stoic exterior was just that, an exterior shielding most compassionate thoughts and actions. They were a lot alike, he mused. Both regularly confronted frustrating situations, and both were generally restrained in their responses to them.

"If we're to pursue them to Caracas, someone had better arrange transport." Schmitt's use of 'we' was quite intentional. Though the others might only grudgingly admit it, he was indispensable. It was a position he relished.

"Actually, we already have," Colonel Cooke volunteered. "The lads and I came via a supersonic Concorde. It can get us to Caracas ahead of them. Which means we can scout the place quickly, choose our ground and prepare. Once they land we strike almost instantaneously. Leaves no time for them to attempt anything."

"Are your men up to a second try?" Randall asked.

Cooke looked hurt. "I daresay they'll be wantin' another go. It'd take a bit more'n a brief encounter like this mornin's to wear them down. They'll be ready." There was more than a hint of pride in the tone.

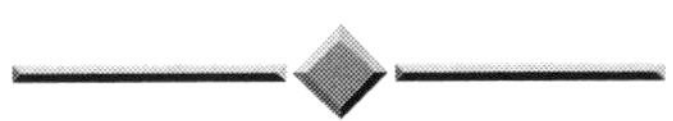

The After-Take-Off Checklist complete, the 747 continued its steady climb. It leveled off at thirty-five thousand feet without incident. The blister-like domes, which the fuselage sported on either side, remained firmly in place. The pressurized cabin remained intact. The careful calculations and precisely fitted modifications had proven sound.

Malin's features were grim as he stood stooped forward just behind the pilot's seat and looked out through the windscreen. Deep blue sky spread out ahead, at higher elevations it merged into blackness. Far below wisps of cloud drifted lazily. Malin's mood had soured. The constant pain throbbing in his shoulder could be credited in part, but he had never been one to let a little physical pain significantly hamper him in spirit or action. Nor did mental anguish generally hinder him. In battle such emotions could prove fatal. Nonetheless, having extinguished Price's life weighed heavily on him. He knew there had been no alternative. But Price had been a good friend, something Malin had too few of. And then there was Price's recent bride. How would she cope? Death was a difficult thing to confront. They had been very close, Malin knew that much.

Visions of the past flooded his thoughts. He and Price fighting side by side in the Angolan bush; the two of them cavorting with local whores in some of the nameless villages; both men fleeing the atrocity of the mercenary massacre; he and Price posing as soccer players in the botched Seychelles operation. They had been through much together. They had shared dingy, fly infested hovels, whores who were every bit as dingy, but available, and most importantly, a mutual respect and trust cultivated over the years. Malin felt as though part of himself had perished on that runway. He resolved to break the news to Price's widow personally when circumstances permitted. It would be difficult, but he owed Mark that much.

"Beautiful day, huh?" The flight engineer asked, glancing up at the bearded man who leaned on his seat.

Shaken from his reverie, Malin looked blanking at their acting pilot. "What?"

"I said, it's a beautiful day isn't it?"

"Yeah, I guess so."

"Couldn't have asked for better flying weather," Higgins interjected lightly. "Fact is, we can expect about the same all the way. If, that is, you put much stock in forecasts."

"Not that it matters much one way or the other, does it? We're committed." Malin stated dryly and stalked back to the lounge.

Larson looked up from the twin radar screens when Malin entered. "How's the arm?"

"Still there," he replied sourly. Melancholy seemed so out of character. Noting the slight rise Larson's brows made, Malin shrugged and forced a smile. "Will ya listen to me? Moping around and everything. Damnably depressing soul, aren't I? And just when things seem to be movin' smoothly along. Leave it to ol' Keith to be a spoiler."

He began to strip off his ruined T-shirt in silence. Three holes were punched across its chest. The shoulder was torn ragged and blood soaked the side. The three neat holes were made by slugs that would have killed or at the very least incapacitated him had all three not been stopped by the vest beneath. The relatively lightweight garment was made of bullet resistant Kevlar. The remarkable fabric's stopping power was such that it could leave a fiber imprint on a flattened bullet on impact. Malin peeled off the bloodied vest and crammed it into a duffel bag together with the remains of the T-shirt. Three purplish bruises marked the impacts on his chest.

Forcing a smile, he tapped Larson on the shoulder. In his hands he proffered the medical kit. "Care to play doctor?"

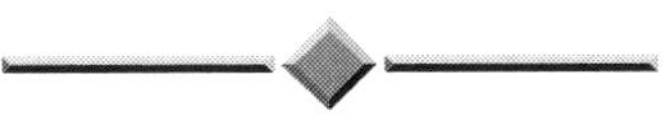

The door to the flight deck had been surreptitiously closed before Malin, his shoulder neatly bandaged, slipped below. Moments later he returned with one of the passenger's belongings. In his absence Larson had gathered a handful of items, the case with the diamonds among them, on a lounge table. Upon Malin's return, the pouches with the diamonds were taken from the case. The gemstones were carefully dumped from the pouches only to be replaced by remarkably realistic, yet completely valueless fakes. The next half-hour passed while the two men busily completed a task crucial to the success of the entire operation. It was a task to which the others were not to be privy, particularly so in light of the inexplicable turn of events at Kennedy. The task finished, all signs of their work were diligently removed and Malin returned the borrowed item to the lower deck.

The all-important clandestine work behind them, Malin and Larson decided to check on their hostages. Moving in a fashion more akin to a leisurely stroll than an inspection tour, they started aft. Had any passenger been in a somewhat more animate state, he or she would surely have assumed the two men were flight weary travelers up to stretch aching legs and revitalize tired corpuscles.

Malin glanced side to side as he followed Larson into the second cabin section. His assorted combat experiences had brought him face to face with death often. He himself had extinguished the lives of many people. More often than he cared to recall, his sights had lined up on a man only to leave a tattered corpse sprawled on the ground an instant later. Until that day in Amsterdam, he had enjoyed a several year hiatus in killing. And now he had killed again. The once familiar, slightly uneasy feeling that had been a constant unwelcome companion during combat, made its reemergence back there on the runway. It continued to nag as he stared wearily at the corpse-like passengers. It wasn't fear or even remorse, he was certain of that. Whatever the feeling was inspired by, he had long since come to the conclusion that it was something to be ignored, however much he despised it. Perhaps Price had been right, he was getting too old for this kind of thing.

"It's kind of eerie," he said. "I mean, with everyone out cold, it's kinda like they're all dead."

"They'll be alright." Larson stepped across a fallen flight attendant and proceeded down the aisle. "I should be the one with the willies, though. No offense intended, but death isn't exactly something far from your repertoire."

"Unless you're a sicko or something, you can watch a hundred men die and each time it still impacts, each time some inner consciousness seems to pity the poor slob who bought the farm. Just for the record, I may be good at what I do, but I sure as hell don't enjoy killing. I'm a mercenary, not a psycho." Both men lapsed into silence.

The scene in the last cabin section was the same; dead silence save for the constant, reassuring whine of the engines, and a total dearth of movement. Tourists with their families, the inevitable students, and businesspersons whose expense accounts couldn't meet the higher first class fares made up the bulk of the slumbering mass. The panorama exemplified serenity in its own macabre way.

A narrow aisle near the rear of the aircraft joined the starboard and port aisles. On this passageway wall hung a chart of the world with the originally intended flight path highlighted in red marker. Larson studied the map. An awfully long distance remained. Distance meant time and time afforded the authorities the opportunity to regroup after the shock and surprise of events at Kennedy wore off. The element of surprise, coupled with a display of enormous, unprecedented destructive capability, had favored Larson and his compatriots. He was acutely aware that with time, despite all the in-depth meticulous planning, the margin of advantage diminished inexorably.

Back on the upper deck Larson glanced thoughtfully around. Aside from the curved ceiling, the room could have been a den in someone's house. The wide, comfortable armchairs and couches did not seem to belong in an aircraft. Nor did the wood-grained tables and bar. If only Lindbergh or the Wright brothers could see it. To think that aviation had progressed so far in the scant sixty-seven years that separated the Wrights' achievement and the first flight of a Boeing 747, the fuselage of which is almost twice as long as the distance covered by their first flight. It made for a sobering thought.

He passed onto the flight deck.

"Been below?" Higgins asked as he punched some figures into a laptop computer lying on the flight engineer's workspace.

"Yes. Everything is quiet."

Higgins nodded as he studiously finished entering data. The little monitor displayed a series of figures that he consulted as Larson peered over his shoulder. "Fuel consumption and range data," he said superfluously. "So far, so good. The domes are having a negligible effect. I've run a quick projection for the remainder of the flight," he looked up at Larson briefly, "including course modifications." There was no need to elaborate on the latter. Larson knew what he meant and it was imperative that the plane's genuine flight engineer did not. "She'll be pretty close to running on fumes when she gets to Caracas, but she'll make it."

"Excellent."

"Company," Malin stated matter-of-factly as Larson returned to the lounge. The bearded mercenary sat comfortably ensconced in a chair by the radar screens. "Two blips came up from behind like bats out of hell. Matched course and speed and took up station behind and a little above us."

"Fighters?"

"That's how I'd make it."

"With all the turbulence this beast kicks up in its wake, I don't envy them. Must be getting a hefty buffeting out there."

"Probably." Malin shrugged impassively. "What do we do about them?"

Larson stared thoughtfully at the radar screens. Another seemingly excessive precaution had paid off. "Well, they serve two purposes. First to test our defenses. Some wiz kid may have surmised what the domes are all about. Second to keep an eye on us. To ensure that we don't opt to plunge to a lower altitude and bail out or something. For now they're quite harmless. On the other hand, we don't want anyone around later, nor do we want to be perceived as weak. We must prove that we're still potent adversaries. Hence, we force their withdrawal."

Surprise registered on Malin's face. By his reckoning no explosive devices remained.

A raised hand silenced his protest. "I know, I know," Larson said solemnly. "It's a bluff, but they won't know that."

On the flight deck he selected the appropriate military frequency band on the modified radio and flipped the toggle switch to engage it. The radio equipment on a 747 can be set for two frequencies simultaneously, thus enabling the pilot to switch frequencies and still keep the last locked in so that he can return to it with a mere flick of a switch, as opposed to resetting it. Larson listened patiently. A wisp of a smile crossed his features when one of the pilots contacted base. The communication was mired in military jargon, but the gist of it was clear enough, he and his wingman were in position.

"Bluejay Leader, this is Atlas 923. Do you read?"

Only static answered Larson's transmission. Unperturbed, he repeated his call with the same lack of result. The fighter pilot had undoubtedly been startled by the transmission. By approaching the 747 from the rear, under normal circumstances, he and his wingman should have been undetectable to anyone aboard the jet. Standard radar equipment on a 747 only faces forward and could not have betrayed their approach.

The pilot remained silent. His base did not. "You are using a restricted frequency, Atlas 923. This violates Federal law."

"So arrest us," Larson responded coolly.

Another voice came on. "This is Major Osborne. Civilian use of this frequency is strictly prohibited. We are well acquainted with your purpose. Should you wish communication with the proper authorities, you must use standard frequencies and vacate the military bands."

"I'm growing impatient, Major. Call them off!"

"Call who off? The police authorities?" Osborne asked with feigned ignorance.

"Let's not play inane games, Major. Two aircraft swung in line about a quarter of a mile aft and some two hundred feet above. We clearly specified that this corridor was to be cleared for us. We never asked for military escort and, in fact, your aircraft's' presence violates the rules for this affair. Withdraw them immediately or you leave us no recourse but to take punitive action. Do I make myself perfectly clear?"

There was a brief silence while the major consulted his superiors.

They in turn weighed the situation and instructed him on how to proceed. "Assuming that any military aircraft were in your vicinity, and I am not saying that there are, why should we accommodate your demands?"

"You've undoubtedly been briefed, Major."

"True, and you are undoubtedly bluffing," the major replied evenly.

Larson remained unfazed. "Are you prepared to run that risk?"

In quiet fascination Malin watched the sleek gray aircraft with its twin tails. It was an F/A-18 Hornet, a lethal weapon from the Navy's arsenal. The fighter was so close that he could gaze at the white helmeted pilot who stared right back at him from behind a darkened visor. Sunlight glinted off the helmet. An identical aircraft hemmed in the other side of the 747.

The little jet seemed suspended in midair as it maintained its position for what seemed an eternity; less than a minute in reality. Then it rushed ahead, effortlessly leaving the lumbering airliner behind. Face pressed to the window, Malin sought to follow its progress. He caught a last glimpse as it rolled gracefully to the side and dove away beneath the airliner.

"My dear Major Osborne," Larson chided patiently as though scolding a child, "don't play me for a fool. Your pilots are good. Their theatrical departure, with its coordinated rollout, was impressive. But don't insult my intelligence by having them sidle up beneath our belly. Admirable flying. Truly so, but it won't be tolerated. Do I make myself perfectly clear?"

A crackle of static preceded the major's stentorian voice. "Our aircraft withdrew as ordered. You're all alone out there."

"Bull. I should think that by now your people would have surmised that, among other modifications, we've added a rather effective rearward facing radar capacity to this aircraft. No matter how cautious, no one can approach us undetected. I trust that this clarification will end future futile attempts to keep an eye on us."

There was strained silence as Osborne again consulted his superiors. The F/A-18s had been ordered to try a second, radio silent approach from beneath the airliner on the assumption that radio transmissions had betrayed their presence the first time. Their immediate detection and the proffered explanation dispelled any such thoughts. The technical sophistication of the terrorists was becoming painfully clear.

"The domes on the upper deck?"

"Give yourself an A for the day, Major. Now that we understand each other, let's quit playing games before I tire and take punitive action. Recall your planes!"

Maintaining their excellence, the two F/A-18 pilots throttled up and left the airliner in their wake. In a precise maneuver, they rolled to the right in unison and were soon lost to sight as they thundered their way back to base.

CHAPTER EIGHTEEN

11 April

12:30 to 2:00 PM

The sun was high overhead when the last of the strike team boarded the sleek, delta-winged shape of the Concorde. The supersonic airliner stood high above the apron perched atop its spidery struts. With its nose dropped, the aircraft looked like a gargantuan white bird plumed with blue and red tail feathers, or so Randall thought.

The cabin was every bit as narrow as Randall had imagined it would be. A long thin corridor ran down the center flanked on either side by double rows of seats stretching aft. The cabin's dimensions and lighting gave the impression that it was longer than it actually was.

Besides Schmitt and Colonel Cooke, the first few rows were empty. The next seven rows hosted young men dressed in mottled green and brown battle fatigues. Tan berets similar to Colonel Cooke's proudly crowned the heads of the elite group of highly skilled commandos. Randall studied the countenances of those nearest him. All were physically fit with intelligent faces. But their eyes told more. There was a certain hardness there, hardness born of training and experience. These were extremely competent soldiers who yielded only stubbornly. Grim expressions bespoke of the morning's fiasco. It did not take an expert to see that each of them eagerly relished the opportunity to redeem the unit as a whole.

Beyond the troops, most of the seats were piled high with their specialized weaponry and paraphernalia.

Randall settled into the vacant seat beside Cooke. The Colonel seemed lost in thought, oblivious to the high pitched whine of the engines coming to life.

Everyone aboard remained silent, locked in his own reverie as the jet taxied onto the runway. There was a noticeable increase in engine noise before the needle-shaped aircraft rapidly gained speed. Several thousand feet after starting the take-off run, the Concorde rose gracefully into the pale blue sky.

The Concorde winged its way rapidly southward. An hour and a half had elapsed since its hasty refueling and departure from JFK. In that time additional bits and pieces of information had been relayed to those aboard. The most recent such message in hand, Randall regained his seat. He was glad to be out of the cramped cockpit. He had never liked flying. To him it was a modern convenience one occasionally had to endure. Despite the statistics, he preferred to plunk himself behind the wheel of his Ford Mustang and take his chances. The blare of horns, the snail's pace of rush hour traffic, the frustration of finding the elusive parking spot, the bone jarring potholes; all were preferable to a man who felt uncomfortable when aloft. It didn't seem right to be zipping along in an aircraft that quite literally 'pushed the envelope' when at speed. Friction left the skin temperature very hot as the needle-like jet rammed through even the rarefied atmosphere found at sixty thousand feet.

"What gives?" Schmitt queried. His seemingly eternal optimism made him a difficult person to rankle.

"Not much." Randall was very much aware of Colonel Cooke's avid attention. "They've gotten a rundown on the van. Bought in New Jersey at a dealership in Newark three months ago. Paid in full with a certified check." Schmitt's brows arched slightly. Criminals generally paid cash for all purchases in an attempt to make it harder to trace them. The only disadvantage was that police, aware of the practice, monitor utility and other payment records. When cash payments of notable size or frequency turn up, a brief investigation sometimes follows. If any further irregularity is discerned during the inquiry, additional investigation is instigated. "The check was drawn on an Elizabeth, New Jersey bank by one Charles Hobson, who is the duly registered owner with proper title, tags, and insurance. You'll never guess where our mister Hobson resides."

Schmitt nodded in understanding. "Same address where the hostages were kept. The one I found for you," he added as though to reinforce his importance.

"Give the man a cigar. Same address. Same name on the mailbox. The house was taken on an annual lease basis four months ago. Security deposit and rent paid by checks drawn on the same bank. The bank employees who might have seen our man will be thoroughly questioned, but since our dear Hobson has not set foot in the bank since he picked up the certified check some three months ago, I doubt the descriptions will be of much use. The hostages, the airport personnel recruited and the neighbors are also being grilled for information, but I'm afraid it'll be more or less a waste of time. This Larson chap is damned careful. I'm frankly surprised that he let you latch on to him, Schmitt. Such carelessness is quite out of character."

Colonel Cooke looked pensive. "And my men? Any word on their condition?"

"Nothing new. Nor has any positive ID been made on the dead terrorist. No papers of any kind on him."

"Somehow that comes as no surprise."

"Agreed, Colonel."

"Like you said, Randall, not much of consequence." Schmitt leaned forward so that he could see both men. "Which brings to mind a nagging question of mine. Has it occurred to anyone else that, as I believe I already mentioned, Larson and his band of merry men may not be going to Caracas? As I see it, the consensus is that we are not dealing with amateurish idiots here. They know that given another crack at them, we'll be sure to take full advantage of the opportunity. Telling us where such a chance might be offered would favor us immeasurably. Do we understand each other?"

"All too well," Randall retorted. "Others have given the matter considerable thought too. The last item on this communication," he waved the paper covered with his scrawled notes, " addresses just that possibility. Seems a fully fueled 747 has a potential range in excess of 6000 miles. Gives us one hell of a lot of territory to cover. Conceivably, the bastards could come down anywhere in the continental US, Central America, the Caribbean, Europe, parts of northern Africa, and a goodly portion of the northern half of South America. Contingency arrangements have been made accordingly. The US Army's Black Berets, who apparently have a training regimen conducive to this sort of thing, will cover any points within the US, Central America, and the Caribbean. Germany's Group 9 of the Border Guard is on alert and will cover Europe in the unlikely event that our friends divert there, while Israel's 269th Headquarters Reconnaissance Regiment is prepared to cover potential African locales. All provided the host countries are amenable."

"That could indeed be a sticky problem," said Cooke. Lack of cooperation in host countries infuriated him. It was the sort of senseless abrogation of international cooperation in the fight against terrorism that had to be eliminated if terrorists were to be denied safe havens. He remembered all too well the 1977 skyjacking of a Lufthansa 737. Though never officially substantiated, it was generally understood that the then West German government had paid the Somali government $25 million just to be permitted to employ their strike team and liberate the hostages in the spectacular raid at Mogadiscio. The Americans had also been blackmailed into promising future arms shipments to insure Somali cooperation. It was a disgraceful display by the African regime. In Cooke's eyes it was one that should not have been tolerated by the international community.

One of the special flight's two flight attendants brought Cooke a cup of steaming coffee. He sipped it cautiously, then added. "Are there contingency plans if we don't happen to get an agreeable host country?"

Randall shrugged. "If there are, they didn't see fit to confide in us at this juncture."

"Let's hope it doesn't come down to an Entebbe style conflict."

"Amen," Randall concurred while stirring some sugar into his own coffee.

"You know, in a bizarre way it's a pity they didn't kill any civilians." From Randall's shocked expression, Cooke decided clarification of his sentiment would be prudent, and hastily so at that. "What I mean is that had they actually killed civilians we'd be in a substantially better position to deal harshly with them."

"How so?" Randall still looked somewhat incredulous.

Schmitt nodded knowingly and cut off Cooke's response. "So far, Randall, they've pulled off a remarkably well-rehearsed crime. With almost every conceivable use of technical sophistication and gadgetry, they've become the sort of criminals who can command a type of underdog admiration. They've beaten the system with its own technology. Seems a popular theme these days."

Understanding dawned on Randall. "Kinda like those guys holed up in a New York bank many years ago, the one they made a movie about. Al Pacino played one of them, but I forget the title. Anyway, I see your point."

Schmitt finished his Coke. "I saw the film you're thinking of. Pretty good flic. Bad news for the law enforcement people involved though."

"Precisely my point," Cooke chimed in. "Which is why we would be in a better position if some innocents had been butchered back in New York and not just some of my lads. Right or wrong, public perception in this age of instant media coverage is bloody well tough to keep squarely in our favor."

"True, but purely academic at this point." Schmitt motioned the flight attendant for a refill. "On a more practical level, there's the possibility that they are indeed going to Caracas. Which raises all sorts of intriguing questions. Do they have back-up defenses pre-set there? Do they have influential government contacts? Why let us know in advance? And fundamentally, why Caracas?"

"More charges?" Randall asked.

"Just because I didn't get to see them place them, does not rule the possibility out."

"Be reasonable," Cooke advised.

To Schmitt's utter amazement, Randall took up his defense. "Reasonable? Like it or not, Schmitt knows more about the bastards than any of us. Add to that the painful facts of the past few hours or so and I'm beginning to think that about anything would fall within the realm of reason with this Larson fellow.

"This morning if anyone had told me that a team of the world's finest anti-terrorist troops would be beaten back by a couple of gunmen, ETA or otherwise, I'd have had a good laugh. I'm not laughing, am I? If someone had told me that some maniac would destroy all that has been destroyed, I'd have thought that person mad. Had someone told me that a 747 could be commandeered and quickly refitted with special radar and God only knows what else, I'd have thought the person an avid and rather gullible reader of science fiction. I doubt if the F/A-18 pilots who were picked up on the newly installed radar would concur."

Cooke waved the FBI agent to silence. "You've amply made your point."

"Good." Randall tasted his coffee, then emptied another packet of sugar into it. "Bombs aside, I've another little scenario in mind. Some of the junk hauled aboard at Kennedy could have been parachuting equipment. Maybe this Larson fellow intends to drop to a lower altitude, bail out with the diamonds and let the plane and any and all evidence aboard crash into the sea. His demand for the air corridor and the considerable trouble that he has gone to in order to detect violations of that corridor would fit neatly with that scenario."

Schmitt took a refreshing gulp of his new Coke before saying, "Not Larson's style. Not the mass murderer type, our Larson. He went into this venture prepared to kill, but only as a contingency, not for bloodsport. Wholesale slaughter is far too messy for him. He fancies himself as much too refined.

"A crash *would* eliminate evidence and potential witnesses," Cooke interjected. "All he would need is a small boat to pick him up at a pre-arranged spot. Makes for a smooth getaway with just about no tracks left behind."

"Think about it. He's already let us have equipment that he was finished with, *intact*. That note found with the flight plan in the van proves he's not afraid to let us see his handiwork. The location of every explosive device was on that list. Nothing he could leave on that plane would be likely to be any more incriminating. Besides we already know who he is and he knows that we know. That fact should be driving him right up the wall by now. He'll be racking his brain trying to decide where he messed up. He may even conclude that one of his men sold out. Think of the animosity and distrust brewing aboard that airliner. It's fitting!" Schmitt twirled the can of Coke idly in his hand. The thought of an anguished Larson amused him. But the central thought occupying Schmitt's mind was quite different. He was calculating how best to capitalize on his knowledge and the months of groundwork he had invested in this crime. He wondered just how much he should reveal and how soon he should do so. He felt certain he knew exactly where Larson was headed, at least initially. It was an interesting quandary for Schmitt to wrestle with.

The Concorde sped southward at twice the speed of sound. There was a lull in the conversation and planning while Colonel Cooke walked aft to brief his men. The break gave Randall opportunity to speculate on what lay ahead. Besides the current case, there was the unpleasant fact that whenever one hijacking occurs, others inevitably seem to follow. Maniacs would have to try their luck. The only thankful thing was that none would be as technically adept as Larson.

And what of Larson, the quarry? Randall had matched wits with criminals of every sort. Occasionally someone with a hint of finesse or a clever MO surfaced, but never in all his years of law enforcement had an adversary such as Larson even haunted his wildest dreams. Where did he get all of the special equipment? And what of the capital to finance the project? Had investment moneys been sought from thrill seeking millionaires? Was there a new breed of techno-criminal in the offing? Was Larson's band the forerunner of a new trend in crime? It made for chilling, and frighteningly plausible thinking.

CHAPTER NINETEEN

11 April

2:00 to 6:00 PM

"Power . . . on." The laptop strapped to the jump seat booted up, its display coming to life. A pair of coaxial cables connected modified computer the with the modified autopilot console substituted earlier. Larson's fingers flew over the keyboard. "Destruct sequence . . . disengaged. Course programming . . . ready," he said flatly. "Switch to autopilot on my mark . . . three, two, one, engage."

"Autopilot engaged." Higgins responded mechanically, attention riveted on the controls.

The computer began to whir softly as the complex program began its work. Seconds ticked by. Nothing further happened. Larson continued to time events with a stopwatch. Maybe the unit would not work. It was purely theoretical, never tested. To have done so would have greatly alleviated the difficulties of design. Sadly access to the flight deck of 747s is limited, and access to the flight deck of a 747 with time alone to conduct the requisite tests had been impossible to get.

The unit was based on existing systems modified only slightly to enable it to perform its specialized task. From drawing board to completion, it was untested, unproven. There were a hundred sound reasons why it should not work and only the talents of one man saying that it should. Larson grew anxious as his unit's critical moment neared.

Ever so slowly, the yoke began to turn without human assistance. The aircraft executed a gradual banked turn. By the time it had steadied on the new heading, it had begun to add power and climb. Higgins read off the new course and rate of climb. Larson checked them with figures typed neatly on an index card. They matched. So too did the interval between engaging the autopilot and the maneuver.

Tension on the flight deck eased considerably when Larson announced the success of the test. "Alright, disengage the autopilot and get us back on course." Fingers flew over the keyboard and aborted the guidance program. He shut down the laptop to conserve battery power.

Larson sat stiffly in the lounge. He absentmindedly twisted the end of his mustache. From time to time he ran a finger along the scar on his chin. The scar was the kind of thing people would notice and remember. With it to trigger memories, witnesses probably would recall his dark-brown hair and bushy mustache of the same color. They might even remember his hazel-colored eyes. The whole thing was, of course, a carefully prepared illusion. From the contact lenses to the artfully applied scar, it was a sham.

His clenched fist pounded the armrest angrily. So much trouble to conceal his identity and for what? His cover was blown. Somehow they knew the impossible. Yet, they had relinquished the diamonds. He looked at the briefcase. A fortune beyond most men's wildest dreams had been in it. But the luster of that wealth diminished greatly with the realization that he could never return to the life he had known. He was a marked man destined forever to be a fugitive, however rich.

The queer thing was that the authorities had made no mention of the identities of any of his accomplices. Which could only mean that they did not know who they were. This baffled him.

His gaze fell upon Malin. The mercenary lay stretched out comfortably on a couch. He seemed to be asleep, but the instant Larson's attention focused on him, his eyes slid slowly open to gaze steadily back. Malin had that sort of uncanny sixth sense that seemed to border on the psychic. Larson presumed it was an acquired talent, nurtured in the Vietnamese jungle, a place where such an instinct could spell the difference between life and death.

Seeming to read Larson's troubled thoughts, Malin said, "I didn't spill it."

"I know. It's hard to believe that anyone did, at least willingly or intentionally." Larson turned to watch the video monitor of the lower deck.

"Look at the bright side, Erik, we can afford to run in style."

There was a strained silence. Only the subdued whine of the engines permeated the cabin. Nothing could be heard from the flight deck, the door to which was closed.

At length Malin opted to comment further. "Higgy's sure been actin' cagey since we got underway."

"Small wonder. I had to draw on him to shut him up earlier."

Malin straightened. "You pulled a gun on him?"

"Had to. He was acting crazy once he heard them use my name. Said that was the end of the whole thing. I had to shut him up fast."

The mercenary shut his eyes as he digested this news. A pensive look came over him as he drew a deep breath. When he spoke his tone was low, barely audible. "Suppose Higgy sold out. He might have arranged to set us up in exchange for a percentage deal. Hell, how else could they have known where nearly every charge was? He was there when I planted them. All except the one they didn't catch wind of. Think about that."

Larson did. In fact, he already had and did not like the obvious conclusion. "They could never offer more than his split. It doesn't figure somehow."

"Of course they couldn't top his split. But they sure as hell could offer immunity and a cash bonus." Malin stabbed his index finger at Larson. "No lookin' over his shoulder for the rest of his days. He's a spooky sort too."

"He came highly recommended. Luftin, the same guy who put me onto to you, vouched for Higgins as a reliable man and a damned good pilot to boot."

"Maybe he was good at slipping in across the border with a planeload of drugs and other shit, but that doesn't make him good for a long-term operation like this. Higgy flew one shot at a time smuggling runs. Maybe he just don't have what it takes to handle real pressure. Maybe he plum chickened out. I've seen better men than him crack under pressure."

Larson met Malin's concerned gaze. "We could never be sure until it was too late."

"I don't cotton to runnin' unnecessary risks." Malin looked incredibly intense.

Frustration plagued Larson. Uncertainty etched itself into every line of his face.

"I don't like it any more than you do," Malin said quietly, "but one's got to protect oneself. Higgy's become a terminal liability."

"A *possible* liability." Larson corrected, still torn.

"Nope. A bona fide one. An operation like this depends on mutual trust. Neither of us ever again will be able to place that kind of trust with Higgy again. That makes him a liability of the worst kind."

Larson frowned. "We could minimize his involvement from here on out."

The mercenary shook his head. "Uh-uh. No way. That's not good enough. No, Higgy's outlived his usefulness. I say we terminate his contract permanently." His voice was cold, chillingly so.

"Not yet. First we let him get us to our destination. Then maybe we'll terminate him. The final decision is mine, understood?"

Malin nodded reluctantly. A good soldier always followed orders. "Just so long as you'll take it under advisement."

"Count on it." Larson fell silent again. He was mildly surprised at how easy it was to subjectively consider whether another person should live or die. Perhaps the instinct for self-preservation overrode moral considerations.

A movement on the video monitor caught his eye. A gentleman on the lower deck shifted uneasily. With a perplexed expression he studied his fellow passengers.

Drawn by Larson's sudden rapt attention, Malin joined him by the monitor. "Looks mighty confused, huh?"

"Understandably so," Larson mumbled.

"Do we gas 'em now?"

"In a few minutes." He jerked a thumb at the two unconscious members of the flight crew lying on the floor nearby. They were securely bound with heavy duct tape round their legs. Somewhat unusual handcuffs restrained their hands behind their backs. Blindfolds, isolating headphones, and tiny gas masks were all taped securely in place. "Sure the masks are on tightly?"

"Yeah. Besides there'll be no gas released up here."

"Never leave anything to chance. Pass a couple of masks to the fellows up front and lets be done with it."

Malin did as ordered while Larson picked up the control unit for the gas cylinders below. He waited long enough for the others to don the protective masks, slipped into his own, and threw the toggle switch.

On the lower deck all four gas cylinders spewed forth their contents in a long loud rush of escaping compressed gas. The handful of passengers who had begun to stir, lapsed back into the enveloping darkness of unconsciousness.

CHAPTER TWENTY

11 April

6:00 to 6:30 PM

The South American continent loomed ahead. The 747 skimmed along just above the tiny swells on the relatively calm sea. The sunlight was fading and a few scattered clouds made their appearance as land was sighted.

The greenish blur quickly took shape and form as the distance diminished. The Barima and Waini Rivers of northwestern Guyana appeared slightly off to the left, their muddy brown waters spilling into the sea. Higgins pulled back gently on the yoke, gaining some altitude to safely clear the dense tall trees lining the coastline. The luscious green carpet slipped beneath them as he banked slightly to bring the jet onto a heading of 165 degrees. It was not long before the Cuyuni and shortly thereafter the Mazaruni Rivers were left behind. Major waterways, they were no more than momentary breaks in the green as the 747 sped past. For Higgins, the man in the pilot's seat, it was just like any other low-level radar-evading smuggling run of the past. The notable difference was the size of the aircraft and the nature of the illicit cargo. He stroked his bearded chin thoughtfully as old memories of past exploits stirred. Reverie thrust aside, he returned his rapt attention to the ground sweeping beneath in a blur of motion. If he failed to spot any of the landmarks and thereby failed to make a maneuver on schedule, the whole operation would be blown. Eyes strained, neck craning, he kept very alert. If anyone screwed up, he was determined it wouldn't be he.

Since the plane had dropped down to wave top level to avoid radar detection, fuel consumption had increased considerably. The jet's voracious appetite for aviation fuel was about to be furthered. Malin undid the locks and heaved on an emergency release mechanism. The rearward door on the starboard side fell off into space, crashing into the jungle below. The thunderous roar of the engines blasted into the cabin. Turbulent air whistled about near the open hatchway.

Together with Larson, the mercenary jettisoned all unnecessary equipment. Everything, including the machine pistols, vanished into the dense green mat rushing by below. The lot of it disposed of, Larson left Malin where he was and hurried back to the upper deck. Hands gripping the edge of the table, Larson anxiously made one last inspection of the radar screens. The scan lines swept back and forth several times before he was satisfied that all was indeed well. Adrenaline pumping with excitement, he raced onto the flight deck, catapulted himself into the co-pilot's seat and took the controls. Higgins scooted back into the lounge where he slipped into his parachute harness. The junction of the Potaro and Essequibo Rivers swept by. Time, which had dragged during the long hours of the flight, was fast running out.

Larson's probing eyes darted around the instruments as he climbed over the rim of the Pakaraima Escarpment. The low altitude made him feel uncomfortable. The airspeed dropped slowly as he brought the 747 up an additional couple of thousand feet. All else remained normal.

Higgins struggled awkwardly into the pilot's seat. Steady hands firmly grasped the yoke. "I've got her!" Excitement infected his quavering voice.

Larson rebooted the laptop computer. This time he engaged the destruct program before the guidance program was engaged. Once the plane was released from autopilot, the destruct program would destroy all content in the computer's memory by unleashing a fast and highly voracious virus in the computer.

In the lounge he knelt beside the bound members of the flight crew. The flight engineer, whose assistance had been most useful, had joined his fellow crew members, his bonds a duplicate of theirs. The only viable assumption was that he, like the rest of the hapless crew, had been a helpless victim throughout the entire unsavory affair. Though he had no way of knowing yet, he would never see the share of the ransom that he'd been promised. To pay him would be too dangerous and Larson was never one to take chances.

The handcuffs used on the flight crew were specially made. The metal bracelets themselves were conventional, but instead of being joined by a short chain, a short rectangular block connected them. A seam ran around the midpoint of these blocks. Next to each seam, a small plastic push button graced one surface. Larson pressed down hard on this button on each of the three sets of manacles. The action ruptured a small vial of acid inside. The acid, in turn, would slowly eat through the thin metal rod joining the two halves. In roughly twenty minutes the halves would separate. With their hands freed, the flight crew could easily undo the remainder of their bonds and regain control of the aircraft.

Larson covered the all too familiar distance back to the rear door. Once there, he hastily shouldered into his parachute harness just as the plane banked steeply to starboard. That was the signal that the drop site was almost beneath them. Deft fingers secured his harness as the plane leveled off again. He pulled on his helmet and adjusted his goggles as Higgins came awkwardly running down the aisle, his comical gait the result of his cumbersome chute pack.

On the ball as usual, Malin stood by the open door. A duffel bag containing among other things the briefcase with the fake diamonds, hung securely from his harness. A Savage rifle was strapped across his stomach. He tossed another to Higgins as the pilot drew up gasping for breath. He didn't bother to mention that he had emptied its magazine. Larson also had a lightly laden duffel bag and rifle with his outfit. Each had a machete, a hunting knife, and a powerful flashlight clipped to his utility belt. Under different circumstances and in different garb they could have passed as a team of commandos preparing for a foray behind enemy lines.

Hands pressed firmly against both sides of the open doorway, Malin poked his head into the powerful air current. The force of the rushing air tore at his goggles. He scanned the ground ahead as it swept by in the rapidly diminishing light of dusk. A few seconds elapsed before he made out the break in the jungle he had sought. A grassy section of savanna lay just ahead. He jerked his head back into the comparative shelter of the cabin and shouted, "There it is! Let's go!"

Without a moment's hesitation he catapulted through the doorway into the evening sky. His companions were close behind. Seconds later three camouflaged, steerable chutes opened to begin their swaying descent towards the grassy opening in the jungle that Malin had spotted.

The 747, guided by the instructions on the laptop's programming, regained speed slowly as it disappeared in the distance, executing a sharp turn to avoid the mountains that lay in its path. It would continue to work its way southwestward for the next thirty minutes guided by the navigational program prepared by Larson. After that, the fate of aircraft and all aboard rested in the hands of the as yet securely bound, flight crew. Their ability to save the airliner depended on three small vials of acid, now crushed inside the manacles, eating away the thin metal rods in time.

ROUGH ICE

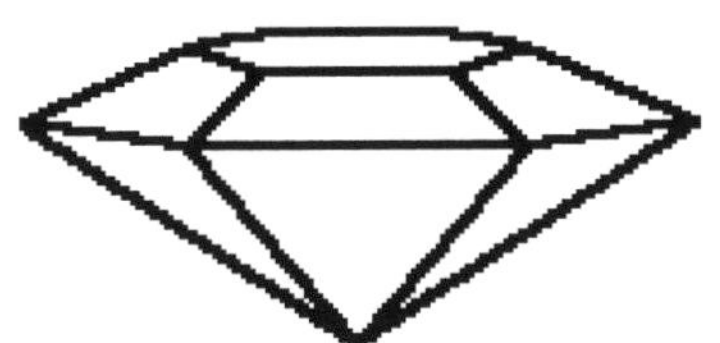

BOOK THREE

AFTERMATH

CHAPTER TWENTY-ONE

11 April

6:30 to 6:45 PM

In Atlas 923's first class lounge the flight engineer lay quietly alongside the other bound crewmen. He'd been told that by binding him exactly as they were, his alibi would be firmly established. So far as the investigators would be concerned he was just another hapless victim. 'Patience', he repeatedly told himself, 'just a little longer, then these damned, cumbersome handcuffs will automatically release me so that I can loose my other bonds and take control of the plane.' Or, so he hoped. Every minute or two he gingerly tried to pull his hands apart, each time with the same disheartening result. An eternity passed and still the manacles remained tightly locked together.

A terrifying thought occurred to him. Suppose these fancy handcuffs just did not work? What if the amount of acid was too small to eat through the rod in time? Maybe they weren't supposed to work at all. What if he had been double-crossed? No one would be able to regain control of and then safely land the mammoth airliner. With him and the jet neatly disposed of, there would be no loose ends left behind by the hijackers, men, he reflected, he really knew remarkably little about. Had he been too gullible? Too greedy? He could have kicked himself, but trussed as he was, it was a physical impossibility.

He tugged at the bonds again. This time it was no longer a gentle act to check them, it now took on an almost panic stricken motion. The tugging caused considerable pain as the metal bracelets dug into softer flesh. Cuts and bruises soon covered his wrists.

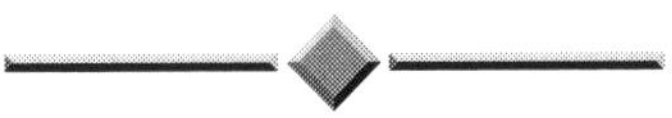

Appropriately, Atlas 923's flight engineer was first to find his hands freed. He rolled roughly onto his back and sat up stiffly. His hands still encumbered by the dangling ends of the manacles, he tore away the layers of tape pinning the blindfold, gag, and gas mask firmly in place. He winced in pain as tape tore away from hair and skin taking a not inconsiderable amount of hair with it.

With the blindfold off, the sudden abundance of light forced him to squint. Gradually his eyes adjusted as the familiar surroundings came into focus. He hurriedly unraveled layers of the thick tape wrapped around his legs. When he tried to stand, he experienced a surprisingly severe lack of coordination after having lain motionless for so long. He flexed his muscles until they limbered up and his circulation was on its way back to some reasonable semblance of normality.

Five minutes later his two crew members were also unfettered.

Understandably bewildered, they joined the flight engineer on the flight deck. Minutes later they carefully disengaged the auto-navigational system and took manual control of the aircraft as per the typed instructions left on the pilot's seat.

Atlas 923 then took up a direct heading for Caracas as the note further instructed. Only then did the pilot make a hasty tour of his aircraft. All the while he marveled at the incredible installations left by the terrorists in the lounge and on the flight deck.

CHAPTER TWENTY-TWO

11 April

6:30 to 8:00 PM

The relative quiet of the jungle evening was rudely interrupted by a boisterous mechanical bird as it whined swiftly overhead. Had anyone been there to look up into the darkening sky, he would have seen three tiny, seemingly insignificant dots drop away from the airliner. He also would have seen a dark, rectangular patch of material mushroom above each within seconds. But, as suited Larson's intricate planning, no one was there to watch and the three intruders descended unobserved towards the jungle clearing.

Larson worked hard to guide his chute away from the dense jungle toward which he seemed to drift inexorably. His lines became entangled and lack of experience further hampered his efforts. Off to his right his two companions alighted near the edge of the grassy savanna for which he was desperately aiming. The parachute's rapid descent jerked to an abrupt stop, fouled in a large tree at the jungle's edge. He was left helplessly suspended nearly twenty feet off the ground.

Like a giant pendulum, he swung from side to side in a broad arc. Unclipping his flashlight from his belt, he aimed its powerful beam towards the others. Within seconds Malin dropped the chute he was gathering and came running.

He laughed heartily when he saw Larson's predicament. "Imagine blowing the whole deal by snagging a tree! Pretty sloppy," he chided. "Suppose you'll want us to cut you down."

"The thought had crossed my mind."

"Be back in a flash." Malin turned and dashed away to help Higgins with the rest of the gear and chutes. Ten minutes later they had Larson safely on the ground and his chute cut down from the offending branch.

"Well, by God, we made it!" Higgins said rather jubilantly.

"Looks that way," Larson agreed. "Still, we've got a long ways to go. He looked out across the short expanse of grassy savanna where they had touched down. Besides the handful of scrub trees dotting the narrow slit in the jungle, it had successfully fended off the encroachment of the dense forest that hemmed it in. It existed in defiance of the jungle, a stark contrast to its environs.

Voice somewhat somber, Larson said, "Wrong savanna. With all the trees dotting this place we could never get picked up here."

Malin thoughtfully bit his lip. "I was afraid of that. When I tumbled out of the plane I was momentarily disoriented. Given the short drop this seemed the best target."

"I'm not criticizing . . . "

"Too late to adjust for it during the drop, but I noted that the larger section of grassland we were shooting for is about a couple of hundred yards from the western perimeter of this little oasis." He pointed at the wall of trees. "Just over yonder."

"I saw it too." In the fading light he scanned the slit of savanna where they stood. "I can't see David chancing a landing in this place. Too many blasted trees. We'll have to make for the other bit of savanna and fast."

"I was kind of afraid you'd say something like that." Higgins sounded suddenly sullen.

Larson ignored him. "We've a good while until the pick-up, so we should be able to cover the ground easily with time to spare, but let's not stand here flapping our jaws and wasting minutes just the same. First off let's get the chutes buried. It'll be pitch dark soon. I don't want to be wandering about out here in the black of night any longer than absolutely necessary. Never know who or what one might run into."

"Cheerful thought," grumbled Higgins, his spirits waning still further. Despite his visits to Central and South American countries in connection with drug smuggling operations, he never liked being in the tropics, especially not in the bush.

It would indeed soon be completely dark. Night came quickly in the tropics. Gloomy shadows of the impending night already engulfed just about all of the savanna. High overhead a multitude of stars, far more than any person living in civilization could ever hope to see, twinkled to life in the darkening sky.

Higgins and Larson dug a hole large enough to bury the parachutes and their harnesses. The lot was soon covered by a layer of dirt and clumps of vegetation.

Finished with the folding Army surplus shovels, the men heaved them into the tangled vegetation of the jungle. As if in protest, a shrill screech sounded from somewhere within the dark, forbidding forest. A second unearthly screech soon followed. The deepening gloom of night coupled with the loud cries of unseen birds served to heighten apprehensions all around.

Cutting a trail through dense rain forest, even in daytime, is a tiring and unpleasant enough task in the semi-darkness prevalent near the forest floor. In the pitch darkness of night it could be positively unnerving.

Gathering their remaining equipment and weapons the little party walked the short distance to the western perimeter. Every now and then, the quiet was broken by some unseen creature's cry. On several occasions the powerful beam of Larson's flashlight fell on the reflecting eyes of some otherwise unobserved creature. It was unsettling to know that potentially dangerous creatures lurked in the shadows of the bush observing their every move.

Reaching the westernmost portion of the little clearing Larson consulted his watch nervously. He preferred not to think of the consequences of missing their rendezvous. Safe escape from the continent rode on being at the appointed place at the appointed time. One slight consolation was that the pick-up was scheduled to come a relatively long while after their parachute drop to lessen chances that anyone would connect the helicopter's presence with that of the passing jet. On the surface, this might have seemed an extravagant precaution, but in reality the rain forest sported many human eyes and the human tongues to which they were connected wagged freely. News and rumors spread with remarkable alacrity for such a "primitive" place.

He glanced round as though to get his bearings. At length, he said, "If I'm not mistaken, the pick-up site is just beyond this patch of woods." The gleaming blade of his raised machete waved expansively at the tangled wall of vegetation. "Time to put our jungle survival skills to work."

"Thrilling," Higgins replied dryly. He fervently hated the jungle. A comfortable suburban dwelling somewhere in the southwestern United States was far more to his liking.

A metallic singing sounded as the others pulled out their own machetes from their scabbards. Well-oiled blades glinted in the lights. Without further preamble Larson attacked the dark, menacing wall before them. Each blow sliced into the interwoven web of vegetation with a savagery not usually akin to Larson. It troubled him that they had missed their intended drop site. It was a careless error. One that could mean failure. Unlike Higgins, he bore no animosity towards the jungle, but it had to be crossed and quickly, a fact that led to his attacking it with a vengeance. The physical exertion allowed him to vent some frustration. Each blow became a blow against himself, for he invariably blamed himself for any miscalculation in his intricate plans.

Every swing of the sharp blades began with a gentle whoosh and ended abruptly with a loud chop as the razor sharp edges slammed home into the tangled mass of vines and brush. Sometimes the blow would slice clean through the impeding vegetation. Other times several blows might be required to sever the growth. The air was heavy with moisture; rich with a myriad of scents. Yet it was not the dank steaming jungle of Hollywood celluloid. In fact, the temperature was perceptively dropping now that the sun had set. They were only a few degrees from the equator which seemed to dictate higher temperatures, but the altitude on the escarpment blessed it with surprisingly moderate temperatures not common in that latitude.

Progress through the labyrinth of lianas, trees, and underbrush was vexingly slow. The path chosen was as straight as the jungle would permit, which is to say it was not very straight at all. Standing and fallen trees frequently blocked the way. As if the trees themselves were not enough immovable obstacles, there were also the buttress-like roots sported by some. Thick entwined vines stretched up into the canopy of the jungle growth in the constant search for light, a scarce commodity on the forest floor on even the brightest of days.

Tentacle-like claws of the over exuberant plant world tore at their clothes, resisting every exhausting step of the intruders. Given the circumstances and their fatigue after the long eventful day, all nature seemed to conspire against them.

After what seemed like hours in a living hell, but in fact was less than thirty minutes, a weary Larson finally heard what he had been straining to hear from the moment he had plunged into the jungle - the sound of running water. A few more swipes with the machete and he was able to see the stream. Only fifteen to twenty feet wide, it didn't appear to be very deep. His light sparkled on the surface and threw dancing reflections upon the jungle on the opposite bank. The forest provided an arched roof overhead making the stream appear to be in a haunting subterranean passage.

The others were still a pace or two behind when Larson stepped gingerly into the water. It felt refreshingly cool as it filtered into his boots. He waded across the shallow stream that reached his thighs at its deepest point. On the far bank he attacked the equally dense jungle growth with renewed vigor. Behind him Malin splashed across the stream.

Larson turned to the mercenary when he had climbed up the tangled embankment. An unusual grimness set Larson's face. "Remember our discussion in the lounge?"

Malin nodded solemnly as both heard Higgins plunge into the cool waters of the stream.

"Do it now," Larson said simply. Not a flicker of emotion showed as he condemned Higgins to death.

The mercenary turned. He unslung his rifle and pointed it almost casually at Higgins. The stunned pilot stopped in midstream.

"What the . . ." He stammered hoarsely. His flashlight dropped from his hand, splashing into the stream. The bobbing light swayed about as it floated off and round a bend in the stream. Higgins fumbled for his rifle, aimed, and squeezed the trigger in a frenzy. Nothing happened besides a dull 'click' as the weapon sought to discharge a nonexistent bullet.

"Empty, pal. The cartridges are in my pocket." He patted his jacket as though to confirm it. "The pistol's got nothing in it either."

Higgins drew and pulled the trigger several times. The hollow clicks of the hammer seemed unnaturally loud. He flung it contemptuously into the stream. The rifle almost followed, but he thought better of it and kept it loosely clutched in one hand. "I've done my part! We had an agreement!"

"True," Larson conceded as he stepped up behind Malin. "Trouble is, someone sold out. I know it wasn't me. Kristine surely wouldn't have. Aside from the fact that she is my wife, there is the trifling fact that she helped formulate the original plans. Keith, here, didn't, because if he had, then *every* single explosive charge would have been compromised, as opposed to just *most* of them. The flight engineer couldn't have betrayed us because he didn't know a damned thing of any consequence. He didn't even know what day we were going to move on until less than 30 minutes before the flight when Malin passed him his gas canister and mask. Price laid down his life defending us, so that clears him of suspicion. That leaves just you, Harry. No one else could have known the disclosed locales or my name. Not even van Troje knows my name. But you do or rather, ***did***."

"Jesus Christ! What the hell for? I want my share of the money too! I didn't squeal to anyone! Hell, look at my rep! You think an ass who can't be trusted gets to run big shipments of drugs, millions of dollars' worth! Wise up!"

"Strange things happen every day. Maybe the law caught on to you for one of your past exploits and this became a way to buy your freedom. I don't know, and frankly, I don't care." Larson sounded bone tired.

"You know," Malin said suddenly, "he might have blown our LZ and escape route too."

Larson licked his lips nervously. "The thought had crossed my mind. If he did, at least we'll have the satisfaction of knowing that he didn't live to profit by his treachery. Come on, let's get . . ."

In desperation, Higgins flung his rifle at Malin and dove into the stream. A swirl of bubbles that moved swiftly away with the swift current marked his entry point.

Malin deftly parried the rifle. It clattered against a rock on the bank and slid into the dark waters. All else was silent, except for the gentle rush of water.

Two beams of light played across the water, one upstream and one downstream. The dancing images and eerie shadows thrown revealed nothing. "Blast it all," Larson said as he drew his pistol. "Why didn't you shoot?"

The patience of the skilled hunter filled Malin. He set his rifle carefully against the trunk of a tree. His duffel bag and pistol landed beside it. A finger touched his lips. "Douse the torch. He'll surface any moment now."

Somewhat bewildered, Larson obeyed. The darkness became complete. He heard Malin wade into the stream and then silence reigned. More seconds passed. The faint sound of disturbed water came from a short distance upstream. Silence settled in again. Larson licked his lips nervously again as he strained to hear the slightest sound. The urge to switch on his flashlight was stifled.

Near midstream, Malin had heard the faint movement too. He turned and moved silently upstream, senses acutely tuned. The haft of the hunting knife rested easily in his right hand. Some thirty paces later he heard a swish in the water about fifteen or twenty feet ahead and slightly to his left. The watercourse was thigh deep as he adjusted his course and moved stealthily toward the source of this new disturbance. By then his eyes had fully adjusted to the darkness. Through the rare breaks in the foliage above, stars could be seen.

He slowed his pace; stopped, listened. Malin held his breath and stood in perfect silence. The musky scent of the jungle filled his nostrils. The cool water swirled round his thighs. Ever so slowly he turned until he judged that he faced the bank. He listened for a few seconds more. In slow motion he fished a bullet from his pocket. With his left hand he flicked it the six feet he reasoned remained between himself and the near bank. The shell rustled some leaves and plunked into the water. Something just right of it moved suddenly.

Without hesitation Malin flung his knife at the sound. Before he even heard the primal scream, his machete came singing out of its leather scabbard. He lunged forward, the long bladed bush knife swinging. The blade hacked aside Higgins' machete that had been raised reflexively. Higgins' weapon disappeared in the murky water. Malin took several steps back from the gasping pilot. He unclipped his flashlight and switched it on.

Higgins threw up an arm to shield his eyes. Blood soaked his stomach and dripped slowly into the water. The haft of Malin's knife protruded from his gut, just below the rib cage. The pilot drew his own hunting knife and staggered forward. He stumbled, slipping to his knees. Hatred surged in his eyes as he fought to get back to his feet only to slip again, this time tumbling headlong into the water. Another primeval scream left his lips as his head bobbed to the surface. The water round him seemed to erupt in a furious boil.

A slightly stunned Malin hurriedly scrambled up the far bank. Steadied against an enormous buttress-like root, he again found the hapless pilot with the beam of his light. Within seconds the screaming ceased and Higgins disappeared forever beneath the dark waters. The frenzied turbulence where he had been continued for several minutes as the voracious piranha finished their evening meal.

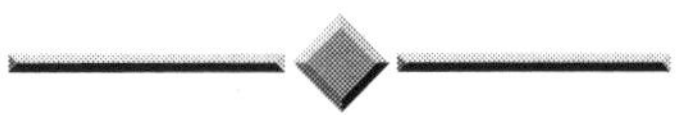

"By now the little buggers'll have picked the bones clean. No one, besides you and I, will ever know what really happened." Malin clipped the duffel bag back on his utility belt and retrieved his weapons. "Neat way to dispose of a corpse, eh?"

"You should just have shot him right off." Larson sounded sour. His stomach churned at the thought of the horrendous death Higgins had endured. It made his skin crawl to think that he had blithely waded through those same waters only minutes before.

"No. If he did sell us out completely, then a shot here and now would draw attention. A knife is quieter."

"He screamed like a bloody banshee!" Snapped Larson.

"Rifle shots still carry better and further."

Larson shined his light upstream. Occasional movement still marked the spot where Higgins had fallen. "Ravenous little bastards."

"I've heard they can strip a full-grown cow to the bone in about five minutes."

This comment drew a strange look. "Let's get the hell out of here!" Larson pulled out his machete and advanced on the tangled vegetation.

His hacking seemed to embody a new sense of urgency, or perhaps it was bona fide fear.

The two men took turns at breaking trail as they moved through the blackness of the jungle night. Only the slowly dwindling beams of the flashlights provided an inkling of a sense of security and that was only a false illusion. It seemed they would be forever hacking and chopping in the hostile nightmarish world. To someone given over to panic or unreasonable fear, it would have been a nerve racking and utterly terrifying trek. For Malin it was merely a nuisance; for Larson something between the two.

By chance, Larson led when the last vestiges of jungle fell away to reveal a large grassy expanse of savanna. More stars than he could remember seemed to fill the clear, unsullied, night sky. He was understandably extremely relieved as he pulled away from the last clinging branches and stepped clear of the jungle growth. The starlit plain stretched off for hundreds of yards before being swallowed by the black shadows of the dense forest. To the south the wall of jungle curved round towards the opposite boundary of the grassy oasis. To the north lay a couple of grass covered rises. It was towards these that he set off.

"How long do you figure we'll have to wait, Erik?"

"Roughly half an hour, maybe a little less." He took another step and froze in his tracks. The rattlesnake's distinctive warning demanded immediate compliance.

Swinging the light slightly to the left of his intended path he soon saw the coiled serpent. The slit-like eyes met his coldly from a head cocked back to strike. Larson found himself remarkably calm. "Can you get him, Keith? If I so much as twitch I'm afraid he'll strike."

Malin stepped carefully to one side, machete raised. Just as the snake's head reared back further preparatory to strike, he swung. The razor-sharp blade swished through the air and lopped off the serpent's head. His blow sent the steel cleanly through the snake, leaving two convulsively jerking parts.

A shaking hand wiped a bead of perspiration from his brow as

Larson lowered his light. "That's one I owe you, my friend. Thanks." It was not the first time that the generally soft spoken mercenary had saved his life, nor was it likely to be the last given the way things were going. Whatever the circumstances, Malin repeatedly proved himself a good man to have around.

The two moved on, though more cautiously than before. Atop the first of the small rises they used their machetes to mow down a small patch of the tall grasses. The little clearing would give them a somewhat safe haven in which to rest and wait. Two extremely fatigued men plunked down in darkness as they extinguished their flashlights.

"You know," said Larson, "this place could quickly drive one crazy. Thank God we don't live here."

"Oh, it's not all that bad. Actually it's quite beautiful. Just takes a little getting used to."

"Just a little," came the sarcastic response. Larson smashed a mosquito on his neck. "Between the blasted snakes and damnable insects this place is like a living nightmare."

"I never claimed that it was the most comfortable or safest place on the face of the Earth. Funny thing is, that rattler shouldn't have been out and about at this hour. Probably had a bellyful and was slow getting in for the night. Besides we're lucky that wasn't a bushmaster you happened across back there. If it had been, rest assured that at least one of us would be dead. Compared to them, rattlers are downright friendly, sociable creatures. Bushmasters mark out a territory. Anything that ventures into that territory is fair game and likely to die. They're outfitted with long fangs and inject large amounts of venom when they strike." Malin looked up at the spectacular night sky. "Good night for mayhem."

"Such a cheerful thought. Think there are any of these bushmasters close by?" Apprehension marked Larson's question.

"If there are, we'll know soon enough. Wilson told me that the natives call it the shadow snake because a man seldom walks the length of his shadow before dying when bitten."

“Are you vying for an award as an authority on the blasted snakes of the region?” Obviously Larson was not developing any newfound love for jungle living.

“Just trying to convince you that things could be much, much worse.” He smiled wryly. “Besides, I always try to learn as much as I can ‘bout a place when I’m going to be working there. Of course, past experience with the bush helps, but this place, like any other, is unique in special ways. Helps to know what natural enemies and dangers one might stumble upon. Stuff like snakes, for instance.” Realizing that his friend no longer listened to his banter, he too fell silent with a sullen, drawn out sigh.

Habitually, Larson’s mind sifted through the day’s events searching for flaws or errors that might aid the authorities in locating them. Aside from the baffling exposure of his identity and the location of some of the explosives, he found no appreciable problems. His thoughts drifted off. Vivid images of what might lay ahead materialized. As usual, every possible angle became fair game for speculation and the foundation for creation of probable scenarios. Always the perfectionist, he contemplated each detail surreptitiously. This trait had proved invaluable in the past. Now, in the midst of his most ambitious endeavor, it was doubly so.

CHAPTER TWENTY-THREE

11 April

8:00 to 10:00 PM

Daydreams of how to spend his share of the money in years to come consumed Malin's thoughts as he reclined on the new mown grass. Some new firearms for his collection, a classic sports car, perhaps he would even consider purchasing a parcel of land and put down some real roots. Maybe out in Wyoming or Montana. Maybe his old buddies were right; a man needed to establish roots somewhere during his life. He rolled his shoulders. They ached. He hated to admit it, but age was taking its toll. This should be his last outing, his last mission, yet something inside him had a hard time accepting that thought.

Larson simply wanted to put the whole operation behind him. Undoubtedly, years from now he would look back on the hardships and dangers with that fond nostalgia to which humans are prone. For now, he longed simply to be back in an American suburb lounging by a large built-in pool, a tall cool drink in his hand, with Kristine by his side and not a care in the world to bother them. But then, that could never be now that his name ranked high on the Most Wanted list of law enforcement agencies. How did they know? Where had he blundered? Had it indeed been Higgins? Somehow it had to have been Higgins. How else could the unexplainable be explained? Mental anguish wracked his brain as he wrestled with the quandary.

Their reverie broke as a faint hacking sound became discernible in the distance. It grew steadily in intensity. There could be no mistaking the racket made by approaching helicopter. Off to the south a bright white light flanked by smaller red and green ones, moved swiftly in their general direction. The intense searchlight illuminated a broad swath of the savanna as the helicopter drew nearer.

"Right on schedule." Malin, already on his feet, yanked his flashlight from its clip and switched it on.

"I've never known David to be late for an appointment, especially where money was involved." Larson clicked on his own light. Gathering their gear, the two men moved away from the center of the rise while aiming their twin beams of light at the spot where they had been relaxing.

The instant their lights switched on, the helicopter headed straight for them. It spun around once overhead while the pilot made certain that it was a safe spot to land. The two weary men shielded their eyes against the spray of dust and grit kicked up by the rotors as the flying machine settled gently to the ground. Once the helicopter came to rest, the side door popped opened and a silver-haired gentleman gestured from the doorway for them to board. They anxiously obliged, hurrying over to the aircraft and climbing into its relatively comfortable interior.

The door closed and, the cabin isolating against some of the din of the rotors, they were able to hear themselves think again.

"Good to see you chaps made it. 'Ave you got the diamonds?" The silver-haired gentleman spoke congenially. The accent was unmistakably British which was perhaps not so surprising given the fact that Guyana was a former British colony.

"How on earth could you think that we'd fail to deliver? Worse yet, the gems seem to mean more to you than our own well-being." Malin feigned disappointment.

"Infinitely more!" The silver-haired gentleman who looked to be about seventy-five, grinned broadly showing a mouthful of yellowed teeth. "Of course, I know that you wouldn't 'ave let me down. To do so would mean letting yourselves down, eh? I take it the diamonds are in the duffel bag."

"Every last one. It took a bit more convincing than I'd have liked, but as you can see, they finally relented. They never really had much choice," Larson said. There seemed no sense in talking about the inexplicable knowledge the authorities in New York had had.

"Good show, Erik." He looked his passengers over with a cursory glance. "It would seem that you're two men short."

"Like Erik said, it took more convincing than we'd hoped for. Heavy casualties," explained Malin.

"Well at least the two of you seem no worse for the wear."

"We managed fine until we landed in this blasted jungle," an intentionally surly Larson stated flatly. "This is where the danger is. First we miss the drop site and have to slog our way through a few hundred yards of rain forest. Then Higgins slips and gets slaughtered by piranha. Finally I nearly make the acquaintance of an insomniac rattlesnake."

"Always does take newcomers a while to adjust to life here." Wilson grinned again. No doubt he relished the idea of having fewer partners with which to divide the spoils of the enterprise.

"I don't want to seem impolite by breaking up our little reunion, but I think that we'd better get underway. The sooner we're off the continent, the sooner I'll be able to relax."

"Of course, of course. Business as usual." Wilson turned in his seat and taking the controls lifted the Jet Ranger into the starry, cloudless sky.

Once airborne, he flew over the nearby Echilebar River. The helicopter steadied above its murky dark waters. The side door opened and everything that Larson and Malin had brought with them, except the case with the gemstones, was jettisoned, consigned to the river bottom.

Arms and equipment safely deposited in the Echilebar, they set off on the relatively short flight to Wilson's main camp. Within minutes the lights by the airstrip and the mining encampment twinkled in the distance.

Drawing closer it was possible to distinguish a row of small buildings lining one side of the dirt airstrip. On the opposite side a small hill rose about a hundred fifty feet above the surrounding plain. Atop the hill stood a larger structure, obviously a headquarters of some sort. Besides it stood a wooden tower crowned with the fifty-five gallon drums of water that supplied the building. At the base of the hill were three more buildings and a circular patch of ground surrounded by tiny lights aimed at its center. It was the heliport on which they landed seconds later in a voluminous cloud of dust.

The word camp, Larson mused as they settled to the ground, was being grossly misused by Wilson. His mining establishment, although isolated in the bush, was far more reminiscent of a small town than a camp.

The Jet Ranger's rotors still revolved slowly as the three men piled out. Stooped over for safety, they hurried away from the helicopter and across the short distance to the nearest of two twin-engined aircraft parked there. Their arrival had been expected, the plane's door was already open, the lower half providing steps. A giant of a man stood silhouetted in front of the steps. He said nothing as Larson and the others scrambled into the Cessna 441 Conquest, an aircraft whose name seemed oddly appropriate to Malin as he stooped over and climbed aboard.

Wilson, the owner of the Guyana highlands mining operation, dropped the briefcase on the rear seat in the slender cabin. With the others looking on, he slowly, almost reverently, opened the case. He took a pouch, opened the drawstrings and poured a few of the uncut stones into the palm of his hand. In the relatively faint light available, he ogled the rough stones, occasionally turning one over with a finger. At length he said, "Excellent, excellent! I trust the rest are all here?"

Larson watched Wilson's reaction carefully and was relieved to see that the aging miner did not examine the merchandise more closely. Had he done so, he soon would have recognized the stones as the fakes that they were. Despite his numerous social and technical deficiencies, David Wilson could not by any standard be called an amateur where diamonds were concerned. The man had devoted all of his adult life to the oft risky pursuit of the most precious and elusive of all gemstones.

Wilson was, of necessity, a knowledgeable expert in the field. It was said that he could estimate the weight, in carats, of a rough stone just by visual examination with such incredible accuracy that he practically did not require the standard scales of the diamond trade. Such a man would not easily be deceived, but given the superb quality of the phony diamonds, the poor lighting, the limited time, and the high improbability of substitutions, his failure to detect the fraud was perhaps understandable. So too was Larson's relief when the miner pronounced that he was pleased with the fruits of all the months of labor.

"They're all there, David. Now, if you've no further objections, I think we'd better be on our way."

"Of course, of course, got to stick with the s'hedule." He replaced the stones in the pouch, completely satisfied that they were the genuine ransom diamonds. "And here you go, my boy." He pulled a bulging envelope from his pocket. "The first of many, I trust."

Taking the envelope Larson opened it and fanned out the bills. There were twenty-five thousand dollars in well-used U.S. currency. He smiled and replaced the money. "Let's hope so."

It was strange how easy it had become to lie straight-faced.

The three shook hands before Wilson climbed out of the aircraft, briefcase firmly locked in his grasp. Accompanied by the large man who had waited patiently outside the plane, he disappeared in the shadows. By the time the two men had gone from sight, the Conquest's twin engines were coming to life. Larson had no intention of hanging around any longer than absolutely necessary.

Shortly thereafter, in a cloud of dust, the aircraft lurched forward onto the dirt airstrip. As if on cue, the landing lights along both sides of the runway came on. Maintenance was sadly lacking; a number of lights were burned out. Larson taxied to the far end, turned, held the brakes on hard and eased the throttles to full take-off power before releasing the brakes.

He was slightly nervous about the take-off, not because of the poor lighting, but because a short dirt strip was hardly the best for a fast aircraft like the Conquest, and then there was the Echilebar River that lay somewhere just beyond the end of the runway. The only favorable point, as he saw it, was that they were making the take-off in the cooler evening air which would improve lift and shorten the take-off run. All in all, it was probably the most nerve-racking take-off Larson would ever make. When the seemingly impossible had been done and the plane was airborne, he was grateful for its excellent rate of climb, which more than enabled it to clear the jungle beyond the river's far bank.

Designed to accommodate up to ten passengers and a pilot, the Conquest afforded the two men more than ample space, though it could scarcely compare with the enormity nor offer many of the creature comforts of the 747 they so recently had vacated. The flight to Georgetown, the capital of Guyana and the largest city in the small country, would take nearly an hour even when pushing the Conquest to its maximum cruising speed. In spite of the apparent abundance of time they would be hard pressed to complete their next chore before their arrival.

Taking turns at the controls they made a quick change of attire, donning casual sportswear that they found in two of the four locked suitcases stowed aft. Their new garments seemed appropriate for their new role as businessmen who had been out to inspect a possible site for a joint mining venture. Carefully constructed to legitimize their presence in the area, their cover story was also designed to permit a quick unobtrusive exit from South America as part of a routine business schedule when the time was at hand, and the time was most definitely at hand. It was a cover Larson knew would quickly disintegrate under the scrutiny of any investigation such as that which would surely follow in the wake of their exploits, but it would suffice while they made good their escape.

Once off the South American continent their chances of survival would be greatly enhanced. Time would be the only major obstacle, as it had been so often during the past twenty-four hours and in the many months and days preceding. The more efficiently they used time, the greater the distance they could log before the authorities picked up on their trail. With each successive step that trail was designed to become harder to locate until, if all went according to plan, it vanished altogether, leaving a very frustrated team of investigators.

The new clothing would have been a frivolous gesture had they done no more to alter appearances. The passports tucked away in the cases contained photographic images of two similar but distinctly different men. To assume that Larson and Malin and the businessmen portrayed in the photos were one and the same required a vivid imagination. None-the-less the two men knew how to work the superficial changes and stowed in the cases were the implements requisite to the task.

By the time they made their final approach to Georgetown's airport they looked convincingly like the passports. Their damp discarded clothes, Price's and Higgins' unopened suitcases, and the mass of make-up paraphernalia had long since been jettisoned over the jungle. No trace of the transformations remained.

CHAPTER TWENTY-FOUR

12 April

Predawn to 1:00 PM

Daybreak was not far off. To the east the sky had long since begun to brighten with the faint luminescence of the approaching day. As the minutes passed, the darkness far below gradually materialized into a sea. A sea that stretched off in all directions only interrupted occasionally by some pinnacle of land poking its green head above the surface. It was a spectacular sight as the sun finally made its appearance in fiery splendor. Through it all, the constant drone of the Conquest's twin engines continued as it had for most of the night. Many miles lay behind. Many more miles lay ahead.

Off in the distance, an island much larger than any of its neighbors, protruded from the sea. The island was Puerto Rico, the next stop on the twisted path Larson and his colleague had selected for their escape.

The night had been long and fatiguing, but all had gone smoothly, everything had followed their taut schedule. The customs check in Guyana went smoothly with the aid of a rather lax inspector. Maybe he was ill suited for his occupation, but Larson thought it more likely that the man was weary and anxious to call it a day. Their arrival had been timed to be among the inspector's last before his shift ended for just that reason. The stopover took little more than an hour. During that time they passed the hasty customs inspection, had the plane's tanks topped off, and filed a flight plan for San Juan, Puerto Rico.

The original plan called for Larson and Higgins to take shifts at the controls. Circumstances dictated otherwise. Malin was not a pilot. Until Larson had let him take the controls and monitor the instruments on the leg of the flight from Wilson's camp to Georgetown, he had never even sat in a pilot's seat. The flight to San Juan could be made without switching pilots, but when the pilot had already gone twenty-four hours without sleep, that didn't seem prudent. Larson explained the rudimentary details to Malin, who not surprisingly proved a quick study. Aided by the autopilot he mainly had to monitor the gauges and verify that they were on course.

Thus, since leaving Georgetown, they had alternately flown and slept. Though the Conquest lacked beds, their extreme fatigue and the lulling drone of the engine made it easy to doze off.

The sun rose in all its fiery splendor while Larson pulled a stint at the controls. He yawned wearily. The serenity of the vista surrounding him seemed soothing. The magnificent beauty was inexplicable, myriad shapes and colors. The dawn of a perfect day, he assured himself. He longed for Kristine. He wanted her to share the moment. It was at such times he realized just how much he had come to love her in their years together. She was an integral part of his life, a part he trusted and relied on and never, never wanted to lose.

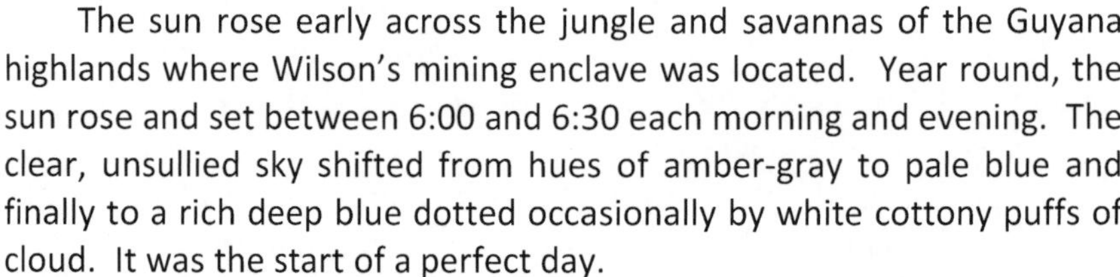

The sun rose early across the jungle and savannas of the Guyana highlands where Wilson's mining enclave was located. Year round, the sun rose and set between 6:00 and 6:30 each morning and evening. The clear, unsullied sky shifted from hues of amber-gray to pale blue and finally to a rich deep blue dotted occasionally by white cottony puffs of cloud. It was the start of a perfect day.

Wilson rose at daybreak with little thought of the natural beauty surrounding him. A single thought occupied his mind. The same one that had possessed him since the remnants of Larson's team had left the briefcase with him the previous night - the diamonds. His examination of the gems in the plane had been cursory at best because he knew that Larson had already scrutinized a random sampling before accepting them in New York. Wilson respected his judgment, having personally spent many lengthy hours schooling him in the subtleties of recognizing quality gemstones. His own cursory inspection had been a mere formality the night before. Now it would be an exercise in pleasure.

Together with Peter Shurcliff, his six foot ten aide, Wilson settled at a cleared table in the north facing living room. The contents of one pouch, then another and another were scrutinized in a proper light for the first time. At first the two men proceeded at a leisurely pace, but with each passing second the pace quickened until it became a frenetic scramble.

They stared painfully at one another. Wilson's mounting rage was echoed in the younger man's face. "They're fakes! They're bloody awful fakes! The stupid bastards accepted paste!" He shouted vehemently. "The blasted coppers duped 'em!" His fist hammered the table, then swept the worthless glass away, scattering it across the room.

CHAPTER TWENTY-FIVE

12 April

1:00 to 6:30 PM

Lost in thought, Schmitt pensively gazed through a window in the Lockheed C-130 Hercules. The canvas jump seat on which he sat was anything but comfortable. Far below, the mottled green carpet of the jungle swept by. It reminded him of man's insignificance in the primitive world of the rain forest. Although he was unable to see any movement in the tangled mass of trees, vines, bushes, and tall grasses, he knew that the forest teemed with life, some deadly and hostile, some beautiful and alluring, and some docile and quite harmless. It was a world of stark contrasts. Beauty and death walked hand in hand through its twisting labyrinths.

It was Schmitt's first visit to the South American continent. Until his arrival aboard the Concorde the preceding day, he had never come closer to its forbidding jungles than the average armchair explorer. Like many, he had watched some television documentaries about the rain forest and its inhabitants with interest, but that was the extent of his knowledge. The vista currently afforded him somehow didn't conform with any of the programs he had seen. It seemed somehow vastly more magnificent, much more impressive. It would take a great deal of courage to parachute into that menacing world as dusk plunged it into darkness. The lengths to which some men were driven by greed never failed to intrigue him.

Randall's scathing remarks concerning Schmitt's own apparent greed, had been blithely ignored as the shrewd European negotiated an agreeable fee for the information locked away in his superb memory. When the airliner turned up minus the terrorists over northern Brazil, Schmitt's earlier supposition as to their ultimate destination was confirmed. It had to be the diamond-mining outpost that van Troje had repeatedly contacted after Larson's initial visit to Amsterdam. Tucked away in the remote jungles of the Guyana highlands near the Brazilian border, it offered a haven for the fleeing terrorist band. Schmitt reasoned further that it might offer a conduit for the ransomed gems to reenter the diamond trade as legitimate shipments of newly mined diamonds. The real trick would be to irrefutably prove van Troje's connection and nab him as well. The obese Dutchman was, after all, the original target of Schmitt's probe.

The plane shuddered briefly as an air pocket buffeted it. None of the passengers seemed to mind being jostled, or maybe they just didn't notice because their thoughts were focused on the near future. Schmitt shared the roomy cabin with thirty of the most taciturn traveling companions he had ever known. Besides Colonel Cooke, twenty-four of his men and Randall, there were two Venezuelan air crewmen and two Guyanese police officials picked up a short time earlier at the small border town of Lethem, Guyana. The Guyanese government insisted on their inclusion when it grudgingly agreed to allow the strike force to act within its borders. Guyana's long-standing territorial dispute with Venezuela as to exactly where their common border lay, prompted an initial reluctance to cooperate by allowing a Venezuelan military transport to bring in a British strike force. Promises of future economic aid by the U.S. government soon squelched the problem.

The operation was designed to make maximum use of the element of surprise. And yet, until Schmitt's supposition was confirmed, forceful moves against those at the mining compound could not be taken. It made for a potentially sticky situation, but Cooke tackled it unflinchingly with supreme confidence in his plan and his men.

Aboard the Concorde the previous day, Schmitt had learned that standard SAS practice dictates that its members are trained to act with what in more conventional military circles is oft viewed as an unprecedented freedom of action and independence. SAS troops generally function in tightly knit four-man teams whose members become extremely competent as a unit and develop an unusually high degree of camaraderie. Each man knows exactly what he can expect from his mates and they from him.

The Spartan interior of the military transport aircraft offered no amenities for its passengers. Narrow canvas seats stretched over gray metal frames lined gray cabin walls. For the taut young men of the SAS it was just another transport like many others in which they had passed many weary hours. With typical aplomb they sat quietly on the back-less seats and made the best of it. They were a hardy lot; alert, powerful, and possessing great stamina.

The plane banked sharply, leveled out, banked again and started its final descent. Off to the side Schmitt noticed several stretches of grassy savannas, the only breaks in the dense jungle. It was into the largest of these that the Hercules now headed. The hard packed dirt of the airstrip made for a rough touchdown as the pilot made a fast landing. A swirling cloud of dust rose in the big plane's wake as it barreled down the short airstrip. The dust cloud obscured the entire aircraft as it executed a tight turn at the far end of the runway, the end near the river. Twelve SAS commandos were through the open rear cargo door and into the tall grass beyond the runway by the time the plane completed the turn and began to taxi back towards the scattering of buildings near the midpoint of the airstrip. The cargo door swung shut before the swirling dust hiding the aircraft cleared enough for anyone to see the aircraft clearly.

A small, twin-engine aircraft was parked off to the side near a blue and white Jet Ranger helicopter. The Venezuelan C-130 pulled off the runway and parked near them. Before the plane even halted, the remainder of Colonel Cooke's men were on the ground. They formed a neat line, weapons at the ready.

Several men from the camp, all wearing side arms and carrying rifles or shotguns, warily approached the military aircraft. The menacing group of grizzled men fanned out and stopped a short distance away, their motley assortment of weapons leveled at the intruders. Their clothes were soiled. Bearded or stubble covered faces were etched with deep lines. Leathery skin, the price of lives spent toiling outdoors, covered their swarthy features. All were either Latino or black.

A veritable giant of a man joined them. He towered over the men who composed his motley fighting force. Broad, powerful shoulders sported long, sinewed and heavily veined arms whose raw force rippled through the muscles with each movement. The clean shaven European face was as deeply tanned as the arms. The rugged features might have been hewn from granite. An aquiline nose separated pale blue eyes. Shortly cropped light brown hair poked out beneath the sweat darkened Stetson atop his head. His khaki shirt and pants were also dampened by perspiration, as were the filthy garments of his ragtag force. Clearly the giant directed while they toiled.

He was the only man not to have a weapon drawn and pointed at the intruders, although one massive hand rested gently on the butt of a holstered .38, dwarfing the pistol. One had to wonder whether his fingers could fit inside the trigger guard. The expression on his face said that it could and like the gunfighters of yore, he knew how to use the pistol. The deep booming voice was no less imposing than the man himself. It was authoritative, with a decidedly British accent. "I trust you've a good reason for this sudden intrusion."

Neither of the Guyanese police officials made any move to speak as though the action might trigger gunplay. Randall stepped forward. "We do," he replied stoically. He was acutely aware that a single blast from any of the shotguns aimed casually at him could slice him neatly in two. "Name's Randall. I'm with the American FBI. We're here under the authority of the Guyanese government," he gestured towards the police officials from Lethem, "to investigate an airline hijacking that took place yesterday."

The big man swatted away a noisome fly. His roughhewn features remained immobile. Only his blue eyes registered any change at all. They seemed to lose some of their harshness, as did his voice. "Hijacking? Ah yes, there was some mention of it when the supply plane arrived earlier. One of the largest ransoms ever paid according to Ned, the pilot, but then he tends to exaggerate things a mite. But what's it got to do with us then?" His tone became almost cordial and his rock steady right hand slid away from the sidearm after snapping the holster cover shut. He motioned for his men to lower their weapons.

Schmitt brazenly pushed past the two reticent Guyanese policemen and introduced himself. Then he said, "We believe the terrorists bailed out in this general vicinity. Now, if you'd be so good as to take us to the man in charge, I'm certain that we can get all the answers we need. We're busy people with little enough time to stand about dawdling on some hot, dusty airstrip."

"Perhaps." The big man turned. He spoke rapidly in fluent Portuguese to one of his men who wore a sweaty, red bandanna wrapped around his head. The man turned and hurriedly left. Facing about, the big man smiled in a manner that reminded Schmitt of a leering crocodile. "I 'ope you'll forgive our somewhat unfriendly welcome. Alas, we've 'ad bad experiences with bandits. Your sudden unannounced appearance, naturally 'ad us somewhat worried. The Venezuelan markings on the plane also baffled us a bit." He extended his hand. "Peter Shurcliff, Mr. Wilson's assistant. Mr. Wilson owns the mining operation 'ere and 'olds the lease on the property. Everything for about five miles in every direction; almost one 'undred and five square miles in all."

Schmitt strove to look duly impressed. He hastily introduced his party. Shurcliff led them to a path near some buildings at the base of the hill atop which stood the mining operation's headquarters. The Venezuelan aircrew and eight SAS men stayed with the plane. Shurcliff dispatched the remainder of his men, then he and the party of strangers hiked up the slope to the headquarters building.

The buildings by the airstrip were all constructed of grayish-brown adobe bricks with high, steeply pitched roofs made of palm fronds. The steepness of the angle ensured proper runoff during the torrential downpours of the rainy season. The buildings had been constructed by local Indians hired for the task at obscenely low wages. Many of the structures were old, but remained in reasonably good shape. One of the oldest sported a new roof, the fronds for which had been cut during the new moon a couple of months earlier before being laid out to dry in the sun and then woven into the roof. The natives long since had learned the trick of cutting leaves for roofs during the new moon because at that time of each month there are fewer insect larvae present that will subsequently ruin the roof. Such a roof, if properly thatched and pitched can endure upwards of twenty years as opposed to only about five years if cut at other times.

Although also built of adobe, the headquarters building was unquestionably the most impressive structure. It was the largest building and unlike the rest, sported a red tile roof. Many wide windows afforded spectacular views across the surrounding savannas, swamps, and jungle. A tower constructed of long poles bolted together, rose behind it. Here, as with the wood used to build the buildings themselves, the interloping Europeans relied on the ingenious natives with their jungle skills acquired over the eons. The wood used for construction was selected by taste. Only bitter tasting wood was acceptable because termites would not attack it so long as sweeter fare was at hand. Atop the tower a raised platform hemmed in numerous red and white painted fifty-five gallon drums. Water pumped into them supplied water pressure for the headquarters building. A diesel generator in one of the adjacent sheds provided electric power. Running water and electric lights were rare commodities in the isolated areas of the jungle interior.

It was late afternoon when the party reached the big headquarters-cum-home atop the hill. The air was surprisingly cool, a pleasant reprieve from the expected tropical heat. The sun, already low on the horizon, reminded that night was near. They were greeted at the door by the Latino with the red bandanna. Colonel Cooke posted two men outside and followed the party inside. He was glad that no one seemed to have taken notice of the three teams dispatched from the Hercules as they landed.

The visitors were led into a spacious living room just off the entry. The colonel posted his last two men in the entry just outside the room. If they had indeed stepped into the lion's den, Cooke was determined to have an easy exit available.

The furnishings were simple yet adequate. Handmade Indian works adorned the adobe walls. Intricately woven shallow baskets with jaguars patterned in, hung beside a rack with what at first glance appeared to be spears. Shurcliff pointed out that they were in fact arrows. He picked up one with a barbed wooden head and handed it to Schmitt, then Randall, and finally Cooke to demonstrate how incredibly light it was. The shaft, he explained, was a hollow reed that would float in water, bringing the skewered fish up with it. The other arrows all had equally specialized purposes. One with a blunt wooden head was for hunting birds, while another with a more typical angled point was for hunting small game. The long, straight stick with a woven bowstring served as an effective bow.

Shurcliff also pointed out a long, slender blowgun hanging on the opposite wall. A small quiver of very thin, foot-long splinters of wood hung beside it. A tiny wad of cotton-like material clung near one end of each dart; a tiny notch was cut into the shaft about a half inch from the other. The notched point would be dipped in the curare poison kept in the small half gourd atop the quiver. When the dart hit the intended victim, the tip would break off inside the skin with the poison thus effectively implanted to do its deadly deed. Shurcliff finished his brief explanation of the Indian weaponry by saying that, in the right hands, it was unfathomably accurate and effective. The worst thing was that you couldn't hear where the blowgun's dart came from. It was a silent killer.

He was just suggesting that they all sit down when a fairly short man entered the room via one of the two other entrances. He had aged slightly since the photo in his dossier had been taken, but the face was unmistakably the same. Schmitt instinctively reviewed the contents of the dossier in his mind as he studied the man. The silver fringe round his balding pate and the bushy mustache made him resemble the archetypal Hollywood stereotype of a British colonial-era gentleman off to conquer new challenges in the often perilous colonies. David Wilson had, in fact, been solidly established with his mining venture long before Guyana had shucked its colonial ties with England and in so doing altered the country's name from British Guiana to simply Guyana. At the time of transition he had feared the change in government. Realizing the potential value of good relations with the new authority in Georgetown, he had acted quickly to cultivate valuable new allies within the ruling factions. His wisdom and occasional bribes paid off. The lease on his property was extended for a fifty year period and his operation was spared from nationalization in return for 50% of his net annual profit. A few greased palms in the right places enabled him to slip by for less than half of that, which pleased him immeasurably.

David Wilson was that kind of man. A slightly less than honest businessman who was not beyond stretching legal boundaries when to do so would improve his position. Born and raised in the colonial setting of Hong Kong he learned early the value of well-placed bribes. His father was a mildly successful exporter who in his dealings with the Chinese often overlooked certain rules and regulations. The young Wilson became equally skilled and worked side by side with his father until the outbreak of World War II when the family fled to Australia and in so doing lost most of its assets.

For five grueling months the young Wilson fought with the British Eighth Army in the North African campaign. A severe leg wound ended his combat days. It also left him with a slight permanent limp. At the close of the war his family tried to reassemble the pieces of their abandoned life. Wilson dutifully returned to Hong Kong, but within a few years his restlessness grew too great and he set out to seek his fortune elsewhere.

The lure of adventure and possible prosperity drew him into the remote regions of the Guyanese interior in the early 1950s. Gold and diamonds were to be had. The combination of the two precious minerals proved irresistible. A year of primitive living in the bush convinced the ambitious newcomer that the general approach of the scattered prospectors, locally referred to as porknockers, was all wrong. Most worked alone or in small groups with meager tools in search of the alluvial riches strewn throughout much of the region. Wilson opted for a more regimented, systematic approach that would draw on every available technological aid. With enthusiastic fervor, he sold several backers, Peter Shurcliff's father among them, on the viability of the venture as he envisioned it. For many years it proved an unparalleled success and was generally credited with helping to establish methods employed at the newer Venezuelan boomtown of Guanaimo. By the end of 1960 he was able to buy out all but one of his backers. The coming Guyanese independence loomed on the horizon and most were eager to bail out. Only Shurcliff's father remained as a junior partner, and that because Wilson felt that he could prove helpful during the governmental transition. The elder Shurcliff worked at Government House in Georgetown, the capital. As Wilson had calculated, he proved useful as an ally during the turbulent change of power.

By the mid-1970s Wilson finally bought out the elder Shurcliff, who was anxious to return to his native England and avoid the racial tensions prevalent in Guyana. To his dismay, his youngest son Peter decided to stay on and work with Wilson.

The rewards of Wilson's many years of toil were great. He was a self-made millionaire with most of his assets safely tucked away in a numbered Swiss bank account for that oft mentioned, but never honestly considered, day when he would sell out his diamond operations and retire. When the time came he expected to reap rich rewards from the operation's sale. The prospects for a profitable sale had waned during the past several years. Like so many diamond and gold fields of the past, the resources being painstakingly sought within his concession were dwindling. Times were bad with no indication of improvement. This at a time when even the sprightly Wilson had to admit that there were days when his age was beginning to tell, days when even he had to admit that however much he savored his lifestyle, change loomed on the horizon. If only output from the operation could improve markedly, it would allow a real killing when selling the concession. Hence Wilson, never one to quibble over minor things such as laws when it was to his advantage, eagerly leapt at the proposition laid before him by the adventurous Americans. For a man of Wilson's wealth the sum invested in the scheme was nominal, particularly so in light of the potential returns. To begin with there would be a fortune in diamonds bought for a paltry million dollars paid out over a five year period after delivery of the gems. Top that with the profitable sale of his concession being assured when investors noted the impressive gains in output. Doctored records showing the mass of diamonds as having been mined on his land would inflate the value of the concession many times over. He could sell out and start to enjoy life, making a killing on the way out. His last hurrah would be spectacular!

Then something had gone awry. The gems accepted by his seemingly inept associates and subsequently delivered to him had been well-made fakes. He believed Larson and the others had been duped by the authorities because they took absolutely nothing with them when they boarded the Cessna and headed north. To compound the bitter agony of having wasted tens of thousands of dollars bankrolling the operation for absolutely nothing, Wilson now found himself the focus of an investigation into the crime. How the authorities should have drawn a connection was as baffling to him as it had been to Larson. He was extremely angered by this cruel turn of events, yet acid feelings were contained for the time being. The intruders must be dealt with politely, he reminded himself.

Wilson's step was lively, the limp almost imperceptible as he strode into the center of the room where he struck an almost comical pose. Hands on hips, he shook his head in dismay. "Gentlemen, you're in my home!" His alert eyes focused on the two armed commandos. "A strict rule of my home here is that no one brandishes firearms. In general, no one is allowed to bring them through that door. Either the two of you will lay your weapons aside and join us or I shall have to ask the lot of you to depart."

The two SAS soldiers looked expectantly to Colonel Cooke, who nodded. They found empty chairs, carefully leaning their automatic weapons within easy reach. One point hammered in throughout their grueling training was that one's weapon was never to be beyond arm's reach. If an SAS soldier left a rifle, etc. unattended, even to take the few steps down to a stream to slake a burning thirst, ridicule was sure to follow. Harsh words and penalties such as knocking off fifty push-ups, were handed out liberally for such an infraction.

"Much better," said their host whose frown was replaced by what was clearly intended to be a sincere smile. To Schmitt's attuned eye, it was as phony as a three dollar bill and he remained on his guard.

The introductions were brief but courteous. While the social formalities were being observed, one of Wilson's men appeared with a tray of drinks. The strange, reddish colored liquid resembled some sort of cloudy red wine with a fine sediment. A rather pungent odor somehow seemed to rule out that possibility. Noting his guests' curiosity, Wilson volunteered the answer.

"Indian beer. Stuff called *cassiri*. Rather unusual flavor. Do try it. Cheers!" He raised his own glass to his lips and the others hesitantly followed suit. The Guyanese police officials refrained, broad smirks spreading across their swarthy faces.

True to Wilson's word, the *cassiri* possessed a most unusual flavor mildly reminiscent of a sour Burgundy wine. Once everyone had gotten a good taste of the *cassiri*, they found Wilson looking at them with the same bemused grin sported by the Guyanese officials. "Most whites won't even try it. Bloody shame really, I rather like it myself. Uncivilized is what most men call it."

"Just what is it?" Randall asked the question half-heartedly, afraid that the answer wouldn't agree with his sensitive stomach.

Wilson quaffed the last of his glass before replying. "Derived from the cassava root. Poisonous at first, you know, but these ingenious people extract the poison and make a kind of soup with the stuff. Then the women sit round the pot, take bits of the pulp out, chew them up and spit them back into the brew. They do this over and over until it's all fairly well broken up. The saliva is what makes *cassiri* ferment. Rather tasty result, don't you think?"

It was obvious that whatever liking any of his visitors might have begun to develop for the beverage, vanished forever in the moments it took him to relate its manufacturing process. Each set his glass down, thoroughly repulsed by the contents. Randall and one of the commandos looked positively ill, neither man quite certain how to handle the situation.

Wilson set his glass on the proffered tray of his servant. "Quite popular with the natives. So much so, that women who are particularly good cassava chewers are rewarded with short lines tattooed out from the corners of the mouth. The more lines, the better a chewer." He cleared his throat loudly. "However, I am sure that you gentlemen did not venture all the way out here just to sample the local spirits." His jovial manner faded as he leaned forward looking from Schmitt to Randall. His tone became very businesslike. "Now, what can I do for you chaps?"

"I presume that you've heard why we're here," Schmitt said.

"I fail to see just what an American hijacking has to do with me or my place of business. New York is hardly around the corner."

"Maybe nothing. That's what we're here to ascertain. A little cooperation on your part and things should run along very smoothly. I'm sure that this is a colossal waste of time and tax dollars," Randall lied. "Before you know it, we'll be on our way."

"Why here? What connection between myself and these terrorists can there possibly be?"

Schmitt watched the elderly Britisher's face closely as he replied. If there was even the slightest hint of anything reflected there, he was determined not to miss it. "The ransom paid amounted to just over ten million dollars."

"I still fail to see a connection."

"The ransom consisted entirely of uncut diamonds. You mine and cut diamonds. Add to that the fact that the airliner carrying the terrorists had to have passed with a hundred miles or so of where we now stand at about the time that they must have vacated the plane. I think you'll agree that these facts make for a tenuous, yet logical connection. Maybe not to you, but perhaps someone like you."

Wilson remained unruffled, his face unchanged. If he were involved it would be difficult to rankle him into betraying the fact. And yet, he had to be the man. Schmitt had bet everything on it.

"Yes, yes, now I see." Wilson looked down for a moment. The hint of insincerity was gone. If he was acting, then he deserved an Oscar for his performance. "Naturally I'll cooperate in every way possible. Let me assure you, gentlemen, I'm as much against terrorism and crime as you." His gaze fell upon Cooke. "And you, Colonel, from the mother country, no less. Our dear old England has seen its share of terrorism. What with the bloody IRA fanatics blowing up things for their twisted aims. Eh, Colonel? And now these Spanish bastards, the E . . .T . . . something or other. Oh, what wicked webs some men weave. No, no, can't have people running around blowing things up wantonly. And then there is the question of my honor. Like yourself, Colonel, I served Queen and country. I've the stiff leg to prove it, by God! Unless things have changed radically these past fifty years or so, honor is an integral part of the British military psyche."

"Still is."

"Ah, my dear Colonel, then you especially can understand the great insult you and your associates have made by impugning my dignity, my honor, with the assertion that I might even deign to associate with such rabble."

"Questions were raised. Answers are demanded." Cooke was in taciturn form. "I believe it was a German mercenary fighting for England in the war with the American Colonies who said it best. *'Honor is like an island with sides steep and high. Once you fall off, it is hard to get back on.'*

"As a servant of the crown, I salute you for your past service to our country. However, the record shows that the letter of the law has not always lain close to your heart. Honor is something to be earned every day, sir, not just when it suits."

Wilson reddened at the rebuke. His verbal offensive had been neatly parried. "The caliber of Her Majesty's armed forces has obviously declined drastically, when a loyal subject has to endure such insults from an officer."

"Truth and honor go hand in hand. You made your own truths." Cooke said with a shrug. "But past indiscretions do not prove quilt in the current affair. I trust you'll help us establish the truth promptly."

"Just what the devil do you want?" Cordiality was on hold.

During the exchange Schmitt had eyed Wilson speculatively. There had been no mention of the destruction wrought at JFK. Had Wilson's mention of it been a slip of the tongue or had he heard news from the supply plane?

"Relatively simple things, Mr. Wilson." Randall sought to be courteous though he had no wish to be so. "We'd like to see your production figures for the past year or so, some of the diamonds mined here recently, uncut naturally, and we'll need to question some of your men. Hassles all around, to be sure, but unavoidable, I'm afraid. I'm sure that by the time we're done, we'll owe you our sincere apologies for the inconvenience and for having questioned your honor."

"Yes," Wilson's cold gaze fixed momentarily on Cooke. "I trust you'll have the good taste to apologize too, my dear Colonel."

"When warranted, sir."

Wilson ignored Cooke. "All of those things can be arranged, but you'll never finish tonight. It's already getting late. Be dark soon." As if on cue everyone turned to look out the room's large windows. The afternoon sunlight was waning. Night came quickly in the tropics, especially as near the equator as the camp lay. "Despite our differences, might I suggest that you accept my hospitality for the evening?"

"At least until we've gathered the data we're after. Then, I fear we'll have to incur the wrath of one of the other operators in the region."

"Splendid." Wilson's countenance rebounded to its former exuberance. He rubbed his hands together and smiled broadly, flaunting his yellowed teeth. "We rarely have company. It'll be a bit of a treat at dinner. I'll have my cook put together something most palatable."

"Begging your pardon, but will there be any . . . ah . . . local dishes?" After the episode with the *cassiri* Randall had no wish to experience any further culinary adventures.

"Nothing quite so unappetizing to the American palate as the *cassiri*, I'm quite sure." Wilson replied evenly.

CHAPTER TWENTY-SIX

12 April

6:30 to Midnight

Ambling along with his curious gait, Wilson led two of his unexpected quests down a corridor and into his office. Because it was the one room in the whole camp where temperature and humidity were maintained at a constantly comfortable level, the office doubled as a remarkably well-stocked library. The walls of the large, windowless room were almost entirely covered with shelves straining under the weight of thousands of volumes. Titles ranged from highly technical geological and mining reference tomes that would be beyond the scope of most readers, to the latest best-selling novels. One corner of the room lay dominated by a large, pale-blue cabinet with many wide, flat drawers. Wilson explained that it contained detailed maps of the immediate area, as well as, most of the northern half the continent.

In the center of the room two huge desks seemed to spar with one another. Handsome examples of the furniture craftsman's art these were no run of the mill desks. They were hand crafted works of undeniable beauty. Their rich mahogany was polished to a high gloss and adorned with gleaming brass hardware. They would enhance any room, let alone so fine a library. Beside each stood an equally marvelous chair created with the same attention to workmanship and detail.

The only other furnishings in the room were two four-drawer filing cabinets placed like sentinels on either side of the sole entrance. The scene seemed so out of place in the midst of the South American jungle.

"A superb library," commented Schmitt as he scanned some titles. Randall walked over to the desks and ran a hand along the woodwork.

"I like to think so." There was a hint of pride in his voice as Wilson settled into the chair behind his desk. "Isn't much to do here in the evenings; cable TV still hasn't reached us out here. Reading passes the time pleasantly." He unlocked his desk and pulled out a small vial that he tossed to Schmitt. "Is this what you're after?"

Schmitt eyed the vial's contents with interest. "Diamonds?" He asked dumbly, feigning ignorance.

"In the rough. Not terribly spectacular in that state."

"No, I suppose not, and yet some are nicely formed crystals." He twirled the vial around letting the stones tumble about. "How much is a vial like this worth?"

"All depends on what's in it. Quality, size, color, inclusions, things like that. Those aren't particularly good. Worth very little actually." He swung open a hinged door on the desk to reveal the faceplate of a safe. "Now lets get those documents you wanted." Wilson spun the safe's dial back and forth several times, turned the handle and opened the door. The inside was crammed with ledgers and files. He pulled out two ledgers. "Here you are, gentlemen. I think you'll find what you're looking for in these. They cover the past twelve months or so."

“Thanks. Tell me, aren’t you afraid that someone will break in and steal the diamonds from your desk?”

Wilson grinned, yellowed teeth on display. “It’s a very solid desk. Seriously though, the entire place is guarded by what I like to think is a very trustworthy security force. You see, being very near the Brazilian and Venezuelan borders, it’s not unheard of for small bands of raiders to try and steal some gold and diamonds, then slip back across the border for protection.”

“I see,” Schmitt replied simply. He was suddenly very glad to have some of Colonel Cooke’s men stealthily lurking about somewhere outside. He wondered how the Colonel and the Guyanese police officials were faring in their interrogation of workers down by the airstrip. Would the Colonel be able to help in time if trouble brewed for Schmitt and Randall in the headquarters building? More importantly Schmitt wanted to know what had become of Larson and the rest of the terrorists themselves. Patience, he chided himself.

The two investigators began to deliberately page through the ledgers while Wilson busied himself with some paperwork at his desk. The better part of an hour slipped by in relative silence.

When he looked up, Schmitt cleared his throat to get Wilson’s attention.

“Yes, what is it?”

“Well, something puzzles me a bit. I noticed here that during the last three to four months your operation has increased production by nearly fifty percent. Queer thing is that prior to that the figures show a steady decline in output. What happened?”

“We opened a new sector back about that time. Appeared to be very rich. Gave splendid results.” Wilson was smooth as ice.

“I’ll buy that.” Schmitt spoke as pleasantly as he could. “But why has your gold output continued to dwindle?”

“Unfortunately we’re in a business full of quirks. The vagaries of mother nature often confound logic. Sometimes . . . when one is damn well lucky . . . gold and diamonds are to be had in quantity from the same deposits or general area. At other times nary a flake of gold dust is to be had amongst a treasure trove of diamonds or vice versa. Besides which, in our case, our gold output has always been tiny. A sideline, you might call it.

"I don't know how much you chaps know about the business, but most people seem to think that we work a lot like the big outfits in Africa. A complete fallacy, that is." Wilson vigorously shook his head for emphasis. "The big mines o'er there work volcanic pipes of Kimberlite. Kimberlite tubes are sometimes rich in gem quality diamonds. They can sink a few test shafts with galleries at various depths to determine whether or not to invest the staggering sums required to go into full scale operations.

"To date, no one 'as ever found a Kimberlite tube on the South American continent, which is not to say that there aren't any, or at the very least weren't any at some time in the geologic past. Hence, South American diamonds are sifted out of diamondiferous alluvial gravel deposits or crushed out of conglomerate rock." Wilson sounded like a university professor in a lecture hall. "These gravels and conglomerates are scattered about vast areas. This makes large scale industrial development so bloody tough. This drawback is why the majority of work done in South America was abandoned long ago with the discovery of the Kimberlite pipes in South Africa.

"In this particular region we've been rather fortunate. There are large deposits of diamondiferous gravel on my concession. The only trouble is a most annoying twenty to thirty foot layer of diamond sterile soil and gravel overlaying them. Even with the few pieces of heavy machinery I own, that becomes a tricky lot to remove. We also work holes or 'pots' in the stream and riverbeds. Because of their weight, gold and diamonds tend to settle in the pots.

"The surge in production you've noted comes from one of the buried gravel deposits that was markedly deficient in gold. We did have one positive thing in our favor though, as I'm sure you've observed. The ratio of gem quality stones to industrial grade ones was higher than the forty to forty-five percent we generally experience." He smiled congenially, the picture of the sincere elder statesman, Schmitt thought.

"As for the diamond production itself. Given the nature of our work, rises and drops in production are not uncommon. Check further back if you've a mind to and you'll see we've experienced similar slumps and sudden successes in the past. Somehow we always manage to find a rich new deposit that spurs us on and keeps the whole place chugging merrily along with the hope of more to come."

"Remarkable risks," commented Randall.

"All goes to add to the excitement."

"I imagine so." Schmitt spoke softly as his mind raced. From the beginning of the actual hijacking he had assumed that the terrorists demanded uncut diamonds for one very important reason - cut diamonds can be traced. Sophisticated techniques in coherent optics using a laser and special camera, made positive identification of cut diamonds very feasible. The photographs of the inner light refraction through the gem showed intricate patterns. Like human fingerprints, these Gem-prints are unique for each specimen. Large cut stones would therefore have been tricky to unload. Given the large quantity they would have to sell, Larson and his associates probably would have had to settle for a small fraction of their actual value.

Schmitt now realized that a second, purely monetary reason led to the call for uncut stones. When cut, their value would increase by upwards of a factor of ten to one. Thus, the ten million would be transformed into roughly a hundred million while all chances of tracing the diamonds would be greatly diminished if not extinguished.

But to take advantage of this multiplier effect, Larson would have to be aligned with a diamond cutter. To further legitimize the caper, he needed to affiliate himself with a genuine working mine where the rough diamonds could be introduced gradually. What more natural place for rough diamonds to show up than in a diamond mine? A rich new pocket or deposit. Nothing wrong about mining diamonds so long as everyone believes that they're coming out of the ground you're working and aren't being imported. Wilson's new pocket, registered in his ledgers, was undoubtedly meant to be the ransom gemstones.

Schmitt stroked his chin thoughtfully. "Tell me, since your mining output has soared so during the past few months, why hasn't your cutting operation seen any commensurate surge?" Schmitt's intent blue eyes tried to probe beneath Wilson's friendly demeanor as he listened to the reply.

"Excellent observation," retorted Wilson. "First off, just because I own a modest cutting operation, it does not follow that all of my production is cut there. It isn't. In fact, very little is. My cutting operation is very small, might even be called minuscule. It certainly could not handle our output even if I so desired. Hence, many diamonds are sold rough to dealers, while some are kept for speculative reasons. In this case, the surplus stones are being stockpiled. The value of quality stones inevitably rises over time, no doubt aided by inflation. If the trend continues, as I think probable, the stones that I could sell for say five thousand dollars now, will be worth many times that in due time. It makes good sense to hold back some production. Pays to speculate. Right now we sell only enough of our yield to enable the operation to go on producing. Regrettably the recent surge you've noted played out rather suddenly. Had it continued, we'd soon have had a sizable reserve." Just a hint of bitterness crept into his voice.

"I'm sure you'll find most other similar operations do the same. All part of the perpetual game."

Of that, Schmitt was certain. "Most intriguing. Of course, it's a bit involved for someone not wholly familiar with the business. Especially so when one considers the enormous sums of money involved. How much does an operation like this gross in a year?"

A coy smiled greeted the question. "Privileged information, my boy. Can't tell you that, but I will say that I'm not about to become a pauper. You might go so far as to say that I'm independently wealthy."

Schmitt closed the ledger and returned it. Randall following suit with the other ledger.

They were soon tucked away in the locked safe. The desk too was carefully relocked. As Wilson withdrew the key, there was a knock on the door. An Indian servant announced that dinner was ready.

"Shall we?" Wilson waved magnanimously towards the door.

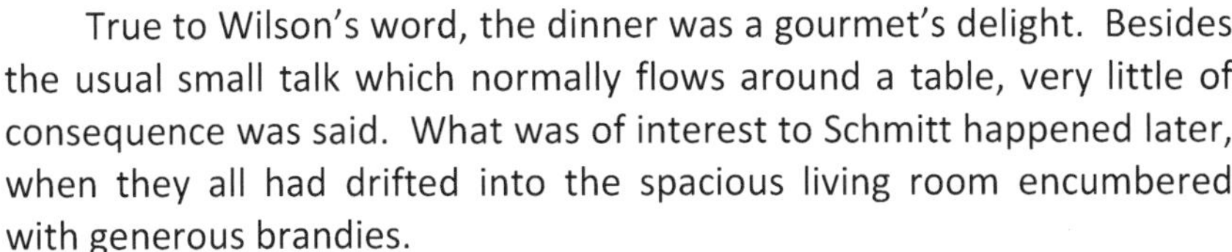

True to Wilson's word, the dinner was a gourmet's delight. Besides the usual small talk which normally flows around a table, very little of consequence was said. What was of interest to Schmitt happened later, when they all had drifted into the spacious living room encumbered with generous brandies.

It was so subtle, so innocuous, so seemingly unimportant that even Schmitt almost missed it. He was certain that no one else caught it, except perhaps Wilson himself. Something told him that the wily old man realized the blunder almost as it happened.

The conversation had been touching on how the terrorists had miraculously withstood the SAS assault, when Wilson muttered, "Yes, Erik's got the luck of the devil in him. A crafty bastard to be sure. How many of those explosive devices did they actually have left?"

The sudden lack of vitality in Wilson's voice indicated he knew that he had erred. No mention of Larson's identity had been made. The link was forged.

Trying to act nonchalant, as though the slip had gone unnoticed, Schmitt answered. "None at that point, although we didn't know that until too late."

"Pity, what? Strange how such little gaps in knowledge can forge the outcome of events on such a grand scale. Tell me, Mr. Schmitt, how is it that you, a European, find yourself mixed up with an American crime?"

Wilson's undivided attention riveted on him. Somehow the old man sensed that he knew. The link had been irrevocably forged. Only physical proof lacked. To drop the charade and confront Wilson immediately might trigger a serious conflagration. With Cooke's men scattered and out numbered, it seemed prudent to play along a while longer.

"Chance really. I'm a private investigator. A case had me in New York and I stumbled into the hornets' nest, so to speak."

"Sounds like a proper cock-up all round, to me. On the subject of which, if I don't give my supervisors their instructions for tomorrow's work assignments, this place will be just as muddled. I'm sure Peter can entertain you gentlemen for the few minutes it will take." With that, Wilson shuffled out of the room and down the corridor leading to his office.

Pitch dark reigned the night beyond the large windows as Schmitt glanced casually about. The two SAS soldiers were still there, but their weapons were not in hand. The machine pistols lay beside their chairs on the tiled floor. Two more of their number still should be posted just outside the headquarters' main entrance. Then there were the eight down by the plane. As for the twelve that had deplaned and vanished upon landing, they probably lurked somewhere outside in the shadows, their presence still cloaked in secrecy.

Randall had just commented about how quickly darkness had come, when Wilson ambled back down the hall flanked by four armed members of his rag-tag security force. Three hefted pump shotguns that had been conveniently sawed-off to enhance their killing power at close range and in close quarters, and by no stretch of the imagination could anyplace within the room be considered anything but close range. The third held an M3A1 machine pistol, better known as a grease gun because of its uncanny resemblance to that tool.

Instinctively, one of the SAS soldiers went for his own machine pistol. An explosive roar ripped through the room and the commando, or rather what was left of him, toppled backwards with the chair to crash against the wall in a bloody heap.

If his mate had entertained similar thoughts of heroism, they were quickly abandoned. Like the others he remained perfectly still, lest he should upset an itchy trigger finger. Schmitt refrained from glancing towards the main entrance. Any moment the door would burst open and the two men stationed there would burst in with a murderous fury. Nothing happened.

Shurcliff, now on his feet, rested a big hand on his pistol's butt. Not without a hint of satisfaction, he explained. "They're dead. Some of our Amerindian employees are still remarkably proficient with their native 'andicrafts and skills. Blowguns and curare tipped darts make fine weapons. There's no one to help. The blokes below can't hear anything from up here. Even if they could it would make no matter. Like yourselves, they're dead men. If they try to assist you, they simply shorten wot little time's left 'em." He smiled his crocodile smile.

Wilson shook his head sadly. "Most regrettable. My own fault, of course. Careless mistake. You chaps were supposed to come and go without getting any the wiser. Bloody stupid of me to blow it. Well, Peter, my boy, it's a bit a sticky mess we're in."

Shurcliff agreed. Wilson was like an uncle to him. "They 'ave to die." His tone rang of finality. "Explaining it will be the tricky part."

"Not so bad, actually, Peter. We take the lot of them aboard that nice Hercules they came in. Radios malfunction all the time, you know. It seems theirs is now broken. They came and left after dinner. Tragic crash into the side of Mount Roraima. Terrific explosion, the fireball will be seen for miles. All aboard dead." He caught Schmitt's eye. "Naturally, being good, law abiding citizens, we'll even volunteer to help find the crash site. Pity that the corpses will all be so badly smashed and burned that identification will be next to impossible."

A grin spread across the big man's face. "I like it. Neat and sweet. 'Course it means we'll have to let things cool off a bit afore we go after the others."

"What others?" Schmitt interrupted loudly.

"Shut up!" Snarled Shurcliff.

"Easy, Peter." Wilson ignored Schmitt, turning to face Randall. "Tell me something, Randall. Were the diamonds surrendered at JFK genuine?"

"Genuine? What kind of question is that? You're the diamond expert here!"

Wilson was surprisingly calm and patient. "Were they?"

"Of course, they were! How could we chance fakes? We had no way of knowing whether or not your pals could make good on any more of their threats." He instinctively thought of his shoulder holster, but dismissed the idea. Shurcliff would kill him before the gun ever cleared leather.

Wilson's brows knit. "You gentlemen were at Kennedy. You gave the men on the plane about ten million in genuine diamonds. Most interesting." He looked at Shurcliff. "It appears that you were right, Peter." The big man nodded solemnly.

"Right about what?" Schmitt ventured. This time he met no swift rebuke.

"It's a pity we can't join forces. We're all after the same men now. You want them because of duty and all that rot. I, because they've bilked me out of a small fortune and left me to take the rap, as I believe you Americans phrase it. You see, Erik and his sole surviving henchman brought me a case full of quality paste. Don't look so surprised, Randall. Any bastard who could pull off this caper would have to be the devil's own spawn."

"More so than you know." Schmitt muttered.

The tired eyes turned to Schmitt. "How so?"

"Remember the ETA hijacking in Texas? We have sound reason to believe that Larson somehow orchestrated it as a decoy."

Despite everything, Wilson found himself laughing. "Did he now? A terrorist playing another terrorist for the fool. It seems the joke is on all of us. Our friends will be very popular indeed." Wilson half turned to Shurcliff. "Escort our friends to the airfield and take care of . . . "

When Shurcliff's eagle gaze lifted for that moment, Schmitt saw what might be his only viable chance. He launched himself boldly at the giant with all the strength he could muster. Shurcliff's reaction was every bit as fast as expected, but not fast enough to draw and fire the .38 before Schmitt hit him squarely in the chest. The tackle would have impressed any professional football coach. Locked together, the two men tumbled across a squat table that splintered and collapsed beneath their combined weight.

The sudden flurry of activity caught the ill-suited security guards' attention for a split second. A split second was all that trained men needed. The SAS commando rolled out of his chair, retrieved his weapon and loosed a burst at the scattering guards. Colonel Cooke dodged an errant shot and tumbled to the tiled floor with one of the shotgun toting guards. Within seconds he wrenched the man's neck and the struggling guard was dead.

The Guyanese police officials frantically sought cover. A hail of buckshot cut one down and wounded the other severely. Randall dove behind the nearest couch, which seemed to disintegrate to the accompaniment of a staccato buzz and a snow flurry of tattered upholstery and stuffing. He felt a stinging sensation in his right arm and realized that he had been hit. With his good arm, he fumbled for his gun.

The first burst from the SAS commando's machine pistol eliminated the trigger-happy guard who had extinguished his comrade. The second caught another shotgun toting man. Wilson, who sought refuge behind the bar at the outset, scurried out on hands and knees to recover the fallen guard's shotgun. A well timed shot from Randall left the aging miner in agony, his right arm useless.

The man with the grease gun retreated down the hallway, firing a short burst to cover his escape. He never made it. True to his intensive training, Colonel Cooke rarely missed. He hurled the weighted throwing knife with deadly accuracy.

Schmitt and Shurcliff remained locked in mortal combat. From the look of things, the giant's size and strength were too much for his mismatched opponent. Schmitt was no slouch when it came to fighting, but none of his blows seemed to have any effect. Before long he was hopelessly pinned, head jammed into the crook of a massive, hairy arm. Seconds remained before already tortured neck vertebra gave way. There was no time for caution. Randall took quick aim. The weapon felt strange in his left hand as he squeezed the trigger.

Shurcliff let out a primal yell. Face contorted with rage and pain, he glanced at his shattered shoulder. Most men would have been sent reeling from the concussion, but Shurcliff was not like most men. He dropped the gasping Schmitt and charged Randall like an enraged bull.

At that precise instant two SAS commandos crashed through the front picture window in a shower of glass and splintered woodwork. Another pair burst in through the hall leading to the rear of the building as the men in the first pair rattled off a burst from their machine pistols into Shurcliff.

The big man staggered backwards in a daze. Lethargically, he pulled his .38 and sought to raise it. Another rattle of small arms fire slammed him against the wall and briefly held him there. Moments after the gunfire ceased, he seemed to lean there. Suddenly his gigantic carcass toppled forward to the tile floor. The battle ceased as abruptly as it had begun.

Colonel Cooke was only mildly surprised to see that the two men who had smashed through the window were the ones that had been posted outside the headquarters, the ones supposedly killed by poisoned darts. The one, Staff Sergeant Smith, reported that all resistance outside had been neutralized. The entire camp was secure. Smith was a veteran of the advance team sent into the Falkland Islands before the main British landing in 1982.

Brushing off his bloodstained uniform, Cooke nodded matter-of-factly. Never had he doubted the capabilities of his command. Picking up his beret, he set it carefully back in place.

It was up to a more than slightly shaken Randall to ask the sergeant the obvious.

"Oh that," Staff Sergeant Smith replied with archetypal SAS pluck. "McDonnell and Richards slit the throats of the lil' buggers with the blowpipes." To the Colonel he added. "Figured you could 'andle things 'ere while we rounded up the lot below."

"Casualties?" Cooke asked impassively.

"Richards got a scratch. Other 'an 'at about a dozen foolish lil' buggers'll be pushin' up daisies."

CHAPTER TWENTY-SEVEN

13 April

Guyana proved costly in lives and time. The one Guyanese police official and one of the SAS team left in makeshift coffins. The entire operation, including mop-up and interrogations, took the team nearly a full day from start to finish. This afforded Larson an abundance of time.

The Guyana mining camp yielded information, but not nearly the treasure trove hoped for and expected. Larson's funding source had been located, but his major backer had been duped too. Revenge is a powerful motive and Schmitt believed that the faint hope of foiling Larson's escape, prompted Wilson to eagerly volunteer all that he knew. He described Larson's initial contacts, the moneys provided to finance the operation, timetables, and the escape route. He knew vexingly little about the latter; only that Larson and another man had left aboard a leased twin-engine Cessna Conquest. They were supposedly bound for the United States via Georgetown, Guyana.

Confirmation that a Conquest with two passengers had landed and passed customs inspection in Georgetown on the night of the hijack came quickly. The same plane turned up in San Juan, Puerto Rico the following morning, but had flown no further. It had been leased at the local airport by a man named Collins who redeemed his sizable cash deposit upon its return. Oddly enough, none of the descriptions of the pilot and his associate obtained from any of the sources matched. Larson and his accomplice were blessed with a bit of the chameleon it seemed.

Another frustrating fact gnawing at Schmitt was that Wilson vehemently insisted that neither terrorist had taken anything aboard the Conquest at the jungle airstrip. They foisted off the satchel with false diamonds and left empty-handed. Where then were the genuine ten million dollars' worth of gems? Had they been cached and left in the jungle? Schmitt thought it unlikely. Instinct told him that somehow Larson had managed to spirit the gems off the continent. The ten million dollar question remained, how?

The thought that Larson was content with the twenty-five thousand dollars Wilson had made as a down payment was ludicrous. Somehow the seemingly impossible had been accomplished with the gems and with himself. The trail to San Juan was relatively easy to piece together, yet the traces were cleverly disguised to afford sufficient time for the fugitives to vanish. Of course, Schmitt knew the probable end destination of Larson's twisted path, but for the moment that knowledge would remain his little secret.

Dried blood still smeared furniture and the floor of the mining camp's headquarters. Shattered furnishings, swept off to the sides, provided further grim reminder of the preceding night's carnage. Schmitt slouched uncomfortably in a rattan chair. He sipped a lukewarm beer. It was almost unbearably bitter.

"Beats the local hooch, eh Smitty?" Randall crossed the room and dropped onto a chair. He puffed slightly having just made the climb up the hill from the airstrip below.

"My name is not *Smitty*." Schmitt's lips curled menacingly as he spat the name out contemptuously. "Kurt Schmitt," he said crisply. "You can call me Kurt or mister Schmitt or even just Schmitt, but don't call me *Smitty* again."

Randall merely looked exasperated. Moving his bandaged arm gingerly, he leaned back. "I thought you'd be interested to hear the latest about the fancy gizmos your pal Larson used on the airliner."

"A brilliant deduction, Randall." Schmitt was in a provocative mood. Since the diamonds had not been recovered, no fee was payable. More toil and sweat would be expended before he could terminate the job and get paid. "Let's hear it."

Randall took his sweet time snapping open the tab on a can of beer. He took a swig, then grimaced. "I hate warm beer."

"You Americans have to have everything chilled. Why, I'll never know. Though in this instance the flavor leaves a lot to be desired."

"Yeah, it does at that." Agreed Randall. "Well, you know about the nav unit used. The computer hooked to it ran the plane along a pre-determined flight path. It was rigged so that once a destruct program was engaged, the entire memory would purge itself whenever the crew regained control of the aircraft. All that's left is a bunch of gibberish created by a form of computer virus.

"From serial numbers on them, the laptops have been traced to a discount chain outlet in Detroit. No attempt to hide numbers, so the trace was easy. Some pieces used to modify them and other equipment have been traced to Radio Shack. Could have been bought darned near anyplace in the US."

"Which, simply stated, makes them dead ends. Onwards, Randall."

"The modified radio and auto-nav consoles substituted in the plane appear equally fruitless. From serial numbers that were again left intact, they've been traced to a theft at Boeing's Seattle plant about a year ago. The theft was investigated at the time with no appreciable results.

"The radar equipment is also pretty much a waste of time. The scopes and hardware were bought in Miami about eight months ago. Naturally, the specialized installation in the aircraft required considerable technical modifications, such as the heavy metal plates and the fitted domes. If we can track down their origins we may have something."

"All you would get is the name of a legitimate business that fabricated some equipment to specifications supplied by a bogus corporation or business used as a front by Larson. Tracking them down is a waste of manpower. What else have you got?"

"The closed circuit TV monitor is standard video equipment purchased two months back in New York. The handcuffs come from a wholesale police equipment distributor out of Atlanta and the modifications to them appear to be homemade. As for the acid used, without a container to narrow the field, it could have been bought in any of the fifty states."

"So, to put it succinctly, your people have nothing to go on." Schmitt said dryly.

"I'm afraid so. But Larson's got to surface sooner or later." He paused, then added as an afterthought. "Some good news to report. The genuine ETA bastards in Texas got nailed. Four dead and two wounded, one critically. Blue Light took 'em in a successful pre-dawn strike. Only one passenger suffered a wound of any consequence and only one member of the assault force was wounded slightly."

"Hurray for Blue Light." The words were uttered sullenly, without elation. Schmitt had vastly more pressing concerns. More than ten million dollars' worth of diamonds were at stake and he wanted to be the man to recover them while nailing Larson. Randall rambled on about the technical sophistication of the crime, but Schmitt essentially ignored him. He relished the thought of boarding the Venezuelan transport plane within the hour. It would take him back to civilization and his next round of negotiations with authorities. He knew where Larson was headed, the question was when?

CHAPTER TWENTY-EIGHT

15 April

"I'm beginning to think that if it came down to it, you could cheat the devil himself. You've more luck than any one man has a right to expect, Kurt."

"I don't believe in luck." Schmitt responded with a smirk. He propped his feet up on the corner of Determeijer's desk. The cramped office swirled with a bluish haze of tobacco smoke.

Peter Determeijer scratched his head irritably before lighting another cigarette from the glowing stub of the last. The black, stone ashtray overflowed with smashed butts and ash. "Filthy habit, this smoking. Keep telling myself I'm going to get serious and quit. Then I find a plausible excuse and puff merrily on." His gaze met Schmitt's.

"You know, you're an extremely churlish person, Kurt. You take it for granted that everyone will always be willing to fill in the gaps whenever you need a little help."

"I honestly do appreciate everything you've done, Peter. They might have detained me for days otherwise."

"And well they might!" Determeijer snapped. "If you'd come clean with everything you knew or suspected about this Larson fellow at the outset, this whole messy affair might have been averted. Now some good men are dead, the United States' government is out ten million dollars in ransom money, an airport was laid waste, thousands of people were terrified, and Larson has gone to ground. Hell . . . you even let him know that we knew his true identity!"

"That was the decision of the Americans, not mine. They hoped that the added pressure would prompt a careless mistake. They were wrong."

"Obviously. To compound the error, that blunder means that we can rest assured Larson will not surface in any of the places where he might otherwise have been reasonably expected to appear sooner or later." He shook his head dejectedly. "I should never have listened to you. It was against my better judgment to give him room to roam in hopes of targeting bigger game."

"The contest isn't over yet." Schmitt was keenly aware of the great trust placed in him by his friend. The sense that he had betrayed that trust gnawed at the edges of his thoughts.

"Face it, Kurt, for you this one has been a massive fiasco. You've invested months of time and God only knows of the expenses incurred, but the payoff was a bust. You got the chance to play bigshot with the Americans, got whisked to South America and all, but only because you are a shrewd hustler and ***had*** something with which to bargain."

The anger directed at him was justifiable. Schmitt forced a weak smile. "You should know me well enough by now, Peter, to know I've still got something to barter."

"I thought you'd come clean with the Americans?"

"In large measure. Through a bit of . . . ahhh . . . strategic misrepresentation sounds fair enough, I neglected to mention van Troje's connection."

Determeijer straightened, incredulity etched into every line and crease of his face. "You lied? After I went out on a limb to expedite matters for you?" His head shook sadly as though he had just suffered a severe emotional blow. "I thought you had explained van Troje was Larson's link to this Wilson, chap?"

"I did. I also gave the impression that van Troje is a law-abiding, God-fearing citizen duped by the inscrutable Larson."

"We both know better. Yet from what you've said, I too thought him an unwitting accomplice."

"Van Troje is the key. He can convert the ransomed diamonds to cash. In due time I'll give you Larson AND van Troje."

"This thing is too big for one man to tackle, Kurt. I insist that you let them know everything you've got. Everything!"

Schmitt sighed plaintively. His eyes flashed. "I'd like to oblige, Peter, but I won't. I'm too close to the payoff, as you put it, to toss everything aside. I came here today to lay the groundwork for the trap that will net me my fee and you fame."

He stifled Determeijer's protest with a jerky wave of his hands. "No, hear me out! I'm not looking for favors. We're talking a bona fide team effort. So long as I get due credit with the appropriate authorities for having put it all together, you can bask in the limelight of a major success on the international level."

"Psssh . . . don't try and hustle me, Kurt!"

The right words would sway the detective, Schmitt instinctively knew that. "I can't explain how he spirited them away, but Larson has got a fortune in uncut diamonds. To him they are utterly worthless bits of crystal! That is, until he can establish contact with a buyer. This operation has been too big to leave that to chance. A pre-determined route to profitable disposal of the gems would have been essential to his planning. Van Troje is that outlet."

Determeijer nodded. "Logical. However, odds favor a long wait before reestablishing contact, if indeed that is the conduit Larson intends to utilize. Thanks to you, he knows his organization has been breached somehow. Even if the original plan called for prompt return to Amsterdam, circumstances may now dictate otherwise. Were I in his shoes, caution would reign supreme."

"True." Conceded Schmitt. He happily noted Determeijer's improving temperament. "On the other hand, Larson now must bury himself deep, very deep. His name has hit high on the international hit parade of terrorists. To burrow deep enough, he'll need cash, prodigious quantities of cash. The diamonds must be converted quickly. Trying to establish a new conduit for their disposal would be time consuming and extremely hazardous. Even if he could align himself with a buyer willing to assume the risks, he'd undoubtedly be forced to settle for a fraction of their value." His feet dropping to the floor, Schmitt suddenly leaned forward, hands pressed against the edge of Determeijer's desk. "I can't tell you how he got away with the diamonds. I can't tell you where he went from San Juan. But just as sure as I'm sitting here, I can promise you he'll be in Amsterdam very soon to close the deal with van Troje."

Determeijer's dull gray eyes seemed to ponder every detail of Schmitt's face. Smoke curled from his nostrils as the detective slowly exhaled, furrowed forehead knit in concentration. Torn between his own tendency to do things by the book and the grudging respect anchored to Schmitt because of the young man's penchant for sound hunches, he weighed his options. The deciding factor proved to be the fact that he had already gambled on Schmitt with regards to Larson. Perhaps the hustling investigator's arguments bore merit. Nagged by reservations, Determeijer opted to give Schmitt some additional leeway. He chain-smoked three more cigarettes as Schmitt outlined specifically what he envisioned.

CHAPTER TWENTY-NINE

16 April

A certain uneasiness plagued Schmitt as he opened the door to his apartment. He couldn't quite put his finger on it, but an obscure sixth sense seemed to be doing overtime. Undoubtedly the result of a fruitless day with Determeijer, he concluded as he closed the door behind him. It was late. He was tired.

Lisbeth greeted him from the sofa where she sat stiffly, a bathrobe clutched round her. Her eyes warned him too late that they had company.

"Stand very still." A deep voice said flatly from the kitchen. The silenced Makarov pistol in the steady hands of the swarthy man dictated obedience. So did the fact that a similarly armed man appeared from the bedroom. Yet a third person rose from behind the sofa, her weapon aimed at Lisbeth.

The man from the bedroom was fair-haired with a ruddy

complexion. Like his accomplices he wore jeans, a knit shirt, and a light jacket. The skin-tight gloves and his easy manner attested that he was no novice in these matters. When he spoke, the accent was impossible to place. "Welcome home. Be a good lad, now, and don't try anything foolish. I'm going to relieve you of any burdensome materials." He walked nearer to Schmitt as the dark-haired woman lightly stroked Lisbeth's hair with the silenced barrel of her weapon.

A sinister look in her dark eyes, the woman said, "I'm sure you'll cooperate, Mr. Schmitt, for her sake."

Options were limited. Resistance seemed futile and certain to bring harm to Lisbeth. Reluctantly Schmitt allowed the grinning man to search him. He felt strangely naked when his Mauser and switchblade were pocketed by the muscular brute. Ignoring him, he glared at the lithe woman. The form-hugging, black leather pants and knit pullover left little to the imagination. There was determination and power in her intelligent face, a face that was at once beautiful and sinister. Schmitt instinctively knew that she was the leader.

"It's always easy to act tough when one is holding a lady hostage and has a three to one advantage."

"True." The woman concurred, surprisingly agreeable despite the obvious contempt leveled at her. "Favorable odds have always lain dear to my heart. They lessen the probability of failure and make the winning no less sweet, Mr. Schmitt. From all of what we've learned about you, I think you'll understand my reasoning quite . . ."

"What the hell do you want?" Schmitt interrupted fiercely.

"Temper, temper." She motioned Schmitt to the sofa. "Seat yourself. Make yourself as comfortable as possible under the circumstances. We've a bit to talk about."

After a moment's hesitation, Schmitt settled down uneasily beside Lisbeth. Her hand trembled as he took it in his.

"I couldn't help it. They broke in a couple of . . ."

Gently caressing her cheek, he shushed her. "Not your fault, darling." Then to the intriguing woman he added, "If you harm her or have already done so, I swear you'll die painfully."

The gun-toting stranger plunked herself onto a chair and sighed. "I can be called many a thing, but an abuser of innocent people is not one moniker that can rightly be applied. I've killed several people, maimed others, but always for a reason and always when it was justified. I am not as cold-blooded as my adversaries would have everyone believe."

"Then why don't you tell us just what you are?"

"Well, Mr. Schmitt, I'm known by several aliases, most notably as *The Black Widow*. To the scant few people I call friends and a handful of trusted associates like Gregorio here," she motioned at the blond man, "I am Louisa."

"The notorious Louisa Lopez Sanchez of ETA fame?"

She laughed genuinely. "Fame is it? Being pegged as a brutal, insentient killer hardly rates as fame. And as for the ETA affiliation, a few scant weeks ago few people outside of my homeland and the nearby areas had ever heard of the ETA or its purpose."

"They sure as hell have now." Schmitt noted.

"True." She removed her glasses and blew a piece of lint from the one lens. For an instant she seemed vulnerable, almost defenseless. Slipping them back on, she continued, "You see, I love my country. So much so, that I and my friends here devote our lives to patriotic service as we strive to stamp out the pestilential invaders of that country."

"I doubt if many people outside your band would consider you particularly patriotic."

"Opinions are a subjective thing, that much is true. Be that as it may, a few days back, some of my good friends and fellow patriots came in harm's way in America. In fact, four of them died. Two others would have been better off had they been so lucky. The brilliant scheme in which they were involved went terribly awry. It now seems the gentleman who betrayed them is an acquaintance of yours."

Understanding dawned on Schmitt. He was duly impressed that they knew of his involvement. "I don't follow."

"From your face, I see that you do indeed, but to squelch further argument, thereby saving aggravation for all concerned, let me explain a bit more." She leaned back comfortably and crossed her legs.

"Like you, we have sources. From all sorts of fascinating places, even Scotland Yard and La Sûreté. A little investigative work and we learned that you, Mr. Schmitt, were at Kennedy when the sham ETA hijacking began there. And it was you who identified the gentleman responsible to the US authorities. A man known to us as Thomas Collins. A smooth operator is Collins. He penetrated our hierarchy with an ease that has left more than one eyebrow raised. Fools he made of us. Surely you'll agree that such a thing demands retribution of a sort?

"I had the pleasure to make his acquaintance once in Copenhagen. Since you managed the seemingly impossible and fingered his true identity, then I believe that you are the right person to help me renew that acquaintance. You see, I'd like to meet Erik Larson again, for old times sake, if you catch my drift."

Schmitt stroked his chin thoughtfully. The admission of Larson's involvement in the ETA hijacking was intriguing. "Did you know he killed one of your couriers here last summer?"

"Is that a fact?" She looked at Gregorio. "That explains the lost money."

The man nodded. "Mr. Larson's generous donation . . . stolen from our own people. What a saint!"

"And he only gave back about half of what he stole!" Her attention returned to Schmitt. "You are sure of this?"

Schmitt nodded. "And three others to boot. I knew he pocketed some cash earmarked for your organization. But until now, obviously I didn't know that he had used some of it to help ingratiate himself with you."

"All the more reason to speak with him. Certainly you can see why we want to find him rather badly?"

"I'm sure you would. Sadly I haven't the foggiest idea of where to find him."

"It's true! Larson seems to have vanished into thin air." Interjected Lisbeth. "Kurt hasn't even been paid because he cannot find him yet. Check that with your sources!" Defiance dominated her voice.

"We have." The woman responded patiently.

"Then why this?" She indicated the intruders.

"Because your man, it seems, is quite good at what he does." The intense dark eyes left hers to focus on Schmitt again. "Surely you've no intent to drop things where they stand?"

Schmitt leaned forward. "Tell your muscle boys to put their weapons away and take a walk. If you've checked me out, then you know I stand by my word. I'll not try anything while you and I talk. On my honor."

"Honor is it?" The woman grinned slowly. "So be it." To her men she said, "Gregorio, I'll be fine. Wait for me at the hotel." When they hesitated she added, "Go on, be off with you!"

"Not with my weapons!" Schmitt demanded.

The fair-haired man looked at Louisa who assented with a nod. The Mauser and knife were placed on the coffee table by the powerful man.

"Have you any Remy Martin Louis XIII, per chance?" Louisa asked when they had gone.

"Cognac?"

"The best. Aged to perfection! Each drop began its life over 80 years ago!"

"Scotch is the best I can muster." Schmitt rose to fetch a bottle of Black Label from his liquor cabinet.

"Kurt," Lisbeth inquired, "can I go to bed? I've an early appointment at the magazine." She knew Schmitt wanted Louisa alone for whatever was about to transpire.

"Of course." He kissed her lightly on the lips after pouring the Scotch and passing one glass to the enigmatic woman known to police as *The Black Widow.*

"To better days." Louisa proclaimed as she belted down the liquor.

The toast was ignored. After sipping his own drink, Schmitt met the Basque woman's steady gaze. "Listen, Louisa, or whatever your real name is, if you or your friends pop up and eliminate citizen Larson, I don't stand a snowball's chance in hell of collecting my fee."

"And a sizable fee it would be. If you expect me to match it, I'm afraid you're in for disappointment. We're just poor working class terrorists."

"No. I don't work for your kind." Distaste dripped from each word.

Noting this, the woman looked at the bottom of her empty glass contemplatively. "It's been said that the line between a freedom fighter and a terrorist is a fine one. One that depends on perspective. A bit like asking is the glass half full or half empty? It all depends on your point of view." When she looked up again, a certain sadness permeated her visage, a vulnerable look seemingly alien to the tough, competent demeanor of the past few minutes. "Had you grown up in the Basque country, maybe you'd think differently."

"Perhaps. But I didn't, and your plaintive plea has not changed my scruples."

"Nor would I expect it to."

"Good. At least we understand each other."

"A start, anyways. So, Kurt, where do you suppose Larson is now?"

"I told you the truth. I don't know. He's a slippery character."

"Truer words were never spoken." Louisa helped herself to a refill. "Seems we're at an impasse. Suppose we let you put the finger on Larson for the law first? That way you can collect your fees."

"What about the diamonds?"

"Though they would be a most welcome bonus, a small price to have Larson in hand. My word on it."

"Just what the devil do you have in mind?"

"When you find Larson, you let me know. That way I can pay my respects to him *AFTER* you get credit for nailing him, but *BEFORE* he's in true custody. It'd be a lot messier if we waited until the authorities really had him in the bag."

"Do you really think you can coerce me into cooperation?"

"Having finally met you, I think not. I regret now, not coming alone to speak with you in a less threatening manner. No, Kurt, I'll not force you. We'll see Larson again, with or without your help. The only difference is the body count of innocents if you don't help and we have to take him another way. So, though you've no reason to do so, I'll ask you to help me."

Replenishing his own drink, Schmitt pondered the possibilities. A butterfly or two roamed freely in his stomach as he thought.

CHAPTER THIRTY

17 April

Shipol International Airport in the Netherlands was crowded. Several flights had arrived during the past half-hour or so, each adding to the noisy milling throng. Hundreds of people passed the bench where a nattily dressed gentleman in a slate-gray, three-piece suit had been sitting for some twenty minutes or so. His piercing green eyes intently watched the numerous people as they sauntered by. He sat erect, lips drawn together. Beneath an aquiline nose he sported a neatly trimmed mustache the same silvery color as his hair. If appearances could be counted on, he looked to be about fifty and of probable Nordic descent.

His impassive, slightly wrinkled face suddenly gave way to a boyish grin, followed closely by a wide smile. He got anxiously to his feet.

A woman with flowing silky blonde hair hurried towards him. A clinging magenta dress highlighted a stunning figure. She too smiled warmly, lovingly. It was the same dress she'd worn when last they'd seen each other a few days earlier. Drawing near, she dropped her small suitcase and large make-up case to throw her arms around her husband's neck. Lips met in a long impassioned kiss.

The grand old Hotel De L'Europe lay near the heart of Amsterdam. The luxurious hotel, one of the city's finest, embodied all of the old world charm so endemic to Erik Larson's sense of pleasurable accommodations. He regretted that on this trip his stay would be a brief one. Predictably, the face he wore was markedly different from the one assumed during the hijacking and also from his own. Three times since executing the caper his appearance had changed radically. Three times artful alterations to hair color, eye color, facial features took place. Three times new passports, each as false as its predecessor, had come into play. Three times attention to minute detail, even to the point of voice and speech modifications, had paid off. Thrice transformations had confounded and all but eliminated any trace of the twisted trail that led him from the jungles of the Guyana highlands to a luxury hotel in Amsterdam.

The silvery hair obscured his natural honey blond. Green lenses disguised his true blue-gray eyes. The mustache was an accessory. So too were the special shoes that made him appear taller. The life of a chameleon had become second nature.

Kristine, the ravishing blonde Larson greeted at Schipol airport, provided the critical key to their success. She was his most trusted and valued accomplice. Her strong will and sharp intellect proved invaluable throughout the planning phase of the operation, but the passive role she assumed during its execution virtually guaranteed success. The mystery of the vanished diamonds was no riddle to her. A seemingly hapless victim aboard the hijacked airliner, she coolly answered the barrage of questions the investigators had posed, then confidently smuggled the gems through customs and off the South American continent. Such was the level of trust she enjoyed. But she was more than just a trusted and useful accomplice. She was also the loving wife whose presence gave Larson's life its long absent sense of meaning. Sensual sex appeal proved as overpowering as her rapier wit and sharp intellect. Delicately beautiful facial features and a curvaceous body could devastate. Fiery emerald eyes could make most men melt.

Larson considered himself fortunate to sport such a mate. Not without a touch of satisfaction did he enter the luxurious hotel's lobby with her on his arm. The spacious lobby was opulently decorated in turn of the century elegance. The short, jet black-haired assistant manager greeted them cordially.

"Ah, Mr. Collins, I see that your lovely wife has finally arrived." He bowed and kissed her hand lightly. "Shall I reserve a table for two at the Excelsior?"

"Make it for three."

"Eight o'clock?"

"Nine."

"Very well. Have a pleasant afternoon, Mr. and Mrs. Collins."

Kristine smiled politely as the fawning assistant manager nodded and left to attend another guest. Trailed by the bellman they retired to their room overlooking the Amstel River. The room proved as magnificent as the lobby, with gorgeous period furnishings and decor. On one side a breakfast nook lay nestled near a balcony where one could sit comfortably immersed in the peaceful vista beyond.

The bellman deposited Kristine's bags, collected his generous tip and departed. He was barely gone before there was a knock on the door. Malin, casually dressed in sports jacket and navy slacks, entered the room jubilantly shaking hands and kissing Kristine lightly on the cheek.

Malin's beard had been trimmed to a goatee and mustache. They were flecked with gray. The make-up case caught his attention. "No trouble I see."

"Not a one. Erik tells me that you fellows fared well too."

"Aside from my old buddy, Price, and of course, Higgins." A touch of bitterness entered Malin's voice.

Consulting his watch, the gold Piaget was back in place, Larson said, "We've got to get moving. The meet with van Troje goes down soon."

"Right," Kristine agreed as she slipped into the bathroom to change quickly. She left the door ajar. "Are you guys ready to deal with all eventualities?"

Malin produced a silenced 9mm automatic from where it had been tucked in his belt at the base of his spine. He expertly checked the weapon before stuffing it back into concealment.

Having seen the weapon in the mirror, Kristine, who shared her husband's aversion to murder added, "Let's hope it won't be necessary."

"Knowing van Troje, I wouldn't want to bet on that. With us out of the picture, he bags it all and it won't have cost him any sweat or money to speak of. I expect a less than friendly encounter." Larson picked up the big make-up case. "Anything in the case you want to keep, Kris?"

Coming out of the bathroom she shook her head. Nothing in it bore any fingerprints and an empty case would raise suspicions in the unlikely event that someone other than van Troje should see it.

"All right then, let's get started."

He and Kristine left together, make-up case in hand. The assistant manager was conspicuously absent when they crossed the main lobby and exited. They walked briskly into the street where an ancient barrel organ nearby strained to create beautiful music. Shortly after their cab pulled away from the curb, Malin followed suit.

The overcast had visibly thickened and threatened imminent rain. The twin spires of Sint Nicolaas Kerk pierced the gloomy sky just behind where Larson stood. The church dated from the late 1800s and blended in perfectly with its environs. He was across the road from the large structure in a small parking area by the edge of one of Amsterdam's numerous waterways. Cars sped past on the street while glass enclosed tour boats, brimming with gawking tourists who looked from side to side in wonderment and snapped picture after picture, glided along the canal. How many of them would ever bother to look at the volumes of picture records more than a few times? Not many he decided.

The dark-blue make-up case rested at his feet. Many people had undoubtedly thought it strange to see a man carrying it, but Amsterdammers are noted for their tendency to ignore the affairs of others. They generally respect the privacy of another's actions, regardless of how queer they might seem; no one questioned Larson's reason for toting the large make-up case. He leaned back against the fender of a convenient auto. "Where the devil is van Troje?" He muttered under his breath when the Dutchman was five minutes late.

As if in answer, a chauffeured, chocolate-brown Mercedes with darkly tinted windows pulled into the adjacent space. Van Troje climbed out of the car. Invariably he was clad in the same dark suit that he always seemed to wear, puffing on the same obnoxious cigar that always seemed to be clamped firmly in his teeth. He was a repulsive man, short and fat, with a round, heavily jowled face dominated by a bulbous nose. Nervous dark eyes set deep in his head hid beneath a pair of bushy gray eyebrows that almost made up for the lack of hair on his nearly bald pate.

Despite his physical repulsiveness and obnoxious cigars, he was a shrewd adversary. Van Troje used people. He used them in every way possible, then discarded them cruelly. Whether they ended up at the bottom of one of the canals or in jail for the crimes he committed, made little difference. What mattered was the expansion of his personal goals and fortune.

Wilson provided a prime example. Van Troje knew the diamond miner professionally, knew how greedy the Britisher was, and had taken full advantage of it. Without ever revealing his connection with the American hijackers, he shrewdly managed to manipulate Wilson into financing nearly the entire operation only to leave him holding the bag in Guyana.

Now that Larson had the diamonds and was on van Troje's home turf, he was keenly aware of the dangers. He was vulnerable, something he had not felt in such large measure since leaving Copenhagen. Given half a chance, the fat man would gladly eliminate the last two participants in the crime. Thankfully he knew nothing of Kristine or her involvement, which was the way Larson wanted things.

Van Troje's face contorted into what was clearly intended to be his version of a friendly smile. "Good to see you made it through all right, Erik. Have you got them?" He spoke with a heavy accent.

"Do you have the money?" Larson asked flatly.

"In the car." He gestured for Larson to get in. "The diamonds, they are in the case?"

"It's for the money." Larson replied as he slid onto the soft leather seat.

There was the loud blast of a boat whistle as the fat man got in beside him and shut the door. The uniformed chauffeur remained motionless, eyes straight forward, seemingly oblivious of their presence. He was no novice.

"Where are the diamonds?" Van Troje persisted.

"Once I've got the money."

The fat man snapped his fingers and the chauffeur half turned and passed a leather flight bag across. When van Troje relieved him of it, he returned to his mannequin-like posture, eyes staring forward.

The bag was unzipped. It was filled to the rim with well-worn American currency, the smallest visible bundle composed of twenty dollar bills. “It’s all there, I can assure you.”

Larson had learned not to trust van Troje, particularly not where money was concerned. He took several bundles out and checked them. They were indeed genuine. He dug to the bottom of the bag. The same. There was no time to count the lot of it, not now anyway. He checked some more bundles. It certainly looked like a million dollars ought to look. He zipped the bulging bag shut.

“Satisfied?”

Larson nodded. The foul smell of the noxious cigar smoke was rapidly giving him a headache.

“The other six million dollars were transferred into the Geneva account this morning as agreed.”

“I know.” The American answered. He didn’t bother to add that the funds should already have been transferred out of the account into three separate accounts in three different banks.

“Now, perhaps you’ll be so good as to give me the merchandise.”

Larson proffered the make-up case. The fat man made another futile attempt at a smile and opened it. Besides a handful of make-up paraphernalia and a particularly bulky Styrofoam insert, the case was empty. The disappointment on his face was profound. “Not very funny, my friend.”

“Oh, they’re there alright. You’re just not looking right.”

Van Troje’s face registered comprehension. Eagerly he pulled the bulky Styrofoam insert out. There was nothing beneath it. Again he looked deeply disappointed.

“Not very imaginative, are you?” Larson took the Styrofoam and broke off a corner. He held the broken piece for van Troje to see. The coarse surface lay studded with diamonds. “The whole thing is full of them. Just flake off and clean away the Styrofoam.” He returned the piece to the make-up case. “I think the time has come to bid you adieu, my friend. It has been a pleasure to have worked together." The extended hand went unmet.

"Not so fast." Van Troje spoke quickly. "Where are your associates?"

"Stateside. Probably quite anxious for my prompt return."

"Most unfortunate."

Larson saw it coming. He prayed that Malin was near. Cautiously he moved his hand towards to the door handle. Unperceived by either man, he also pressed his left elbow down hard against his knee. By doing so he compressed a thin contact switch. This, in turn, completed a circuit and sent a signal racing up thin wires taped to his arm to a minuscule transmitting device in his jacket pocket.

The fat man snapped stubby fingers. This time when the chauffeur turned, the silenced barrel of a Luger appeared half hidden beneath his outstretched right arm. Despite almost mechanical movements the chauffeur proved himself a competent henchman. The lackluster eyes now fixed upon his quarry were those of a professional assassin.

"What's this mean, van Troje?" Larson shouted indignantly.

"The meaning? I should think it crystal clear. Why split the rewards when you don't have to?"

"You'll still be out the six million."

Van Troje smiled gleefully. "Among my vast array of associates there are those who can forge authorization signatures. Since I know the account number and will be able to produce the proper countersignature, the money will soon return to one of my own accounts."

"My friends will not let this lie. They'll be after you."

The chubby face acknowledged this with a nod. "I presume so. They can join you at the bottom of the Amstel or one of the canals. No one can possibly harm . . ."

The flight bag full of money slammed squarely into the chauffeur's face. Instantaneously the Luger spit flame with a muffled plop. The bullet vanished harmlessly into the plush leather upholstery missing Larson by millimeters. Van Troje tried vainly to grasp Larson, but a vicious elbow jab to his face threw him back into his side of the car. Nose bleeding, lip cut, and with one or two broken teeth, he tried again.

Larson had more pressing concerns. Leaning across the seat he struggled to wrest the gun from the chauffeur as van Troje's stubby fingers clawed at his neck. In that same instant the front passenger door jerked open. Two muzzle flashes accompanied with the soft plops of a silenced weapon shot into the car. The chauffeur went limp.

His windpipe choked off, Larson strove to free the clinging hands round his neck. He tore them away and slammed van Troje back into the paneled door. The gunman who had dispatched the chauffeur so efficiently, leaned in the front door. The silenced weapon fired once more with its muted plop.

A red flower bloomed on the left side of van Troje's chest. In the instant before death claimed him, he stared dumbly at Larson, mouth agape. Sickly eyes then rolled up as he slumped backwards, a lifeless mass.

The weapon vanished back into Malin's belt as quickly as it had appeared. Then he hefted the chauffeur into an upright position and locked both front doors. Larson grabbed the hunk of Styrofoam he had broken off and tossed it back into the make-up case. To his chagrin, a portion of the chunk had been crushed in the scuffle. He scooped up most of the bits and stuffed them in his pocket. There was no time to worry about the rest. Leaning across van Troje, he locked the door before climbing out with the money and make-up case and locking his own as well.

Schmitt rounded the corner in his rented Volvo. Van Troje's Mercedes had pulled into a little parking area alongside a canal. A tall man stood waiting there. Schmitt immediately knew it was Larson. His hunch had proven sound. The American sought to peddle the ransomed gems.

Careful not to stare, Schmitt drove past them, swung up a side street, and pulled to the curb. He left the Volvo illegally parked. Walking quickly, but not so quickly as to draw attention to himself, he headed back towards the rendezvous site. A daylight meet right out in the open surprised Schmitt. It seemed almost reckless on either man's part. But then if something went awry, van Troje could always claim he was merely checking out a potential sale with an unknown seller.

His pace became almost lackadaisical as he sauntered along. He gawked like a wide-eyed tourist out to see the sights for the first time. Looking this way and that in wonderment, Schmitt surreptitiously watched the Mercedes. When Larson climbed in, Schmitt steeled himself for a mad dash to the Volvo. With mild surprise he noted the luxury car remained where it was. Suddenly he became aware of a man walking aimlessly along the canal side in the direction of the parking area. An earphone was jammed into this man's right ear, the flesh toned wire trailing down his neck into his shirt collar. Schmitt turned away, ostensibly to stare at the ancient stonework of the enormous church. He tugged a compact walkie-talkie from his pocket. "Hurry up, Peter! It's going down right now in a parking area by the canal at Sint Nicolaas Kerk!" Without awaiting a response, he slipped the radio back into concealment.

Turning to gaze across the serene canal, he noted that the aimless man now strode purposefully towards the Mercedes. He disappeared momentarily through the front passenger-side door. When he emerged seconds later Schmitt saw the silenced weapon vanish beneath the folds of the man's jacket. A second or two later Larson climbed out of the car. A large make-up case was handed to the gunman while Larson kept a leather satchel for himself. Schmitt didn't need to see the gory details within the car to know what had transpired within. The wily Dutchman had finally been bested.

The two Americans walked calmly away from the parking area. Schmitt maintained what he deemed a prudent distance and followed.

Shortly, the radio in Schmitt's pocket beeped softly. He switched it off. Undoubtedly Determeijer and his men had found the Mercedes and its grisly contents. Schmitt had no time to answer. He continued to trail the Americans as they maintained their brisk pace and threaded their way through the city.

Schmitt was vaguely aware of an attractive blonde as she brushed past him. For him not to have noticed a woman would be uncharacteristic.

Some fifteen minutes later the same woman stood selecting post cards from a wire rack in front of a little shop as he passed in stealthy pursuit. Given the aimless, twisted nature of the Americans' movements, he thought nothing of the chance encounter. Not until he witnessed the same woman sidle up alongside Larson and his companion in front of the Grand Hotel Krasnapolsky on the East End of Dam Square, did Schmitt suddenly realize that the winding path had been a ruse to ferret out anyone following the two men.

Larson maintained his pace, pausing only when he neared the soaring white stone monument in the midst of the square. By then his accomplice had passed the bulky make-up case to the woman. The man said something to Larson, shook hands, and started away through the milling mass of standing and seated people congregated near the memorial.

Cobblestones bore Schmitt's tread as he strode on across the square, painfully aware that his presence lay unveiled, his sentence probably already passed. He rounded the stone base of a roaring lion statue. A little girl there bent over to sniff some flowers planted round the base. Intent on his quarry, Schmitt tripped and lost balance when he bumped into her.

The stumble saved his life. A chip of stone flew off the statue as a bullet whined into space with the unmistakable whistle of a ricochet. Schmitt pushed the little girl gruffly to the ground and darted round the base. An old woman scolded him for his unprovoked rudeness to the little girl. Schmitt ignored her, senses on high. The old woman gasped when he drew his own weapon.

Trained eyes surveyed the situation. In the distance Larson and the woman leisurely moved away, threading slowly around the towering pillar. The gunman was nowhere in sight. Keeping to a crouch, Schmitt ran towards Larson.

The American saw him coming. Something was said to the woman, then they were momentarily obscured as Schmitt skirted a group of longhaired youths. Suddenly the woman reappeared, a silenced weapon firmly clasped in a double-handed grip.

The first bystanders thus realized that a deadly duel was being played out in their midst. Terrified screams arose. People began to scramble away.

The shots missed the remarkably nimble Schmitt. One of the longhaired youths didn't fare as well. He yelped as his thigh felt two searing lances plow through the edges.

No clear return shot offered, so Schmitt held his fire as he dodged beneath one of the jutting stone platforms around the base of the memorial. He and the gunman spotted each other simultaneously. Schmitt dove sideways onto the unforgiving cobblestones, firing as he went. The explosive blasts of his weapon reverberated across the square. The cobblestone in front of him splintered, the bullet whining past his ear, stone chips spraying and cutting his face.

Schmitt rolled right knocking over an elderly man. As he brought his weapon up again it became obvious that he need not waste the bullets. The gunman wavered on unsteady feet, his arms hung limply at his side. A thin trickle of blood ran down his chin. His perforated brown sports jacket seemed to darken in spreading splotches. The silenced automatic clattered to the ground, followed briefly by the gunman.

Body bruised and aching, Schmitt climbed slowly to his feet. Larson and the woman had vanished. Jamming his weapon into his belt, he leaned wearily against the sun warmed stone of the memorial. He flexed the fingers of his bloodied right hand to stimulate circulation. Ribs hurt with each breath. He would give odds that one or two cracked when he hit the cobblestones. Some stone fragments were plucked from his face before he dabbed the cuts with a handkerchief. Fishing in his coat pocket for the radio, he found only smashed bits of plastic and bits of pieces of useless electronics.

A uniformed policeman ordered him to freeze. Gun drawn, the police officer approached cautiously and relieved Schmitt of his pistol. Schmitt did not protest, a man named Determeijer could explain everything. Thank God for good old Peter, he thought as the police officer was joined by others. The Ba-buu, Ba-buu siren of emergency vehicles approached. He suddenly felt exhausted.

CHAPTER THIRTY-ONE

17 April

"The couple of diamonds found in van Troje's car are from the New York ransom, alright. Soon as they were under the black light the fluorescent dye became glaringly evident." Determeijer's face looked grim as he spoke, a cigarette clamped in the corner of his mouth.

Schmitt grunted as the unmarked police car rounded a bend. "The Americans took a big chance by marking the diamonds."

"Apparently not. I'm no expert, but from what I'm told, the technique is virtually unknown. Even within the industry very few people realize it can be done. Queer thing is . . . it only works with rough diamonds."

The car took another turn making Schmitt wince in pain.

"You know, I could have you taken directly to the hospital."

Schmitt smiled weakly. "Not even you'd be that callous, Peter."

Determeijer shrugged. "Suit yourself. If you want to be a masochist . . . then so be it." He fumbled in his coat pocket until he located a pack of cigarettes. It was empty. "Damn." From his other pocket he pulled a big cigar. "Found it on van Troje. Figured it would be a shame to let a fine Cuban cigar waste away in the property room downtown." With obvious relish he bit off the end and lit up. After a few luxuriating puffs, he continued. "A quick check of major hotels found Mr. and Mrs. Collins lodged at the Hotel De L'Europe." He paused as they drove past the red brick and stone facade of the Hotel De L'Europe, crossed the adjacent canal and turned down the tree lined road paralleling the canal. The car nosed to the edge of the embankment beside the canal and parked. Rounded red awnings sprouted above every window and balcony on the hotel that stood grandly on the opposite bank. "A man answering Larson's general description is in there now. So is his wife."

A plain-clothes policeman walked slowly over to the car. He stooped by the driver's side window as Determeijer cranked it open.

"Everything set?" The detective asked.

"We've got a team staked out in the lobby. Others all around the building." He started to point towards the hotel.

"Don't point, you idiot!" Determeijer barked angrily.

Chastened, the man stammered. "Sorry, sir. I was just going to say that his balcony is second from the left, second level above the restaurant."

Four members of a special police squad were on the balcony directly above the one to Larson's room. They squatted behind the stonework in the shade of a red awning.

Determeijer tapped Schmitt lightly on the shoulder. The younger man sat peering absentmindedly at the balcony. "I guess I stand corrected. You didn't miss the payoff on this one after all, eh?"

Schmitt remained pensively silent.

"Shall I give the word to go, sir?" The curly haired plain-clothes cop inquired nervously.

Probably his first big assignment, Determeijer thought. "Be patient, lad." He turned to Schmitt. Several loving puffs on the cigar later, he said, "This one's been a bit rough on you, Kurt. Care to give the word?"

"With pleasure." Schmitt looked at the anxious policeman. "Have the men proceed." There was more than a hint of satisfaction in his voice.

Moments later the four men on the balcony sprang into action. Swinging out on ropes they rapidly descended to Larson's balcony where they landed on cat-like feet. They charged through the doors and were lost to sight.

Louisa Lopez Sanchez walked back round the corner to the little delivery van. She too had seen the assault team descend to the balcony. Once in the van she told the driver to get started. The yellow van, trailed by two men in an old dark-green Mercedes wound quickly through the streets. Before long, the two vehicles paused a short distance from the Hotel De L'Europe.

The wait was a short one. The expected police van and two escorts pulled up by the hotel. The prisoners were about to be brought out.

"Now!" Louisa commanded sharply. The driver put the van in gear. Trailed by the car, it drove along peacefully enough until just opposite the police van. By then Louisa and all members of her team had donned ski masks. The van slewed violently across the road and drew up by the police van just as the prisoners were being hustled out of the hotel.

Two men leapt out of the rear of Louisa's van. So too did the two men from the Mercedes. Grenades were lobbed under both the police cars and the police van. The flat crunch of the explosions joined the staccato buzz of machine pistols as Louisa and her men cut down startled police with deadly fire.

At the outset, Larson and his wife were shoved roughly to the pavement by their guards. Moments later the guards lay wounded, their weapons kicked out of reach by the crack team led by Louisa. Amidst the stunned confusion, the Larsons found themselves being dragged towards the yellow delivery van.

More grenades landed in the hotel's entrance to dissuade pursuit from that quarter. Forty-five seconds after the bloody events began, both Larsons were in the van and it was driving off. As it pulled away in a squeal of burned rubber, the Mercedes exploded. The burning wreck blocked the road, preventing immediate pursuit by the other police units rounding the block.

The boldness, unexpected nature, and bloody severity of the attack ensured total success.

The yellow delivery van bounced into the garage. Doors swung shut behind it. Within the darkened confines of the big garage the Larsons, still manacled, were hustled out by their captors. The open trunk of a Volvo indicated their next mode of transport. None too gently they were loaded into the trunk where they lay in an extremely uncomfortable heap.

"Who the hell are you people?" Larson demanded harshly.

A masked man was about to jam a dirty rag into Larson's mouth when another, smaller masked figure stopped him. The woman pulled her ski mask off to reveal the intriguing visage Larson remembered from Copenhagen.

"Oh my God!" All color drained from Larson's face.

"Prayers won't help much. Your list of sins is too long. God has far better things to attend to than the likes of you!" She spat out the words defiantly.

Mind racing, Larson pleaded desperately. "My employers staged the second operation to raise even more funds for . . . "

"And I'm the resurrected Mother Teresa come to bless you."

"We've got about six million dollars! Surely that should count for something!"

The dark eyes narrowed. "Six million, you say?"

The glimmer of hope shined brightly for the desperate American. "Yes, yes! Six million dollars! That kind of money could finance a lot of campaigns."

"Indeed, it could that." The Basque woman looked at one of her accomplices. "What a fine gesture of support, eh Gregoria? And from a condemned man, no less." With that she jammed the dirty rag in Larson's mouth.

Larson's eyes begged mercy, but they found none in the cold eyes that bore down on him. There were only hatred and disgust to be found. Louisa spat on the American.

She spoke slowly. "Money can buy many things. Honor, respect, loyalty are not among them. Our cause has paid a dear price thanks to you. Several good people are dead. And as God is my witness, you'll pray you were with them long before you are."

She reached out and slammed the trunk shut.

EPILOGUE

Schmitt winced in pain as Lisbeth hugged him dearly. "Careful or you'll finish what they started."

"It would have served you right if they had killed you." She chided. "You've been driving me half mad with worry. Thank God you're not hurt worse."

It felt good to be back in the apartment; good to have Lisbeth near again. He smiled lovingly. "A few cracked ribs and some bruises here and there are a small price to pay to collect my fee for this one."

There was a stout knock upon the door. Lisbeth answered it and soon returned with a package. "It's for you."

Somewhat cautiously Schmitt opened the hefty carton. Inside was a generous supply of Remy Martin Louis XIII, the two ornate bottles being separated by a pair of crystal cognac glasses, and a gift card. He read the card aloud. "To Kurt. Thanks for being an honorable man. I regret the inconvenience the other day. Hope this, in some small way, makes amends. It will at the very least be a welcome addition to your liquor cabinet. May you savor it!

"The merchandise we discussed is on ice, no pun intended, and will be dealt with properly. Until our paths may cross again. Louisa"

"That evil Basque terrorist woman?"

Schmitt nodded, looking again at the card. "I almost pity Larson and his wife. The ETA will not be gentle in their vengeance."

The package slid onto the table as Lisbeth settled lightly on his lap again. "Thank God they're gone." A sly expression suddenly graced her features. "So tell me, how much did you con the Americans out of on this one.

"Earn. How much did I *earn*, literally with my sweat and blood, is what you should be asking. Between you and Peter, my splendid character is unfairly maligned constantly."

"He and I know you too well, Kurt." Her hands gently felt along the edges of the brace enveloping his midsection.

"They grudgingly agreed to five percentage points. Five hundred thousand dollars, U.S.."

"Half a million dollars! And you never even phoned once! Not from America or Venezuela! When I'm on assignment I can always find the time."

"Latent Dutch frugality."

Her arms encircled him tenderly, careful not to put too much pressure on his battered chest. "Never again." She whispered as her mouth locked onto his.

THE END

ABOUT THE AUTHOR

A local newspaper account dubbed me the "Modern Indiana Jones" due to some of my life experiences. Although I have experienced some unique things, I doubt that the good Dr. Jones has any need to fear being eclipsed.

I have been fortunate to have visited countries on three continents including the jungles of the Guyana highlands in South America. In the latter location I was blessed to explore the beautiful wild realm with natives and learn about how they lived and some of their customs. A bona fide Amerindian blowgun, bows, and arrows hang just outside my office.

Off the coast of an obscure little island in Massachusetts I led on an archeological exploration seeking a possible clue to the location of Leif Eriksson's Vinland. Working with the US Navy I was able to relocate an inscribed stone in the sea that bears the date of 1001.

I have flown in a great variety of aircraft ranging from Beach Bonanzas (one of which crashed in South America) to venerable DC-3s (in the South American jungle – where else?) to spacious 747s bound for European adventures. Flying with the US Navy helicopters during my work in Massachusetts was an awesome experience. So too was a trip into the Atlantic off the Virginia coast on board CVN-73, the USS George Washington, a nuclear aircraft carrier.

Writing professionally since school, my first published article was an Op-Ed for the New York Times. Numerous articles followed, appearing in three languages to date.. I have also written various user manuals and training materials for various companies. I pride myself on accuracy and strive to deliver quality work.